Incline
Our
Hearts

By the same author

The Sweets of Pimlico
Unguarded Hours
Kindly Light
The Healing Art
Who Was Oswald Fish?
Wise Virgin
Scandal
Gentlemen in England
Love Unknown
Stray

*

The Laird of Abbotsford
The Life of John Milton
Hilaire Belloc
How Can We Know?
Pen Friends From Porlock
Tolstoy

Incline
Our
Hearts

A. N. Wilson

VIKING

VIKING
Published by the Penguin Group
Viking Penguin Inc., 40 West 23rd Street,
New York, New York 10010, U.S.A.
Penguin Books Ltd, 27 Wrights Lane,
London W8 5TZ, England
Penguin Books Australia Ltd, Ringwood,
Victoria, Australia
Penguin Books Canada Ltd, 2801 John Street,
Markham, Ontario, Canada L3R 1B4
Penguin Books (N.Z.) Ltd, 182–190 Wairau Road,
Auckland 10, New Zealand

Penguin Books Ltd, Registered Offices:
Harmondsworth, Middlesex, England

First American Edition
Published in 1989 by Viking Penguin Inc.

1 3 5 7 9 10 8 6 4 2

LIBRARY OF CONGRESS CATALOGING IN PUBLICATION DATA
Wilson, A. N., 1950–
Incline our hearts.
I. Title.
PR6073.I439I5   1989   823'.914   88-40308
ISBN 0-670-82358-9

Printed in the United States of America by
Arcata Graphics, Fairfield, Pennsylvania
Set in Palatino

for
Christopher and Deb

ONE

'Will you be eating with us?'

Aunt Deirdre, a tin-opener in hand, spoke over her shoulder to her husband without looking round. She let out a little explosion of annoyance at the bluntness of the instrument. It had a large, wooden handle, and a curved blade, much dented from use.

'We really should get a new one,' she said.

I watched my uncle's handsome, pampered, mildly effeminate face. Whether he would be eating his supper with the rest of the household seemed, for that moment, as though it depended upon Aunt Deirdre getting the tin open. At the best of times, she kept us on rather short commons, and my uncle's expression appeared to indicate that if she were prepared to give him some tinned meat, he might spend rather less of his time 'up at the Place'. In those days of austerity, no source of protein was to be sneezed at. The odours given off from the tin, once the opener had punctured it and begun its jagged journey round the top, made my mouth water. But the meat was not for us. She scooped out a couple of spoonsful (in their jelly they made an appetising slurping noise) into an enamel bowl and with sharp, violent gestures she mashed it into the Winalot. Then with the playfully affectionate tone which she more often adopted with animals than with human beings, she called out: 'Tin-ker! Din-dins!'

Still without looking at my uncle (the pair seldom exchanged glances) she held the spoon under the cold tap to rinse off the remaining bits of meat. It was heartbreaking to see good meat go to waste like that. Tinker, a wire-haired dachshund of uncertain temper, devoured his food with greedy gulps and much rattling of the dish on the cold, stone kitchen floor. When she spoke again, my aunt had resumed the slightly cross tone with which she normally spoke. There was usually a vague sense that she was having to argue a case and that her hearers had threatened to turn nasty.

'Only I've made a rice pudding,' she said.

I was not old enough to know whether this was offered as a means of persuading Uncle Roy to dine out or as an inducement to stay.

'I *think* I'd better . . .' My uncle paused. He ate half his meals at the Place, but there was always this apologetic rigmarole before he set out there. 'Promised Sargie a game of chess.'

'Just so long as I know,' said Aunt Deirdre. I could not tell whether she would have been less cross if he had said he would be eating with us.

'He gets lonely,' my uncle added. Then, with meaning, he said, 'As we *all* do.'

I do not know whether the last bit of that sentence is true. People appear to have different levels of tolerance as far as solitude is concerned. How much Uncle Roy allowed his mind to dwell on his own loneliness, let alone that of his wife, is something I shall never know.

During the period when I was getting on badly with Uncle Roy, I liked to tell myself that he was a moral coward. It was only much later that I came to reflect that the opposite of moral cowardice is a tremendously rare quality in human beings and, when found, not always particularly attractive. The rice pudding conversation took place, however, before the period of the quarrels. I was still taking my uncle and aunt for granted. However annoying I might find either of them, they were unalterable facts of life, that afternoon in the kitchen as I sat looking first at one, then at the other.

My uncle's crinkly, white hair was his own, but it sat on his head like a wig and somehow gave him the appearance of some Victorian humbug – perhaps one of the cheery old gents in

Dickens, or more likely a sybaritic minor canon in Trollope. Probably this was the effect he was aiming for. He had very clear blue eyes which – again, a Victorian touch – were boyishly innocent, childish. His silky, pink cheeks were quite as soft, when you kissed them, as my aunt's; if anything, they were softer; and his lips, too, were prissy and womanish. My aunt, on the other hand, whose Eton crop emphasised a rather stout neck, was much more obviously masculine. She never, to my recollection, wore trousers, but there was always something mannish about her clothes. The tweeds were of a kind dubbed (and perhaps, by some, deemed) 'sensible'. She always dressed in the same style: in summer a skirt and blouse, in winter, a skirt and jumper; little tweed coats almost identical to a man's hacking jacket.

The outfits were very slightly too smart for gardening (which she did all the time) but a bit too countrified for anything else. She never, however, modified what she wore. On the extremely rare occasions when I met my aunt off home territory (at speech-days or, very occasionally, in London) she always seemed less dressed up than any of the other mothers or female relations.

No one, by contrast, could accuse my uncle of being insufficiently dressy. His wardrobe was extensive, idiosyncratic and, in its own way, stylish. Standing there in the kitchen, he wore some beautifully cut, very wide Oxford bags of the palest grey flannel, a tweed coat of brilliant russet with a waistcoat of the same hue. The high collar and the white bow-tie must have been old-fashioned when he first affected them in the 1920s.

When my uncle turned to me, I knew that he had abandoned the conversation about supper. It was by now established that he would be eating with Sargie Lampitt. I could see from his expression that he was about to begin one of his disquisitions about the Lampitt family in general. These speeches could burst from my uncle at almost any moment and in any company. When waiting for trains on station platforms, I have seen him accost total strangers – porters, guards, or fellow passengers – and immediately engineer some general observation about the weather or the time of the next train into an account of the family whose history, doings and affairs appeared to dominate nearly all his thoughts.

Usually, if you talk to strangers in England, they resist being drawn. Fear of boredom, quite as much as the possibility that one might be mad or sexually unreliable, explains their reticence. My uncle was impervious to any of the signals which might be given off on such occasions that the stranger would rather be left in peace. So urgent was his need to talk about Lampitts that any excuse must be found.

'Train's late,' he might say. Trains were a good introduction. If the stranger replied, 'What d'you expect with all this nationalisation?' – a familiar enough response at that date – he could proudly announce his divided loyalties.

'No one can blame the Honourable Vernon *personally*' – he laughed aside this unvoiced suggestion, which no one had made, as an absurdity. 'But then, as all his cousins say, "Vernon, you are in the Cabinet." Dear Vernon replies, "I suppose I am." On the other hand, no one should suppose that the Honourable Vernon has the last word to say about railways.'

My uncle referred to Lord Lampitt's son as the Honourable Vernon to distinguish him from another Lampitt cousin of the same first name. By now, his interlocutors would be truly puzzled, possibly edging away, wondering why this snowy-haired stranger, an Alice-in-Wonderland figure, sometimes in tweed knickerbockers, should be addressing them on the subject of a family of whom they had never before heard.

'I am old enough,' he would continue, 'to remember old Mr Michael Lampitt, and he was a director of the L.N.E.R. Now the trains really *did* run on time in those days.'

Regardless of whether this assertion met with agreement, he could then get into his stride. Railways forgotten, he could concentrate on Lampitts *tout simple*. 'What an extraordinarily nice man Michael was! Eton and Trinity – I *do* beg your pardon.'

'That's all right, sir,' the porter on Norwich Station might answer.

'I was momentarily confusing Michael with Hugo. It was *Hugo* Lampitt who was at Trinity. Michael was up at Clare. Most of the Lampitts have been Cambridge men, except, as you perhaps know, Mr Sargent Lampitt, who is the one I know best. His father Michael was one of the very kindest men I ever knew.'

Such floods of information would have been too much to absorb, even had his listeners been interested. In spite of a distinctly rocky friendship with Sargent Lampitt, my uncle was constant in his devotion to Sargie's family. All Lampitts, great and small, were the object of fascination for him, and it can never have occurred to him that other people might not share his enthusiasm. No moment and no audience ever seemed inappropriate, as far as he was concerned, for the rehearsal of some anecdote in which Lampitts figured prominently. And when the wells of anecdote ran dry, he was quite happy (even the greatest concert pianists need to practise their scales) to give a simple verbal rundown of their family tree.

It followed, that having lived for over four years under my uncle's roof, I had become, willy-nilly, something of a Lampitt expert myself. Almost my only conversation had been that of my uncle, and that had been primarily devoted to his theme of themes. If required, I could have passed an examination on the Lampitts. Which uncle had the misfortune to develop phlebitis while staying in Mombasa? In what year did Sargie's father join the Labour Party? Which female member of the Lampitt family was deemed by Sargie and others to be a complete doormat? Which member of the Lampitt family was the author of *Lagoon Loungings*, a distinctly sub-Ruskinian work of the Edwardian era, and went on to achieve minor fame as a popular biographer, most notably of the Prince Consort and of Swinburne? Which Lampitt was married to a Strachey?

Even at twelve, I could have answered all these questions with the same alacrity with which other children of my age could have rehearsed the names of cricketers. I actually knew more about the Lampitt family than I did about my own. This was all the more bizarre since I seldom met any of them except 'Uncle Sargie', a reclusive and mysterious figure who was our neighbour up at Timplingham Place.

Sargent Lampitt was no relation. The 'Uncle' – never a formula employed or accepted by my Aunt Deirdre – was a pleasantry devised by Uncle Roy. Kinship with Sargie was something which my real uncle would love to have claimed. As a child, I was dimly aware of this, but unable to explain it. Since, I have had moments of disgruntled anger about the matter. Viewed from a common-sense point of view, it seems outrageous to esteem one group of people more highly merely because they seem to have attracted to themselves money, fame or chic. Furthermore, with an illogical flight into the values which I professed to despise, I might recall that the Lampitts were not, in class terms, anything so very special. True, the Honourable Vernon and his father Lord Lampitt (Sargie's uncle) were in *Debrett* but this was only a Lloyd George peerage. In terms of literary fame, the distinctions were analogously muted. A Lampitt had once edited *The Nation* before it amalgamated with *The New Statesman*; and there was James Petworth Lampitt (Sargie's brother Jimbo), the belle-lettrist. But this was small beer. Why, if he wanted to disown his harmless suburban origins, did my uncle not aspire after something rather more distinguished?

The answer, I suppose, is that snobbery does not really work like that. Like lust, it is seldom omnivorous and nearly always it will look about for particular, attainable objectives. My uncle idolised the Lampitts for the same reason that the man climbed Everest: they were there. Norfolk was sparsely populated. My aunt's taste for society was almost non-existent. Sargie was their nearest neighbour in a village of less than a thousand souls.

Uncle Roy would probably have been horrified to hear anyone accuse him of snobbery: the more so since he had absorbed much of the Lampitt, vaguely leftist, ideology.

If asked to explain his Lampitt-preoccupation, he would have said that it had nothing to do with their money (they were a fourth-generation brewing family) or their modicum of good marriages and worldly success. It was hard to avoid the impression, however, that Uncle Roy regarded his own mother as vaguely infra-dig. The occasions when Granny came face to face with Sargie Lampitt were a torment to Uncle Roy. The reason given was that she spoke her mind – in other words, she saw *through* Sargie. But since she never said anything particularly abrasive, it was hard to see why Uncle Roy hovered so nervously on these occasions, unless it was for fear that she might let slip in her speech signals, unnoticeable to most of the world, but excruciating to her son, of his background and origin in Putney: 'pardon' for 'what', 'settee' for 'sofa'; the usual string of shibboleths by which the socially mobile in the British Isles have chosen to torment one another.

Although in my moments of bitterest hostility to my uncle I

have dismissed his fondness for the Lampitts as 'pure snobbery', I have since revised my view. In time, one comes to revise all views, just as one comes to see that very little is 'pure' anything. Snobbery itself, embarrassing as it may be when identified, is not explained simply by being qualified with the epithet 'pure'. In any case, I rather doubt whether my uncle's first call at the Place (years before my own birth) was conducted in a mood of social aspiration. Uncle Roy was enough of a romantic, at that stage before his addiction began, to regret that the Lampitts were not one of the old Norfolk families, like the Whatleys, now extinct, whose tombs and brasses adorned the parish church. Nor could the religious history of the Lampitts (originally Unitarian, now predominantly left-wing atheist) have made an immediate appeal. To give him his due, Uncle Roy always expressed disapproval in that area. At some stage, he and Sargie had become fast friends. And if I supposed that the terms of the friendship were ignominious (my uncle always having to play Sancho Panza to Sargie's Don Quixote) that was really their business, not mine. What was my business was the fact that when he was at home, Uncle Roy was able to speak for hours on end about the Lampitts, and to expect me to listen.

That afternoon, for instance, as though he had first thought of the fact, he said, 'Your Uncle Sargie is an *extraordinarily* intelligent man, but he can on occasion be exasperating.'

Uncle Roy laughed, a sure sign that one of his anecdotes was to be trotted out. We all knew them by heart. My aunt, who had got the rice pudding from the bottom of the Aga, stirred it with particular vehemence, as if she would really prefer to be stirring Sargie's wonderfully powerful brains.

'Some time ago – it was before the war – when *was* it, Deirdre?' There was never any 'Stop me if I've told you this before' about Uncle Roy.

'Oh, I don't know,' snapped Aunt Deirdre. '1933.'

'It could have been. Anyway, the telephone rang and it was old Sargie. "Roy! I'm fed up!"' Already my uncle's voice was trembling and it was uncertain whether he would get through a recitation of this thousand-times-told story without a collapse into laughter. '"Let's drive to Cromer and spend a couple of nights in that nice hotel there." I said, "Honestly, Sargie, I can't simply drive off to Cromer at a moment's notice."'

Taking a silk handkerchief from his top pocket, my uncle mopped his brow. If he took the story gently he might manage to tell it without the giggles, or actual hysterics, setting in.

My aunt, after her little flare of temper about the date of the historic drive to Cromer, now showed no emotion at all. She knocked the side of the spoon against the edge of the pudding dish and put it back in the oven. A bit of skin clung to the spoon and, rather than waste it, she said brusquely, 'Here!'

I opened my mouth obediently and then protested at the heat of the spoon.

'Get off with your bother,' said Aunt Deirdre.

By now, our gleeman had resumed his tale, and reached the stage of the anecdote where he and Sargie were on the road to Cromer. Uncle Roy was at the wheel of Sargie's nice old Lagonda and Sargie was starting to imagine that the tyres of this noble vehicle had gone flat. They pulled in at the next garage. Sargie leaned over my uncle and tooted the horn to alert the attention of the garage man. Sargie's imperiousness with underlings was a regular feature of the stories. It did not appear to trouble Uncle Roy – if anything, the reverse. On this occasion, when the garage man appeared, Sargie insisted in ill-mannered tones that he blow up the *something* tyres. Swearwords, in my uncle's version of events, were always censored.

'You should have seen the man's face!' said my uncle. 'I really think, for two pins, he'd have struck old Sargie.'

At the next garage, Sargie made my uncle pull up. He railed at the garage man because the tyres were too hard. They had been blown up by a *something* maniac. At the next – somewhere near Fakenham – toot-toot. The tyres were too soft. And so on, all the way to the coast.

By the time he got to the closing stages of this anecdote, one of his favourites in the repertoire, my uncle was nearly crying with mirth. The fact that it was (as I came to feel) a vaguely ignominious story never came into it. For example, he never suggested that he himself had been wrong, at a moment's notice and purely on Sargie's whim, to abandon his wife and child – and his job – and drive off for a few days by the sea. Nor did he ever suggest any resentment at being treated, when Sargie was in one of his moods, like a dim-witted servant, brought along simply in order to drive Sargie's car and fight his crazed battles for him with petrol-pump attendants, hotel clerks and all the multifarious figures whom Sargie suspected of being out to get him. One of the most mysterious facts of all was why Uncle Roy consented to stop at all those garages, rather than protest that there was nothing wrong with the tyres and that if Sargie wished to be driven to Cromer, he should stop being a prize ass. On the contrary, part of the pleasure they seemed to derive from one another's company was precisely Sargie's exploitation of my uncle's good nature. The Cromer saga in its longer version continued with Uncle Roy having to swap bedrooms with Sargie because his own room had a better view of the sea and because Sargie's bedding was somehow damp or uncomfortable.

'And goodness, it really was uncomfortable!' my uncle would laugh, in a tone which suggested that Sargie's insufferable behaviour was something we would all half admire.

On this occasion, however, my aunt cut him short with, 'We're going to eat at half-past six. Couldn't be easier.'

Those were the actual words, but her tone implied that the whole business of putting a cottage pie and a rice pudding in the oven had in fact been fraught with difficulties which she was too stoical to reveal. 'You'll be at Sargie's.'

With this, she clumped up the back stairs which led directly from the kitchen to one of the landings aloft.

There was over an hour before my uncle was due to set out, but this was her leave-taking, for she said, when out of sight and halfway up the stairs in the mock-jokey tones of reproof which she used for upbraiding Tinker if he chewed a newspaper or shat on the carpet, 'Not too much to drink, mind!'

My uncle, as if man to man, gave me a look suggestive that my aunt's words were somehow preposterous. They seldom complained openly about one another, but their mutual discontent was not a secret. Perhaps they let me know about it because I was not their child. Felicity, their grotesquely misnamed daughter, was not, I guess, treated to any such conspiratorial signals as that glance which my uncle gave me. Nevertheless, the emotional discord of her parents' house was, for Felicity as for me, part of the air we breathed.

Philosophers, such as Felicity was to become, like to remind us that some questions are not worth asking because there is

no possibility of verifying the answer. Most of the questions
which I have ever found interesting have fallen into this category, not least the question of why my uncle and aunt ever
chose to get married. I could never tell – and I don't think they
could either – whether they were what is called 'happy together'
or whether they hated each other's guts. Perhaps a bit of both.
Although both Laodiceans who deprecated displays of emotion,
they were both ardently, strongly married. It was a strange
thing to grow up with. They weren't capable of leaving the
thing be. They were addicted to their marital routines, but
somehow aware that whatever was going on between them, it
was not for public display. It was as though there was some
strangely pungent smell in their house of which they were half
ashamed. I went through a phase of believing that my aunt
would have seemed less cross all the time if Uncle Roy had
taken her out more. But where would they have gone? And if
out, would they have wanted to be seen?

The world was kept firmly at arm's length. Sometimes relations or old schoolfriends of Aunt Deirdre's would come to
stay. Very occasionally, she would ask a female friend for lunch.
But, for most of the time during my school holidays, the four
of us were walled up together with Deirdre and Roy's unhappiness, breathing it, avoiding it, allowing it to warp and change
us.

An hour or so after my aunt had gone up the back stairs, my
uncle sauntered down the front stairs. He had discarded his
tweeds and assumed evening clothes which had known better
days. The 'black' tie was really a dullish green; so were the
lapels on his dinner jacket. In the hall, there was a large
hat-stand with a looking-glass set into the middle, encircled
with pegs. An array of headgear depended from this hideous
object of furniture, all of them in their different ways suggesting
versions of Uncle Roy which at one stage or another he had
thought of adopting. He paused now, unaware of my lurking
presence in the hall, and stared at the glass with undisguised
admiration. It was quite surprising to me, what my uncle did
next. I have suggested that the variety of hats represented
different aspects of Uncle Roy, but it might be equally true to
regard these strange objects as items from a child's dressing-up
box. If my uncle had ever been able to distinguish between

charades and real life he would probably have possessed fewer hats. The deerstalker would have been ideal for playing Sherlock Holmes but looked absurd in the village. The solar topee – Dr Livingstone, I presume. The Mickey Mouse gas mask was in point of fact Felicity's. But what of the *Daily Mail* hat? Uncle Roy must have been the only person in the world to own such an object – apart from Winston Churchill, at that stage out of office thanks to the unpatriotic (in my aunt's terms) activities of the Attlees, Crippses and Lampitts of this world.

My uncle paused before the glass, as though unable to decide between becoming the greatest private detective or the formidable wartime Prime Minister. For the time being, he rejected both possibilities and reached instead for a tall, silk opera hat which, as soon as he had perched it on his head, gave him the look of Burlington Bertie, the decayed toff. The sight of himself thus attired made my uncle smile and then titter. Having had his moment of fun, he put the hat back and reached for his daily wear, a rather battered black trilby.

'Byee!' he called.

The house could have been empty for all the response he got. At that moment a feeling of tenderness for my uncle seized me and I wanted to call out an affectionate good night. I could not do so, however, without revealing my presence in the shadows by the green baize door at the back of the passage, and thus betraying the fact that I had witnessed his innocent charade. So I let him go out comfortless into the night. My aunt never responded to his cries of greetings or valediction as he entered or left the house; and my cousin Felicity, at that date, never used her vocal chords unless positively forced to do so. There was something tremendously sad about my uncle's figure as he sloped out into the spring evening. It was still light and the colours of the garden seemed especially vivid since, after that long winter, there had at last been a thaw.

*   *

Within seconds of his departure, my aunt emerged from her bedroom on the first-floor landing and made her brisk descent, this time down the front stairs.

'Nearly time for "The Mulberrys"!' she announced to the world in general.

This wireless programme, to which my aunt was devoted, purported to be a realistic account of life in some fictitious, rural village of England. It had begun, a few years previously, during the war as part of the Government's propaganda, the object in this case being to persuade the populace to dig for victory, eat carrots for their supposed efficacy as optical stimulants and save scraps for pigswill. 'The Mulberrys', however, soon outgrew their origins as a vehicle for Government information and took on a narrative life of its own. The family in question were supposed to live in a village called Barleybrook and run a farm of a few hundred acres. Even by the restricted standards of rural life, it was astonishing how, in this particular village, the Mulberrys got everywhere. Dick Mulberry, the paterfamilias, ran Daisy Farm with his wife Elsie and their son Stan. These three all spoke with an invented rustic voice, 'z's for 's's, 'oi' for 'I', loosely based on the dialect poems of William Barnes. Dick's other children were Reg, who spoke with the accent of a completely different region (vaguely North Country with presumably accidental lapses into Irish), and the Cockney Mag who had married rather rakishly and was always getting into scrapes. The supporting cast included farmhands, a doctor, the vicar and a rival farming family, supposed to be less amiable than the Mulberrys, called the Swills.

No village on earth ever bore the remotest resemblance to Barleybrook and no human being ever spoke, thought or behaved like a member of the Mulberry lineage. How my aunt, a countrywoman all her life and deeply acquainted with villages and their ways, derived pleasure from the programme I don't know. But she did. When my uncle was out, supper could be timed to coincide with the latest drama from Barleybrook. It was an addiction which Aunt Deirdre had passed on to Felicity and, to a lesser degree, myself.

Consulting the little watch which she kept pinned to her bosom, my aunt called again in her jokey voice; it was sort of mock-pompous, as if she were announcing a hymn number in church.

'Nearly Mulberrytime!'

Felicity did not waste breath answering if she were called. She showed that she had heard by opening her bedroom door and galumphing down the back stairs into the kitchen. When it was just the three of us we did not bother to sit in the dining room. It saved the business of the trolley, one of whose casters was loose, and all the palaver of place mats and glasses.

'Kitchen living' is now universal. At this date, I suspect it was slightly unusual, one of the many examples (marrying Uncle Roy had been the most glaring) of my aunt's willingness to behave eccentrically when she chose.

Cottage pie, with some cabbage which had been swimming in boiling water for a good three-quarters of an hour, was dolloped on to our plates and borne to the kitchen-table just as the 'Mulberrys' theme tune crackled from the large bakelite speaker on the dresser. I little knew then how ominous that tune was to become in my life.

'Now, old Silas, doan' you stan' there a-leanin' on the gate. You come up to Oak Meadow – there be some ewes a-lambin'.'

'Sorry, Marser Stan.'

The familiar bilgewater of Mulberry-dialogue dripped over our heads.

'Wonder if Mag's *really* bought those black-market silk stockings,' whispered Aunt Deirdre; but a glare from Felicity, whose concentration on the programme was total, was enough to silence her.

Of her two parents, Felicity more resembled her mother than her father. She had my aunt's massiveness; I do not mean that either woman was tall, but they were both then – before Felicity lost so much weight – strikingly full-featured. My aunt's large round face never aged much until she got into her sixties. With her short hair and ruddy cheeks, she could have been almost any age from truculent teens to moody menopause. My cousin Felicity had some of her mother's ageless quality in her late teens, only in her face the truculence was much more marked. In some lights, Felicity at eighteen actually looked older than her mother. They did their hair differently. Instead of Aunt Deirdre's short crop (which, like the tweeds, seemed to be announcing itself as sensible), Felicity had a long, thick plait. She seemed, and I think was, permanently cross. Since it was obvious that she did not like me much, it was hard not to take the bates personally.

We ate our cottage pie, which was greyish and devoid of all flavour. The scene of lambing at Daisy Farm changed to the back bar of the King's Head where Reg Mulberry, with his mysterious semi-Lancashire voice, was making up to Flo, the barmaid.

'Lay off, Reg Mulberry.'

'I jus' said how nice you looked in those stockings, love, that's all.'

'You've been drinking, Reg Mulberry.'

'Hic! I 'aven't.'

'I don't know what you're implying, Reg Mulberry, about my stockings, but I'm not the only person who has them. Your sister Mag's got silk stockings, and there are plenty of people who'd like to know where she got them.'

'Oh, they would, would they?' said Reg in his drunken voice. 'Then if you like, I'll tell you, Flo. I'll tell you straight out . . .'

At this exciting point the Mulberry tune interrupted the dialogue, leaving us on tenterhooks for twenty-four hours. I was every bit as gripped by the programme as the women were, an added excitement being the sense that the vaguely sexual overtones of the final scene had disturbed them both. I knew it had been sexual, without knowing how or why, because my aunt, when she switched off the set, said, 'A pity when Reg starts getting silly.'

Aunt Deirdre thought all male lapses from sobriety or chastity were 'silly'. She was probably right. She had even once said that she did not like Sargie making Uncle Roy drink so much because it made him silly, an observation which offered a strange glimpse into the impenetrable world of their private life. By the severest standards it could be said that it did not need drink, or anything else, to *make* Uncle Roy silly; he was, in fact, never anything else. This, however, was not what she had meant by the word.

'Don't let the other boys get silly,' was the only piece of sex education offered to me by my aunt, before returning to school one term.

The small cottage pie which had been dolloped out of its Pyrex dish had been finished at its first serving. There were seldom seconds at my aunt's board. I would have happily eaten another plateful of cottage pie; though dull, it was far from unpalatable and hunger in those days was a perpetual condition.

'All finished?' asked Aunt Deirdre.

'It was very nice,' I said.

Felicity got up and piled our plates.

'The pud's in the bottom of the Aga, darling,' said my aunt, a remark to which Felicity did not reply. Trying to make the silence seem more 'normal', my aunt exclaimed, 'Good old rice pud!' One felt it was the reply which Felicity was *meant* to have given herself.

The pudding dish was brought to the table and its contents were dispersed into three willow-pattern soup plates. Then my aunt spoke again.

'We'll have to start packing your trunk tomorrow, Julian. There's no point in pulling a face, old thing, it's *got* to be done.'

Packing the trunk was always the signal that the school holidays were drawing to a close. About a week before term began, all my uniform, beautifully laundered and with name-tapes sewn into it, was laid out on one of the spare beds – grey shirts, grey socks, games things (cricket flannels this term): prison clobber. Knowing how difficult I found transitions between home and school, Aunt Deirdre always adopted an attitude of breezy jollity about the whole thing.

'I hate packing,' I said.

'Poor old boy! Back to the Dump!' This was a playful allusion to a judgement of my own, sincerely passed on the school after a couple of terms there. 'Still, summer terms aren't so bad, are they?'

Seeing tears start to my eyes, my aunt swiftly turned her attention to Felicity.

'Darling!'

Felicity was 'Darling'; I was 'Julian' or 'old thing'; my uncle was usually nothing at all in my aunt's vocatives.

'Darling, you're all packed up, too, aren't you? Well, you don't need to pack so much because they let you leave quite a lot of your books there, didn't they? Very sensible. Do you have a lot of beastly exams this summer? What are they called? Prelims, isn't it?'

'Part One,' said Felicity with some ruthlessness. The tone implied that any fool, even one who had married an Oxford graduate, could get the names of Cambridge exams right. My uncle, as a tiresome sort of joke, affected not to remember any of the Cambridge slang; my aunt, who had not attended either university, innocently came out with her 'quads' and 'scouts' instead of 'courts' and 'gyps'. Felicity looked furious. She hated talking, but she hated inaccuracy even more; the one had prompted the other.

'Whatever it's called,' said Aunt Deirdre. 'I wonder if you'll go rowing this term – rather fun! Your father said that the girls' colleges do sometimes have a boat. Pity to do nothing except work.'

The idea of Felicity, a poorly co-ordinated girl, being a welcome member of any rowing crew was one which maternal love allowed to take its place in Aunt Deirdre's brain, but it was an incredible one.

The rice pudding was very hot. We all put a spoonful of jam in the middle. My policy was to eat the cooler parts round the edge, working my way gradually into the middle of the bowl. If one gauged it carefully, one's last spoonful could be pure jam. Felicity, by contrast, eighteen years old and an exhibitioner at Girton, stirred up her jam and rice, spattering some of it on the oilcloth. Then she took up great spoonsful to her lips, blowing at the pudding with noisy smacking of the chops until it was cool enough to eat.

She ate with lightning speed and began to clear the table before my aunt and I had finished eating. Then she started to wash up. Within quarter of an hour, she was back in her room. Those two syllables – 'Part One' – were the only ones to have been uttered by Felicity in the course of the whole evening.

Trivial as its events were, I shall always remember that evening, and the morning after, as the beginning of the story which follows. For a while, after Felicity had gone upstairs, my aunt and I sat in the freezing drawing room. She turned collars and I turned the pages of my *Boy's Own Paper*. Then we played a couple of rounds of Snakes and Ladders. She won hands down. Then she pecked me on the cheek and said good night.

Later, long after I had switched out my light, I became aware of my uncle and aunt talking animatedly in the hall. I was too full of sleep to make out what they were saying, but it sounded as though something was up. Probably I am reading back into the situation a significance which I only discerned later on, but

I *think* I felt excited, the sort of feeling you have when it is your birthday.

The next I knew, it was seven o'clock, which, because it was Thursday, was the time I got up. There was an early celebration on Thursday mornings and during the school holidays I was an altar server. Later on (from about the age of fourteen onwards) I developed very decided views about these matters and felt sure that Christianity was based on various moral and historical falsehoods. At twelve, I just regarded it as something you did, like compulsory games or going to school or wearing a tie. I am not sure that in so many words I believed it, if by 'it' is meant the abstruser formulations of theology. Certainly, I did not associate my uncle, or any of the things he did in church, with what I would have later called 'genuine' religious aspirations of a kind which I had come across in books or wondered if I had not experienced myself. There was certainly no connection between what went on in church and such questions as whether life had a meaning, or whether there was a personal god. As far as I was concerned, it was drill, a matter of certain words, clothes and actions.

The walk from the vicarage to the church in the early morning was never for some reason frightening, even though the same walk in the half-light of evening required a great act of will. Every bush and shadow in the evening felt as if it were inhabited by a hostile stranger, a ghost, a village lout, or perhaps some man (my aunt had given me hints about their existence) wanting to be silly. In the shadows of morning, everything was different. The grey sky was getting brighter each moment. Though it was still cold, there was a feeling of spring in the air. The birds sang overhead in the long avenue of beeches in the vicarage drive, on either side of which, in thick green clumps, the foliage (but not yet the blooms) of bluebells grew in abundance. Once through the gate and out into the lane, the grass verges were thick with primroses, campion and aconites. The walk was a mere quarter of a mile.

We always entered the churchyard not by the wicket gate but through a little gap in the wall on the south side, from whence a path led up to the church, a large, flint, fifteenth-century building with clear glass in its perfectly proportioned Perpendicular windows.

It is for its carvings that most visitors remember Timplingham Parish Church – the rood screen and the misericords which somehow survived the Reformation, and, most distinctive of all, the beam ends in the roof of the nave. Other East Anglian churches are famed for their angel-beams, but Timplingham has a row of choristers in what Uncle Roy certainly regarded as highly 'correct', full-sleeved rochets. The row of plump carved faces and of hands clasped in prayer could not be more demure, or so one thinks until one has made a careful examination of each figure. All down the south aisle, they stare down, these male wooden innocents, with pudding-basin coiffures reminiscent of Laurence Olivier in the film of *Henry V*. Up the north aisle they appear to present a similarly pleasant if dull picture. Carmelites in choir, my uncle always said. (Timplingham had been a friary until the Reformation.) All figures, that is, save one, three from the end, who gazes down just over the pulpit. The face of this figure wears the same placid expression as all the others. But its hands are not clasped in prayer, nor is the linen enfolded at its neck. Rather, the choir garment has been pulled down to reveal not the flat chest of a Carmelite friar but the ample bosom of some fifteenth-century East Anglian girl. My aunt always said that it was a 'pity' that Timplingham should be famed for this *risqué* piece of sculpture, but my uncle enjoyed pointing it out to visitors. Sargie Lampitt, never known to attend divine worship, was also a devotee of what he called the Timplingham Titties.

Uncle Roy always got to church before I did. By the time I arrived, he would be half vested, in amice, alb and girdle, sitting or kneeling at the back of the Lady Chapel. My job was to light the candles on the altar, check that a quantity of bread (my uncle deprecated the use of communion wafers) was on the credence table with the wine and return to the vestry to wait for the service to begin. Sometimes I wore special rig for this, sometimes not. That morning, I seem to remember, I did not dress up.

All the clothes worn in church excited a passionate interest in my uncle. They all meant something. For me, they were just fancy dress. The fact that I knew anything about it, still less that I *wore* it, was a jealously guarded secret which I should hate to have been known by my contemporaries at school.

Wearing albs and knowing the word 'alb' was both pansy (almost, in my aunt's sense, silly) and creepy: only a short step away from witches' robes and dabbling with the occult.

Not so for Uncle Roy who was punctilious about the exact shape, colour and function of each liturgical vestment, and who prided himself on being much more 'correct' than other High Church clergymen in the neighbourhood. The idea was that one should be Catholic without imitating Rome. The clothes and rituals with which Uncle Roy cluttered the church services were all in his view authentically English: the full conical chasubles, for instance, were of a kind which you might see in some fifteenth-century English book of hours and were quite unlike the cut-away, fiddle-back chasubles worn at that date by the Roman clergy. Times have now changed and Uncle Roy's vestments would nowadays be all the rage in Rome. Not that he was trying to be in the vanguard – quite the reverse. My uncle's outlandish rig in church was all part of his desire to cut a dash and differentiate himself from the rest of the world. As such, it embarrassed me quite a lot and I would have given anything to see him dressed like an 'ordinary vicar' in church, just as I would have preferred him not to attend school speech-days wearing bright green golfing trousers, a matching Norfolk jacket and the inevitable white bow tie.

The claim that, by wearing extraordinary clothes in church, he was getting back to some more ancient or authentic mode of carrying on later struck me, however, less as a piece of Uncle Roy tiresomeness than as a symptom of the almost universal human tendency to rewrite and readjust the past. The so-called Sarum Rite, of which my uncle was so enthusiastic an exponent, had really been invented by a Hampstead clergyman in 1899 and probably bore no more relation to anything which had happened in the Middle Ages than did the deliberations of the Honourable Vernon at the Labour Party Conference. No matter. The important thing was that Uncle Roy and a few others had convinced themselves that what he did in church was the real thing. What was the Judaeo-Christian religion itself, except a creative readjustment of history, a ceaseless rehearsal and repetition of past events which, each time they were recited, became further removed from the original events they described and more a part of the mental furniture of the devotees? So that, events such as the Jewish Exodus from Egypt or the Exile in Babylon had long ago ceased to be matters of pure history, if there is such a thing, and had become mythological episodes by which the present lives of the faithful were shaped and judged. One could see the same thing happening in national mythology, too – Churchill's period out of office actually helping to make the events of the Second World War, Dunkirk, the Battle of Britain and all that had happened since achieve an Homeric status in the common consciousness, so that each retelling of the stories itself re-forms rather than uncovers the past. Speaking about the past is always, therefore, an example of the truth of a line of Russian poetry quoted to me (ages after the period I am describing) by Felicity – 'A thought expressed is always a lie.'

What is true for nations or communities of the religious faithful is equally true for individuals. Our attempts to recover or uncover the past and what really happened are doomed at the outset to failure because it is we ourselves who are doing the investigation. We move on. We become someone else. The self of ten, twenty, thirty years previous is alien to us. And yet, untrustworthily creative as we know our memories to be, we are prepared to invest them with more credence than those pictures created by the inevitably rougher brushwork of outsiders. Our own lives, that is, as remembered by ourselves, are probably fictions, but they are more reliable fictions than other people's reconstructions of our own lives. Of all liars the most arrogant are biographers: those who would have us believe, having surveyed a few boxes full of letters, diaries, bank statements and photographs, that they can play at the recording angel and tell the whole truth about another human life.

Strange to say, it was on that April morning in Timplingham Church that the story began which, more than anything else which has happened in my life, has sharpened this truth and put it into focus: the story of Hunter and the Lampitts.

I have mentioned that the colours worn in church were of particular significance to my uncle. Unbleached linen for Lent (it was considered very infra-dig to wear purple during this season). Scarlet for Passiontide. Green for those long, lazy Sundays after Trinity. Since it was shortly after Easter, I should have expected my uncle to be wearing vestments of white damask. It was something of a shock to see black vestments spread out on the chest in the sacristy. There was no talking before Mass – not so much as 'Good morning' – so the gossipy question of who had kicked the bucket would have to wait. My first horrified instinct was to believe that it was Granny – but then I realised that my aunt would surely have told me and not allowed me to learn so horrible a piece of news in so roundabout a way. On the other hand, since my aunt was the Mercury of the household, why had she not told us the previous evening at supper of the passing which these black vestments commemorated? Her stream of commentary about Timplingham and its affairs provided us with an episodic village drama every bit as interesting as anything dreamed up by the scriptwriters of 'The Mulberrys'. If someone in the village had died, Aunt Deirdre would certainly have told us over the cottage pie.

And besides, if some village person *had* died, it would not have been usual for my uncle to say a requiem mass for their souls. He wore his black vestments on Remembrance Sunday, or for the funerals of those who occupied some special place in his pantheon. I am not quite sure whether 'village people', Uncle Roy's phrase for his parishioners, actually possessed souls. If not, it would clearly have been superfluous to pray for them. Certainly, when soul and body were both in one piece, few enough of the good Timplinghamites ever came to watch my uncle in action. Even by the minimal standards of the day, Uncle Roy's flock was almost scandalously small.

The identity of the deceased would, however, soon be revealed. My uncle had come into the vestry and was putting on the last of what Sargie once disrespectfully called his 'glad rags'. First the black stole, which he always kissed before placing it around his neck; then the huge black chasuble over the head; finally the maniple over the left wrist. Then he picked up the chalice and paten, loosely covered with a cloth (he considered the burse and the chalice-veil Roman and therefore common) and he nodded to me that he was ready for the off. I rang a small handbell and we made our way to the Lady Altar.

The congregation that morning could not be said to be overwhelmingly large. Felicity no longer attended, which eliminated a high percentage of the worshippers. (It was never talked

about, but generally assumed that she had lost her faith.) Mrs
Batterbee, who helped my aunt in the house, sometimes obliged
my uncle by making up the regulation two or three without
whom the Prayer Book decreed that it was improper to celebrate
the Sacrament. On this occasion, she was away, perhaps with
her sister in King's Lynn. Eirene, who did the rough, had the
excuse of being chapel, so was not expected to come to the
services. So, that morning, only my aunt was in church.

My uncle reached the altar, bowed and kissed it. Then he
turned round and spoke in his rather beautiful liturgical tones:

'Of your charity, pray for the repose of the soul of James
Petworth Lampitt, who died yesterday . . .'

So! I might have guessed that this liturgical extravagance
heralded the passing of no ordinary mortal. Sargie's brother
Jimbo had gone to meet his Maker. One could only hope (I
suppose that was the point of the requiem) that the Lampitts
were as highly regarded in the Kingdom of Heaven as they
were in Timplingham Rectory.

All my uncle's judgements of the Lampitts are fixed involuntarily and indelibly in my mind. I sometimes think what a
well-stocked brain I would have if, instead of grinding on about
the Lampitts, he had read aloud to me from Homer and Plato.

'Old Jimbo is in many ways like Sargie – both very highly
strung and *highly* intelligent. What a man Jimbo is! A true
belle-lettrist!' My uncle was innocent of the idea that 'belle-
lettrist', in modern literary circles, is a term of opprobrium. 'I
dare say that there will be fuller lives of Prince Albert, but none
more elegant, none more concise, none more *delicious*.'

I had never set eyes on Jimbo, who wrote under the name of
James Petworth Lampitt and whose flow of mannered prose
had dried up a goodish while before the war. His visits to
Timplingham were rare after their mother died, but he and
Sargie were said to keep in touch, to write letters and to meet
in London. Unless one counted the transitory glory of sitting
in the Cabinet (as the Honourable Vernon now did), then Jimbo
was probably at that stage (even before he was immortalised
by Hunter) the most famous of the Lampitts. The idea of a
requiem, I believe, is that the sins of the dead person are in
some way cancelled out by the power of Christ's sacrificial
offering. None of the three present in church that morning had

the smallest inkling what those sins might be. It was Hunter's task to unravel those for us. Had my aunt been aware of *quite* how silly Jimbo had allegedly been, she might very well have gone home to prepare the breakfast, rather than waste time praying for him.

My uncle was a stickler for the 1662 Prayer Book, so that at each celebration there was a complete recitation of the Ten Commandments.

He stood on the altar steps and peered down into the shadowy aisles and the rows of empty pews.

'Thou shalt not commit adultery,' said Uncle Roy.

Alone in the body of the church, my aunt's Angela Brazil tones responded, 'Lord have mercy upon us and incline our hearts to keep this law . . .'

*   *

Over breakfast, Uncle Roy told us that Jimbo Lampitt had died the previous day at about half-past five in the afternoon. With my passion for times of death, derived from reading detective stories, I made a mental note that 'the deceased' had died at the very moment that Aunt Deirdre had been putting the rice pudding in the oven.

It was an upsetting death, which was at present unexplained. Jimbo (as my uncle referred to him throughout this narrative) had fallen into the area of his London house from a top-floor fire escape: a distance of some sixty feet. He was not quite seventy years of age. Apparently, he was in the habit towards the end of day of strolling out on to the fire escape on the top floor of his house to admire the roofscapes and treetops, the views and the skies. Sargie said this reminded Jimbo of Italy, though why such reminiscences should be afforded by the sight of Manchester Square in the rush hour was never made altogether clear.

'Sargie was very fond of Jimbo,' said Uncle Roy – 'I think we shouldn't say too much about the *way* he died. It really is too upsetting – the worst death really' – he meant the worst Lampitt death – 'since Gerald died of that tumour thing in . . .'

'Mombasa,' said my aunt.

'No,' I said. 'It was Vivian who had phlebitis in Mombasa. Gerald had a tumour in Johannesburg.'

'He's a clever boy, this,' said my uncle, delighted that I should be so well-versed in my Lampitt-catechism.

'Of course,' conceded my aunt.

'I suppose that there'll be a family funeral and then a memorial service afterwards for the *literary* world. And we all know what a hotbed of gossip and misinformation *that* is.'

'Quite,' said my aunt.

As it happens, this was a perfectly reasonable exchange, though I don't know what it was based on; my uncle and aunt were as ignorant of the 'literary world' as I was.

'Sargie's very anxious that people won't start saying it's a repetition of history. Angelica all over again.'

'Angelica?' My aunt really did not *concentrate* enough on her Lampitt-lore. One even got the impression that she was sometimes frivolous enough to think about other things.

Angelica Lampitt, an unmarried aunt of Jimbo and Sargie's, and a keen supporter of Women's Suffrage, had taken her own life – cut her wrists in the bath – upon the marriage of her close friend Miss Bean. The emotional undercurrents of this tragedy were lost on me then – indeed, I am not sure that I understand them now – but the facts were clear enough. Angelica's death was so dramatic that it seemed to me nothing short of fantastic that anyone could have forgotten about them. 'Angelica' was now synonymous with suicide. My aunt couldn't have forgotten this. Perhaps she considered that that sort of thing, the emotional life of the unmarried, was an unsuitable topic to discuss in front of a child.

'You *know*.' My uncle spoke irritably.

Coming quickly to heel and evidently remembering the Angelica incident, my aunt said, 'They surely don't think it's *that*?'

'There's going to be an inquest,' said Uncle Roy.

Again, echoes of Agatha Christie and Dorothy L. Sayers! It was often at the inquest that Poirot or Lord Peter would first see the suspects. I felt thoroughly excited. The violent and unexplained death of a minor literary celebrity whom we hardly knew could not but be the cause of excitement, even pleasure. But death makes hypocrites of grown-up persons. My uncle's line, as a professional, was the reverse of sentimental when it came to the deaths of village people.

Not long before, in Holy Week, my aunt announced the

death of a bedridden old woman whom she had been visiting almost every day for the previous year.

'Evie Tarrant's dead,' she had said.

'At last!' was my uncle's only response. Then, about an hour later, he had put his head around the kitchen door and said, 'Does that mean that I have to take the funeral?'

Lampitt-deaths were different. They required a sort of possessive solemnity. We had to pull especially long faces to show how 'in' we were with the family. Equally, it behoved us to be cagey about the whole thing with strangers, implying that we who were more or less family knew a thing or two which it would be unsafe to divulge to the hoi polloi.

'I think we shan't talk about Jimbo's death in the village,' said my uncle.

'Of course not,' snapped my aunt. 'You always speak as if I were the one who went round Timplingham gossiping.'

My uncle winced as though she were hitting him with a rolling pin. At the same time there was a look of pleasure in his eyes: he liked getting a rise out of her.

'Anyway,' said my aunt, 'I can't imagine the subject coming up. It's fifty years or more since Jimbo *lived* in the Place and Sargie has retreated so much into himself that people hardly *know* about the Lampitts any more.'

Clearly, the idea that people did not know, care or think about Lampitts was too outlandish to be worth answering. My uncle sighed.

'Dear old Jimbo,' he said. 'Do you remember his dropping in here once when he was staying with Sargie?'

'He was rather rude,' said my aunt.

Obviously, this couldn't quite be gainsaid, because my uncle merely replied: 'It was when he was writing that short book on Archbishop Benson. He wanted some advice about the ecclesiastical background. People like that know *nothing*.'

'I didn't like him saying – "Oh, you're Sargie's tame parson."' My aunt adopted the all-purpose mincing tones which in her speech signified 'someone else speaking whom I don't happen to like'. As a matter of fact, Petworth Lampitt *did* have rather a squeaky, mincing voice but, had my aunt taken a dislike to Paul Robeson, her 'imitation' of his voice would have been no different.

'He shouldn't have spoken like that,' she said firmly.

'Oh, it was all right,' said Uncle Roy.

'You didn't like it at the time. You didn't go up to the Place for about three weeks. "I thought Sargie was a friend," you kept saying. "How could he call me his *tame parson*?"'

'It wasn't the only time I met Jimbo,' said my uncle. 'He came to Hilda's eightieth birthday party in Ashley Gardens.'

This was a Lampitt family dinner to which my aunt had not been invited. The memory of it rankled as much as Jimbo's visit to the Rectory.

'It was extremely kind of them to ask me,' said Uncle Roy. 'Jimbo was certainly in cracking form that night, cracking form: memories of Rupert Brooke, Baron Corvo, he even went to see Oscar Wilde in Paris, you know.'

At this my aunt glared. When she was in the mood, my aunt glared easily. I had no idea who Oscar Wilde was, nor what he might have been doing in Paris, but my uncle had clearly sailed too near the wind. He began to generalise.

'Good style and beauty of language are undervalued today, but my guess is that old Jimbo will last. The Prince Consort biography is a classic – and some of the essays. That lovely thing about the death of Tennyson – do you remember it? Him clutching *Cymbeline* and the evening light falling on his beard. "No sound from those lips, no breath"' – my uncle had quite a lot of Jimbo's purple prose by heart – '"He slept, as Arthur slept in Avalon; and, as another Arthur, who lay in the churchyard at Cleveland. The widowed race was run."'

'I expect he'll cut up pretty nicely,' chipped in my aunt brusquely. 'Will Sargie inherit the lot or will they divide it between the remaining siblings?'

'I haven't asked. He seemed much more worried last night about the possibility of an inquest and all the publicity.'

'Oh, *Lord*!' said Aunt Deirdre.

Then with a silent shrug my uncle went to sit in his study to do whatever it was he did there, and my aunt announced that she would be going to the village and would I come with her?

Before we left, we packed the trunk and carried it to the front porch, ready for collection by the railway van.

'One more label perhaps,' said Aunt Deirdre, who was a dab

hand at all activities such as packing, tying parcels, or tidying cupboards. 'Will you stick it on, or will I?'

I let her do so, and stared at its newness, wishing that the name on the label had no connection with the address, but realising with misery that the trunk and the label represented an inevitability.

MASTER JULIAN RAMSAY
SEAFORTH GRANGE SCHOOL
GREAT MALVERN
WORCS

I was always embarrassed by my aunt's continuation of the already obsolete custom of calling me Master Julian Ramsay. It conjured up a picture of Little Lord Fauntleroys, Eton collars and the sort of school stories which my uncle probably read in his own boyhood.

'That's done,' said my aunt. 'Now we can go down to the village.'

'You couldn't get me some stamps if you go into the post office?' asked my uncle, coming out of his study.

'Let's hope we don't meet that wretched woman again!' said my aunt. 'She's *everywhere*. Yesterday, she was in the post office and said' – once more my aunt put on her mincing voice – '"You call me Debbie and I'll call you Jill." Well, I mean, she's only been in the village five minutes!'

'I expect Jill could cope,' said my uncle, lighting his pipe.

'Oh, she ignored it. She gave the woman quite a nice smile, but there was no question of Christian names. It's just so *silly*, trying that sort of thing on.'

I had witnessed the Wretched Woman's blunder. It would be pointless to have told my aunt that Mrs Maddock was only trying to be friendly. That was just the trouble. When my aunt disliked people (she called it 'taking a scunner against them') she could not be reasoned with. It was never explained why she had such a scunner against Mrs Maddock who had moved to the village with her husband not two months before. They still had not learnt that you pronounced it 'Timming 'em', rather than the way it is spelt. Mr Maddock, a weedy little man with glasses, taught in a school in Norwich. She – the Wretched

Woman, that is – did not do anything, but she was a Cambridge graduate. 'And don't we know it!' my aunt would always add when recounting this piece of information. 'I could have told her about Felicity being up at Cambridge. That might have shown her that she wasn't the only person to have been there.'

There was no evidence that the Wretched Woman did sub-scribe to any such extraordinary belief. Just what beliefs she did *not* subscribe to were made all too clear one day in the greengrocer's when she had called out to my aunt, 'You must tell your husband that we'd love to come to support the church, but we just can't believe there's such a thing as a personal creator.'

My uncle seemed most annoyed that the Maddocks had made a joint decision in the matter. It was the 'we' that annoyed him. My aunt averred that the least she could do, the wretched woman, was to keep such ideas to herself and not to go shouting about them in village shops.

The control of information in Timplingham was something in which my uncle and aunt took a strong interest. They did not themselves take a daily paper – Sargie's copy of *The Times* was sent over from The Place several afternoons a week, when he remembered. Otherwise, there was the wireless set. Neither my uncle nor aunt actually said that they believed that these were the only means by which information from the outside world could legitimately reach the village, but they behaved as though this was what they thought. For instance, in the matter of Jimbo's death, they both spoke as if only those within the charmed circle of the Lampitts themselves might be privileged to know of it. Since Sargie was so seldom out and about, the burden fell on the Rectory to decide what the outside world should or should not know about the Lampitts. The previous year, Sargie's Aunt Hilda had died in a nursing home aged eighty-six. There were no suspicious circumstances. Neverthe-less, Uncle Roy treated this story as classified information. He decided that it would be a bad thing if the village 'got talking about it' and we were all sworn to secrecy about Hilda's death. No one in Timplingham had ever heard of Hilda, so it was hardly surprising that bootfaced yokels did not stop my aunt as she walked down the village street in order to quiz her about this most unremarkable passing. Both Uncle Roy and Aunt

Deirdre, however, attributed the village people's silence purely to the efficiency of the Rectory's censorship.

A similar line was to be pursued in relation to Jimbo's demise.

While I put on my blue school gaberdine, Aunt Deirdre adjusted her felt hat in the hall glass. It was her only hat, at least thirty years out of date, vaguely *cloche*. She checked that she had her purse and her shopping list in the bottom of the basket. With her passion for planning everything down to the last detail, she never went out without a list, even if she was only going to post a letter and buy some tobacco for Uncle Roy. She could easily have done the bulk of the shopping on one day each week, but she preferred to do the rounds of the shops every day, disseminating and suppressing news. Like any good agent in the field, my aunt believed in collecting as much information as possible while giving almost nothing away in return.

'Now, we shan't say anything about Jimbo dying,' she repeated to me in the drive.

'Is Uncle Sargie very sad that his brother is dead?' I asked.

'Of course it's a shock – the *way* Jimbo died. But people don't go on for ever.'

It occurred to me – one of the thousand totally false impressions which I harboured as a child – that grown-ups might conceivably not feel things at all. They got into bates; but, by feelings, I meant needing to blub. Grown-ups hardly ever blubbed. I therefore thought it conceivable that feeling was something which you might outgrow, like short trousers.

There had been no mention of Sargie blubbing, even though he *was* one of the grown-ups who sometimes did lose control. Once, when down in the dumps, he had allowed my uncle to buy him lunch in some hotel in Norwich; the salmon was past its best and Sargie had burst into tears. Salmon was worth Sargie's tears, but not the death of a brother. This seemed queer to me.

I agreed with my aunt that nothing should be said of all this in the village; and I believed completely in her power to prevent anyone in Timplingham hearing anything about Jimbo. If Uncle Roy and Aunt Deirdre felt that the village was vaguely hostile or alien, their feelings can have been as nothing to my own. I dreaded the place, hated the idea of having to talk to anyone encountered there, and believed, when I did show my face in the village street, that they were all talking about me. Just going into the shops could be embarrassing; I always had to screw up my courage to do so.

The first port of call was the butcher's. My aunt had the words 'Scrag end' written neatly at the head of her list, words which heralded one of her Irish stews in the near future. As soon as we stepped into the shop my aunt allowed herself an angry 'Tut!' – which was easily explained by the sight of the Wretched Woman standing at the counter.

'You don't have a chicken, Les, I don't suppose?'

'Sold my last, m'dear.'

Mr Harris, the crimson-faced and game-legged butcher, called all his customers, male or female, 'm'dear'. His glistening, lecherous features possibly suggested pleasure at being called Les by this young lady. One suspected that no one, except his darts cronies – and possibly his wife – had ever called him Les since he was a child.

'It's Derek's birthday on Saturday and I wanted to cook something a bit special, you know, perhaps *coq au vin*.'

Mr Harris leered, entering into the spirit of what he took to be some bawdy joke, while the two women behind Mrs Maddock in the queue turned to my aunt. Everyone exchanged glances of horror. Rationing was still in force and the idea of foreign food in Timplingham was somehow not quite nice.

'What about lamb then? Some chops?'

'Right out of chops, m'dear, but I'll tell you what I could do you. A nice bit of scrag end.'

He wiped the cleaver on his old apron, which had once been white and which was now brown with stale blood. Then he clonked a few bits of red and white bone on to the wooden counter.

'I suppose it'll have to do. I can make him a *navarin*.'

Deborah Maddock was tall, blonde, slim and twenty-five years old. If it weren't for the teeth, she would really have been quite pretty. There was a stylishness about her which I admired. I was also fascinated by her voice. Having just about emerged, by the skin of his teeth, from the lower middle classes, my uncle set enormous store by 'good speech', his own voice being in the highest degree mannered and posh. My aunt, who was anyway of a slightly higher social class than her husband, shared Uncle Roy's feeling that educated people should speak what they called 'B.B.C.'. Those who had the misfortune or challenge to grow up speaking 'ee bah gum', as my aunt called any regional variations of speech (northern or southern), jolly well took elocution lessons.

That was Aunt Deirdre's view. Mrs Maddock, evidently, was brazen enough to think otherwise. Although, by today's standards, her voice was barely 'accented' at all, she was thought at the Rectory to 'make rather a thing of being ee bah gum; I should just ignore it if you come across her'. This meant that Mrs Maddock had short North Country 'a's and a few other hardly discernible local variations of speech. I thought she had a nice voice.

While Mr Harris was wrapping the last of the scrag end in newspaper and rolling it into a small haggis-shaped parcel, Mrs Maddock turned round and caught sight of my aunt in the queue behind her.

'Deirdre!' she called. 'Have you seen the news about naughty old Petworth?'

Readers will simply have to take on trust that this is what Debbie Maddock said. At the time, I admit, it seemed incredible. First, one could not believe that she was calling my aunt by her Christian name. One had felt, until that moment, that all my aunt's signals had been so clear that she was somehow keeping Mrs Maddock under control. Evidently not. Secondly, one was astonished that she should have got hold of this top-secret information about the death of James Petworth Lampitt. Thirdly, she was yelling it over the tops of village people's heads as though the Lampitts were just anyone, and even a bit of a joke.

'Ah,' said my aunt, 'good morning, Mrs Maddock.'

'Debbie – *please*. Doctor Leavis used to say that Petworth Lampitt was the worst writer of this century with the possible exception of Humbert Wolfe,' pursued the Wretched Woman. The extraordinary thing was that she did not seem to notice my aunt's face as she was saying it. Not only was she prepared to insult the Lampitts, she was also prepared to admit that she had been discussing them with her doctor. This was surely not something you shouted about in shops.

'Still,' she said, impervious to my aunt's icy demeanour, 'you feel sad when they go, don't you, these old literary landmarks. They actually called him the Albert Memorial, you know.'

My aunt was icily silent while Mrs Maddock blurted out these phrases, derived, as she freely confessed, from that morning's *Manchester Guardian*. It was my first glimpse into the rather horrifying fact that certain people – authors evidently among them – have private lives which are considered to be public property. Had Petworth Lampitt been a local grocer or solicitor it is questionable whether even someone so avant-garde as Mrs Maddock would have yelled about his death in quite such tones.

'You do know who I mean, don't you?' she tried, when she saw that she was getting nowhere with Aunt Deirdre. The people behind Mrs Maddock in the queue were becoming restive. 'Petworth Lampitt. He was an author. His brother lives up at Timplingham Place. They say he's a tremendous recluse and a bit of a boozer, but that's probably just village gossip. Anyway, Petworth – that's the author – fell out of a window or something, or he might have jumped off a roof. It was in the paper. They do quite often commit suicide, of course.'

'I don't know what you are talking about, but whatever you mean, it is a very dangerous line of talk,' said my aunt, who had blushed tremendously.

'Poor old things. A blackmailer gets hold of them and that's it – or they just get overtaken by the sadness of life passing by. They think of the days of their golden youth. It's sadder for them.'

The mention of suicide made everyone in the queue stare even harder. Mrs Maddock got out of the way, allowing the other women to approach the counter to buy what little Mr Harris had left.

None of us at this date had any idea that Debbie Maddock, with her teeth and her twins in a pram, regarded herself as an author. There must already have been a novel in the pipeline, though it was several years before she got it published. In other words, with the death of Petworth Lampitt she felt it necessary, as a fellow scribbler, to note his passing and salute it as best she could.

Quite unconscious that she had said anything in the least offensive, she pushed back her floppy, blonde hair from her forehead and turned to me. She said the one thing which I was trying not to think about.

'Well, young man, you'll be going back to school soon.'

I was really just as shy as Felicity. Even had I wanted to answer this tactless quip, I would have been unable to do so. I just felt myself going red and left Aunt Deirdre to do the talking.

'Next week.'

'Is it awful?' pursued Mrs Maddock. Seeing that I went even redder, she adopted those 'concerned' tones with which I later became so familiar. 'No, I mean it. If it's awful, you should say so. Some of these private schools are positively medieval, Dickensian. I don't know why you don't go to a day school.'

She spoke as though I had some choice in the matter. She couldn't, if she had tried, have trodden on stickier ground. The school, however inadequate, had been chosen by my parents. No doubt it suited my uncle and aunt to have me off their hands for rather more than half the year, but my suspicion is that they might have considered taking me away from Seaforth Grange had it not been Daddy's choice. There was an element of piety to his memory in leaving me at quite such an expensive place and at such an inconvenient distance away.

'The wonder is they don't do away with private education altogether,' said Mrs Maddock. She got absolutely no response from Aunt Deirdre to this little morsel, but she battled on with a self-confident laugh: 'It'll come, it'll come!'

By the time our turn came to stand by Mr Harris's filthy wooden counter, there wasn't much meat left. He tried to sell Aunt Deirdre a blueish joint of pork which he said he had been keeping specially.

'And keeping for some time by the look of it, Mr Harris,' said Aunt Deirdre. In the end, she bought half a pound of mince.

'If in doubt, give them mince,' she announced, as though it were a useful general principle to carry through life.

Once outside the butcher's, she stood on the pavement to consider our next move. She was badly shaken by her encounter with Mrs Maddock and it was obvious that we must avoid bumping into her again that morning.

'We'll hang back.' My aunt spoke with the quiet seriousness of a platoon commander who knew that enemy snipers were lurking in every tree and rooftop.

One of the most difficult things about constructing a truthful review of the past is knowing how to chronicle feelings: to say just when I felt this, and when I began to feel the opposite. Everything gets coloured by one's most recent feelings; about Debbie Maddock, my feelings have been so different that it is hard to get any of them into focus. I can't actually remember what I felt about her before she began her career as a novelist, but I *think* that even then, on the morning we met her in the butcher's, she represented rather a romantic world to me, one of which I did not yet dare to think I would be a part, but a universe which represented the most exciting contrasts with that of the Rectory.

Even while I relished my aunt's extreme dislike for Mrs Maddock (just as a spectacle, in the way that some cruel people enjoy bullfights) I was aware that Mrs Maddock awoke in me the dream of other worlds. Was this what Uncle Roy had felt when he first developed Lampitt-mania? For him, the excitement was something which I have cruelly dismissed as snobbish, but he was not in the mean sense a worldly man. He did not love the Lampitts because he hoped to get on. Rather, he loved them at first for what they represented and later, quite simply, as people. After he met Sargie, the world was a bigger place for Uncle Roy, it contained larger imaginative possibilities. Rank, status and fame were only part of the picture, not the whole of it. Money, except in so far as it allowed Sargie to do nothing, and therefore to be endlessly available to waste my uncle's time, played very little part in the picture. None of these things would have meant anything to me aged twelve. But Debbie Maddock, from a very early stage, suggested worlds of which one might dream: a bohemian atmosphere in which people spoke their mind, unfettered by the habits of politeness and concealment with which my uncle and aunt chose to imprison themselves, a world of meals served any old time, of foreign recipes and literary talk . . . I don't know, it was all too nebulous to define. But her presence, just her existence, excited me rather. If Sargie had opened a doorway for my uncle into an enchanted garden, perhaps Mrs Maddock, precisely because my aunt disapproved of her so forcefully, would open a gate for me into another.

Perhaps a large part of the charm derived simply from the

fact that she was still a young, personable woman, only about a dozen years older than myself. This too was a new area of things of which I had only the smallest intimations. School, appropriately, was where I was learning. At Seaforth Grange, we had an undermatron scarcely out of her teens called Vanessa Faraday. Her (for those days) short skirts and unmistakably ample figure beneath woollen jumpers made a vivid impression when she supervised bath nights and dormitory drill. In our dorm, she permitted us all a good-night kiss, allowing us for some moments to hold her against our flat pyjamaed chests and to press our lips against her own. In that austere environment, these kisses were deeply consoling.

Among all her admirers there was active speculation about Vanessa's real boyfriend, who was said to live in her home town of Bromyard, Worcs. Was he handsome and what was the extent of the favours extended to him? Although we all prided ourselves on our acquaintance with 'the facts of life', our ideas were almost inconceivably mechanical and crude. In point of fact, there was very little imaginative connection in my mind between the wonderful sensation of kissing Vanessa's full, moist lips, while her breast was clasped to mine, and the cruder levels of dormitory talk after she had switched out the light and left us alone. Although it was a full year or eighteen months since Darnley had informed me how our parents had begotten us, the information had not properly sunk in. A good deal of scepticism remained. If, as seemed to be the case, our mothers had truly allowed this extraordinary invasion of themselves to occur, one could be fairly sure that they did not make a habit of it. Since I was an only child, the evidence suggested that my parents had only had to do it once. Poor Darnley's mother had wanted a large family and had had to do it four times. I now understood, and shared, my aunt's disapproval of Roman Catholics who had been known to do it anything up to eight or ten times.

This being the level of my knowledge and sophistication, it is unnecessary to explain that most of Debbie Maddock's talk about naughty old Petworth, blackmailers and golden youth sailed over my head, and meant absolutely nothing to me. Imaginatively speaking, they still mean very little. The difference between my perceptions now and my twelve-year-old vision of things lies largely in my greater capacity to make connections. Just as I would never have connected good-night kisses from Vanessa with Darnley's anatomical jokes and chit-chat, nor would I have associated Petworth Lampitt (after all, he was a *Lampitt*) with the manifestations of inversion which had so far come my way. These fell into the two general categories of things which had happened to Darnley on scout camp (regaled to the rest of us amid fits of giggles after lights-out) and those more melancholy episodes back at school when the Binker (our word for the Headmaster) was being a Dirty Old Man.

The fact that the Binker was a D.O.M. awakened in us all at various times a mixture of fear, amusement and distress. But, like his cruelty and his verbal mannerisms, it was something peculiar to the Binker, something of which, on his behalf, we felt ashamed and which I would not have found words to describe to any grown-up. I hated the Binker and I should love to have disgraced him; but it was impossible to speak of such things to anyone, least of all to Aunt Deirdre and Uncle Roy. I had never been his victim, but Darnley had been made to go into the Binker's study and take off all his clothes, while many others had suffered one of the Binker's little talks on the sofa, hands straying, or been visited at bathtime – 'Is that water warm enough? Don't move! Nothing to be afraid of!'

The victims imitated the Binker saying this, telling the rest of us in those terrible whispers after lights-out. Sometimes we listened in complete silence and sometimes we let out chilly laughter. No, it never crossed my mind that Mrs Maddock was shouting about *this* sort of thing on that morning in the butcher's shop in Timplingham. I could not imagine why she thought Petworth Lampitt was naughty. Had I realised, I should probably have understood and shared my aunt's rigid horror, as she hovered in the street, determined, at least during that morning's shopping expedition, not to bump into that Wretched Woman again.

*   *

'Felicity!'
Silence.

I was standing outside her bedroom door. I knew she was in there because I could hear her turning the pages of her book. Also, from time to time, I heard her crunching a raw carrot which she had found from somewhere. It is unlikely that my aunt's larder afforded such riches. I suspected Felicity of raiding a neighbour's rabbit hutches.

'Felicity, it's me.'

'Cleo – nmph.' That squelching, chewing sound. Perhaps it wasn't a carrot. Perhaps she was just sinking ravenous teeth into a raw potato.

'Felicity, I really have got an aquarium now. Like to come and look?'

Silence.

It was incomprehensible that anyone could be informed of the existence of a new aquarium in the house without wishing to view it. A mixture of hurt and fury welled through my body to think of Felicity sitting there, with her solid, red face, not answering.

'Oh, come *on*, Felicity.'

Her bedroom door opened. She stood there holding a copy of Camus's *L'Etranger*.

'There's an aquarium in my room now.'

'So you said.'

Triumph! I had actually got Felicity to mouth some syllables. She scowled, knowing that I had scored a point here, and shook back her thick, reddish hair from her freckled brow.

'I was just helping Aunt Deirdre with the garden and it was lying there. You're a lazy pig anyway, not helping – we've laid out the spinach and all the lettuce: we've sown radish seeds and stock. Anyway, I thought it was dead at first and I picked it up to stop Tinker eating it.'

'Eating what?'

On the rare occasions when she addressed me, she had a ponderous way of speaking; I was prisoner in the dock and she was the presiding magistrate, aged a hundred and eighteen rather than eighteen.

'Then it jumped. It's lovely, Felicity, come and look.'

'Is this a joke?'

'Aunt Deirdre says I'll have to release him, poor little chap. I'd hoped I might breed them.'

'If it's a frog . . .'

Felicity obviously did not know what she would do if it was a frog. It was a foolish sentence to have started. She ought to have known that, even with her powers of cleverness, she could not change frogs into other things – handsome princes or anything else. With extreme reluctance, my cousin followed me into my bedroom. On the surface which served as dressing table, desk, storage space and laboratory bench, I had placed a large mixing bowl full of water in which a toad was swimming, a beautiful little creature with black and gold markings and glossy black eyes.

'I knew it would be a frog. Put it back in the garden at *once*, Julian.'

She was trying to act nonchalant, but she was scared as hell. I had not brought the toad indoors with the purpose of tormenting her. I was enraptured by its beauty and genuinely wanted to share my joy. Seeing how rattled she was, however, it was tempting to make her suffer, just a little.

'But it's a toad.'

'I can see that.'

'Why say it's a frog then? Would you like to hold it?'

She wasn't staying for this. She turned and walked back to her own room.

'Look at its lovely eyes,' I said.

'I am aware that toads have eyes,' said Felicity, before she slammed her bedroom door.

Darnley would have understood. He had sisters who were even more putrid than my cousin. He also had an extensive knowledge of natural history. I would have asked him to stay with me during the holidays. Aunt Deirdre often urged me to ask a friend and said that she wished I mixed more with boys of my own age. I think Darnley would have enjoyed it. I couldn't bring myself to ask him, though. I was lonely during the holidays and would have valued a croney, but I was too ashamed of the oddness of my family, of the whole Rectory set-up, to risk a friend coming to stay. Darnley would find out that I helped at church and then next term it would be all round the school. Or my uncle would have waylaid him and talked endlessly about the Lampitts. No, having someone to stay in the hols wasn't on. Besides, little as I enjoyed either, I wanted school and home to be quite distinct. The idea was that the holidays were tremendously enjoyable. I think if I had seen the Rectory through the eyes of a friend, I should have realised that this was not quite true. Instinct made me shield myself from the knowledge.

Whatever the reason, the transition between the two worlds was something which I was unable to manage. There was a half-truth in my aunt's brisk 'He'll be all right once he's *back*,' and 'He's much better off without a lot of fuss.'

When I came downstairs with the toad still cupped in my hand, my uncle and aunt were having one of their conferences. These discussions about arrangements were often unpremeditated; they took place suddenly, often in unlikely places, with one person standing halfway up the stairs while another peered down from a landing, or both sitting on the substantial marble-topped table in the hall. On this occasion, my aunt was hovering by the green baize door, with her apron and her air of crossness a parody of the stage domestic. My uncle (the mad employer? the tyrannical butler?) was standing on one leg in the further recesses of the corridor, a coal hod in hand. He was in the middle of stoking the Aga.

'That may be better in any case,' said Aunt Deirdre.

'I don't think Sargie could object.'

'I mean, it might avert, you know . . .'

I instantly grasped that they were discussing the travel arrangements for my return to school. These always threw them into an unreasonable panic because I was unable to take my leave of them without violent displays of emotion. They were lucky if they got away with tears on the station platform. More than once there had been actual hysterics at Paddington and I had had to be forcibly carried on to the Malvern train. They were always devising new means of conveying me back to school without such an outburst. I was as anxious as they to avoid the embarrassment of such involuntary displays. (I had long ago abandoned any hope that they would take me away from the school and I had only a couple more terms there to run.) They had tried both accompanying me. I had clung to them and screamed. Singly, and the same thing had happened. They had sent me by car with Mr Padley the gardener. That was the time I had to be carried on to the train by a porter, and

Mr Padley had subsequently handed in his notice. Now, it seemed, they had hit on a new method.

'Felicity thought it was a frog!' I said. 'I'm going to start an aquarium.'

I opened my hands and showed the quivering little toad to my uncle.

'Wouldn't he be happier in the garden?'

'Please, Uncle Roy.'

'I'll have to have that mixing-bowl back in any case' – it was always an ominous sign when my aunt sided with my uncle in a conversation. 'Mrs Batterbee will be wanting it.'

I could see the wisdom of all this. We were pretending to have a conversation about the toad. Actually, we were talking about the fact that, in three days' time, I would not be there. It was an example of that touching human propensity to behave as though there were a future even when reason declares that there isn't. The man on his way to the gallows asks permission to stoop down and tie his shoelace. The Jewish woman brushes mud off her husband's shoulder in the queue for the gas ovens, though clothes (muddy or otherwise) and life itself are soon to be surrendered. These are not the actions of foolish optimists. Rather, instinct keeps them straining towards the sun, even when they no longer believe in the future.

Comparisons as strong as this will strike home to readers who reacted as I did to the English Gulag, and will be dismissed by others as tasteless and trivial. English frivolity, the inability to take serious things seriously, the tendency to treat unserious things – dogs or school – as other races might treat war and death – these are difficult waters to chart. As any navigator knows, it is the shallows where vessels come unstuck. Much of the difficulty derives from the fact that emotions cannot be faked up. It may be that we *should* mind about some things, rather than others, but 'sensation is sensation'. I am sure that I am not the only English reader of the Russian prison novels of the Stalinist period, Grossman or Solzhenitsyn, who feels, from the moment of the protagonist's arrest, a complete familiarity with all the emotions through which he passes. The actual deprivations and hardships of an English school may be worse than a Soviet labour camp, and the food about on a level. What counts is that the inner torment is identical – the sharing of insanitary conditions with too many uncongenial people, the strange friendships and distrusts which grow up among fellow prisoners, the same fear of the system which never quite leaves you. The only major difference is that *their* Gulag is something of which the Soviet Government is ashamed, denying its very existence, whereas the English system of private schools is openly boasted about, one of the glories of the world. So powerful is the effect of propaganda that even those who have been through the system and know what it is like are prepared to whitewash their memories and pretend that the dear old place was not so bad as weeds and sneaks such as myself might claim. The other day I had an invitation to the centenary of the foundation of Seaforth Grange. It is a bizarre fact that people will have attended this function and even paid £5 for a buffet lunch. It is rather as if former inmates of the Bastille or the Lubyanka were eagerly to revisit their place of torment, attending a service of thanksgiving in the chapel for all the benefits which such institutions have showered upon humanity; hear a sermon by some former inmate, now a bishop, extolling the virtue of warders whom he knew at the time to be cruel or insane; and even contemplate putting down the names of their own children for a spell in clink.

All this is as much as to say that I could see that there was no future in my aquarium. My aunt told me to give her back the bowl and to dispose of the toad, which I did. I suppose it was cruel, because I might have guessed the ultimate fate of that beautiful creature.

That afternoon, standard Lubyanka procedure, I was taken to the village barber to have my hair cropped. It might be thought strange that there was a barber in such a small place. Haircutting was only by appointment with Mr Sykes, a retired man who operated from his front room in a small house near the Methodist chapel. 'He cut hair in Kingsway,' was always the boast, though I have never heard since that this London thoroughfare was particularly famous for its high-quality barbers.

Uncle Roy, who always accompanied me to the barber, used to say it every time we approached Mr Sykes's door.

'It's a jolly good bob's worth – and don't forget, he used to cut hair in Kingsway.' Evidently, in my uncle's belief, it was like saying a doctor had once had a Harley Street practice or that a tailor, though now operating from a front room in Timplingham, had once cut clothes in Savile Row. Sometimes, when recording in Bush House, I have walked up Kingsway and tried to identify the barber's shop where Mr Sykes was once employed. At some periods, unless I am mistaken, there have been no hairdressing establishments there at all. More recently, the kind of unisex salons which have sprung up all over London have seemed a world away from the smelly little parlour where this alleged expert in the coiffeur's art spluttered over his combs and razors, and hovered, with blunt scissors and quivering hand, so perilously close to one's ears.

'I hear there's been a sad bereavement up at The Place,' said Mr Sykes, solemnly blowing some of the scurf from his comb before applying it to my scalp.

'It is very sad, a great loss,' said my uncle's voice behind me. I could see his face in Mr Sykes's looking-glass. For the quarter of an hour or so which it took Mr Sykes to give me the shorn appearance of a Soviet army private, my uncle lectured him on Lampitt-lore. Mr Sykes, before his illustrious career in Kingsway (I often wondered whether sweeping the floor rather than cutting the hair had not been his vocation, wherever the barber's shop in question), had been born in Timplingham and lived there for much of his life. He probably knew as well as I did who all the Lampitts were and could remember the days of their youth. On one occasion, he had even told me how Sargie had run away from Winchester. But he was patient, while my uncle recited his *credo*.

'The eldest brother you may remember – Sir Michael Lampitt.'

'He who was a director of the railway, sir? Yes, yes. I remember Master Michael, though him we always thought of as the second son, sir, there having been young Master Martin who died when he was a lad.'

'I meant the eldest survivor,' said my uncle shortly.

'And then there was Mr James.'

My uncle smiled tolerantly. This was the mistake people often made, to forget about Vivian Lampitt. Mr Sykes fully conceded defeat here.

'Went to live in Africa, did he, sir?'

'Mombasa,' I chipped in.

'And *then* it was Mr James,' said Mr Sykes.

'Martin; James Petworth; Michael, who was killed at Mons; Vivian, Sargent, Sybil,' said my uncle, just to make sure that there would be no mistakes in future.

'And Miss Sybil, she's now Lady – what *is* her name?'

'Lady Starling.'

'And still going strong, sir – her ladyship, I mean?'

'Oh, rather!' said my uncle. 'What a *charming* person she is. Gentle to a fault and of course a very great beauty. In her youth, as you will know, she really moved in very high society indeed.'

'Well, is that *so*, sir?'

'Oh,' said Uncle Roy airily, 'presented at court. The lot. But completely modest with it. Too kind, some would say. Mr Sargent always says that his sister is a complete doormat, lets people walk all over her.'

'Is that so, sir?'

'Yes,' said Uncle Roy, and they paused for a moment's respectful silence as they contemplated the beauty of Lady Starling's character.

'And then there's Mr Lampitt who's in the Cabinet, isn't there, sir?'

'Ah, that's the Honourable Vernon – he's the son of *Lord* Lampitt, who is Mr Sargent's uncle. They live at Mallington Hall.'

'Out beyond Downham Market, that would be, sir?'

'That general direction. It's one of the most splendid houses in the county,' said Uncle Roy.

'And to think they just started off no better than you and me, brewing beer in King's Lynn,' said Mr Sykes with a sigh.

This egalitarian line of talk would not do. My uncle leaned forward to survey the few hairs left on my head and said, 'Just a little more off the back, if you please, Mr Sykes.'

'More off the back, sir? Right you are.'

I was never consulted about the length of my own hair.

'We'll have you all nice and smart for the summer, won't we, young sir? Be playing a lot of cricket, I expect.'

'Not if I can help it,' I said sourly.

I was fed up with Lampitt-talk. I loathed having my hair cut. I rather hated Mr Sykes and I hated all forms of organised sport. Mr Sykes attempted a weak laugh which evolved into a lung-wringing torrent of coughing, only relieved by taking a somewhat crinkly cigarette from behind his left ear, applying it to his lips and lighting up. The rest of the work with clippers and scissors took place in billows of Woodbine smoke, so that in this incense cloud I was more than ever like some shorn, sacrificial victim.

My uncle went on reciting the names of Lampitts all day. Evidently, he was going through in his mind all the members of the family who could be expected to put in an appearance at Jimbo's funeral. Rather as at certain times of year the rabbis recite those enormous genealogies from the Book of Numbers, rehearsing the names of the Hebrews who crossed the Jordan with Joshua into the Land of Promise, so the Rector of Timplingham spoke of Lampitts throughout the morning and the afternoon. Technically, he had an audience: at lunch, my aunt, myself and Felicity; during the afternoon, a mixture of myself and Mr Gillard who did rough work in the garden; and during the evening, the family once more.

I am fairly sure that the recitation would have continued even if he had spent the day alone, interrupted only for the quarter of an hour when, clad in Canterbury Cap and M.A. gown he went over to church at four p.m. to read evensong. And perhaps, even then, there was no controlling a man's thoughts. It is hard to imagine a recitation of the *Magnificat*, with its mention of the mighty in their seats, without the mind involuntarily straying to the Honourable Vernon in the Cabinet, or to Dame Ursula Lampitt, the Principal of an Oxford college. Similarly, the exaltation of the humble and meek, promised in the same canticle, could not be read without some thought of Lady Starling.

I cried a bit during that evening's episode of 'The Mulberrys', hoping that nobody could see. Supper, which, my uncle being present, was at seven, after 'The Mulberrys', was sausages with mash, followed by Eve's pudding with custard. These were my favourite dishes. On any other day of the holiday, I would have wolfed them down. The eve of departure, however, was always enough to bring a sick dread into my stomach. I pecked at custard which on other days would have not had time to cool on my plate.

When the meal was over, we all played cards. When the

silently erubescent Felicity had twice, by the luck of the draw, been declared an Old Maid (a verdict which Fate, in real life, looked all too likely to endorse) her parents hastily switched to gin-rummy. Then bed – and a good-night kiss from my uncle and one from my aunt. Even Felicity grunted before slamming her bedroom door, an action which was normally accomplished without utterance. She treated me like a brother, that girl.

I went to my own room and listened. Felicity was a long while getting undressed. I began to fear that I might fall asleep before I heard her. Probably, it was not much more than half an hour, but it seemed like an eternity. Then, more satisfyingly loud than I could possibly have hoped, her under-worked vocal chords were given more exercise than they had had for years. Her screams could have been heard in the village.

'Oh – the *pig!*'

Doors were flung open.

My aunt, who was still downstairs, called up to ask what was the matter.

'The frog –' gasped Felicity. 'Julian put the frog in my bed. I felt it on my toes.'

*   *

'Put your cap on, I should,' said Uncle Roy.

'I should' was his strongest imperative. In this case, was his sentence, taken literally, believable? Would he, in any circumstances, be prepared to walk through the village wearing an electric-blue school cap, with the initials 'S.G.' (for Seaforth Grange) emblazoned above the peak? Perhaps he would. I was made of feebler stuff.

I had eaten my breakfast. My bag was packed and in my hand. My mac was on.

'Goodbye, old thing.' My aunt pecked my cheek. 'I'll write. And Granny will come down to see you in a few weeks. We'll get down when we can – anyway for the sports.'

I was being phenomenally good. There was not so much as a crack in my voice as I bid farewell to Aunt Deirdre.

Felicity, who was also standing there in the hall, smiled with unconcealed relief at my imminent departure. The toad incident had not been mentioned. I heard my aunt, while I was dressing, telling Felicity not to start getting me upset; to which Felicity had replied, not unreasonably, what about her?

'You have *got* your cap, haven't you?' asked my uncle when we were in the drive.

'The thing is, I packed it in my bag,' I improvised. Actually, it was in my mackintosh pocket.

I could see that Uncle Roy would not force a showdown about the cap. Already his mind was full of the day which lay ahead. Within a matter of hours, he would be feasting his gaze on a crematorium chapel packed with Lampitts. He wore a white shirt and a black tie to mark the occasion. Aunt Deirdre had talked him out of wearing the opera hat.

'They'll think you're one of the undertakers, especially since you're driving.'

In the event, he wore the *Daily Mail* one and a black suit which was unseasonably thick.

'Your Uncle Sargie will be very upset,' said my real uncle as we walked along. 'He hates funerals. He always expects me to . . .' Here he began to laugh. '"Save me from my relations, Roy!"' he said in his Sargie voice. 'The last family gathering of any size to which I accompanied him was Gloria's funeral. He somehow managed to quarrel with his sister Sybil. It was about the transfer of some shares, I seem to remember. Good old Sargie.' More chuckling. 'He said, "My sister drives a *very* hard bargain." And this of Sibs, who's the most charming girl and submissive to a fault, as Sargie, in more enlightened mood, is the first to admit.'

'Does Uncle Sargie not really like his family?'

'Sh, sh, sh. You mustn't say things like that! The Lampitts are all very highly strung. They are apt to fly at one another's throats somewhat,' he said admiringly.

By now we had crossed the road, passed the lodge cottage, where Sargie's housekeeper lived with her husband, and followed the drive up towards Timplingham Place, a rather handsome, red-brick affair, 1750s, with two wings and a graceful flight of steps leading up to the grand, central front door. This was the entrance we used. My uncle invariably walked in without knocking.

'Coo-ee!' he called as we entered the large hall. 'We're here! Oh, good morning, Mrs Marsh.'

'He's not up yet,' said this long-suffering domestic. She savoured the shock produced by this remark and then, out of pity, she began to mollify it.

'Well, he's *up*, but not dressed.'

She cast her eyes upwards.

('This time, Mr Sargent, you've gone too far,' Sargie liked to imitate her saying. Unlike my uncle and aunt, he was a good mimic and captured Mrs Marsh's Norfolk lilt to perfection.)

'Is he in the bedroom?' asked Uncle Roy, putting the *Daily Mail* hat on the huge refectory table which stood in the hall.

'Oh, no. He's in the library.'

Another raising of the eyes aloft.

Completely ignoring me, my uncle strode through the passage and the drawing room which led to the library. As Uncle Roy opened the door, I could hear Sargie's anguished voice call out, 'Mind! Don't let Joynson-Hicks out!'

There was a rush to the door and my uncle just managed to prevent the exit of Joynson-Hicks, a rather flatulent marmalade Tom who, though all of fourteen, was still quick on his pins.

'All ready to go?' asked Uncle Roy hopefully.

'Roy, you'll have to go without me,' said Sargie in pathetic tones. 'I find that, after all I can't face it.'

'Say hallo to Uncle Sargie,' said my real uncle. He was flummoxed by Sargie's announcement and played for time by turning attention to myself.

'Hallo,' I said, going round to shake Sargie's hand. Although the days had passed when my uncle made me kiss Sargie, I could still smell the distinctive, spirituous flavour (almost neat gin with a dash of dry vermouth) of Sargie's breath.

'Poor old man,' he said to me, with a gesture to my uniform which made clear what he meant. For some reason Sargie's allusion to my imminent departure to concentration camp did not upset me. It was genuine boy-to-boy stuff. There was nothing of adult condescension in it. 'Let's both do a bunk, eh? I don't want to go to this bloody funeral and you don't want to go to your bloody school.'

I would have welcomed the scheme, even in Sargie's company.

'If we don't set out soon, Sargie, there won't be any time for lunch and Julian will miss his train.' My uncle could plainly see the whole day going wrong. There was panic in his voice and face.

'Joynson-Hicks says I don't have to go,' said Sargie, slowly, seeming to savour the effects of the gin on his sibilants. 'And he says that Julie doesn't have to go back to school either.'

I was close enough for Sargie to ruffle my hair. Then he picked up Joynson-Hicks and stroked him instead.

'You're a wise old campaigner, aren't you, Joynson-Hicks?'

Sargie had all the Lampitt features too strongly to be in any sense handsome: a long, bony face with a pronounced Roman nose, beneath which was cultivated a moustache, at that date a brindled grey though the hair on his head, sleekly combed back and perhaps even brilliantined, was mysteriously dark. He wore horn-rimmed spectacles and the smouldering cigarette in its bone holder was so often between his lips that one thought of it as a permanent extension of his physical features, like a tusk or a unicorn's horn.

'Come *on*, Sargie,' said Uncle Roy, nearly stamping his foot.

'You see, I think Cecily will be there. She's always at these things.'

'She won't necessarily be.'

'Yes she will. She and Jimbo were as thick as thieves. You know how she poisoned his mind against me.'

'I'm sure that's not true.'

'Well, we were reconciled a year or so ago, in spite of her. Otherwise, I shouldn't be able to stay on here. I really need Jimbo's money. Well, it's not all his money, it's Mama's. Did I tell you I was the sole heir?'

'No.'

'Well, the idea was that the others were more or less set up. Now it's just me and Sibs anyway, and she's rich as Croesus. And I have this place to keep up. I've been thinking of some of the improvements I shall make here now I have a bit of cash.'

'Does the Place need improving?' I asked.

'Lord, yes.'

He stood up, holder still between his lips, dropping ash down the front of his dressing gown.

'You don't mean that I have to come to this bloody thing of Jimbo's?' he asked.

'I should if I were you,' said Uncle Roy.

'Oh, Julie! He's a hard taskmaster, your uncle!' And then the next sentence Sargie intoned. It was hard to see its relevance, but perhaps it just signified that he was getting in the mood for a funeral service. The voice was not mock-parsonical; on the contrary, it was sonorous, almost moving. 'Now we see through a glass darkly, but then face to face. Well, I'm half done as you can see, my dears.'

He flung open his plaid dressing gown to reveal a long shirt, whose tails stretched to his knees; a stiff collar, black silk tie, black socks, suspenders tied from the knee, highly polished black shoes.

'I got disheartened before I put on my trousers. What are we meant to be wearing anyway? I can't tell from your rig-out, Roy. It won't be morning coat will it? Surely they won't have all that bloody nonsense just for Jimbo. A black coat and striped trousers, I thought.'

'I'm sure that will be all right.'

'What are you wearing?' – he turned to me – 'Oh, you're not coming.'

He left us for a remarkably short space of time, coming downstairs as smart as paint and carrying a well-brushed bowler.

'Michael's old hat. Used to wear it to meetings. Look here, Roy, you're going to have to drive, is that all right?'

'Perfectly.'

'Will you be safe on the back seat, Julie?'

'Oh yes,' I said. And soon, with my little case, I had sidled on to the large soft back seat of the Daimler.

Sargie's life had been sadder than most, the turnings falser, the ends deader. Uncle Roy could not avoid hyperbole when talking about that family, but I have heard others say that Sargie had been brilliant. He was a scholar of Winchester, a Fellow of New College and then had come the rather surprising marriage to Cecily. No one ever told me exactly what had gone wrong here, but his dread of his wife was something about which he was always vocal. It was some time during the First World War that they had got married. Asthma made it unthinkable that he would join up. Instead, he watched all the young men go to the trenches.

By the end of the First World War, Sargie must have been

about thirty. The distinguished monograph on the House of Lords (written from an abolitionist point of view when he was only twenty-one) had never been followed up by the large work of grand political analysis of which everyone had believed him to be capable. Felicity, after she became a don, heard someone say that Sargent Lampitt was the only Englishman since Hobbes who had it in him to be a great political philosopher and thinker. Something happened, though. By the time the Great War had ended, so had his marriage. There was, I believe, a spell in an asylum. The attempt to resume an academic life had not been wise. Not long after my uncle, very young, had been appointed to the living of Timplingham, Sargie had come home to live with his mother at The Place. When old Mrs Lampitt died (not long after the outbreak of the Second World War) the rest of the family were all settled elsewhere. They had no wish to come back and run what Sargie, with a mixture of irony and true snobbery, used to apologise was 'only a bought house'. So he stayed there and ran the place as best he could, with the help of Mr and Mrs Marsh, and one or two other makeshift domestics and amateur gardeners. His only companions were my Uncle Roy and the gin bottle.

The desire to chicken out of that morning's melancholy expedition was typical of Sargie's neurotic behaviour. In later years, I need hardly say, the whole day had become one of my uncle's anecdotes.

'We've got plenty of time,' said Sargie.

'Oh, plenty,' said Uncle Roy.

'That doesn't mean that you have to drive at a snail's pace.'

Although in a nannyish way my uncle bullied and cajoled Sargie, he seemed fully to accept his role as a sort of glorified servant. Rather than question Sargie's right to nag about the driving, he put his foot on the accelerator and the car sped out on the road towards Newmarket. It was a reasonably straight bit of road and the scene was one of haunting beauty. The vast sky dominated. The picture was seven-eighths sky; the rest, elms and horse chestnuts coming into leaf, fields and hedges tinged with the first green of the year, thorn and may already in blossom. After a very few minutes of swirling through this canvas by Hobbema, Sargie let out a deep moan.

'Do slow down, silly. Are you trying to kill us?'

This fast-slow nonsense punctuated the whole drive, a very merciful accident, because although I felt slightly sick in the back of the car and I was dreading my handover to the prison guards at Paddington Station, I found the bickering of the two men wonderfully amusing.

Uncle Roy obviously thought that I was crying when I tried to disguise my giggles by stuffing a handkerchief into my mouth. I could see him in the driving mirror, avoiding my gaze. Sargie was far too absorbed in his own thoughts to be thinking about me. Occasionally he resorted to a small hip flask and that pleasantly spirituous exhalation which I had discerned in the library at Timplingham filled the limousine. The more he imbibed, the more the death and the approaching funeral of his brother appeared to impinge on his consciousness; the higher, too, grew his estimation of Petworth Lampitt as a prosewriter.

'He wrote some books, didn't he, old Jimbo?'

'He certainly did,' said Uncle Roy. 'Particularly the Prince Albert.'

'It's a little masterpiece, isn't it? Bloody little masterpiece. And the one about Swinburne. And you don't need to go to Venice if you've read his Venetian thing, you know, whatever it's called.'

'*Lagoon Loungings.*'

'That's the fella. Another bloody classic.'

'It is excellent.'

'And yet – I say, Roy, slow down on the bends, can't you?'

'Sorry, Sargie.'

'They had it in for him, those buggers, didn't they?'

'I'm afraid they probably did.'

'Any excuse to denigrate quality, to run down good writing, genius.'

One of the views which appeared to unite Sargie and my Uncle Roy was the idea that there was a gang of people – their precise identity remaining something of a mystery – who were committed to bring to pass all the things of which they themselves disapproved. It sounded as though the motive of these people, the buggers, was pure spite. No erotic preference was indicated by the term. Debbie Maddock was in this sense a bugger, who had learnt from Dr Leavis (a bugger if ever there was one) to denigrate Petworth Lampitt's work, when in fact all Jimbo's books were masterpieces.

'Bloody masterpieces,' concluded Sargie. 'So were the articles he wrote in the Sunday papers. I know it's a sad thing when people descend to writing for the papers, but Jimbo made an art of it. Gems, they were. Did you read the thing he wrote only last week about the French merchant?'

'I hadn't heard of him before,' said Uncle Roy. 'Jewish, I think. Jimbo made quite a lot of that.'

The Lampitts were famous pro-Semites. There is even a Lampitt Street in Tel Aviv, in consideration of the numbers of refugees from Hitler rescued by Sargie's uncle, Lord Lampitt. But everyone in that circle still spoke about the Jews in terms which would nowadays sound offensive.

'Proust,' said Sargie. 'He wrote this bloody great novel all about his own childhood and then a whole lot of characters all linking up with the big house where he used to spend his summer holidays. They all turn out to be pansies.'

'As you know, I don't really read novels, except for 'tecs,' said my uncle.

'We all read them when they started to trickle over here. Haven't looked at them since. Jimbo had. He read everything. I thought his thing on Proust was bloody brilliant.'

The vehemence with which this was spoken was really addressed to all those who had asserted otherwise, the philistines, the buggers, Mrs Maddock, Dr Leavis and all.

'You're right,' added Sargie. 'He was a Jewboy, now you mention it. All happened at the time of Dreyfus. The French have different ideas about all that sort of thing – I say, for Christ's sake, Roy, we may be going to a funeral, but do you *have* to drive so slowly?'

Although unused to the Daimler, Uncle Roy got us to London remarkably smoothly and, considering all the fuss Sargie was making, in a remarkably good temper. There was the occasional expostulation ('Sargie – honest*lee*!') but no sharp retorts.

Seeing London always thrilled me as a child. It thrills me still. The passing seasons are no less marked there than in the country. As we drove westward, we passed bombsites vivid with green; daffodils in window boxes; beneath trees, grass was purple and gold with crocuses. We purred along to Sargie's club in Mayfair.

'Like to come in for a snifter?'

Sargie was quite without side. If I had said that I would like a glass of brandy and soda, he would have had no hesitation about taking me into his club, clad in blazer and shorts.

'I think . . .' Uncle Roy consulted his fob and had no need to finish his sentence. My train left Paddington in not much over half an hour.

We had parked by the kerb and were standing on the pavement in Brook Street, awkwardly sniffing the air before we took our farewells. Suddenly departure was chillingly imminent.

'I'll come back to lunch with you,' said my uncle to Sargie. 'We can either eat at the club or go to Claridges. There'd be time.'

'Plenty. The funeral's not till three.'

Their ability to talk about these events, which were to take place after my own departure, was intolerable to me. A figure lying close to death would have felt the same if watchers round the bed began to discuss their plans for what to do after his demise. Sargie became aware of their insensitivity. He had been far from a model schoolboy himself and I always knew, without his having to explain anything, that he *understood*. He turned on me a look of genuine, unmistakable sympathy, the one thing at that moment which could have been calculated to topple my equilibrium.

'Well, my dear, chin chin,' he said.

Even as he pressed a large, white, crinkly five-pound note into my hand, I burst into tears.

TWO

My earliest memories are of screaming and crying. In my dread of being separated from my mother, there must have been some element of premonition. As a young child, I always screamed myself to sleep unless one of my parents, nearly always my mother, consented to sit by my bed, stroking my brow with her hand. If she were to leave me a moment before I actually fell asleep, I woke up completely and started to cry with panic. Telling Felicity about this phenomenon, years later, I discovered that my good-night screams were already a part of family legend.

'You were a spoilt little tick,' was her probably quite legitimate judgement.

If spoiling was the reason I screamed, my parents must have rued their mistaken softness towards me. My involuntary demand for companionship last thing at night was so powerful that I was incapable of releasing them from it, even when I was old enough to reason with myself and to long *not* to be a nuisance. If they were at home, one of them had to sit with me. On those occasions (and, poor things, I suspect they were pretty rare) when they allowed themselves to go out for the evening, I screamed and screamed until exhaustion brought its own comfortless, unsatisfying sleep. Quite often, they would return from the film, or the meal out, to find me still wailing at ten or eleven o'clock. I can vividly recollect every stage and element of these paroxysms. First, the eyes watering, tears uncontrollably falling down my cheeks and that unpleasant feeling in the back of the throat which heralded the start of a weeping fit. If my mother was at hand, this first stage could be averted by her smoothing my brow and singing 'Golden Slumbers', sometimes dozens and dozens of times. No other lullaby worked. Mummy must have sung it to me thousands of times, millions. If I hear the tune now, it turns me to gooseflesh.

Granny's anarchic way of getting round the problem, on those evenings when she was in charge and my parents were enjoying a rare snatch of respite, was simply to get me up. She was far too sensible and too self-protective to put up with two or three hours of someone else's unhappiness, whatever Dr Trubie King may say or write. My parents would therefore get back to the house to find Granny and me building with wooden bricks or, later, for the annoying trick lasted until I was seven years old, playing Beggar My Neighbour.

By then, war had broken out and everything was changed. My father, who in peacetime had been a manager in a shirt factory, joined the R.A.F. Mummy, whose parents were both dead, moved to a small house in Fulham to be near her mother-in-law, who lived in Parsons Green. It was in the garden of that house in Alderville Road that we had the air-raid shelter built and those best of all nights were spent, Mummy and I curled up in the same makeshift bed, clutching one another for fear of the Luftwaffe who never came, for the whole of that autumn.

It was for the first Christmas of the war that we all went to Timplingham – Mummy and Daddy, Granny and I. Apparently, though this was something broken to me at quite a late stage of the holiday, it had always been the plan that Mummy and I should become evacuees and live with Uncle Roy, Aunt Deirdre and Felicity until London was safe again. Before we got to Norfolk, a journey accomplished by train, I can remember my father, in his R.A.F. uniform, imitating the way Uncle Roy said 'invole-ved' rather than 'involved', and 'accomplished' rather than 'accumplished'. There were a whole range of 'aristocratic' pronunciations – 'larndry' for 'laundry', 'blooze' for 'blouse' – which struck Daddy as funny. It made it hard to keep a straight face when we arrived and Uncle Roy's voice was exactly as his brother had rendered it.

Both the brothers had been to one of the 'good London day-schools', as Granny called them. Mummy had been to some awful-sounding boarding school on the south coast. I have no idea what education they would have planned for me in peacetime, but the prep school in Malvern was an idea they had hit upon at the same time as deciding on our evacuation from London. Aunt Deirdre said that it had been recommended to my father by a business colleague: there was no opportunity to inspect it because – that phrase which covered everything – because of the war.

That Christmas was awful. Without the slightest intention of being unkind (never having stayed with us in London, they were entirely unaware of the problem) my uncle and aunt had put me to sleep in a maid's bedroom on the second floor while Mummy and Daddy slept below in a much larger and colder room designated the guest room but hardly ever occupied. The first night that I was left alone, I screamed myself hoarse. I can remember the awful jerks in my voice as I cried out, increasingly incoherently, 'STAY WITH ME, STAY WITH ME!' After ten or twenty minutes of this, the words got lost in mere sound, my cheeks were scorching, my eyes scalding, spittle and snot in great loops like egg-white were festooned across my face and dribbling down the corners of my mouth, and I could not stop.

Not long after the holiday, Daddy went back to his squadron and Granny (wearied, I suppose, by so much talk of the Lampitts and the Sarum Rite) decided to chance what the Luftwaffe could bring. She spent the whole of the war in London, which, as her friend Mrs Webb sometimes said, might have accounted for her nasty heads. Mummy and I were left behind. My nocturnal screamings got no better.

The Rectory policy was that I simply *mustn't* cry and scream. Mummy was forbidden to come to my bedroom after her all-too-brief good-night kiss. After about a week of my regular screams, my uncle was sent up to hit me. If I did not stop crying, he would tell me, he would take me out of bed and give me a jolly good walloping. He was much too nice ever to carry out such a punishment. He had been told to say this by Aunt Deirdre. Felicity, then about thirteen or fourteen, suffered from no such scruples and her bedroom was nearer to the noise centre than Uncle Roy's. More than once, she came in and biffed me. This did nothing to reduce the noise level nor to increase the love between the cousins.

The idea of sending me away to school had been planned, I am assured, before my uncle and aunt were aware of the screaming habit. For over two years my nightly shouts made life in the Rectory well-nigh intolerable for everyone else. I have since watched the parents of difficult children and seen how they suffer, both on the child's behalf and from embarrassment. How much anguish I must have caused Mummy! She did not know (nor, I suspect, like) Aunt Deirdre and Uncle Roy very well. She was staying in their house very much on sufferance. Rectory ways were very different from the much more homely atmosphere which surrounded us in London. We did not know anyone who lived in a big house or had relations called the Honourable Vernon. I remember how tense Mummy often looked, frightened probably, that I was going to scream or, in other moods, worried that I was going to be clumsy. It was hard to imagine that Felicity had ever been a child. Uncle Roy and Aunt Deirdre seemed so very disconcerted by any manifestation of childish behaviour on my behalf. I can remember when Mummy and I were playing French cricket with a tennis racket and an old ball in the garden. Aunt Deirdre came running out of the house.

'Doesn't matter a *bit* if you want to play, so long as you do it well down the lawn, away from the house.' Afraid that she had sounded too severe (and, indeed, her tones would have been rather too panicky if we had been juggling with sticks of dynamite) she added an unconvincingly playful, 'Jolly dee!'

Her fears that I would smash one of the windows with the ball entirely dominated that particular little patch of fine weather. Then, the inevitable happened and, driven indoors by sleet, I had taken to bouncing the ball in the hall. I knew perfectly well that it was a dangerous thing to do and I was not even particularly interested in ball games; simply addicted to bouncing the wretched thing. Mummy's face was so sad on the day I smashed that looking-glass in the hall. The more often Aunt Deirdre said it didn't matter, or that there was no use crying over spilt milk, the nearer Mummy looked to tears.

They had told me that I would eventually be sent to Seaforth Grange, but the reality of it meant nothing to me. Nor did I really imagine that this sending-away would happen for a very long time. There were dozens of warning signals.

'You poor girl, you're simply worn out by that child,' I heard my aunt telling Mummy on one occasion.

And, 'This weepy habit is one he'll jolly well have to break.'

My aunt was quite right; by her lights, she was not being unkind. No one was. I don't blame my family for being unable to understand a phenomenon which, to this day, baffles me. But I do now believe that my mysterious weeping whenever I was separated from my mother was premonitory. My aunt's idea was that, by some accident of upbringing, I had grown too soft. School would toughen me up and stop the caterwauling each evening, since you simply can't shout and wail in a dormitory. If this was the idea, it was a perfectly sound one. I was so shocked by being sent away, shortly before my ninth birthday, that I hardly protested at all. Mummy took me on the crowded train to London and bought me a poached-egg lunch at a Lyons corner house. Then we had a little stroll in Hyde Park before the unwilling walk to Paddington. I remember how sad she looked.

'It's all for the best, my darling,' she said. And then it was her turn to cry and mine to comfort her. The duty master in charge of escorting the boys back from Paddington was waiting at Platform One. It was September. Almost everyone on that platform was in uniform of one sort or another – school uniform, army or other service uniform, railway uniform. It made those few women who were in civilian clothes look especially nice. Mummy was in a summer frock, a pre-war print thing. That's how I remember her – her thin arms waving, her springy, light brown hair blown by steam and wind; her lovely blue eyes red with crying, her lips very red with lipstick, trembling as she stood there, and we pulled out in our third-class carriage. I didn't weep then.

Five weeks later, she went down to be near my father at Cranwell. They had a few days' leave together and spent it in a nearby hotel. My father had already become a pilot and survived over three years of the war. He had already taken tremendous risks. It seemed as though Providence would spare him for that peaceful little interlude at an out-of-season hotel.

A Heinkel, returning to Germany from an unsuccessful raid, dropped its load of bombs on my parents' hotel, a direct hit. There were only a few guests there that May. It just so happened that Mummy and Daddy were among them.

Thereafter, farewells, partings, transitions from one place or condition to the next have always been difficult for me. From the moment I went away to Seaforth Grange, I was cured of my habit of screaming before bedtime. I did not cry when the Binker's wife told me that Mummy and Daddy were dead. I don't know why that is. But forever afterwards, when being shoved on to trains by my uncle or aunt, I hollered. On that day of Jimbo Lampitt's funeral, for example, my uncle and the duty master had to lift me on to the train, wriggling and shouting.

'Please! Come on!' my uncle kept saying. 'Think how sad your Uncle Sargie is and he isn't crying.'

I wouldn't have been crying if I had been sitting in the bar of the Savile Club with a large martini and a cigarette, but I was in no condition for repartee.

'Come on! Jimbo's dead. You only have to go back to school, I've got to go to a funeral.'

There is never any point in trying to cure another person's unhappiness by suggesting that someone is worse off than they are. While these reasoned arguments were adduced, I was beside myself, flailing about, kicking and shouting. But when I had been put in the corner of the compartment on the train I did not try to escape. I was so out of control that I was beyond embarrassment. I did not mind that five or six other boys were all staring at me. Though the tears continued to flow, I wasn't making much noise.

'I expect he'll settle down once the train starts up,' said my uncle hopefully. Poor man, I now realise that he must have been in an agony himself, wondering whether he should leave me in the hands of strangers and in such a state of distress. It was rather a spurious character called Mr Rhys who was in charge of the expedition.

'He'll be all right, sir,' said Rhys to Uncle Roy.

'I was just reminding Julian as we carried him in,' said Uncle Roy, 'that we are burying James Petworth Lampitt this afternoon. The author, you know.'

I wonder whether Greasy Rhysy did know about Petworth Lampitt.

'A remarkable loss to literature,' said Uncle Roy. 'Altogether a remarkable family. Jimbo – as they all called Petworth Lampitt – was one of the most succinct and I think I would say *elegant* popular historians in our language. The brother I know much better, of course, is Sargent Lampitt. Again, a man of prodigious accomplishments.'

Greasy Rhysy looked about him anxiously. He had a delicate job to do, herding us all on to the train, counting us, making sure we were all in our seats, attending to other parents and guardians. But, even when he had got off the train and was standing on the platform, my uncle was still talking. He rapped on the window with his fist and made Rhysy stick his head out to listen.

'Mr Asquith himself – Lord Oxford as he became – commended that book on the House of Lords even though, as you probably know, he was far from being an abolitionist.'

'Indeed, sir?'

Snivelling in the corner, I could hear Rhysy's puzzled voice attempting to reply to what had seemed like an urgent summons from my uncle.

'No,' said Uncle Roy, 'old Sargie's a bit of a prodigy. His sister . . .'

He was still talking about the Lampitts as the train pulled out of the station and the summer term had begun.

The prediction that I would be all right, once I had settled back into the routines of Seaforth Grange, was amply confirmed. A fortnight later, if my uncle had been able to witness me talking to Darnley in the queue at break, he would hardly have recognised me as the same being that he had helped to carry on to the Paddington train. The strongest emotions, in my experience, are the most transitory. The despair induced by homesickness or love affairs has always passed away like a squall. Conditions such as my aunt's permanent mild crossness seem unshakable.

'How many did you get?' I asked Darnley.

'Four.'

'Bloody-oo.'

'He's in a bad mood, I expect.'

'Thanks a lot! We've got him next period. But four, just for talking after lights-out. It's usually three at most. Two, even. If talking's gone up to four, what will we get for serious things, like going in a shop?'

'We shall be *beheaded!*' To pronounce this sentence, Darnley bent double and did a war dance accompanied by extraordinary facial grimaces.

'Be-head-ed! Hung, drawn and quartered! Cas-trat-ed!'

When he had stopped chanting, he stood up straight and said, 'If we went into the bushes, I could show you.'

'No thanks – we'd lose our place in the queue.'

'Garforth-Thoms thinks the Binker's drawn blood this time.'

'What did you show them to Blowforth-Bums for?'

'He showed me his. He got four too – but he handed in prep late.'

'Oh, well.' Four for late prep was usual. 'What were his like?' I asked, intending no satire.

'Horrible.'

We both laughed.

This showing of the scars and bruises inflicted by the Binker's instruments of torture (he had a cupboardful in his study) had nothing to do with Eros. We were entirely innocent of the idea that anyone might give canings for fun, and as for the idea that one could enjoy being beaten, I never heard it so much as mentioned in nearly ten years of life in institutions where beatings were a regular occurrence. Nor did I feel the slightest interest, aesthetic or otherwise, in Darnley's bum. The closest parallel which I know to his (purely standard) offer to show me his bruises came in an anecdote told by Uncle Roy in the course of a sermon. After some Council of the Church, Nicaea I think it was, the Emperor Constantine, recently converted to Christianity, entertained the assembled bishops to some kind of knees-up in his palace. It was only lately that these saintly figures had been persecuted for their beliefs. To make the point, they entered the imperial palace proudly displaying the scars of their martyrdom to the guard – pointing proudly here to an eye socket gouged out in gladiatorial combat, here to a stump where some limb had been munched off by a lion. It was very much in this defiant spirit that one might offer, after a thrashing by the Binker, to show the scars to a chum.

Like all the boys in his care – there were about sixty of us – I did everything in my power to keep out of the Binker's way. This was easier said than done. For a start, he prided himself on teaching every child in the school, so one was bound to get him either for Geography or Scripture or (in unlucky terms) for both. When the other teachers weren't teaching, I imagine that they were sitting in the staff Common Room, sucking at noisome pipes and working their way through piles of exercise books. Not so the Binker, who prowled the school grounds in the fervent hope that he would find a boy infringing one of the innumerable regulations by which our lives were governed: having your hands in your pockets; going out of bounds (this meant not merely stepping outside the school gates, but going anywhere within them except a few paths and a couple of asphalt playgrounds); eating sweets, except on Sundays and Wednesdays; running between lessons; not running on runs – all these offences were punishable by the cane if the Binker was in that sort of mood. At mealtimes it was the same. He was always there, pacing up and down between the four refectory tables where we ate, looking for breaches of table manners, and insisting that we consume every inedible morsel which was placed before us.

'What's that piece of gristle doing on your plate, Ramsay?'

'Just about to eat it, sir.'

'Good, good. Otherwise Tammie-tawse would have to help you.'

He did not actually use a tawse, but Tam, Tammie or Tammie the Tawse were among the playful nicknames which he gave to the various rods, garden canes and switches in his collection.

Of an evening, he might turn up at any minute to supervise bathtime and washing. After lights-out, he lurked silently on the landings outside our dormitories in the hope of hearing someone whisper. This had been Darnley's crime on the previous evening. He was a repeated and incurable offender, a compulsive talker quite unable, once a thought occurred to him, of keeping it to himself. Punishment may be enjoyable for those who inflict it. One sometimes questions its deterrent effects. In spite of the severest punishments, we went on talking after lights-out. In the eighteenth century, they went on stealing sheep, even though they could be hanged for it and often were.

The queue in which Darnley and I stood edged its way towards the kitchen window where Mrs Binker, a warty lady of uncertain years, dispensed pieces of bread thinly spread with red jam. There was no marg – we only had marg at tea.

When I put out my hand to receive my bread she rapped it sharply with a spoon, taking the skin off my knuckles. One learnt not to question such unexplained outbreaks of violence. Then she gave me my bread. As I knew quite well, there was no reason for this assault. She had a very understandable dislike of boys (in general, boys *aren't* nice, and they could be said, in this particular situation, to occupy too much of her husband's attention). Mrs Binker therefore lost no opportunity for tweaking a boy's nose or twisting his ear or thwacking him with an umbrella if she happened to be passing and he happened to be in range. Her acts of violence, unlike those of the Binker, were seldom ritualised, but she did on occasion get the gym master to line us up on the edge of the swimming bath so that she could have the pleasure of pushing us in, one by one. The especially timorous ones she liked to push off the diving board.

Unlike her husband, Mrs Binker (their real name was Larmer; I don't know why we called them the Binkers) was very stout; stout and pale; her warts and moles all sprouted healthy shoots of coarse black hair.

When the boys had collected their bread at the kitchen window, the queue bifurcated to two corners of the playground, where there were milk crates. You helped yourself to a third-pint bottle (courtesy of Messrs Attlee, Bevan and Lampitt). Very welcome it was to swig with that bread which was usually a bit dry. You put the milk-bottle top in the box provided. The tops were collected by Mrs Binker for some charitable purpose (she was well known in the town for her tireless works of charity) and if you failed to do this, you either got a beating or, at least, a week's litter duty.

'Anyway,' said Darnley as we threw our silver tops into the box, 'it's the Binker next. India again.'

'I hate India,' I said.

'I wouldn't mind seeing tigers and elephants. My grandfather was in India. Dad was born there.'

'I don't mean real India. That's great. I mean the Binker's India. Sketchmaps.'

'Then after Joggers, there's *Art*,' said Darnley meaningfully. Somehow, he had discovered my feelings for the new art mistress, Miss Beach, who had arrived that term. He swigged down his milk in a couple of mouthsful. Darnley had enormous lips which, rather grotesquely, encased the whole of the upper part of his bottle. Thus refreshed, he began to enact the lovesick swain.

'Oh, Miss Beach, I love you. Let me clean your dirty brushes, Miss Beach. Let me kiss you, Miss Beach.'

And with his slobbery lips he kissed the air, sending forth a shower of milky spit.

'Shut up, Darnley.' I felt myself blushing and gave him a rough shove.

'Steady on,' he said. 'Just 'cause you're nuts about Miss Beach isn't my fault.'

'Shut *up!*'

I now got an arm round his neck and prepared to scrag him. Scragging involved getting your opponent's neck in the bend of your elbow and holding it like a vice. He could then choose between standing up and getting his neck broken or being bent in half. Then you could either pull him to the ground (if he was a friend) or (if you didn't like him) you could punch his face with your free hand, kick him in the balls or generally mess him about. It left your options open.

'Hey! Less of that, you two!' The voice was that of Timpson, the head boy. Darnley, in what struck me as a phrase of near genius, had once described Timpson as a 'prize ten-out-of-ten pillock'.

'Any more of that ragging, and you will be sent to the H.M.,' said Timpson. He was the only boy I ever met who referred to the Binker in this way. 'You two should be setting an example to the younger boys. In less than a year you will have gone on to your public schools.'

'Sorry, Timpson,' I said.

Darnley's specs, permanently bust and held together with bits of Elastoplast, had been dislodged by our horseplay and one of the lenses had somehow got splashed with milk. This clownish appearance did not prevent him following my lead and adopting an attitude of sheepish seriousness.

'So am I, Timpson. Really, really sorry.'

'You were less to blame than Ramsay. He had his arm round your neck, I think.'

'All the same' – Darnley never could resist overdoing things – 'frightfully sorry.'

'I shall overlook it this time,' said Timpson. 'Don't let it happen again.'

He was a cherubic, portly child whose very pursed lips seemed always shocked, forever on the point of giving voice to some well-considered admonition or rebuke.

Carried away by Darnley, I added, 'It was a jolly poor show, Timpson. I should like to put it on record that I am extremely sorry. I should never have scragged Darnley. Not with our both going on to public schools.'

'I am glad that you see it now, Ramsay. As I said, you are both fully old enough to know better.'

'Timpson.'

'What is it, Darnley?'

'I think we've both behaved like nanas – sorry, brutes – and it was frightfully decent, well, sporting . . .'

'The very word,' I said.

'Sporting of you, Timpson, not to send us to the Binker.'

'You mean the Headmaster?' This sage thirteen-year-old had the tone of a High Court Judge who had never heard of baked beans.

'Quite, Timpson. H.M. Sorry to have called the H.M. a Binker, Timpson.'

'That's all right, Darnley.'

'Timpson.'

'What, Ramsay?'

'Can I second that apology of Darnley's? I mean, he should never have spoken flippantly like that.'

'Hear, hear,' said Darnley. 'Terrifically, extremely sorry, Timpson.'

Only at a very late stage of all this did Timpson's porcine features register the fact that he was being teased.

'I hope you aren't trying to cheek me,' he said threateningly.

Darnley, a lanky creature already, at twelve years old, at least five foot six or seven, towered over our plump little *generalissimo*.

'Good Lord, Timpson, no! Wouldn't dream of it.'

It was one of Darnley's particular gifts (being able to fart tunes was another) that he was always able to keep a straight face on these occasions. I couldn't. We both rushed into our classroom as the bell went. In the couple of minutes before the Binker arrived, we put our heads in our desks and howled with merriment.

When the Binker entered the classroom all mirth vanished and we stood in silence. He was a noticeably short man (shorter than Darnley) and his tweedy clothes, slightly too large for him, were suggestive of some Scottish country houseparty. Brindled hair *en brosse*; a slightly florid complexion; glossy brown eyes like a dog's. He spoke in a refined 'Morningside' Edinburgh voice, but would often playfully break into different varieties of Scotchery, as when reading aloud from the novels of Stevenson, Scott or Buchan, something which he did supremely well. This habit also extended to his reading from the Scriptures. Figures such as prophets or judges were often given special voices by the Binker, so that I always irrationally think of Elijah and Gideon as having spoken with strong Glaswegian accents. Quite often, his heart north of the border, he put on Scotch voices just for the hell of it. This morning, for instance, refreshed by the recent castigation of Darnley and Garforth-Thoms, he had assumed the character of some rustic from the pages of the Ettrick Shepherd.

'And wha's tae distribute yon sketchmahps?'

This was a rhetorical inquiry. Having pointed them out he then placed the small pile of papers on Craster's desk and this boy (I never kept up with him – I believe he went into the Foreign Office) dutifully dished them out to the rest of us.

Sketchmaps were the Binker's passion – or one of the Binker's passions. Nearly all his Geography lessons began with a distri-bution of a blank map, drawn by himself (he was a delicate draughtsman) and run off on a stencilling machine. He would then call out the names of places and we had to fill them in on a blank map. Last term, it had been the industrial towns of England. This term, it was India. Since we were only a fortnight into the term, the Binker could be sure that very few of us, except Darnley, would have much grasp of Indian geography. We would not necessarily be thrashed for our ignorance, but there might be the need to be called up to the Binker's desk while, with one hand on the atlas, and the other creeping about our persons, he pointed out the whereabouts of Madras or Hyderabad. ('There's Hyderabad, Craster, and there's no need to flinch – we're all similarly composed'; he was quite open about it.)

Without further announcement, the test began.

'Delhi.'

Phew! He *was* in a good mood. It wasn't going to be a Binker-stinker.

'The Deccan.'

Easy-peasy.

'Karachi.'

Oh, peezeroo.

Like some Homeric deity who sensed *hubris* in his victims, the Binker smiled.

'Vishakhapatnum.'

After twenty, he had us all on toast. No one got more than about four questions right.

Another boy (Dorset-Lemon, now a publisher) collected up the maps and we then opened a textbook dating from the nineteen-twenties. Dorset-Lemon was then required to read out some stuff about tea plantations. Darnley's dad had been a tea-planter, but they had come home before the war. His mum had married someone else quite recently. It was all much more high-powered than anything in my own background.

'Thenk-yor, Dorset-Lemon,' said the Binker.

He laboriously consulted his watch, a thing which he kept on the end of a chain in his waistcoat pocket. Twenty minutes of the lesson had elapsed and there was a quarter of an hour to go. The Binker held forth about India, how it was ours by right since we got it from the French in the eighteenth century, and how Clive of India had showed enterprise and courage ever since he climbed to the top of the church spire at Market Drayton. Another thing was that the King was a King-Emperor who was being betrayed by wicked men who pretended to be his Government but were in fact Communists, determined to hand over the Government of India to another Communist, Mr Gandhi. It amused me to hear the Government spoken of in these terms. It was also baffling. In the Binker's view, Sir Stafford Cripps, the Hon. Vernon Lampitt and others were a gang of ruthless hooligans and pirates, intent on gouging out the finest jewel in His Majesty's Imperial Crown. It was amazing to think of Uncle Roy consorting with such rough-necks. And then I thought of Sargie (who although he wasn't in the Government was the Government's cousin) standing on the pavement in Mayfair and asking me into his club for a snifter.

But it was from the Binker that I heard of the most exciting of all the Government's schemes, something which made me realise that Mr Attlee and his piratical crew were Good Things in spite of so unsportingly beating Mr Churchill in the election.

'There is something worse,' said the Binker, 'worse by far than their desecration of His Majesty's Imperial Crown.'

This was fascinating. I was full of admiration for the Honour-able Vernon even before I heard what it was that was *worse* than pulling down everything Clive and his friends had built up and handing over the best-ordered society in the Orient to a lot of ignorant savages (i.e. the people who actually lived there). It was a scheme which would, if once enacted, make all my nightmares vanish away.

'They openly talk,' and in his precise angry tones the last word became 'tok', 'of making private education itself illegal. And we all know what that would mean. Seaforth Grange would be closed down by Mr Attlee's *cheka*. And himself a Haileybury man.'

I had no idea what a 'checker' was, but the thought of it kept me going during the blacker moments of the next couple of terms. I half assumed that it was someone who came and checked up on you. But, by a process of irrational association, the Binker's clipped Scotch manner of saying the word brought into my mind the memory of Robert Donat in the film of *The Thirty-Nine Steps*. At various exciting moments, Donat is chased through the glens and highlands by Scottish policemen, whose peaked caps are encircled with checked bands. O checker! O rend the heavens, come swiftly down!

The Binker's tirade against the Socialists took up the rest of our lesson and then, as Darnley had not needed to remind me, it was Art.

There was a very rapid turnover of art mistresses at Seaforth Grange. Usually, they were young women who could not keep order. They left, usually for mysterious reasons and sometimes in the middle of term. Yet more mysterious than their reason for leaving was their reason for coming in the first place. The money can't have been good. The conditions of work were appalling.

There was a new art mistress, as I have mentioned, and her name was Miss Beach. I had fallen very seriously in love with her. Before it happened, I had never before spoken to anyone about love (I mean the sort you fall into). The subject was aired during Vanessa's dormitory chats, but as something which had happened to her. Clearly, it had happened to Darnley's mother. 'She's still jolly fond of Dad, but you see, she's fallen in love with this other chap,' he had sheepishly confided in me about a year before; it was really the beginning of our friendship. Like all forms of pain, it is totally unimaginable until it happens. I was now in the depths of it.

I took it that Darnley had never been in love himself. In the light of the catastrophe which had befallen his life when the condition afflicted his mother, he could be forgiven for taking a dim view of love in general. This did not make his crude teasing any easier to stomach. Even as we entered the art room, he was moving into his Romeo routine, one hand on his chest and a pink, smooth, knobbly knee looking as if it was about to genuflect.

'I warn you,' I said.

But already my voice was weak, my heart was palpitating, my stomach was churning; for *she* was near and we could hear her surprisingly stentorian tones.

'Come in, no talking – put your smocks on – Garforth-Thoms, where's your smock?'

We all had to wear smocks for Art, even though as it happened we were doing netting, which involved no glue, no paint, nothing with which we might splash our grey prison uniform. Typical, this, of the Binker's unthinking, Stalinist approach to things. Some boy's grey-flannel shirt had probably once been splashed with powder paint. The rest of us, world without end, had to wear smocks.

'There wasn't a smock on the peg, please,' said Blowforth-Bums.

'Nonsense – I can see a whole row of them out there.'

'But they've run out of blue ones, please. The green ones don't match my eyes.'

This playing to the gallery, very annoyingly, worked. The whole class was having the giggles.

'Don't call me "please".'

'Sorry, please.'

The idea was to break the nerve of any new teacher and normally I joined in the ragging with gusto. But, when they ragged Miss Beach, I boiled with indignation. I could easily have killed Garforth-Thoms for his joke about the overalls. I hated it, too, because it established a sort of intimacy between him and Miss Beach. There was something flirtatious about it, to which she responded. When he came back into the room with his smock on, she said, 'Very pretty, Garforth-Thoms.'

This time, the laughs were on her side and Blowforth-Bums was blushing.

She had short, dark brown, bobbed hair and glasses which rather dwarfed her tiny features – a nose so small that it hardly stuck out from her face, miniature ears. She wore a plain green skirt like an Irish kilt; black stockings over wonderful legs; an open-necked man's shirt rolled up to the sleeve to reveal nougat-coloured, freckly arms. The eyes were the liveliest I had ever seen, full of satire and laughter. They seemed to understand everything. She was not in the ordinary sense pretty; certainly she lacked the glamour of Vanessa. She was rather flat-chested. But my adoration for her was not just a spiritual thing. I adored her whole being, I longed for her. Probably at that date she was about twenty-two; no older, because she had only just left art school in London.

Each time I saw her, the being in love got worse. This lesson, for example, when we were meant to be learning the rudiments of how to make nets, everything made me suffer. I was tortured by the fact that I was not able to paint for her, to do something truly artistic. Nets lacked soul. I suppose, to judge from the sketches she did of us while we made our nets, that she thought of us as fisher-boys, like something in the Newlyn School. But I did not see that and it would have given me no pleasure if I had done so. I had loathed being a child ever since I was aware that I was one. Being in love just made it even worse. I did not want her to think of me as a little boy. Then again, I was unhappy because, to her eyes, there was nothing to distinguish me from all the other little boys. I was hatefully conscious of this. Love allowed me no illusion. While Darnley and the rest teased her, I was quite aware that she thought of me as just a silly little boy, misbehaving like the rest. Infuriatingly, she did not seem to *notice* that I was not ragging her. It would have been terrible if she had not been able to control the class. As it happened, she did possess the mysterious gift of making children behave as she wanted them to.

After a while, she put down her sketchbook and wandered among us as we stitched with our string.

'Well done, Tromans, that's coming on very well.'

I hated Tromans for being good at netting. I knew I was not good at it. I kept trying to persuade myself that it was not her idea that we should be doing it, that netting had been forced on her by some higher authority. But there is no reason to suppose that this was true.

'Come on, Ramsay,' she said when she got to me. 'You can't make a net just by sitting looking soulful at it.'

She had a mock-vehement way of speaking which went down well with boys. The tone implied that she was cheering on laggards. Her reference to my 'soulful' expression produced immediate titters all round the art room.

'And Ramsay,' she said, 'your tension is all wrong.'

I could have told her that.

It gave me the chance to be near her, though. Her tiny little white hands took the netting from mine, and for quite ten seconds our fingers were touching.

'Well, let it *go*, Ramsay, or you'll tie us both in knots. Shut up, the rest of you. Get on with making those nets. Sounds like something in the Bible,' she added as a throwaway line. When I got to know her better, I realised that she had a line in very mildly blasphemous jokes. There was nothing offensive in what she said – there was just a tendency for irony about loaves, fishes, walking on water, that sort of stuff.

'Just look at this!' she wriggled my net with more mock anger. 'I know a net is holes tied together with string, but yours is nothing *but* holes. You've dropped about six stitches here.'

I was trying to say sorry, but words would not come. Already, love's terrible tendency to create false hopes was at work in me. Why had she stopped to look at my netting? The rational explanation was that my netting was in a mess. But love did not want this to be the reason. Love wanted me to hope that she was secretly falling in love with *me*. She had stopped just as an excuse, because she wanted our fingers momentarily to touch. She had wanted me to be able to stand with my nose only inches away from her throat, to note the softness of that white, pulsating skin and to smell the wonderful smell of *her* – a particular soap she used, blending with the smell of her hair which was like honey.

In time, she moved on, but I tried to tell myself that whenever she helped another boy with his tangled little bit of netting, it was because his string was really in a mess, whereas she had paused by me because she *knew*.

Some people I have met have told me that they have never been in love. And I have usually replied that they don't know what they are missing. Much the worst thing they are missing is this desire to kid yourself which comes over you whenever you fall in love. You become a kind of lunatic, looking out for tell-tale signs and secret messages where they do not really exist.

At the end of the lesson, I told myself that she might want me to linger behind. There had been a sign in the half-touching of our fingers as they got entangled in the string together.

'Coming to lunch?' asked Darnley.

There was amusement in his voice, but also the beginning of annoyance that I was making a fool of myself.

'I'll follow you,' I said.

'Aren't you going to lunch, Ramsay?' asked Miss Beach.

'I thought you might need some help tidying up the art room.'

'There's not much to do, is there?'

The way that she peered at me suggested that she thought my staying behind was part of some elaborate tease. There were wary glances at the others, who were drifting out.

'I suppose you could help me put out paper for this afternoon, if you liked,' she said.

I eagerly accepted.

'It's the really little boys this afternoon – Lower III. So that's twenty sheets of paper – distribute them far apart. We don't want them splashing one another with paint.'

'Did you go to an art school or what?' I asked.

'What!' She laughed. 'No, I went to one called the Slade, actually.'

'But I thought the Slade was really good.'

The colossal rudeness of this remark did not occur to me. I took it for granted that everyone knew Seaforth Grange to be a dump, a stinking, hateful pit; the appearance there of anyone intelligent of their own free will demanded some sort of explanation.

'Anyway, how did you come to have heard of the Slade?'

I liked her for not condescending. She did not say, 'Aren't you a bit young to be asking me where I did my training?' She spoke as if we were equals.

With a certain amount of dread, I heard myself having to trot out a line of talk which, if allowed to continue, could have been endless.

'Well, there's this family called the Lampitts. They are terrific friends of my uncle – well, one of them is. Sargie Lampitt. And he's got a cousin who teaches there. Design or something. I've heard my uncle talk about it.'

I thought, when I mentioned the Lampitts, that an expression of faint strain passed over her features.

'There are a lot of teachers and lecturers there,' she said. 'Is your uncle an artist?'

'No,' I said, highly embarrassed. 'No, he isn't.'

She did not ask me what my father did. Had someone already warned her that my parents were dead, or was it just natural tact?

Inescapably, I heard myself being a Lampitt bore.

'They live in the neighbouring large house and they've got hundreds of cousins. One of them is in the Government,' I said.

Miss Beach ignored all this.

'The Slade is *wonderful*,' she said. 'Guess who we had teaching us sculpture last year?'

'I can't.'

'Henry Moore!'

'I've never heard of him, I'm afraid.'

There was a pause.

'I'm really a sculptor more than anything else,' she said. 'Henry Moore is the greatest living sculptor. One of the greatest sculptors in the history of the world. Imagine what it was like to be taught by him. And he is so kind, and so unassuming and modest. And yet he understands so much.'

I wanted to say that I should rather be taught netting by Miss Beach than sculpture by this unheard-of. At the same time, I felt immensely flattered by her treating me to this snatch of grown-up talk. The few sentences about Moore, like Mrs Maddock's Cambridge chat in the butcher's shop in Timplingham, opened up a tiny chink of light: songs from a distant land, promises of future blessedness. I walked on air when I left the art room.

This was the first of many little talks with Miss Beach, talks which began my education. They were always snatched at odd moments – the ten minutes before lunch, the five minutes before the end of break when she was getting the art room ready for a lesson. Sometimes, in a rare moment of free time (and there were precious few of those in an average Seaforth Grange day) we might have as much as half an hour together: for instance, if she were on duty on Sunday afternoons. She was always attentive, she never treated me like a child. For instance, on the first occasion when we met after our Henry Moore conversation, she produced some photographs of his work to show me. I was bitterly disappointed to discover that it was 'modern art', something which Aunt Deirdre (I had assumed, rightly) regarded as preposterous. Not so Miss Beach, who explained to me that the distinction between ancient and modern in these areas was largely artificial, a division made by people incapable of making the much more useful one between good and bad art. Moore's fascination with plasticity and form, and the problems which he so successfully tackled, would have been familiar, she said, to Rodin, to Michelangelo, to the sculptors of ancient Athens. Next time we met, she had illustrated books ready, to explain what she meant. I did not need convincing. I believed everything she said and became instantly a convinced Modernist. I don't think she was in fact partisan. Like all true artists, she was interested in *all* aspects of her subject and anxious to find merit in undiscovered areas.

Picasso, for example, was a passion with her, which she passed on to me. She even showed me some of her own paintings, angular, two-faced heads in asymmetrical designs which soon seemed very beautiful to me, once I got my eye in. She explained about the growth of abstract painting and showed me reproductions of some of the great early twentieth-century English abstract painters; in particular, we both came to share a great fondness for Ben Nicholson's white paintings, pictures which seemed to combine the purity of mathematics with the romance of snow.

If she had not enjoyed our talks, it is inconceivable that she would have allowed them to continue. She must have early on guessed that I was crazy about her and no doubt she considered that this was an acceptable way of dealing with the situation. How much is it ever someone else's responsibility if you offer them the (usually unwelcome) burden of total devotion?

There were hundreds of other reasons why she might have enjoyed these talks. She was homesick for the arty world she had left behind in London. There were few enough people on the staff of Seaforth Grange who had even heard of Picasso and it was a safe bet that those who had would detest him. To have found an audience was, in a way, a stroke of luck for her; and there were many reasons why she might have thought it unlikely that our friendship could go any further: I was twelve years old, I only came up to her shoulder, I wore ridiculous baggy shorts which flapped about my bare, hairless, pink knees, my voice had not broken, I called her Miss Beach and she called me Ramsay. The embarrassing disparity between our ages was something which, little by little, I came to disregard, though she must have been aware of it all the time. I was deeply, seriously, passionately in love. The pains of it were so terrible that I believed that they must end with my getting what I so earnestly desired: to be with her for ever. I had not worked out the details, but somehow Miss Beach and I would win through. We would be together. I have no idea whether she guessed how very deep the wound was going. Obviously, she was aware of something. Perhaps she called it a 'crush' to make it seem less serious. Perhaps, to her, it was not serious. I was deep in the classic mistake, repeated so often in my life, of thinking that because I cared so passionately, I had somehow bought her, that because I had suffered for her, there was something which she owed me.

Sexual feelings unquestionably contributed to these disturbing sensations but they were very far indeed from being the whole of them. The humiliating activity in which my poor parents had had to indulge in order to generate my entrance into the world was not something which I ever intended to do with Miss Beach. It did not cross my mind, I don't think. I wanted to go for long walks with her on the Malvern Hills. I wanted to stroke her pale, freckled arms. I wanted to kiss her and to be hugged by her. But nothing filthy. Indeed, as the association deepened, and Miss Beach became more and more important to me, I instinctively found that smut had vanished from my mind, so that a lot of Darnley's more hair-raising conversations, and many of the things said or done in my dormitory after lights-out, struck me as repulsively alien.

Even the good-night embraces of Vanessa were now to be loyally eschewed. If I could not kiss Miss Beach, I didn't want to kiss anyone. I expect that this was odiously priggish, but if so, the priggery was instinctive and not willed. I did not have to struggle. I no longer wanted anything in my life except Miss Beach.

That did not stop me from being wholly fascinated, as before, by Vanessa's flow of gossip about herself, the school, the world in general, when it was her turn to come round the dorms in our house last thing at night. When it was the turn of the art mistress to come in for Vanessa's searching analysis, her words were torture to me and yet I wanted to know everything. And it was in this way, from Vanessa, and not from my beloved herself, that I began to discover why Miss Beach was in Malvern.

We had all washed and brushed our teeth and got into bed one evening when Vanessa came into the dormitory. As already indicated, she was a Teutonic-looking girl, tall, with a full figure shown to advantage by tight woollen jumpers, pleated skirts, black stockings. Shoulder-length blonde hair was held back from an innocent, oval face by an Alice band. Sometimes the hair was in a ponytail. With her large, blue eyes, her full lips, her little waist and her large hips, Vanessa was what we artlessly called 'a pin-up'. (We did not in fact possess any photographs of beautiful girls and it would have been out of the question to display them if we had, drawing pins being among the thousand items forbidden by the Binker.) Vanessa having entered, the rituals were then gone through. We all knelt in silence by our iron bedsteads for two minutes, hands clasped, eyes shut, little Christopher Robins lost in prayer. My thoughts invariably remained below on such occasions, I think because I then imagined that there was something distasteful, not to say blasphemous, about talking to God at times designated by the Binker.

When we were all in bed, Vanessa came round and said good night to us. There were about ten in a dormitory. For the younger boys, Vanessa's good night was little more than a peck on the cheek, but for the older boys, myself included, they were full-blown embraces, modelled closely on what Cary Grant or Humphrey Bogart appeared to do when pressing their lips against those of a starlet. ('French kissing', appropriately enough, I only discovered when I went to France.) But now, after Miss Beach, things were different. When it came to my turn to be kissed I no longer pressed my lips against Vanessa's, but merely rubbed my cheek against hers, as, once in a blue moon, Aunt Deirdre might do to Uncle Roy – if, say, he were going away for a few days with Sargie by the seaside.

When we had all been kissed and Vanessa was seated at the end of the dormitory captain's bed, the gossip could begin. Like all good gossips, Vanessa was omnivorous, wide-ranging and quite unafraid to swoop from generalities to the particular. Who was the most handsome man in the world (she thought, on the whole, Prince Philip of Greece, who was going to marry Princess Elizabeth) alternated with the really much more interesting question of what was the Maths master's middle name.

We all knew that he was A. J. Rhys and some weeks before Vanessa had let slip that the 'A' was for Alan. When written down, this information looks commonplace, but any information is interesting if it starts life as a closely guarded secret.

'What's the "J" for, Vanessa?'

'Dunno.'

'You do! You must!'

'I don't!' Girlish shriek. (Vanessa was exactly six years older than I was.)

'You're in love with Mr Rhys, Vanessa,' pronounced Bowen,

the dorm captain. 'Vanessa's in love with Greasy Rhysy.'

This suggestion had us all in fits, including Vanessa. We all knew it wasn't true, because she had told us that she had a really wonderful boyfriend back home in Bromyard, who drove over to see her twice a week during term. Also we were all, Vanessa included, young enough and therefore cruel enough to suppose that no one *could* be in love with Greasy Rhysy. We all still believed that love affects only the young and the beautiful and that no heart beats inside such lank-haired, collapsed-looking individuals as A. J. Rhys.

'He's married, anyway!' protested Vanessa. She knew as well as we did that this made the Greasy Rhysy joke all the funnier.

Then someone blurted out, 'What's Miss Beach's Christian name?'

There was a bit of silence; then someone else said, 'Ask Ramsay.' More splutters of mirth. Other people being in love always has joke potential: Greasy Rhysy, me, what difference did it make to them? Anything is good for a laugh.

'That's enough,' said Vanessa. I think she genuinely wanted to spare my feelings. 'Why should I tell *you* things all the time? You tell me what's going on. Are you going to win the matches on Saturday against the Downs?'

'Come *on*, Vanessa, tell us!' some young voice protested. 'What's Miss Beach called? It's B.R.B. Is it Barbara Beach, Betty Beach?'

I could not bear the *tone* in which these questions were being fired off, just as though Miss Beach were some kind of joke in the same league as Greasy Rhysy. At the same time, I was more anxious than anyone to know the answer.

'Beatrice Beach!'

'Bertha Beach!'

'Bottom Beach!'

'Shut *up*, Torrance.'

'Just 'cause you're spoony, Ramsay!'

Perhaps to allay any further unpleasantness, Vanessa just came out with it.

'It's Beryl,' she said.

An extraordinary wave of sadness came over me. The others were jabbering, repeating the name, laughing about it.

'How common,' said Bowen: exactly the words my aunt

would have used had she heard of someone called Beryl.

I loved her no less. If anything, were such a thing possible, I loved her more, being in possession of that hitherto secret talisman, her name. But I was in love with someone called Beryl. I must confess that I would have been happier with a Beate, a Bathsheba, a Brünnhilde. Beryl lacked poetry.

'Has Miss Beach – has Beryl – got a boyfriend?' asked some cheeky little voice.

'Ramsay!'

More laughter. I got out of bed and prepared to sock Torrance, but Vanessa suddenly turned all schooly and told me to get back or she would send me to the headmaster.

'That's quite enough,' she said.

By then it was time for lights-out and she had another dormitory to do. But it was too tantalising to leave things in the air like this. When she had switched out the lights in dorm five across the landing, Bowen, who, needless to say, was himself crazy about Vanessa, called out to her in a whisper and begged her to come and sit on his bed once more.

'Oh, just five minutes.'

In a remarkably short space of time, Bowen and the others pumped her for information about Beryl Beach. She was, they learnt, someone who had done really well at an art college in London, Vanessa forgot the name, and she had already had pictures hung in exhibitions – and statues had been put on show. Everything had been going well, but then she had fallen hopelessly in love with this chap.

(This time, Torrance's repeated interjections of my name struck the others as unfunny and someone, either Pell or Aaronberg, really belted him one.)

Who was this chap?

'He's called Raphael Hunter,' said Vanessa.

'Is he handsome?'

'Very.'

'Vanessa's in love with him, too!'

'Shut your mouth, Torrance, or we'll do it for you.'

'Sorry, Bowen.'

'Does he live in London, this bloke? Who is he? Is he an artist too?'

'He lives in Malvern, or his parents do. That's why Beryl took this job, to be near him, you see. He isn't famous yet, but he's going to be a . . .'

We did not, at that point, learn what Hunter was going to be, for at that moment, someone said 'Sshh!'

There was only one reason for hushing: the stealthy approach of the predator. In the darkness we listened, terrified and silent. To any but the most hardened listener, there would have been nothing in that silence. But instinct told us that the Binker was on the prowl. There was no chance that he could not have heard us all whispering. That could easily mean a beating for the whole dorm, as well as being very awkward for Vanessa. But she was a quick thinker and she was on our side. She went at once to the window, opened and shut it noisily and said, 'There! Off you fly! Settle down now, everyone, it's gone.'

And she briskly left the room. On the landing beneath we heard her voice conversing with the low murmur of the Binker. He was clearly furious that his cover had been blown.

'A bat, you say?'

'It's gone now, sir.'

'Could they not get rid of a bat without tokking?'

Vanessa whispered something inaudible.

Then there was a black silence. None of us knew how long the Binker paced the landings stocking-footed, torch in hand, ear cocked. Better by far, from his point of view, than a mere whisperer after lights-out, would be the detection, by the rustling movement of sheets, of some onanist in the act. But all was still that night.

It was hours before I got to sleep, days before I absorbed all the information imparted that night by Vanessa, weeks before I understood her own silence on the question of whether Mr Hunter was handsome, years before I began to see a connection between this and Miss Beach's own little silence at the name of Lampitt, and decades before the stories which began as gossip about Miss Beach and Hunter took on the distinct shapes and meanings which they possess for me today.

*   *

At first, I felt so hurt by what Vanessa had told us that I found it impossible to believe. Miss Beach was in love with a man called Raphael Hunter. That was her sole reason for having taken a job in Malvern. This information scalded me when I heard it. All the more terrible was that something which affected me so secretly (could *they* know the depths of it?) and so profoundly, should have been the subject of common chat – on the same level of farce as Greasy Rhysy's middle name. This was something on which I felt that not only my happiness, but my actual capacity to survive in this life, depended. The idea that Miss Beach was capable of feeling for a man as I felt for her was something which offered its own cruel sprig of hope. Hitherto I had not so much as considered that she, or anyone else, *could* have feelings which were as strong as those which had taken possession of me. Now that I had learnt that she did feel, that she *was* in love, things were different. If Vanessa had been able to tell us with some infallible and completely reliable authority that Miss Beach was not capable of love, I think I might have felt the beginnings of relief or cure. For the time being, Miss Beach could have remained on her pedestal and I could continue to pour forth to her my secret devotions and oblations. But to learn that she was in the same humiliating and yet glorious condition as myself, but enchanted with Mr Raphael Hunter, this somehow changed everything, made it more highly charged. Since it was knowledge too terrible to be borne, I gradually began to doctor the facts. I forgot Raphael Hunter's name. Then I persuaded myself that Vanessa had invented him in order to spice up her dorm gossip, that he was not real. After a couple more days and another brief encounter with Miss Beach herself, I even managed to persuade myself that Vanessa had been hinting something quite different, namely that Miss Beach was really in love with me. Knowing, as she did, that the other boys teased me about Miss Beach, Vanessa could hardly have been so cruel as to blurt out the true facts of the case to the whole dormitory. I never had any other opportunity to see Vanessa and to talk about things. Supposing Miss Beach had *chosen* Vanessa as her intermediary! Supposing Miss Beach wanted to tell me that she loved me as I loved her, but supposing she didn't dare. She *might* have asked Vanessa to say that she was in love, in the knowledge that I alone would interpret this information correctly, leaving the other boys in the dorm still in the dark.

This theory looks pretty improbable when written down, but

I wanted so deeply to believe it that I soon discovered that all the facts of the case fitted. For instance, during our five-minute encounter before lunch two days later, Miss Beach did not call me 'Ramsay', as I was fairly sure she always had done. She did not call me anything at all. And she had found another photograph of Henry Moore's work. It was one of those strange family scenes – a massive mother shape and a tall figure standing behind her, the whole group photographed against some rough bit of country. She explained to me that the sculptor had got his first inspiration as a child when massaging his mother's back; and that while philistines would say that these sculptures were 'unrealistic' I was to admire their qualities of form, plasticity and strength. I did, I do. But, at the time, this talk of an artist rubbing a woman's back (even though it was the innocuous story of a child rubbing its mother) seemed like a code. When, almost casually, she remarked that I could keep the Moore photograph, all my hopes were confirmed. I could not have been surer of her love had the picture been of Rodin's 'The Kiss' and had the back of the picture, instead of being left blank, been covered with declarations of Miss Beach's undying love for me.

During this phase of conceited optimism, I must have been, even more than usually, an embarrassment and a bore to her. Although I did not dare to snatch many little talks with her, I followed her everywhere and was unhappy unless I could be reasonably sure of her whereabouts in the school. There were very few school buildings as such, Seaforth Grange consisting of five neighbouring Victorian houses and their gardens, enclosed by high hedges and purple granite walls. There was a rudimentary gym and a hideous little chapel, put up a few years before the war on the crematorium model. Otherwise there were few new or specially designed buildings, with the exception of the art room, a lean-to arrangement with large windows at the back of House Five, opposite the rabbit hutches. Above these hutches, there was a rockery and, by clambering up it, one commanded a clear view of the art room. Between lessons, or at other odd moments when she might be there, I would stand and look in. Sometimes she acknowledged my presence and waved, but more often she pretended not to see me.

As soon as she left the art room, I would dash round to the

front of House Five and wait for her to come out of the front door; occasionally, I would have the courage to offer to carry her books, or to walk along with her. Sometimes, as I now think, to avoid me, she scuttled down the drive, out of the school gate, where I could not follow her, into Albert Road North. (Apart from our walk to the games fields, it was strictly forbidden to set foot outside the prison confines.) Her own room was in House Two. By a brisk walk across the school grounds, I could be waiting at the gate by the time she had walked all the way around Albert Road North and up Como Road. House Two, much the most handsome of the school houses, was Italianate and faced with creamy stucco, unlike the lumpy granite of Houses One and Three, and the brick of Houses Four and Five. House Two contained the school offices, the staff room, the Binker's study, the secretary's office and so on. On the first floor there was a small dormitory for the very youngest boys, who were allowed teddy bears. The other rooms in the house were all inhabited by female members of staff: Miss Duffy, who taught the younger boys and, throughout the school, English verse; Vanessa herself; Miss Beach. Vanessa and Miss Beach were next door to one another on the second floor. The fact doubtless explained Vanessa's familiarity with the art mistress's business.

Miss Beach's window looked eastward into the school; over the roof of the gymnasium she would have been able to see House Three where the dining room was, its lawns and shrubbery leading down past the large Spanish chestnut tree to the gardens of House Four. I spent hours walking about in these regions, with my eyes trained on Miss Beach's window. Sometimes I was rewarded with a glimpse of her. Once, when our eyes met, she had looked troubled, rather cross in fact, and closed her curtains, even though it was only the middle of the day. Sometimes at night, however, she left her curtains open and her lights on; and once or twice I took the supreme risk of pretending I needed a lavatory and sneaked out on to that lawn to gaze up at the lamp-lighted room. It consoled me, though there was no vision of her on such occasions, to think of the presence which the room contained.

The window itself now appears in my memory like a picture framed by the great green mass of the Malverns which undulated immediately above the school and on whose lower slopes we nestled. Seen with the painter's eye (and by then I wanted to be nothing if not an artist) there was an interest in the fact that this large creamy house stood out against a background not of sky but of green, for the hills sloped steeply upward behind the town. Even these huge, solid, geological phenomena which had come into being as a result of volcanic eruptions, aeons before Miss Beach was conceived, appeared to conform obediently to her own taste for abstract mass, tactile shape. Had one of the hills, *à la* Moore, developed a hole in its side, I should hardly have been surprised. As it remains, the icon in my mind is of a window full of light. Whereas the sky, in reality, is the source of light, in my picture of that window, it was Miss Beach who herself radiated and lit up the surrounding forms.

And it was through this window of hers that I first set eyes on Raphael Hunter, knowing with the immediate instinct of the rival in love that it was he and thereby I discovered, in a horrifyingly short space of time, that everything which Vanessa had told us in the dormitory was true.

It was towards the end of a cricket afternoon. We had come back to the school from the playing fields and there was an hour or so of free time before we had high tea at six. Instead of going directly to change, with the others, I made my way round to the lawn of House Three for a routine glance at Miss Beach's window. I did not expect to see her at that hour, but the sight of the window itself would have been enough to provide comfort of a kind. It was open wide and, as I looked up, I saw at once that the back of her head was framed by the curtains. Her short brown hair fell straight, just covering her pale neck. Her back and shoulders were bare. At first I thought that she was completely naked; then I could see the line of her print frock, low cut, running across her pale, freckled shoulder blades. Holding these shoulders firmly, and then running up and down her back were a pair of hands, evidently not her own. At first I could not understand what the hands were doing there. They seemed like some weird optical trick. Nor, from where I was standing, were they very obviously masculine. They were just hands. They continued to move, stroking her back. One of them even disappeared within the straight, low collar of her frock. And then, like some absurd conjurer's trick, from behind Miss Beach's head there appeared a second head, resting its chin on her shoulders and kissing her bare back. After a moment of this activity, the head looked over Miss Beach's shoulder, out of the window and in the direction of the lawn where I stood. She turned at that point and then they both disappeared from the window. But for an unforgettable few seconds I had seen Raphael Hunter and our eyes had met.

In the first of those seconds, my agony was compounded by thinking that he was another boy at the school. I do not mean that he *resembled* any other boy, but that he was amazingly youthful in appearance, smooth, sexless. His fair hair was rather short in those days, otherwise I might have supposed that Miss Beach was embracing another girl. His skin was very pale and pasty. Even in the short time that I saw him, I believe that from the very first I was touched by something mysterious in Hunter's face, as though he were not at home in his surroundings. In this case, his air of being troubled, embarrassed, was easily explained by the fact that a small boy was watching him kiss a woman. But I was to see that look of sadness on Hunter's face in other circumstances.

All experience, Uncle Roy had once said in a sermon, has a capacity to change us to a certain degree if we let it, or if we want it to. But there are some types of experience called, in religion, 'revelation', after which nothing is ever the same again. Everything which happens before and after is transformed by revelation, the past as well as the future. If this is the case, then my experience on the lawn, staring up at Miss Beach's window, was a revelation and, like the revelations of Scripture, it was not merely all-transforming, but it was also of so shattering a kind that it took me years to put it into any kind of shape, to interpret it. And this was even more the case because the things which happened over the following few weeks were so completely confusing that the original moment of revelation, the two figures clasped together in the window, the white house framing the window, the green hills framing the house, became for a time obscured. I thought at first that it was a revelation purely about Miss Beach; later, as my interest in him grew, I took it much more as a revelation about Hunter. Only lately has it begun to occur to me that it was both these things, but also a revelation about myself, doomed to be as much the tormented spectator as the actor in my own life's drama.

On the instant, though, I was shocked and bitterly hurt. Before changing out of my games clothes, I went to hide my tears in the bogs.

*   *

Being in love is hell, it dominates life, it makes life painful, but life goes on doggedly around love and in spite of it. So, school went on being awful and for the first time in nearly five years, its awfulnesses were half consoling, like the good thing about the Blitz being that it kept your mind off the war. The school curriculum continued, undisturbed and unaware, while my heart cracked. The collection of oddballs who constituted the Binker's staff continued to impart to us the curious assortment of misinformation which they had at their command. Very little of what they taught us – perhaps nothing – was of the smallest interest or use to me in later life. The chief interest of their lessons consisted in watching them behave according to type. Each lesson provided us with a new, slightly alarming, performing animal. Mr Finch; had he been a deserter, or was he shellshocked? Perhaps neither, but we could make him cry simply by calling out, 'What did you do in the war, sir?'

Poor, wispy Miss Duffy was incapable of making us appreciate the gems of English verse in our reader; she was even less efficient at dodging the paper darts with which we regularly bombarded her. Lollipop Lew, the gangling loon who taught French out of a textbook, had apparently never heard the language spoken. He taught us to speak it phonetically – 'gee swiss' for *je suis*. Was it all some kind of elaborate joke which he was playing against the rest of the world? One can ask that of any eccentric and the answer is never easy. With Darnley at the next desk, an item of furniture in which he bred slow-worms (once one satisfyingly came slithering out of the hole which should have contained the ink well, just as Miss Duffy was passing – what yelps!), lessons were an hilarious agony of half-suppressed giggles and unremittingly anarchic attempts to undermine the system. The level of wit was excruciatingly low, often non-existent. The laughter was cumulative. Someone started to giggle. Then another person. In such an atmosphere, any sort of interjection, any bit of cheek thrown at the unfortunate buffoon in front of us, was enough to make us writhe with laughter.

'Sir!'

'What is it *now*, Darnley?'

'What's the French for a male hen, sir?'

'Isn't that a contradiction in terms, Darnley?'

'Very droll, sir, very funny.'

To show how funny it was, we all shouted with laughter.

'Shut *up*!'

'But seriously, sir, a male farmyard bird. You know, sir. What's the French for it?'

There were two jokes going on here – one of simple bawdry and the other designed to expose our teacher's total ignorance of French vocabulary. We all pretended not to notice him rummaging through a much-thumbed *Hugo's French in Three Months* which he kept in his desk. So intent was he on convincing us that he knew the language that he completely forgot the way in which boys' minds work.

'What are you looking at under your desk, sir?'

'Shut up, Darnley.'

'But, sir, you *are* looking at something. What is it?'

'I think *coq* is the word you are after, Darnley.'

This produced such a roar of anarchic laughter that Greasy Rhysy had to come in from the classroom next door to quieten us down.

Darnley was in a different dorm from mine. I didn't tell him any of Vanessa's gossip about Miss Beach, but inevitably it leaked back to him. He was merciless enough to refer to her henceforth as Beryl. In grown-up life, you can't really get away with being rude about someone else's lover or partner or wife or husband. You just have to accept the fact that the heart plays strange tricks and that friends in all other respects delightful and intelligent have been stupid enough to fall in love. Politeness to or about the current object of desire is only abandoned at peril to the friendship itself. Darnley and I had not yet reached this level of sophistication. (I am not sure that Darnley ever quite did, but that is another story.) It pained me then that he thought of my devotion to Miss Beach as yet another joke, but I accepted this fact and even though I biffed him whenever he mentioned the matter I could not cease to regard him as a friend. I still assumed, for instance, that he would be coming out for lunch with us when Granny came down for her termly visit.

The visits of my grandmother were always something to be enjoyed, but this one was something to which we looked forward most particularly, because of the fact that I owned five pounds – the five pounds which Sargie Lampitt had pressed into my hand. Not only was it a fantastic sum of money – his lunch that day at Claridges with Uncle Roy would have cost him only about a pound – but it was illegal to possess it. Sargie's lavish generosity had in fact landed me in an extremely awkward position. Like many other tyrants in history, the Binker was obsessed by currency control. We were forbidden more than a pound per term in pocket money. 'Ten shillings is more than adequate,' his famous 'Notes for Parents' proclaimed. Whatever money we brought back to school had to be handed in at the school office at the beginning of term. Had I handed in Sargie's fiver to the school secretary, it would have been posted straight back to Timplingham with a brisk letter to my uncle, refreshing his memory of the school rules.

It was therefore imperative that we should convert the five pounds into some commodity which could either be kept hidden when we got back to school or could plausibly be described as a present from Granny. This in itself was not easy. Any sort of food 'except' – I quote again from 'Notes for Parents' – 'one moderately sized cake given on or near the boy's birthday' was forbidden. No sweets or chocolates – which were in any case rationed – were to be bought. Nor – the Binker's pen here got carried away with itself, for in what circumstances would we ever have been able to break this law? – were 'boys permitted to bring within the school perimeter meats, including sausages, firearms, explosives or any sort of tobacco'. Alcohol, of course, was out of the question. So, too, were the whole range of more obviously wholesome distractions, like books. 'Boys are only permitted to bring one book per term back to Seaforth Grange. This must be submitted to the Headmaster for approval at the beginning of term. There are books available on loan from the school library.' This collection chiefly consisted of heavy masculine stuff with an obsolescent imperialist flavour, not at that time to my taste. There were pseudo-historical romances by G. A. Henty, Stanley Weyman and W. Harrison Ainsworth.

There were the memoirs of soldiers and explorers. Then there were the decayed bound volumes of pre-war *Punch*, each joke as fascinatingly unfunny as the last, and a very out-of-date *Chambers's Encyclopaedia*. It was hardly a literary banquet. In consequence I read almost nothing during my time at Seaforth Grange. Even if they had permitted it, though, I would not have dreamed of spending Sargie's five pounds on books. No. This called for the big idea, though nothing much occurred to us as we wandered around together in break or lolled idly on the sun-drenched cricket pitch (there was no rain that term; the weather was an uninterrupted English summer's day) while the others played with bat and ball.

Lollipop Lew, his waist burdened with white jumpers which we had cast off and which he had tied like a cummerbund around himself for safe-keeping, drooped in the slips, tall, red-faced, himself languid.

'Darnley and Ramsay, what the dickens do you think you are doing?'

'Making a daisy chain, sir.'

'Well, get up and go to the boundary. You are meant to be fielding.'

'No, sir, Fielding's batting, sir. Quite a different boy.'

Everything Darnley did or said contrived to be thoroughly puerile and foolish. Yet I have never laughed so much as I did in his company. Instinct must have drawn us together. Ever since, I have been chiefly attracted to those who wanted to make daisy chains while others played the game. Fielding is quite a different boy . . .

My grandmother, I suppose, had reached a rather similar conclusion at an early age, only with her it took the form of being surprised that a game was in progress at all and of needing assistance even with the composition of her daisy chain. Almost everything was either too complicated or too arduous for Granny to do on her own. Certainly, when my parents were killed, it was out of the question that she should have taken any practical part in my own upbringing.

'I brought *two* boys up,' she would sometimes tell me, wide-eyed, as though parents had almost never been so self-sacrificing or adventurous. The effort had evidently exhausted her, and would have been completely impossible had it not

been for the loyal support and help of her very good friend Mrs
Webb. Unlike the saintly Lady Starling (whom I had not at that
stage met) Mrs Webb could not have been described by anyone
as a doormat. She had a forcefulness of demeanour which left
one in no doubt that she could look after herself. Nevertheless,
for her own reasons (perhaps simple kindness of heart) she
seemed prepared to immolate herself to all my grandmother's
whims and needs.

'It's no good asking Thora to *do* things,' Mrs Webb would say
with particular vehemence.

Mrs Webb, for instance, did all Granny's shopping. She had
done so ever since the war started.

'Thora never could master those ration books' – there was
almost triumph in her friend's incapacity – 'and you couldn't
see her queuing, not with those feet.'

Granny's feet, even to the biased eye of her own flesh and
blood, looked much like anyone else's. Each year at Cromer or
(as Mrs Webb much preferred) Westgate-on-Sea, I had seen
them: the full complement of toes and the filmy, delicate, white
skin of her instep paddling in the waves. But it was apparently
an *a priori* truth, requiring no demonstration, that hers were
not feet which you could expect to stand in a queue. 'Mr
Churchill himself would not ask it,' said Mrs Webb, not long
before the end of the war, and this was true. He had asked for
blood, toil, sweat and tears, but not that. Not from Granny.

'Remember, I can't stand too long,' she would say.

I always did remember it. I remembered it again when I saw
the diminutive figure of Mrs Webb waiting at the school gate
on the Saturday of our *exeat*, as the Binker pretentiously called
any permitted outing. Mrs Webb's jaunty little feathered hat,
new-looking handbag and satin costume suggested, rightly, an
air of prosperity not enjoyed by Granny. She had been left, one
gathered, 'comfortable' by the demise of Mr Webb, who had
owned a number of ironmongers' shops.

She and Darnley had met before. He quite often came out for
meals with me when my people were down. Mrs Webb always
embarrassed me, but not Darnley himself, by calling him by his
Christian name.

'Hallo, Miles.'

'Hallo, Mrs Webb.'

'Hallo, young one,' she said to me. 'Your Granny's in the Riley. We could not keep her standing at the gate, not in this heat.'

It was a perfect sunny day, with a balmy breeze blowing in from the south.

Mrs Webb, who had driven ambulances during the Blitz, was addicted to motor travel and somehow managed to get enough petrol to drive her little Riley. Sometimes with a wink she hinted that she knew the right people. I have no doubt that she did. Her proud conveyance, shiny black with a violently sloping back roof, was parked at an angle on the steep street to prevent it rolling backwards. Granny greeted us as warmly as she could without stirring from her front seat in the little car, and Darnley and I clambered into the back.

'You'll be hungry for your lunches,' she said keenly.

I began to explain about having to spend the five pounds.

'If I was you, I'd save it up,' said Mrs Webb. 'Now, we're going to Bobby's. I always like the drive into Worcester.'

'Good,' said Darnley. And he attempted to explain to Mrs Webb why the five pounds must be spent that afternoon, and why Worcester would be an ideal place to spend it. Not only were there more shops than in Malvern, but there was far less likelihood of being spotted by a member of staff from Seaforth Grange. My grandmother's favourite eating place in the vicinity was the restaurant of a department store in the middle of Worcester, some eight miles away from the school. The service was quick. You could get delicious fish and well-cooked chips for only a few shillings, while a palm court trio, three crones, sawed out Indian love lyrics and numbers from pre-war musicals. When Darnley's mum took us out, it was always to the Foley Arms, the largest hotel in Malvern, where the meals were four times as expensive and took four times as long. How restless we used to become, waiting for those hunks of over-cooked meat in their caterer's gravy.

The drive from Malvern to Worcester was soon accomplished – enlivened, after we had turned the steep bend in the road near the lunatic asylum at Powick, by our transformation into loonies, an uncharitable display which made the old ladies laugh and say we were terrible. Actually, on Darnley's part, the loony act was only just beginning to wear off by the time we reached the restaurant. There was a queue, but Mrs Webb walked to the head of it and addressed the manageress directly.

'If we could have a table at once; only on account of my friend's feet.'

This formula was efficacious; we were immediately led through the quite crowded restaurant. Everything at Bobby's was as I remembered it. The waitress, a stubby pencil poised over her greasy pad attached by a piece of string to her waist, was ready to take our order. Against a far wall the three crones shared a tiny platform with a baby grand and a potted aspidistra, and gave forth their melancholy renderings of pre-war songs: 'The Springtime Reminds Me of You', 'The Isle of Capri', and 'Love Is the Sweetest Thing'.

The food came almost instantly; any person anxious about Granny's feet would have been unable to feel equal worries about her appetite. Darnley himself, no mean trencherman, could not compete with her speed when it came to polishing off a pile of chips. The fish was of the freshest, the whole served with thin slices of white bread and butter and a pot of strong tea for four. And it was tea, not hot water poured over a bag.

'Now,' said Mrs Webb, 'I call that a very nice bit of plaice.'

'Enjoy your meal, did you, dear?' The waitress was hovering again.

'Enormously,' said Granny with great emphasis.

'Well, what to follow, what for sweet?'

'Oh, dear,' said Granny.

'Too full?' asked the waitress.

'Certainly not,' snapped Mrs Webb, 'only don't ask my friend to make decisions. She always did find decisions difficult, great or small.'

'There's a lovely bit of Bakewell with custard,' prompted the waitress. 'Or you could have a nice ice . . .'

She had failed to grasp the reality of the situation. Anyone who knew Granny would have recognised that there was something slightly monstrous about expecting her to do a difficult thing like reach a conclusion.

'Oh, *you* decide *for* me!' she said, for a moment vexed.

'What was it, Bakewell tart?' asked Mrs Webb.

'That's right, dear.'

'I think that sounds delicious.'

'I'd rather have the noice oice,' said Darnley.

He was not imitating the waitress's voice. He had an incurable need to embellish, change or improve the world as he discovered it. Mrs Webb and Granny laughed almost constantly in his presence, and kept exclaiming that he really must go on the stage.

Both old ladies, but Granny in particular, had a highly developed sense of humour. They appeared to be approaching life chiefly on the look-out for diversion, preferably of a kind which would make them laugh. Granny loved all Darnley's jokes, and I admired the delicacy and swift editorial expertise with which he made his repertoire acceptable to an elderly female audience. True, this meant that a whole range of his 'jokes' – and some of the funnier ones – had to be scuppered altogether. But he adapted some of the stories about Englishmen, Irishmen and Scotsmen, excising the coarser elements, to truly hilarious effect, so that Granny, having made short work of her Bakewell, was driven to exclaim, 'More, Miles, more!'

'Come on,' said Darnley to me, 'you think of some.'

But he had no sooner said this than he had thought of another. Granny found this particular story, the one about two taxis colliding in Aberdeen and fifty-seven people being killed, so funny that I thought she would choke. As they often say of great performers, it was the way he told them. So conscious was Darnley of this, but so fond of the jokes themselves, that he would sometimes ask, rather anxiously, even when the joke had made everyone laugh, 'Do you get?' Sometimes, he would find that though they had laughed fit to burst, his audience had not understood the point of the joke at all and then he would laboriously explain, 'People in Aberdeen are really stingy, you see, so that they'd all piled into just two taxis . . .'

'They used to make jokes like that about the Jews,' said Granny. 'Before the war, of course.'

Anxious to demonstrate that, Hitler notwithstanding, anti-Semitic bad taste could still raise a laugh, Darnley was about to embark on a series of quickfire question and answer routines; but something extraordinary happened which interrupted Darnley's flow.

'I don't know,' said Granny, already shaking in anticipation, because she knew that Darnley's answer would make her chuckle. 'Why *are* pound notes green?'

There was such a pause that I filled in with the predictable, 'Because the Jews picked them all before they were ripe.' On my lips it was totally unfunny. Not a flicker of amusement was to be derived from the words. And we all turned, even Granny with her neck, in the direction in which Darnley was staring.

'That's our undermatron, she's called Vanessa, she's terrific,' he explained in a gabble. Gossip was as good as jokes as far as the old ladies were concerned and they were prepared for a change of subject. I desperately hoped that Darnley, with his somehow more sophisticated family background, wouldn't tell Granny that Vanessa kissed us all goodnight. I felt, without being able to say why, that my pleasure, or former pleasure, in feeling her large woollen chest against my pyjama jacket was not something which I wanted imparted to the family. But I need not have worried. Beneath the larky exterior, Darnley's impeccable tact was unshaken.

'She looks very young,' said Granny.

'She's eighteen,' said Darnley. 'Most of the staff are ancient, but Vanessa is different.'

'You think anything's ancient,' said Mrs Webb.

'But they're bonkers, as well, aren't they, Ramsay?'

'Yes.'

Darnley then asserted that the thing about Vanessa was that she was a jolly nice person and I agreed. From an aesthetic point of view, she had, perhaps, never looked nicer than on that afternoon. She wore a yellow and white spotted dress with a broad collar cut quite low over the chest. A yellow cardie was draped over her shoulders like a shawl. Her hair was done in a ponytail. She was smoking her Craven A with infinite sensuality.

'I like her young man,' said Mrs Webb.

It was the young man who had arrested my attention. No one else round that table had ever set eyes on him before, but I had. I would have recognised those hands alone, which had reached out to light her Craven A and now were holding her hands across the table. When he turned, it was unmistakable.

'"The oldest, yet the latest thing,"' Granny sang very, very quietly, conducting the music of the trio with her teaspoon. Mrs Webb took up the refrain.

> '"I only hope that Fate may bring
> Love's glory to you!"'

It was not possible to tell any of them who he was. The terrible pain of seeing Raphael Hunter through Miss Beach's window and holding my beloved in his arms had made any subsequent mention of the matter impossible. Although Vanessa had, only a few weeks before, told all the dorm that Hunter was Miss Beach's boyfriend, only I knew what he looked like; only I had the painful evidence of my own eyes that this man in the restaurant had a claim on Miss Beach.

'I wonder who he is,' said Darnley.

'He's very, *very* handsome,' said Granny, quite spontaneously.

Now that I had the chance to survey him at greater leisure, I did so. My feelings about Hunter, before and since, are far too complicated for me to be able to say whether I shared Granny's opinion. I think, rather, that I was looking at Hunter partly in order to find out what handsomeness was. So *this* was what women found beautiful – a completely smooth face, boyish and on the borders of chubbiness; not much colour, not much vivacity in the eyes, but the features framed into an expression which was obviously meant to be amiable. I think – this really is the *point* of Hunter – I think it *was* amiable. Naturally, I can't really remember what it was like to look at Hunter's face for the very first time, nor for the second time, at leisure in Bobby's. My memory of the whole episode is distorted by all the things which have happened since. But even in these first essays in the difficult business of interpreting Hunter's face I think there was the glimmering of a perception in my mind that he was not so much handsome as inoffensive. I have since come to believe that Hunter's strangely youthful and characterless face is a sort of *tabula rasa* on to which his innumerable devotees have fixed their own criterion of beauty and attractiveness, finding there what they have put there themselves. But perhaps this is what we do with all faces? Anyhow, such perceptions, true or false, lay in the distant future.

My instantaneous reaction, which excited an irrational burst of fury against Vanessa, was that he had asked her out to luncheon in order to discuss Miss Beach. It did not occur to me, even when I saw him holding Vanessa's hand, that one could have the sublime experience of kissing Miss Beach and then so much as look at another woman. Miss Beach was not by conventional standards a beauty. But she was The Woman. It was simply inconceivable that Hunter, who had held her in his arms, did not feel as I did in this matter. Vanessa, known to us boys chiefly as a dormitory confidante, was obviously trying to help Hunter through some emotional crisis with Miss Beach.

'Do you know who he is?' asked Mrs Webb.

'The only thing we know is that he comes from Bromyard, don't we, Ramsay?'

'Do we?'

With my literal mind I was on the point of blurting out that Vanessa herself had told us that Hunter's parents lived in Malvern. It was her boyfriend who lived in Bromyard, not Hunter.

'Yes, thicko, don't you remember? Vanessa's told us several times she has a boyfriend at home. They see each other twice a week.'

'I think he looks very – well, *distinguished*,' said Mrs Webb. But, at that point, the waitress blocked our view of the pair and gave us our bill.

'You pay over at the desk, dear.' She indicated a glass cage at the entrance to the restaurant. Granny instinctively peered in the opposite direction for the cash till and began to assume a look of vexed helplessness. The impression given was that it was bad enough to have to pay for our food, but to find a cash desk, even when it was pointed out to her, was insupportable.

'It sounds *awfully* complicated,' she said.

'Anything with a queue is going to be difficult for my friend,' glossed Mrs Webb.

As it happened, there was no queue at the cash desk at that moment. Although it obviously was not part of her duty to do so, the waitress decided to take Granny's pound note over to the cash desk for her. She returned with a fistful of change and was ecstatically grateful when Granny tipped her threepence.

The afternoon, between all the jokes at table, had already

been mapped out for us by Mrs Webb. A short perambulation of the shops would give us time to secrete as many illegal sweetmeats as could be crammed into a blazer pocket. Mrs Webb thought our idea of spending the five pounds all at once absolutely stupid and said that she would take us all on a nice river steamer. Darnley's mum never arranged outings of this kind. After the drawn-out hotel meals, we would simply loll about with nothing to do in her plush hotel lounge. Uncle Roy and Aunt Deirdre (I never inflicted them on Darnley) had outings planned, when they came down, but they were never of a kind which could give pleasure to a twelve-year-old boy. If they had taken me to Worcester, they would have insisted on spending the whole afternoon in the cathedral and we would not have emerged until we had devoted the closest scrutiny to every bit of coloured glass, every tomb and monument, every carved misericord. As for refreshment, in all weathers my uncle and aunt preferred a picnic to 'some awful café'. We always stayed our appetites in some lay-by sitting beside the car, except on those ecstatically happy expeditions to some little-known relation of Sargie's whom Uncle Roy had promised to look up. A tedious drive to Ledbury for tea with Sargie's cousin Peter stays in my mind. Anyway, with Granny and Mrs Webb, there was none of this. We just had to wait while they had one last cigarette in the restaurant and then the afternoon was ours.

The question on all our minds, when we had explained who Vanessa was, was whether to greet her as we left the restaurant. I deeply did not wish to do so, but Mrs Webb, who thought that they looked an extremely pleasant couple, was of the view that it might seem rude not to. Thankfully, wiser counsels prevailed and Granny said, 'Perhaps she'd rather be left in peace on her afternoon off. She sees quite enough of you at school!'

So we left Bobby's without alerting Vanessa to our presence there. Granny heaved herself to her feet, announcing to Mrs Webb that it might be an idea, if they were going on the river, to powder their noses, but how on earth she could find anywhere to do this she could not conceive. Mrs Webb (pronounced by Granny a *genius* for the discovery) said that she could see a sign bearing the word 'Ladies'. Darnley and I thought it might be a good moment for a pee and went off to our own place.

When we were standing at the urinals, Darnley said, 'That was a smashing meal – why can't Mummy be like your grandmother?'

'How d'you mean?'

'Mummy never laughs at things.'

'Doesn't she?'

'Do you think Vanessa's let that man stick it up her yet.'

'They don't want a baby, do they?'

I threw out this swaggeringly worldly riposte partly because I thought Darnley was going too far, partly to disguise the fact that I knew that he wasn't Vanessa's boyfriend, but Miss Beach's.

'Did you see them holding hands?' asked Darnley.

Having finished at the urinal and shaken himself dry, he lowered the side of his shorts once more. I did the same. We never bothered with opening and rebuttoning flies.

'No,' I lied.

'They were holding hands. They had that dreamy look like Mummy and David.' He held the door of the Gents for me (there was never any nonsense about washing our hands). As he did so, he said, 'I hate love.'

*   *

Since Darnley had no idea who Hunter was, he could not really respond to my idea that we shouldn't mention, when we returned to school, that we had seen Vanessa with a man in a restaurant. I begged him to keep quiet about the matter; I felt that it was an area which could only cause me pain and I was equally sure that Darnley had got it all wrong. But he told his dormitory and by the time Mrs Webb's Riley was speeding back to London, all the school knew that we had spotted Vanessa, being kissed by her boyfriend in a really posh restaurant in Worcester. When it was next her turn to supervise our dormitory, the other boys were merciless in their curiosity. Everyone assumed, on Darnley's authority, that this was the boyfriend from Bromyard. She had already told us so much about him – how could she *mind* our having seen him?

Only I knew that this was not quite right; and nobody

reckoned on the seriousness of the whole business. Hitherto, Vanessa had been our friend, a figure who was something between an elder sister and a fantasy figure of perfect womanhood. I always think I understand a little about the conventions of medieval courtly love because of having known Vanessa. How could all the knights of a particular court have loved the same lady? Those who reached out so eagerly for Vanessa's embraces would have known the reason, for there was no rivalry in the love of Vanessa. She distributed her favours equally and this was the convention observed. It was altogether different from the exclusive, secretive passion which I nursed for Miss Beach.

Darnley and I, in bringing back the news of Vanessa in the restaurant, were unwittingly destroying a whole part of our lives: one of the few things which made life at Seaforth Grange bearable. For the Vanessa who was questioned about her lunch on Saturday turned out to be a completely different figure from the dorm pal of yore. It had been perfectly permissible, apparently, to quiz her about the boy from Bromyard and to make outrageous suggestions about her chances of seducing other members of the staff. When we had accused her of being in love with Greasy Rhysy, she had laughed as much as the rest of us. But the lunch in Worcester was out of bounds – we were not to question her about it.

Quite a few of the boys in the dorm were slow to pick this up.

Torrance, inevitably, called out, 'They saw you, they saw you!' as soon as Vanessa came into our room.

She took no notice, but the general, high-spirited uproar soon died down when it became obvious that she was in no mood for japes. She was pale and very, very angry. She strode through the dormitory until she came to my bed. For the first time, her bigness, hitherto merely a matter of erotic attraction, seemed positively threatening.

'You *stupid* little boy!' she yelled at me. She got me by the shoulders and shook me. 'Why can't you keep your nose out of other people's business? Oh, yes, it's all just a big joke to you, isn't it?'

'But I didn't . . .'

'Oh, yes you did, you and your little friend Darnley. I saw you in Worcester! Well, let me tell you, little Master Ramsay . . .'

This terrible transmogrification, by which Vanessa had become a grown-up and one of the most obstreperous kind, held the rest of the dormitory enthralled, but not silent. Some stood on their beds, no longer quite able to speak but showing from their gleeful, foolish faces that this was the most amusing episode yet in the real-life drama of Vanessa: miles better than filmstars and Bromyard.

I was trying very hard not to cry. Other members of the dorm, more sensitive to atmosphere than those who were openly gleeful, sensed that we were about to lose Vanessa for ever, lose her as a friend. They began to support her.

'Honestly, Ramsay!'

'You silly little prat, Ramsay!'

'Ramsay and Darnley do it again.'

There are always people in the world who are prepared to seize on some aspect of one's behaviour which they regard as less than satisfactory and make out that it is a part of a repeated, overall pattern.

Vanessa's little tirade, however, never got finished. Just as she was in mid-sentence, expressing the hope that one day I should find out how much it hurt to have everyone gossiping about me – a more than backhanded curse which could be taken any number of ways – everyone fell silent. Over the shoulder of her blue matron's overall I could see the grey hair, the club tie, the too-large, baggy tweed suit of the Binker.

'Oh hell,' said Bowen.

'Indeed,' said the Binker with grim satisfaction.

The atmosphere was so terrible that one would not have been totally surprised had there been an occurrence like the last scene of *Don Giovanni* in which someone was actually, bodily snatched into the regions of eternal punishment; I took a minute or two to realise that the 'someone' singled out for the role of villain was myself. Foolishly, I had even allowed myself a flash of hope that the Binker's presence would somehow vindicate me, that he would tell Vanessa to stop shouting and allow us all to settle into our beds for the night. This was not the Binker's style and I should have known it.

'Bowen.'

'Yes, sir?'

'Please come to my study tomorrow morning. The offences
– using a swearword of the most obnoxious character and being
unable to control your dormitory.'

'Yes, sir.'

'Woe betide an army, Bowen, when the troops won't obey
the officers.'

'Yes, sir.'

'I shall consider whether or not to allow you to continue as
dormie captain.'

'Yes, sir.'

'And wee Tammie-tawse will settle the rest.'

There was silence. Then, like some horrible witness in a
Stalinist showtrial, Vanessa rose from my bed to denounce me.

'Ramsay is the one to blame, sir. He was the one who started
all this noise and bother.'

'Is this true, Ramsay?'

'No, sir.'

'What! How dare you contradict a member of my staff?'

'Sorry, sir.'

'Well, is it true or isn't it?'

I was silent.

The Binker smiled. He had no idea what was going on,
but there could be no doubt that a serious offence had been
committed, one which needed the most severe castigation.

'You also, Ramsay, will have the goodness to present yourself
at my study tomorrow morning. Now the rest of you are to
remain silent and we will have no more of this matter. Miss
Faraday, if you care to come down with me, you can explain
what these young hooligans have been up to.'

I felt a touch of sympathy for poor Vanessa as she left that
dormitory. She hung her head. She knew that, in the passion
of the moment, she had gone too far and that she had just lost
herself ten friends. Whatever we did to restore things, there
would be 'never glad confident morning again'.

Beatings were so frequent an occurrence at Seaforth Grange
that the sensations of anger and dread which dominated the
next twelve hours were not new to me. Even when you manage
to sleep, in such circumstances, you know in your dreams that
a beating is going to happen. You try to tell yourself that you
have survived dozens of beatings before; that the pain does not

last more than a few days; that, in all the course of the school's history, there have been hundreds, thousands of strokes of the Binker's sticks administered to his pupils and that they have all survived. And yet, for all these attempts to allay fear, it still has its power to torture you. And when you get up you feel sick and the school breakfast seems more than usually nauseating: but the grey, half-cooked pieces of bacon fat must be eaten, partly because it is the school rule and partly as a matter of pride. They all know what you are feeling, the other boys, but you must not show fear in front of them. If one of us had broken down and wept, and implored the Binker publicly for mercy, might not our tears have broken the system? Who can tell? The need to disguise our feelings, to keep a stiff upper lip, was so strong that no one would have contemplated breaking the code. And eventually breakfast ends and everyone stands in silence. Then there is grace, said by Timpson. And then, as if you needed reminding, the Binker says, 'Ramsay and Bowen to see me, please.' And he strolls the leisurely distance from the dining hall in House Three to his study in House Two. The familiarity of the whole routine – it was a daily ritual at Seaforth Grange – did nothing to lessen any part of its horror, and I am only sorry that the Binker is dead and cannot read these words as I write them, nearly forty years on, as a record of all the needless suffering which he inflicted in the course of his career.

That particular morning, Bowen and I followed him at a discreet distance. He would have looked, to an outside visitor from the town, like a charming old gentleman, pottering through his garden. He paused to have a few words with the gardener, who was already at work, watering some petunias in the cool of the morning. By the time we reached the hall of House Two, it was empty.

It was a large hall. Next to the study was the school secretary's office and, opposite that, the staff Common Room; above, as I have said, were the little boys in their dormitory and the female members of staff in their various bedrooms. So there was plenty of coming and going; and all those fortunate people who were not going to be punished would look at us and know that we were miscreants.

Strangely, passers-by more often regarded us with scorn than with pity. I sometimes think of my times outside the Binker's study door when I am watching the T.V. news and some criminal is brought to trial, accused of an offence which at that moment society has decreed to be unpardonable, such as political terrorism or child abuse. The man's head is covered with a blanket, so he is almost invisible. The police hustle him along between the Black Maria and the dock. Yet, the hatred engendered by such figures is so virulent that one sometimes feels it oneself, even while watching them on television. The crowds have hovered to watch, to thump the prison van, to scream abuse at the crumpled, defeated little figure who goes to his punishment.

The Binker's study door opened.

'Ah!' he said genially. 'Bowen, please.'

Bowen was probably in the study for no more than seven minutes, but time is measured by the imagination and not by the clock. My wait seemed interminable. I could hear the Binker's voice meandering on. Occasionally, there was a silence. Probably it was not in fact a silence, but Bowen could hardly find the words to reply. Those about to be thrashed lose their vocal power. What I was anxiously listening for was the actual moment of castigation, for I had told myself that if Bowen got two for his inability to control the dormitory, I might get away with only one. After all, I had done nothing. There was no logic in any of this, but I was convinced of its truth. If he got more than two, I felt that there would be no limit to the Binker's wrath. But, even as I stood there with my ears cocked, Miss Beach came down the stairs.

Because she belonged to the real world and had not yet settled at Seaforth Grange, she did not automatically understand what it signified to be standing outside the Binker's study after breakfast. In fact, she did not even assume that I was waiting for the Binker. Any of the doors in the hall – or none of them – might have been the one I was waiting outside. She probably assumed (what could have been likelier?) that I was hovering about in the hope of glimpsing her. As it happened, I wasn't and the very sight of her on that scene tore me in two excruciating directions. As Miss Beach's aspirant lover, I was ashamed to be doing anything so childish as waiting for a thrashing. I wanted above everything to conceal from her my actual reason for waiting in the hall. On the other hand, still having failed, failed completely, to grasp the significance of my glimpse of Vanessa and Hunter in the restaurant, I believed that Miss Beach was the one person in the world who was capable of saving me from my fate. All she would have to do would be to tell the Binker the truth and I would be let off.

This second view of mine begged so many questions that it is just as well that I never put it to the test. It implied, for one thing, that I was about to be caned purely for spreading false rumours about Vanessa and that the falsehood of the rumour could be established beyond question by Miss Beach. It ignored whatever uncontrollable impulses had actually led Vanessa to lose her temper; still more, it ignored the Binker's need to hit children each morning with sticks. It momentarily ignored the fact that by thus establishing my complete innocence (I had, after all, urged Darnley not to spread the rumour) I would be landing my best friend in the soup. It also implied that Miss Beach would not mind her lover being the centre of this school-boy drama, in fact the talk of the whole school. More than anything, it implied that she knew all about Vanessa's tryst with Hunter. As I was to realise subsequently, she knew nothing about it at all. This is a mistake which I have often made since: assuming, because the whole world knows that X is having a love affair with Y, that this common knowledge is also in the possession of X's family, or Y's other lovers. On the contrary, those most affected by such events are often the last to hear about them; and if they hear about them at all they are often privy to far fewer 'secrets' than might be the common property of gossips at the very outer periphery of things.

'What are you doing here?' asked Miss Beach. 'Do you want anyone in the staff room?'

She was looking wonderful in an open-necked, white blouse. Her intelligent face was screwed up into its expression of comical curiosity, as though any explanation for my presence there could be expected to make her roar with laughter.

I pointed silently to the Binker's door. Boys seldom entered the study for any purpose other than canings or, still worse, one of his little talks. But Miss Beach did not know this. Looking back on the scene I realised that she did not know *anything*. Even my few shreds of knowledge about Hunter and his whereabouts would have been enough to stop her ironical smile. When I pointed to the study door she just pulled a 'solemn' expression, but only of the cheeky kind that anyone might pull when contemplating the pomps of authority.

'You're coming to me today, yes?'

'Yes.' Art was fourth lesson.

'You don't look very pleased about it.'

From behind the study door the noises had begun. Thwack, thwack.

Perhaps Miss Beach did not hear these sounds. Or, if she did, they were to her ears toneless and without significance, as though the Binker had been knocking together a couple of books, or thumping a cushion to make it more comfortable on his chair.

'See you later then,' she said and she stepped airily into the Common Room. Even though the door opened for no more than a second or two, the smell of tobacco which came from the staff room was almost overwhelming.

Then the study door opened and Bowen came out, rather red, but not actually blubbing. In case I had not heard the last stroke (and I hadn't), he held up three fingers and went his way.

'Ramsay!'

The Binker called my name as casually as if I were a patient awaiting treatment from a doctor's surgery.

'Come in, Ramsay, and close the door.'

He had already selected his weapon. It was lying on the desk, but he was in no hurry and he sat down while I stood before him. He began in his usual humdrum way by saying that he set great store, 'verra great store indid, Ramsa' – his voice always became more Scotch when he got excited – 'by the maintenance of discipline in the dormitory.'

Discipline, it seemed, was the beginning of wisdom. Without it, life itself would apparently fall into chaos. Bla, bla, bla.

'But your offence, Ramsay, is very much worse than that. Very, very much worse than a breach of discipline. There is absolutely nothing which more undermines a community such as our own than common tittle-tattle. Gossip, Ramsay. Do you understand what I am saying, boy?'

'Yes, sir.'

'Of course, you cannot be expected to understand that

grown-ups have feelings and that some things, certain very private things, affect grown-up persons most deeply. These things, Ramsay, these private sacred things, you have held cheap. You have chosen to make them the subject of dormitory ribaldry. Am I right, Ramsay?'

One did not in these circumstances ever contradict the Binker.

'Speak up, boy!'

'Yes, sir.'

'Miss Faraday very delicately did not wish to tell me the nature of last night's ballyhoo. It was very understandable that she should have wanted to keep this thing to herself, but I am glad that it has all come out into the open. Although it has yet to be announced officially, I believe that it is only a matter of time before Mr Hunter – the young man with whom you saw her – and she announce their engagement to be married.'

'No, sir, that's not right.'

'Do not interrupt, Ramsay, or you will make things a deal worse for yourself.'

'But you've got it wrong, sir!'

'Mr Hunter's mother told me about it herself only yesterday – before all this disgraceful matter. As it happens, Miss Faraday is engaged, or about to be engaged, to an old boy of the school, to one of my very favourite pupils. His parents are friends of mine of long standing. They live only down the road.

'But, sir . . .'

The wrongness of all this, as I still thought it, gave me tongue and courage. I was not going to land anyone else in trouble. I simply found myself unable to let the Binker say things which were palpably false.

'I wish you to make a personal apology to Miss Faraday in writing. You are to show me the letter before you present it to her.'

'But, sir . . .'

'You are a stubborn little man, Ramsay, but you will hear me out and then I think wee Tammie-tawse will teach you a lesson in manners which you will not forget. You will make a written apology to Miss Faraday for the embarrassment which you have caused her. From what she has told me, your conduct last night was filthy and disgusting. I am happy to say that from what she has further told me there will be a happy announcement ere long. The story has a happy ending. It is not often an Old Granger marries a member of my staff. In fact, I think it sets a new Seaforth Grange record.'

He smiled. It was evident that this particular Old Granger was rather special to him.

'Now bend over, Ramsay, and hold the arms of the chair.'

*   *

'Even so,' said Darnley, later in the day as we changed for cricket. 'Eight! It makes history.'

'I just thought they were never going to stop.'

'And this Hunter bloke was one of the Binker's favourites – a sort of Timpson-style arse licker – about a hundred and fifty years ago or something?'

'Looks like it.'

The whole episode was puzzling and painful. When we had got to the art room for our fourth period and found that all art lessons for the next few days were cancelled, I had told Darnley everything. He promised, this time, not to spread it all round the school, and I now believed and trusted him.

'Crikey,' had been his reaction. 'You should have told me when we first saw this Hunter bloke with Vanessa.'

'I just couldn't. I thought he was still, you know . . .' I couldn't say Miss Beach's name.

'Rather hard cheese on Miss Beach,' said Darnley.

'Very.'

'You see what I mean about hating love.'

For a momentary flicker, as he said these words, I thought that I might release myself, there and then, from the thrall of loving Miss Beach. But then my resolution hardened. I became more in love with her than ever, in love with love itself and, for the first time since I had heard about Hunter, actually hopeful that I might win a place in Miss Beach's affections. After all, if Vanessa could give us kisses, why not Miss Beach? What was to stop Miss Beach kissing me? And then, perhaps, eventually, when I was sixteen, say, we could get married. I was very nearly thirteen. It only meant three years to wait. She could do her sculpture. I could be an artist, too.

'Here, hurry up, or we shall be late for cricket,' said Darnley.

I was still sitting there in the changing room, my studded cricket shoes untied, my white shirt half buttoned.

'There's half an hour,' I said.

'Yes, I know, but we might have business to do on the way.'

'Oh, not more trouble.'

I could see a look of hilarious naughtiness in Darnley's face.

'You know that five pounds you wanted to spend in Worcester?'

'It's always in my pocket.'

'Well, bring it.'

The walk to the games field was the only excursion beyond the prison confines which we were allowed. We were not allowed to deviate to the right hand nor to the left. We had merely to cross Albert Road North, go down a little footpath to the next road, cross that and then follow an unmade-up track to the playing fields. At this point the town touched the countryside. There were open fields. A farm, a smallholding. It was thither that Darnley was bound with my five-pound note. The daring of his scheme was outrageous. I could not believe that anyone would get away with it. He assured me that the smallholder, a Mr Heber, would be only too happy to comply without asking questions, since he had a long-standing row with Seaforth Grange – something to do with the Binker having 'taken' one of his fields before the war to make a football pitch.

'What'll we do if someone asks us why we are setting out so early?' I asked.

'I'll say that Lollipop Lew has sent us on ahead to tidy pads in the pavilion.'

'They'll think we're queering.'

'They won't!'

'Or smoking.'

'Oh, shut up.'

He began to explain more of his scheme. It was impossible, as he outlined its finer points, not to be doubled up with laughter. Our destination was soon reached.

'There we are,' he said. And he pointed to the sign outside Mr Heber's bungalow.

*   *

The reality of the situation – that Miss Beach would not come back that term – was slow to sink in. From day to day, I lived in hope that she would come back – her tears dried, her lover dismissed and forgotten – to be mine and mine alone. The practical implications of a return – she would have had to share a bathroom with Vanessa – did not really occur to me.

There had been something between us, though. It was not all fantasy. About a week before the end of term, I got a postcard from Paris – it was a picture by Paul Klee. No allusion was made to the matter of Hunter or Vanessa. But she would not have sent the card had she not wished to absolve me of any guilt in the whole episode. 'It was fun getting to know you! Let's hope our paths cross one day. Paths have that way with them sometimes, like fingers.' Did she know how much I loved her, or how much in the following weeks I grieved for her? At the time, I was so pleased to have been singled out for a postcard that its sad implications took some time to absorb. She did not sign the card with love. Instead, there were the familiar initials – 'B.R.B., or should I say "Please"!!'

I came across the card not long ago in the bottom of a drawer. It was strange to be revisited by this keepsake of a person who was once so painfully dear to me and by her own youthful sense of life being something all in the future, hers and mine. Gradually, perspectives change. One tries to disguise the knowledge of how much of life has gone by with the insistence that the important thing is to live in the present. Either way, one is indulging onself and viewing one's own life as an entity, something with a storied shape which might be of interest to a chronicler. Another sense within us hints that to explain anything so multifarious and self-contradictory as a human life is an exercise in illusion.

Hunter was intelligent enough to know this, which, perhaps, was why his own practice and advocacy of the biographer's art could be conducted with such *panache*. One accomplishes nothing so stylishly as the thing in which one has no belief: gigolos probably make better lovers than those weak with desire; the best politicians are those who are most like actors; the most influential churchmen are those who seem furthest from the ideals of the Gospel. Hunter wanted to make lives make sense. Perhaps his own painstaking efforts to explain

Petworth Lampitt were all part of a need to hide the lack of sense, thread or meaning in his own life. His charming smiles were those of a juggler who knew that one day the reckoning would come, that his concentration would falter and the various balls which he kept floating in the air as if by magic would eventually bounce into chaos at his feet. What I never discerned in Hunter in the early days was the element of tragic heroism, the element which guaranteed that when he fell, it should be with as much *sang-froid* as he brought to the seduction of girls and the advancement of his own career.

On the simple level of his success with women, many have found it impossible not to be in awe of Hunter. In my own case, there has been an additional factor of coincidence that at times has threatened to form itself into some theory about Life, or Fate, or Women in general. At some periods of existence, indeed, it has seemed as though every woman I knew and a good proportion of those I had ever loved had been in love with Hunter. The desire to explain this coincidental phenomenon has at some periods been obsessive with me. Did it mean that, in spite of all appearances to the contrary, that there are in any individual life only a handful, perhaps a hundred women who are really available? It looks at first as though the field is infinite. Then you start to exclude all those who, at the time of your seeking, are tied up with someone else and you realise that the floating population is actually small. It therefore becomes inevitable, if you take an interest in this population, that you will come across the comparatively few other men fishing in the same waters. For various temperamental reasons, Hunter was incapable of monogamy. So, for a long period, was I.

This is the common-sense view. It is the one to which at present I incline. But for long periods in my life I have veered towards two much more exotic explanations of the fact that my path would keep crossing Hunter's, his mine. Both of these theories, for the time that they possessed my mind, have seemed not merely attractive, but compelling explanations for the coincidental extent to which Hunter and I have almost tripped over one another in pursuit of the same women.

The first explanation is that Hunter is a Don Giovanni who has tasted every fruit and broken every heart in the world.

According to this theory, there is nothing surprising in the fact that most of the women I have known at all well seem, at some stage or another, to have been in love with Hunter. The paltry dozen or so women who have been important to him (I am not just speaking of mistresses or wives, but of friends, too) are just the tip of the iceberg. Supposing, for the sake of experiment, I had known well a completely different selection of twelve or twenty women. The same high proportion of them would turn out to have undergone the Hunter experience.

I have usually entertained this theory at periods when I was angry and hostile to Hunter. Nevertheless, it always filled me with a certain wistful admiration not least for the sheer levels of physical concentration which such wide-ranging exploits must have demanded. Michelangelo is not to everyone's taste. Nor is Balzac. No one, however, can fail to admire the simple energy, imaginative and physical, required to complete the decoration of the Sistine Chapel or the penning of *La Comédie Humaine*.

It is not as if Hunter has been casual or slapdash. It has been no crude matter of notching up a score. In the handful of examples where I have known anything about it, Hunter has devoted not only time but apparent emotional effort to his conquests. To each of his ladies, he has appeared as the first truly sympathetic man they have ever met. Hours have been spent blowing their noses on Hunter's clean handkerchieves because he *understood*. Hunter was always a great believer in all the little appurtenances of heartbreak: flowers, letters, boxes of chocolates. (The chocolates themselves are worthy of a monograph, as, over the decades, I was to discover. How perfectly he always chose the brand. How intimidating the Bendicks girls were; and how reassuring those waitresses and stenographers who opened his gifts of Cadbury's Milk Tray.) A huge proportion of Hunter's existence, when added altogether, must have been spent in the dispatch of these tokens – of what? his affection? This is to say nothing of the time he spent with the girls themselves. A whole lifetime of telephone calls and assignations; of exciting, secret little meals which both parties felt slightly too nervous to eat; of visits to florists and chemists and hotels; a lifetime of afternoons, zipping and unzipping.

If, as I supposed when I subscribed to the Don Giovanni

theory, I only knew the tip of the iceberg, then Hunter's life must rank as something more remarkable than anything he described with his own pen.

Adding up the hours, however, which I myself have spent in florists, etc., I have dallied with a totally different theory, more astrological in tone and which could be called the theory of the Mystic Link. Even allowing for the fact that Hunter was extremely good at organising his time (witness his tireless committee work) it was only possible to fit a finite number of women into a single week, the more so since he liked all his dealings with women to have an extravagant emotional tinge. The love affairs, moreover, only represented the secret, or semi-secret, part of his existence; assuming that he sometimes needed sleep, there must have been some hours each week during which he wrote his enormous books and, more mysteriously, carved out the position of public importance which, from middle age onwards, he began to assume. Certain things followed from this. If Hunter was not a magician, then I knew – anyway at certain phases of life – all about every one of his *amours*. Or so it seemed. I knew, too, that there was an uncanny level of coincidence. I was treading in his footsteps, or he in mine. Miss Beach was the first name in a catalogue. My epiphany, that cricket afternoon, when I saw Hunter's hands running up and down the naked back of the woman I loved, was to be repeated more than once in the years which lay ahead. Very occasionally, the matter would be reversed, and I would discover that Hunter had taken up with someone in my own past. When the Mystic Link theory was in favour, I imagined that Hunter and I had destinies which were conjoined, and that he, like some Fury or some angelic presence, was bound to recur, haunting some of the most painful as well as the most joyous moments of existence.

Into this last category, the joyous, must surely fall the final day of that summer term. The local garage at Timplingham had decreed that the Trojan was no longer equipped for a journey across country. I was therefore spared the supreme embarrassment of my uncle and aunt driving up to the school gates in this vehicle in order to attend the last day of term – always rather an event in the Seaforth Grange calendar. In the morning, as the families of boys arrived, there were various 'displays' arranged for their diversion: some gymnastics on the lawn, a tennis tournament of excruciating incompetence, presided over by Lollipop Lew, a line-up of the more presentable members of the Scout Troop. An exhibition of art and handicrafts, usually a feature of the day, had this year been cancelled.

The morning was rounded off with a service in the little chapel, a sermon by the Binker himself, and a loud rendering of 'Lord Dismiss Us with Thy Blessing'.

So many friends, parents and relations attended this occasion that a marquee was erected on the lawn outside the chapel door, more or less filling the garden of House Two. All boys had to be in their places in chapel half an hour before the service began. The parents then filled up the back rows of the chapel and the overspill sat on chairs in the marquee. It was a claustrophobic arrangement, since the only mode of exit and entrance was the hole at the far end of the tent.

Darnley and I entered the chapel together. His mother had already arrived with her husband. They were standing quite near Hunter and Vanessa, who had something hard and triumphant in their expressions as, rather too dolled up for such an occasion (Vanessa's hair hidden inside a silly hat), they waited with the other grown-ups, but somehow looking like actors pretending to be at Ascot or Henley.

'Do you think they'll really remember?' I asked Darnley. 'What if they just go off with my money?'

'It's worth the gamble. Oh, it's worth it.'

'It's not your money, Darnley!'

He beckoned for me not to talk so freely. Timpson was within earshot. For all his daring, Darnley was as nervous as a bridegroom before his bride arrived at the church. The half hour that we sat in that chapel was intensely exciting. Some of the time, we tried to ignore one another, gazed about us, tied and untied knots in our handkerchieves. Then we would have a spell of noughts and crosses. And three minutes were amusingly absorbed when Darnley managed to lean forward with his ballpoint pen (a present that morning from his mother's husband) and write a word on the back of Garforth-Thoms's neck. It would not seem funny if I wrote it down now, on paper. You had to see it on that pink neck to get the full flavour of the joke. In fact (my nerves were doubtless overstrained) I thought that it was so funny that I might actually faint. However much I bit my fingers and stuffed a grey, ink-spattered handkerchief into my mouth, the word kept looking back at me. Blowforth himself simply imagined that Darnley was tickling the nape of his neck and had no idea of the legend that he was now advertising.

Darnley, the anarchic author of all this merriment – for others in our pew were now squirming with glee – looked facially impassive, his vast mouth drooping in a slightly melancholy way. If you had been told that he had just written a word, you might have guessed, from his expression, that it had been *'angst'* or *'penseroso'*. It was this immovably sad expression, combined, when he raised an eyebrow, with an unmistakable haughtiness, which so enraged his masters and superiors, who were now beginning to show parents to their seats.

Mrs Binker had squeezed herself into position behind the harmonium and, before long, the familiar routine of the end-of-term service was under way – the 121st Psalm, the squeaky suggestion by Timpson, from the lectern, that to everything there is a time and a season, the singing of 'Praise, my Soul, the King of Heaven'. Then the Binker was standing there in his M.A. gown, ready to harangue the troops.

'I want you,' he said, 'to think about John the Baptist.'

It was a curious thing to want. I have sometimes wondered how many of those women in hats or men in their Sunday best, none of whom seemed exactly John the Baptist's type, complied with this desire of the Binker's.

'You see,' he added mysteriously, 'John the Baptist knew that he was born into this world for a purpose.'

How Scotch his voice was then. Borrrrn into this worrrruld for a purrrrpose.

'But so were we all! Ah, yes. Each and every one of us was borrrrn into this worrrruld for a purrrrpose. And it is to help us find that purrrrpose that places such as Seaforth Grange exist.'

This last bit of the sentence was less audible than it might have been because of what sounded like a tractor engine revving up at the entrance to the marquee.

'Sometimes,' said the Binker, trying to ignore the noise, but peering with terrified curiosity down the aisle at what was going on in the drive, 'sometimes that purrrrpose is hid from our eyes for a wee while. But we must train ourselves to seek it.'

There was a clanking noise. A cart was being up-ended. There were voices.

Lollipop Lew's ineffectual tones were saying, 'I'm sure it can't be meant to go there!'

'That's what he said.' Mr Heber's voice.

He?

Darnley and I froze. Surely he was not going to betray us? Not after we had paid him five pounds – a king's ransom.

'You got three guineas' worth there and I had to borrow the cart to bring it round.'

'The way,' said the Binker, 'will sometimes be dark and we shall not see the path before us.'

He all too evidently saw the path leading up to the marquee, and the alarm and anger on his face made the temptation to turn round irresistible. Everyone was now far more interested in the conversation happening outside than in the mysterious purrrrpose for which they had been born. Lollipop Lew, no more capable of asserting himself with Mr Heber than with the third form, had appealed to Greasy Rhysy for moral support. We now heard Greasy's cross, authoritative tones.

'You'll just have to load it up on your cart again, won't you?'

Mr Heber's contemptuous laugh was music to the soul.

'What with? A pitchfork? Load the fucking stuff yourself if you want to. I've got work to do!'

'A purpose,' repeated the Binker, 'a purpose.'

'But,' protested Greasy Rhysy, 'if you leave it all there on the path, people aren't going to be able to get out of the marquee. Besides,' he said, 'there is a service going on and you are disturbing it.'

'Three guineas' worth!' repeated Mr Heber, evidently with some satisfaction. 'He do things in style, your governor.'

'Who did you say ordered this . . . this . . .?'

'Ordure, ordure,' muttered Darnley.

'Like I say,' replied Mr Heber airily. (The Binker was still talking, but none of us was listening.) 'Mr Fucking Larmer, that's who!'

And then we heard the cart and the tractor being reversed out into the road.

The Binker could see quite clearly what we only glimpsed in snatches, over our shoulders: something the size of a small haystack, heaped at the entrance to the marquee, forbidding all exit. While his wife struck up 'Lord Dismiss Us' on the harmonium, the chapel filled with overpowering farmyard odours. The rest – the opening up of a side flap of the marquee, the mothers in high heels teetering through the flowerbeds, the inevitable dozen or so people who trod in what Mr Heber had so liberally bestowed – all this, in a way, was an anti-climax. Darnley, perhaps, had no finer hour. It was with an ill grace, I thought, that the Binker was mouthing the words of the hymn.

> 'Pardon all, their faults confessing,
> Time that's lost may all retrieve . . .'

No one ever did confess to the sin, if it was one, of having paid Mr Heber to unload a cart in that time and place. It remained one of the great Seaforth Grange mysteries. We noticed, by the next term, that the Binker had given up claiming that he would solve this mystery if it was the last thing he did. As to that other matter – the retrieving of Time lost – we were far too young to have thought about it, either its undesirability or its impossibility.

THREE

It was four years before I actually met Raphael Hunter. By then I was a very different person. My short pink legs, the limbs of an androgynous putto on a Tiepolo ceiling, had been changed within a space of eighteen months to long, monstrous, knobbly things, covered with hair: the legs of a caveman. In a world where such alchemy could take place, anything could happen. The transformations effected by Nature on my body were minor when compared with the eruptive changes in my character. Adolescence had taken me by storm.

'I'm afraid that Julian has developed into rather an intellectual snob,' my housemaster had furiously averred on one end-of-term report. At that stage, I held this nice man, with his fondness for the novels of Galsworthy and Nevil Shute, in low regard.

But it was all much more mixed up than that. Very probably I was an intellectual snob, whatever that is. But that was not the trouble. I was angry with everyone and yet longed to be liked; furiously against the system and yet deeply anxious to be in with it. (The same week which had seen me squatting in a little bathtub, ostentatiously reading *The Communist Manifesto* half an hour after I was meant to have been in bed, had also seen me privately smarting, with genuine bewilderment, because I had not been made into a house prefect.)

Treadmill, the senior English master, was one of the few

people who could control me. I don't mean, stop me misbehaving. A number of sergeant-major types could do that. I mean, have some conception of 'the real me'. Harness this being, fill it with enthusiasm, even – though it seems a curious word to use – love it. We were still, perhaps ludicrously, Master and Pupil. There were few stricter disciplinarians in a classroom than Treadmill. (He hardly ever needed to *punish* a boy; the thought of misbehaving in his classes was too terrifying.) I, for my part, like most boys in the school, perfected my Treadmill imitations. Even nowadays, I sometimes find myself drifting into them. It may be that I am wandering into the bathroom in the light of dawn to run my tub and that a dressing gown draped around my shoulders involuntarily recalls that M.A. gown, drooping from the shoulders and sometimes suspended as low as the elbows. And, whether I am alone or in company, I will give voice to that curious noise, impossible accurately to transliterate, which we always made to signal the fact that we were 'doing a Treadmill'.

'Eyair.'

The sound was almost inaudible in the real Treadmill, but all Treadmill imitators said it loudly. They all knew how to hold one hand limp-wristedly in the air (though there was never the slightest suggestion that Treadmill loved his own sex) while the other drooped at his side. Many boys, I think, were disappointed, when they finally reached the privileged position of being in Treadmill's set, to find that his 'Oxford' voice was less strangulated, his vowels altogether less mannered and nasal than their hundreds of imitators. A real imitation would have been quite difficult. Doing a Treadmill, however, was child's play and I prided myself that I could do whole Treadmill sentences, paragraphs; that I could think Treadmill's thoughts, never dreaming until I was hooked that this was the idea and that the success of teachers who are 'characters' depends precisely on luring their pupils into imitation, if not open mockery. The child thinks it is absorbing the teacher, whereas it is the other way around.

Perhaps one of the reasons he appealed so greatly was that there was in itself something adolescent about the paradoxical combination of immiscibles in his overdrawn *persona*. He was an old boy of the school and a passionate devotee of the public-school system. Yet, as he loved to proclaim, he was a Man of the Left, of the extreme Left, who had fought in Spain and known everyone. This knowing of everyone was something which all his cruder imitators seized upon, trying to make Treadmill into a simple snob. As the nephew of Uncle Roy, I knew that snobbery was not simple and that the essence of Treadmill's namedropping was that it was inextricably linked, for him, with the romance of literature itself. He was, as I now realise, a failed writer himself, which is why almost anyone who had ever written a book was surrounded for him by a romantic glow, while at the same time being scorned: for no one had a keener eye for the defects of a writer than Treadmill.

In my Treadmill imitations, I always tried to capture these essences of his nature. It is boastful to describe them as up-market Treadmills, a thousand times truer than the frankly silly Treadmills you might hear down any corridor or dormitory landing. Mine came to me like the visitations of the spirit from some other world.

'Eyair. Will you open *Paradise Lost* at Book Eight?'

One sees again the shredded-wheat moustache, the horn-rimmed glasses, the voluminous Oxford Bags, the oatmeal jacket, the black teaching gown, ragged and worn, which had once (said Treadmill) belonged to Louis MacNeice.

'John Milton, as you may know, was a Cambridge man. Eyair. Woe betide any pupil of mine who thinks of going *there*. Nyair. I never actually met Milton, but of course I have had my days, if I may mention such a thing in petty-bourgeois company such as your own, as a Republican soldier. "Today the deliberate increase in the chances of death."'

He would then look up to see if anyone recognised the quotation. In reality, he would have been astonished if anyone had said, '"Spain", by W. H. Auden'. It would have prevented him from sniffing contemptuously at our ignorance and con-tinuing with his discourse.

'Poor Wystan. How let down we all felt when he went – eyair, to the United States. Though, as he once said to me in a letter, he had never pretended to be brave . . .'

The essence of the parody was that any sentence, however unpromising its beginnings, united an excitement in literature itself with the strange adventure of Treadmill's own personal myth. How very effective this was as a method of teaching, this ceaseless dropping of names and quotations, is shown by the fact that nearly forty years later I can still remember vast amounts of English poetry, not which Treadmill set us to learn by heart but which he merely quoted *en passant*. It was not long, after I started to be taught by him, before I started to search the libraries and identify the source of all his allusions.

'But Wystan, much as we all love and admire him, is a long way from *Paradise Lost*:

> "Think onely what concernes thee and thy being,
> Dream not of other worlds, what Creatures there
> Live in what state, condition or degree . . ."

Ah! I vividly remember Virginia Woolf, of all people, quoting those lines to me. We were at Garsington. I was an undergraduate at the time; my only meeting with the great lady. I felt suitably rebuked. Frieda Lawrence was there. Now what a beautiful woman *she* was.'

These idiosyncratic glosses on the text of *Paradise Lost* took us through line after line, fixing the poem in my memory more surely than any amount of formal explanation. Treadmill's English classes were lectures. He had the required text open on a lectern. If it was poetry, he read it aloud, interlaced with his own highly personal commentary. If it was prose, he spoke more concisely. There was no question of class discussion, nor of audience participation of any kind. The performance was to be heard in silence. If there was the slightest sign of disturbance (a boy dropping a pen) his face assumed expressions of pained outrage. It could have gone either way. A man who claimed so much for himself could, you would have thought, have been treated mercilessly by boys. But it was not so. No one misbehaved in Treadmill's classes, just as no one ever gave him a nickname; with a surname like that, he did not need one.

His comments on our essays, of which we had to write a large number, were almost invariably withering; but they were flatteringly detailed. If you handed in a piece of work to Treadmill you could be sure of getting it back the very next day, scarlet with his semi-legible annotations and corrections. I can still recapture the sinking feeling in my stomach when I had handed in what I thought was a brilliant essay on *Antony and Cleopatra*. It was handed back next morning with the single question – 'Yeair, you have, I take it, *read* the play?' His innumerable marginal notes showed me how utterly ignorant and superficial I was. This was at a time of life when I really resented other grown-ups not minding their own business and judging me by their own infuriating standards. So, the R.S.M. at Corps thought that I did not know how to blanco spats. So what? So what if my housemaster did think it was ill-mannered to slam a door in matron's face? These observations on my character were intolerable, intrusive, irrelevant. But Treadmill was allowed to make really devastating assaults on my ignorance and poor style. He spoke with authority. With naive arrogance, I thought that he was allowable because he shared my values without realising that I shared his, had learnt from him avidly, hungrily.

And I learnt as much outside the classroom as in. Treadmill was a conscientious schoolmaster. He took games, even bothering to change for the purpose. (The billowing garments draped from his narrow hips to beneath his knees could not with accuracy have been described as shorts, but they were, Treadmill claimed, the legacy of a rugger Blue who, while up at the House, had thrown Harold Acton into Mercury.) He was a house tutor. Rather surprisingly (I tried to overlook this embarrassing detail) he was a Christian, who found the liturgical arrangements in the school chapel lamentably 'low'. None of this actually interested me. I completely lacked, and lack, Treadmill's public-school belief in being a good all-rounder.

It was as the producer of the school plays that Treadmill first came my way and was the greatest inspiration to me. One of the reasons Treadmill chose to produce fairly obscure Renaissance drama was unquestionably because he liked it. He took the sensible view that we should all have plenty of opportunity in later life to see mainstream repertoire on stage in London or Stratford; less chance to see the work of Marston, Massinger, Beaumont and Fletcher. Another, less worthy motive but, I suspect, no less strong was a desire to *épater* the Headmaster who, like most potentates, including the King himself, reserved to himself the right to censor and forbid the production of plays within his domains. When Treadmill asked him if it would be permissible to produce *A New Way to Pay Old Debts* or *A Shoe-maker's Holiday*, the Headmaster was never sure whether he was alone in the universe in being unacquainted with these plays and always let the thing through without question, but not without a sense, I suspect, of being put down.

Long before I got into Treadmill's English set, I was Celia in his *Volpone* and enjoyed overacting as Lady Allworth in *A New Way to Pay Old Debts*. My first male role was Jasper in *The Knight of the Burning Pestle*, a melodramatic part ideally suited to a teenage actor. Anne, my first wife, when I used to bore her with Treadmill stories, considered it 'pretentious' to have extended the schoolboy repertoire beyond the usual Shakespeares and Shaws. The stylish thing about it, though, was that there was never the slightest sense that we were posing or doing anything particularly recondite. Once in a blue moon in the army I would (all too rarely) come across some 'kindred spirit' with whom one could discuss books or plays, perhaps a man who had opted to go to university before he did his National Service. He would almost certainly be on his way to work as a clerk or a trainee Intelligence Officer and I would never have more than a few weeks of his companionship. But I often discovered, in such encounters then and later in life, that I knew the works of dramatists who were only names to some of these university men. Then I would feel grateful to Treadmill for giving me something superior to a university education while I trod the boards at New Big School.

The other out-of-school activity which Treadmill organised was a literary club which met once a fortnight in his house after supper – sometimes to read a paper among themselves, but more usually to hear a talk by some visiting speaker. These visits inevitably summoned up those dreams of other worlds, so readily understood at Garsington, so frowned upon by Milton's archangel. However boring the speaker (and some were real crashers) they always brought with them the breath of another atmosphere, usually one which I felt more able to inhale than that of school. This was the sense which I had had to an infinitely slight degree in Debbie Maddock's company long before, that there existed some bohemian society to which all along I had spiritually belonged, some intellectual fellowship from which I had accidentally through birth and upbringing been excluded but to which, once the tyranny of childhood was overpassed, I would return. Our speakers included Shakespearean directors; poets in knitted ties who called Treadmill by his Christian name (Val); lady novelists who had laboured for a quarter of a century to keep the Woolfs from the door; tweedy dons with stammers who laughed conspiratorially when Treadmill mentioned Dr Leavis (he was the enemy now, Treadmill held him in abomination) – all these figures suggested to me a world in which the things I cared about most were valued, a world in which the things I scorned (but which were so vigorously upheld and insisted upon at school) were scorned also.

Treadmill's society was called the Lampitt Club, after one of our more distinguished old boys, James Petworth Lampitt. Lampitt himself had come down to the society's inauguration a few years before he died and Treadmill possessed several Lampitt letters.

It goes without saying that Uncle Roy chose the school because of its Lampitt connections. (A great-uncle of Sargie's and Jimbo's had been headmaster in Victorian times and there were a number of lesser Lampitts connected with the place.) There was even a Lampitt cup for Fives, a fact to which, apparently, Petworth Lampitt had made squeakingly facetious reference on his visit – a facetiousness which was quite misplaced, since all his audience, Treadmill included, were keen Fives players. The distinction between hearties and aesthetes, which was certainly one made naturally in my own mind, was deprecated by Treadmill as inimical to 'everything a school like this stands for'. That was one of my reasons for making it.

Treadmill's attitude to Lampitt was by no means purely adulatory. He had a distaste for 'purple prose' and there was, in his view, a distinction between true satire and mincing malice which Lampitt quite often failed to observe. For two pins, Treadmill could have dismissed Petworth Lampitt as meretricious, Georgian and lightweight. There were two things, however, which redeemed Lampitt in Treadmill's eyes. The first, and much the most important, was that he was an old boy of the school. The second, which spurred Treadmill into action on a number of other occasions, was Dr Leavis's known distaste for Lampitt's works. The gibe about Petworth Lampitt being the worst writer of the century after Humbert Wolfe was not a piece of private knowledge entrusted to Debbie Maddock alone. It had apparently found its way into print and Treadmill had read it. When Lampitt died, his reputation was at its lowest ebb and many of the highbrow papers had apparently written about him in the most slighting possible terms. Treadmill the old boy had simply felt that the honour of the school was threatened and he had devoted a Third Programme talk (one of those discourses given in the intervals of radio concerts) to a restitution of Petworth Lampitt's tarnished name. As he liked to boast, it was the only occasion when a B.B.C. producer had presumed to alter a Treadmill script. Treadmill had written a vituperative paragraph beginning, 'A Dr Leavis . . .' The B.B.C., doubtless infiltrated with Leavisites, had insisted on the deletion of the insultingly indefinite article. (Treadmill did quite a lot of wireless talks in those days and even had his own poetry programme, something which was to have its bizarre influence on my own later destiny.)

It was a curious chance, however, that in all the meetings of the Lampitt Club which I had so far attended there had been no mention of James Petworth Lampitt. We had had talks on a wide variety of subjects but nothing on the man whose name we immortalised each fortnight by crowding into Treadmill's dining room.

In the spring term, speakers were thin on the ground. We were an inconvenient distance from London. Weather that year was poor. Everyone seemed to have 'flu. I succumbed to the worst bout of it which I had ever had, a week of near delirium, aching joints and writhing about in my own sweat. The doctor insisted on a week's convalescence when the fever left me.

I was sitting in the large dayroom of the san, staring across the frosty, fog-laden gardens to the Victorian crescent beyond the cedars. Gables and turrets were silver-grey against a haze of winter light. Matron came in and interrupted my mindless reverie by announcing a visitor. Since it was mid-morning and everyone was in school, I knew that it could not be another boy, and I wondered with a darting mixture of homesickness and embarrassment whether my aunt had been fetched from Norfolk by exaggerated accounts of the seriousness of my condition. Instead, still wearing his teaching gown, Treadmill drifted into the room.

'"God keep thee – yeair – worshipful Master Roister Dois-ter,"' he said.

'"Come death,"' I said responding with another quota-tion from the same play, '"when thou wilt, I am weary of my life."'

'But I heard you were better? I won't come too close. My own susceptibility to influenza is no laughing matter. Indeed, Geoffrey Keynes, one of the nicest men as well as one of the best doctors I ever knew . . . but that's another story. I was on my way home, I thought I'd drop in.'

It is true that Treadmill lived more or less next door to the sanatorium. I didn't at that stage know how appropriate this was, being as yet unaware that, next to the pursuit of literature, the cult of ill health ranked high among Treadmill's list of favourite occupations. It merely struck me as kind that he had bothered to look in, particularly since he at once put my mind at rest about the play which was then in rehearsal.

'You're not to worry about the play. Michael Redgrave – and in my own drawing room indeed – once told me that a bout of illness in rehearsals sharpened the pace at a later stage. We've got six weeks more and it's all going well. As it happens, you're not the only one with 'flu; far worse news is that Margery Mumblecrust's voice sounds perilously as if it is on the point of breaking.'

'I'd hate to let everyone down, sir.'

'It'll be all right and, more important, it'll be fun.'

This turned out to be true. Treadmill's *Ralph Roister Doister*, heavily cut, was one of the high points of my school dramatic career. That and *Gorboduc*.

We spoke desultorily about rehearsal arrangements.

Then he said, 'You'll be fit, I take it, for the Lampitt Society on Sunday evening?'

'I should think so.'

'I've asked down the man who's hoping to edit Lampitt's letters.'

'I hadn't heard that anyone was.'

'My God, the arrogance of the boy! Because he is Hon. Treasurer of the Lampitt Society, he speaks as if he were Petworth Lampitt's literary executor. Editors are apparently obliged to consult you before approaching the shrine!'

'Sir!' This really wasn't fair. I had already told Treadmill of my family reasons for being interested in Lampitt.

'Of course, I was forgetting, your people knew Lampitt's family.'

'We're neighbours of his brother.'

Treadmill did not, on that san visit, think to mention the name of the Lampitt expert who would be addressing the Society.

But, before he left, he said, 'By the way, it might be an idea if at least one member of the society apart from your tired old master had actually read a line of the great man's works before Sunday.'

There was no bluffing or fooling with Treadmill. He knew by instinct what one had or had not read. Lampitt had hitherto not appealed to me. Considering the fact that I had been brought up next door to the man's brother, you might have supposed that I was well acquainted with his work. Probably, Uncle Roy's insistence on their virtue had put me off reading Petworth Lampitt's books. Perhaps, too, I had been put off reading them by that instinctive embarrassment which we all feel when reading the literary productions of those at all close to us. I had not known Jimbo. But what if his prose somehow revealed a self, a world, which in turn cast Sargie and, by implication, Uncle Roy in some funny light? No, that wasn't it. I think it was that I had heard about all the Lampitts so often that I really wanted to think about something else when I had a book in my hand.

Lurking about somewhere in my head, there was, further, the priggish suspicion that Dr Leavis might well have been right. Perhaps Petworth Lampitt was not merely a *bad* writer, but one whom it was somehow discreditable to enjoy. In the intellectually snobbish terms which I was cumbrously working out for myself, liking Lampitt might well have been as bad as, by Miss Beach's standards, liking Rowland Hilder's landscapes; or, perhaps a better analogy, the school of Alma-Tadema.

Treadmill, with a limp gesture, fished a small, green volume out of his pocket and threw it down on my lap.

'It's what used to be called fine writing,' he said, in tones which put heavy inverted commas round the words but which allowed you to take them any way you liked. 'And none the worse for that.'

And, without much of a farewell, he was gone.

I opened the book and I can still remember the tingling excitement brought by its opening paragraph. I dare not quote it here. The austerer tastes of my own maturity, to say nothing of those of the reader, would find much in those perfectly made sentences which was arch, much which was sentimental; for, though regarded by his contemporaries and seniors as an iconoclast, James Petworth Lampitt was more than a little in love with the objects of his derision. I had never before felt the smallest interest in the subject of the book, the life of the Prince Consort. The story was well enough told. But what gripped me was the tone of authorial voice. Now, it slightly embarrasses me, that perfect style and manner. But, that afternoon, it all became so much a part of myself that I cannot consider it dispassionately. The ambition to be an artist, awakened in me by Miss Beach, had still not left me. Treadmill had made me yearn to be an actor. Neither of these desires was abandoned, but to them was added the longing, as deep as love, to write like James Petworth Lampitt. As happens when one is reading a book which is truly absorbing, the world became insubstantial for the next few hours. A domestic brought lunch. I was asked by matron to rest on my bed for an hour. I returned, dressing gown-clad, to sit in the convalescent room. Outside the french windows the mists thickened and by five o'clock night had fallen. But I read on, gulping the paragraphs thirstily and feeling them – again, like love – changing me into a different person by the minute, by the second.

I wanted not merely to write like Lampitt but to *be* Lampitt. Hitherto, I had only thought of him as Sargie's brother. He had come to me filtered not merely through the collapsed, shambolic figure of Sargie but through the distorting lens of Uncle Roy's Lampitt-adoration: a devotion which was unthinkingly applied to Jimbo because he was a Lampitt and could just as extravagantly be bestowed on the Honourable Vernon or Lady Starling. Because Jimbo happened to be a writer, my uncle praised his style, just as he would have praised the expertise of the Lampitts in any field: the delicacy with which a Lampitt surgeon wielded his knife, the astuteness with which a Lampitt broker bought bonds or sold stock at the judicious moment, the eloquence with which a Lampitt Parliamentarian might argue the inadvisability of some piece of legislation. My incapacity to see my uncle as a person, my adolescent inability to be generous, did not allow me to suppose that Uncle Roy might himself have once fallen under Petworth Lampitt's spell, as I did that afternoon in the san and for exactly the same reasons. It did not occur to me that Uncle Roy probably read Lampitt's *Prince Albert* long before he ever went to live in Timplingham or met old Mrs Lampitt or Sargie. It did not occur to me that I was holding in my hands, if not the key, at least the origin of the abiding passion of my uncle's life. Lampitt seemed then purely my own possession. I was ignorant of the fact that a mere thirty years before, he had been an extremely popular writer with a column in the *Saturday Post*, whose vogue swelled the sales of his travelogues and biographies. Rather it seemed, as the light faded, and I read on and on, as if I were the first person in the world to discover this wonderful writer and as if there were only two people in the world with the right attitude to things, what one can best describe as sentimental irony, myself and Lampitt.

I had never before heard the word 'camp' applied to all those things Lampitt's prose reeked of. Pub evenings with William Bloom lay aeons in the future, conversations in which he would put down his glass of beer – 'The only straight thing about me' – and with a nod towards some fantastical creature in drainpipes, tiptoeing towards the Gents, interrupt his discourse about politics or the opera with a toneless, 'That young lady has a camp in both feet.'

On the contrary. I thought then of Lampitt as, on National Service (when I discovered him), I thought of Edward Gibbon – urbane, funny, above all in control of his own manner and material, a writer who not only had mastered completely the apparently simple (actually supremely difficult) matter of making sentences mean what the writer wants them to mean; but had further devised or evolved a style which implied a view of the world without the need to state what that view was.

I think if I were to dwell long with Lampitt's prose today, I would find his manner excruciating, the literary equivalent of an unwanted, well-manicured hand on one's elbow, or the fluttering of the author's eyelashes. The tones which then sounded to me like sharp, Voltairean irony would now be in danger of seeming shrill, flutey. The final paragraph of the famous biography, when the corpse of Albert is laid to rest in Frogmore – 'alone, at last – or, for a little while' – struck me as the most eloquent piece of rhetoric which I had ever read. I read the sentences again and again. They moved me in precisely the way Lampitt had wanted to move the more simple-minded of his *Saturday Post* readers; and like those simple souls, I totally missed the arch implications behind his description of that solitary corpse, allowed at last to sleep on its own without female molestation.

By the time of the doctor's rounds next morning, I had reread *Prince Albert* more than once. I was drunk with it, bleary-eyed. I responded to questions about my health with what I felt to be appropriately Lampittian *sang-froid*, prompting the doctor to say, in slightly aggrieved tones, 'I'm only asking you because I want to see you get better.'

'Ah, but better at what?' I heard myself, rather surprisingly, saying.

'There's not much wrong with you if you can lie there and make jokes,' said matron crossly, reading into my remark an innuendo which had not been intended.

'Doctor, can I take a short walk today?'

'I shouldn't think it would kill you.'

'I need to get to the Reading Room.'

This was a distance of some quarter of a mile.

'Are you asking us to lay on a bath chair?' asked the doctor. He had a murmuring, rather plaintive voice.

So, while the rest of the school was at lessons, I was able to spend the next couple of days convalescing, pottering, swathed thickly in overcoat and muffler, to the Reading Room and returning to the sanatorium for rests and meals.

An almost complete set of James Petworth Lampitt's *oeuvre* was to be found on the shelf. All but his *Lagoon Loungings*. The first two volumes I borrowed were a collection of his essays and his life of Swinburne. The biography of the poet was even better than that of the Prince Consort. I completely entered into Lampitt's schizophrenic ability to admire Swinburne's languorous and over-coloured phrases while making the poet himself a figure of the purest farce. The passages describing his domestic life with Watts-Dunton in Putney remain, by any standards, hilarious. Similar flights of comedy occurred in many of the essays which, if anything then could have done so, deepened my love of Lampitt. Each essay was to my eye so perfectly made. Nearly every one was funny. Yet, even when the laughter was most unfair, there lurked behind the prose a sense that literature itself was something to be taken supremely seriously. Perhaps it was the *only* thing to be taken seriously. I am thinking of his classic essay on Baudelaire; or another, 'The Christ of Gérard de Nerval' (one of the best apologies for the aesthetic point of view extant) or the curiously perceptive essay on the early Ezra Pound.

I do not think that Treadmill had intended to awaken Lampitt-mania on anything like this scale. He probably just wanted to guarantee, when the speaker came to address the club in a couple of weeks' time, that at least one member of the audience should have known who Lampitt was and, roughly, the kind of thing he wrote.

I found as the evening approached that I was looking forward to it. I felt something akin to jealousy, too, as if, having fallen in love with a woman, I had been compelled to spend an evening with twenty other men, poring over her photograph and hearing why they did or did not find her beautiful. At the same time, I was excited at the prospect of meeting the speaker, whom Treadmill had not named, but described as a friend of Petworth Lampitt's. Although I knew the writer's brother, I wanted to cast the *friend* in an altogether more exotic light than poor old Sargie. I would not have been surprised if the friend had appeared wearing a cloak or a wideawake hat like Lord Tennyson's. I think I pictured him bearded, certainly, with thick, snowy white hair and possibly a large, silken cravat tied at the throat in an extravagant bow.

By Sunday evening, I had come to believe in this figure so completely that, as we all squeezed into Treadmill's dining room, I was looking round for him eagerly. I had decided that he would be slightly rosy in complexion and wearing check trousers of a shepherd's plaid.

At the far end of the room, by the mantelpiece, there stood a figure in a pale grey suit and blue shirt. So youthful were his smooth cheeks, pallid face and mousy hair that it did not occur to me that he was our speaker, still less a friend of Petworth Lampitt. I thought, indeed, that it might be some senior boy from the school on whom for some reason I had never set eyes, or some nephew or godson of Treadmill's, staying for the weekend. My man, the friend of Petworth, was doubtless waiting in the wings. Ever a theatrical old boy (probably with memories of the Café Royal, Beerbohm Tree, Granville Barker), he would make an *entrance*.

I only recognised our pale visitor at the very moment that Treadmill said in his quietly reasonable voice (the histrionics sometimes shown in school or on stage were always switched off for visitors) that it was a great pleasure to welcome Mr Raphael Hunter, who had come to talk to us about 'Petworth Lampitt the Man'.

Though these evenings were partially designed by Treadmill to wean us from childish ways and to edge us towards the manners of highbrow undergraduates, we were still *au fond* a lot of schoolboys. We recognised the convention that in Treadmill's house (his wife would appear at some stage of the evening with a tray of tea or cocoa) one could not actually *rag* the visitor as one would a newly arrived teacher.

But, if a man wanted to hold our attention, it would have to be good. For one of those impenetrable reasons which no boy could ever *explain* to a grown-up, the title 'Petworth Lampitt the Man' struck Garforth-Thoms as one of the best jokes he had ever heard. His rather heavy features, by now very different from when we were together at Seaforth Grange, assumed a look of intense seriousness as he tried to ward off the giggles, but I could see that it was going to be a losing battle. His cheeks, on which some half-hearted whiskers and vigorously suppurating acne fought for space, had changed from their usual spatter of pale scarlet to an even, purplish red. His lips slobbered and shook. Then he let out a loud roar of laughter, causing several other boys to do the same.

Treadmill, quietly furious, said, 'Garforth-Thoms, *please.*'

'Sorry, sir.'

But the apology made him laugh all the more. He ran from the room as if he was going to be sick and we heard him quietening down in the hall. Later on, he crept back into the room, dabbing the corner of his eyes with a handkerchief.

After this, the atmosphere was a bit sticky, but the worst of the embarrassment was over. Hunter looked pained by the outburst. This expression was what separated him off from the rest of us even though he looked young enough to be a boy. No boy, however touchy, would have wanted an explanation for Garforth-Thoms's guffaws. Some things just are funny. Once one person laughed, another person laughed. It was all as simple as that. Hunter, being a grown-up, showed by his puzzled brow that he thought that there must be some explanation for the laughter, some secret meaning in his title which, had he known about it, would have made him avoid using the phrase, 'Petworth Lampitt the Man'.

He spoke to us from notes. Considering the fact that I was by now obsessed with Petworth Lampitt, I was surprised to discover that Hunter's talk was extremely boring. My mind kept wandering off and I could not listen as he said phrases like 'in the context of the Edwardian literary situation and early twentieth-century prose generally' or 'Of course, we are now in the post-Modernist situation – Eliot has written *The Waste Land*, Joyce has written *Ulysses*.' Liberal in his use of the historic present, Hunter attempted to fit Petworth Lampitt into his own simplified version of literary history. As he did so, I was astonished to realise that this 'friend' of Lampitt's, who had chosen to journey all the way from London to talk about him in Treadmill's dining room, did not think much of the great man's work.

'I believe,' he said, 'that Petworth's work has already dated, that it won't last and that it *shouldn't* last.'

At this point, his hand came down rather firmly on Treadmill's dining table and his essentially weak features assumed a ruthless coldness. We seemed to have moved out of the world of literary debate and into a universe of power in which Hunter would brook no opposition in this matter of Lampitt being no good.

I mischievously wanted to intervene and say that as a matter of fact Lampitt's intimates called him not Petworth but Jimbo. But with his hand now firmly pressed against the table – the gesture implied that there were spiritual forces present who might at any moment lift the table in the air had not Hunter been so unhesitatingly in control – he turned to his subject: Petworth Lampitt the Man.

'One may as well be honest, Petworth in his last years was a sad man, even a pathetic one. The days of his great success as a writer had really been before the First World War . . . flower of English youth . . . great society hostesses . . . The Souls . . . Bloomsbury . . . the increasing *politicisation* of the literary scene in England . . .' Here the hand pressing the table almost recalled the gestures of a Nuremberg Rally.

In none of any of this was *my* Lampitt to be discerned, that distinctive voice and manner with which I was so entranced. Instead, we were given a catalogue of names which at that time meant absolutely nothing to me: house parties and dinners, Lady Elcho, Lady Horner, Lady Ottoline, oh Lady!

'There were other sides to Petworth's nature, darker sides, but this' – Hunter gave a searching stare in the direction of Garforth-Thoms – 'is neither the time nor the place to expose them. We do him no honour to overpraise him.'

This may well have been true, but so far not a word had been spoken which was not calculated to diminish Lampitt in our eyes. Had this work of destruction been done in Lampitt's manner, one could almost have seen the point of it, but Hunter's dismissal of his subject, though, entirely lacked satire or sprightliness. It was puddingy and at the same time self-righteous, vaguely high-minded.

'He belonged to that rightly obsolete species, the man of letters. He wrote his books, he made his travels, he formed his friendships. In my opinion, as a much younger friend, speaking from the perspective of the younger generation, we will come in time to see that Petworth Lampitt's chief glory was that he had such friends. That is, he can best be seen as a way of viewing a whole literary and social world, rather than as a man who was himself intrinsically interesting. At the present time, I am collecting up the letters of Petworth Lampitt. I think there should be an edition. Petworth was a prolific letter-writer. His correspondents included all the great literary names of the age – George Bernard Shaw, D. H. Lawrence, T. E. Lawrence . . .'

For those of us who might not believe him, Hunter read out a list of famous people to whom Petworth Lampitt had written letters. It was the sort of list he might have read to a publisher to interest him in the idea of printing a selection of Lampitt's correspondence. Its effect on an audience was curiously deadening. As became evident, this was his peroration. He paused.

'Edith Sitwell,' he said, 'and, of course, Osbert.'

He was free with 'of course', was Hunter.

Treadmill stared at him. I thought he was going to say, 'Is that all?' but instead he murmured, 'Eyair, thank you very much indeed.'

There was no particular convention about what happened at the end of talks. Sometimes we spontaneously clapped but applause was not invariable. No one clapped Hunter. We were all bored.

Treadmill sensed this. After a longish silence he said, 'Perhaps I could pose a question – about whether you have found anything out about Petworth's schooldays.'

'A few letters survive, but not many.'

'What house was he in?' asked one boy.

Hunter blushed. He couldn't remember.

'That's what you should be able to tell me,' he said, which Treadmill then did. I could see from the way in which Treadmill was compressing his lips and pushing his moustache upwards to a diagonal, almost a vertical position beneath his nose, that he thought very little of Hunter either as a scholar or as an orator.

I did not want my tenuous connections with the Lampitt family to be a topic of general conversation but I involuntarily found myself remembering the day of Jimbo's funeral; remembering, too, those few days before it – my uncle saying the requiem for Jimbo's soul and afterwards describing the macabre manner of his death, falling from a balcony into the area beneath his flat.

'Was he alone when he died?' I blurted out.

'Who, Petworth?'

Hunter's prickly attitude to my question revealed that he sensed my hostility. Hunter could not possibly have known that for the past four years he had been an object of jealous fascination and loathing in my eyes – ever since I had seen him holding Miss Beach in his arms. The upshot of his betrayal was unknown to me. That anyone could so ill-use Miss Beach remained incredible to me. My love for her, hitherto the strongest emotional experience in my history, was something which time had done very little to heal. I was easily able to be transported back to that period, the few weeks after Petworth Lampitt's death. That was perhaps why I asked my question, which I did heedlessly; as I did so, I discovered that I was curious to know the answer. I had rather forgotten it until that moment but in Hunter's presence it all returned – that morning when my uncle spoke about it; my aunt deciding that the whole thing was much too hush-hush to be mentionable in the village; Debbie Maddock being coarse enough to have read about it in the newspapers.

'Petworth lived alone in his last days. He had a flat.'

'Hinde Street?' I said automatically. I wasn't showing off. I could recite the London addresses of the Lampitts almost before I knew nursery rhymes – or so it now felt. The Honourable Vernon – Great College Street; his parents – Cavendish Avenue in St John's Wood; Lady Starling – my uncle's voice would always sink reverently at the mention of it and his vowels would become strangely elongated – in Cadogan Square.

'Yes, it was Hinde Street,' said Hunter.

'It wasn't a suicide, was it?'

There was laughter when I asked this. Not that suicide was considered amusing. It was my persistence and my suddenly seeming to know more than the speaker which made people laugh.

When the laughter died down Hunter said something which surprised me very much and which had never been mentioned in the version recited from time to time by Uncle Roy.

'As it happens,' he said, 'I was with Petworth on the afternoon he died. I had called round in the middle of the afternoon as I sometimes did. Just to see that he was all right, you understand. He wandered into the kitchen to make some tea. It was a small kitchen – little more than a box with a sink in it and a little oven. But it had a french window which opened on to the fire escape. On fine days he would open the window and stand on top of the fire escape which caught the afternoon sun. On the day he died – it was a spring day . . .'

I suppose Hunter must have told this story a thousand times – to the police, to coroners and, subsequently, at dinner tables and in 'talks' such as this. Like almost all frequently repeated narratives it was too fluent to be plausible. I didn't know whether he was consciously lying or whether the truth had simply been worn away by the repetition. But I knew that I could not believe Hunter. I felt instinctively that he who had betrayed Miss Beach could deceive and lie to us also.

I am not saying that I suspected what the police call 'foul play', but instinct made me think that Hunter was up to no good, not to be trusted. I disliked extremely the way he managed at one and the same time to claim credit for having known the famous writer, and to be condescending in his attitude to 'poor Petworth' and to the writings themselves. One felt (or was meant to feel) that not only was Hunter at the hub of things, but he was also sufficiently discerning not to get carried away; he could see that the 'importance' (a very Hunter word, I was to discover) of Petworth Lampitt was not in his writings but in the world which he encapsulated. In other words, what was important for Hunter was not the imagination but the will, not the outpourings, however unsatisfactory one might find them, but the social climbing, the gossip, the crusts and shell, as they seemed to me, of a life. Hunter thereby blasphemed against art – this was the sort of pompous way I reacted in my fury – as well as letting down an old chum by revealing his secrets to a lot of schoolkids. There was enough of my uncle in me to be shocked that a *stranger* should presume to talk about Petworth Lampitt in these terms.

'. . . and without meaning to be unkind, Petworth was not always steady on his pins after lunch. I heard him calling out, "Oh, *look* at that sun!", and then there was a clattering noise – no cry – just a noise. I thought perhaps that he had inadvertently knocked a kettle off the stove, or a hot pan. "Are you all right?" I called out. There was silence. I went into the kitchen. The window was open, but Petworth was not there. I went to the window and looked down. Petworth was lying at the bottom of the area by the dustbins. He was quite still. I climbed down the fire escape as quickly as I could. I turned over his body – but he had already died.'

For a boy audience this was almost as exciting as a murder story. A 'literary' evening which culminates in the speaker discovering a corpse could be sure of a success. When Treadmill finally wound up the show and thanked Hunter a second time, everyone clapped enthusiastically. Few, if any of us, had ever seen corpses. To have seen a corpse was on the same level of sophistication as carnal knowledge. Therefore we clapped. Over the next week, the tedium of Hunter's actual talk and the embarrassment of Garforth-Thoms's guffaw at the beginning were forgotten. Hunter was alluded to as 'a great bloke' and his talk was said to be 'stunning'; in subsequent weeks when Treadmill consulted us about the kind of speaker we should like to see invited to the Lampitt, the general consensus was that 'we' – that is they – should like more speakers like Mr Hunter.

When the meeting was breaking up, Hunter, all smiles and geniality, came up and asked me, 'Was there some reason for your being so interested in Petworth?'

'Not really.'

'Only, you seem to know quite a bit about him.'

'Ramsay here has relations who live near Petworth Lampitt's nephew – is that it?' prompted Treadmill.

'No, sir. Brother.'

Hunter's face became at once more ingratiating and yet more steely.

'Not Sargent Lampitt?'

'There are no other brothers living,' I said, as though any fool knew that.

While Hunter was getting my name straight, I had to blink to avoid the steadiness of his gaze.

'I'm trying to persuade Sargent Lampitt to let me go through the material in his possession,' said Hunter slowly, cautiously. 'I feel sure that there is a lot of it' – once again his voice assumed its nasal didacticism – 'which could be important, but I would have to look at it before we knew.'

The importance of the Lampitt papers apparently was something upon which only Hunter could adjudicate.

'I suppose the papers might be rather private,' I said, not really intending to get so quickly to the heart of the matter. Hunter smiled to imply that I was being a tease.

'Anyway,' he said, 'should I come down later this summer, we shall probably see one another.'

'Perhaps,' I said. The others were drifting into the hall, where Mrs Treadmill had put a tray of tea and biscuits. Hunter would soon be drawn into the *mêlée*. But I could not part from him without picking at an old wound. In spite of my newly born interest in Petworth Lampitt, I was not really very interested in the fate of the Lampitt family papers. Hunter was primarily, for me, the man who had jilted Miss Beach.

Throughout the previous four years, whenever I thought about it, I had assumed that Hunter had honoured his intention of marrying Vanessa Faraday. With what I considered to be tremendous subtlety, I asked,

'When you and your wife come to Timplingham, where will you stay?'

Hunter smiled and gently touched my arm.

'You mustn't *think* of putting me up! Very kind, but there's a pub, surely?'

'Yes. Not much of one.'

'I'll be quite happy there.'

I had not meant to ask Hunter to stay. Uncle Roy and Aunt Deirdre were thrown into enough of a panic when Granny came for a few nights, or when my aunt's old schoolfriend Bunty made one of her rare visits. The idea of Hunter coming to stay would have been unthinkable had he not so anarchically thought it.

'You see, I think I know your wife.'

Here was real subtlety, real worldly insouciance.

'There must be some mistake,' Hunter smiled. 'I'm not married.'

One could not very well contradict a man when he had just spoken this sentence, but I was so surprised that my reply was unstoppable.

'But you were engaged to Vanessa – Vanessa Faraday. You see, I was at Seaforth Grange before I came here and I remember the whole thing. Even the Binker – Mr Larmer – told me that you and Vanessa . . . I mean, I remember seeing you . . .'

Hunter was less ruffled than I was by these appalling gaucheries, which died on my lips. He smiled and showed two rows of teeth, surprisingly small and discoloured.

'No, no, a bachelor, I'm afraid. Do you still keep up with dear Robbie Larmer?'

This question was incomprehensible to me. Who on earth was dear Robbie Larmer? Before I had composed myself sufficiently to realise that the allusion was to the Binker, Mrs Treadmill was upon us. She obviously found Hunter completely delightful.

'You are being neglected,' she said playfully, allowing herself to touch his elbow, as Hunter had earlier touched mine. She held up a green cup with tea in it and a ginger nut in the saucer.

'Or there *is* something a bit stronger,' murmured Treadmill, with the hesitant tone of a man who did not really know what this something was. Hunter followed Treadmill's gaze to the dusty half decanter – sherry? whisky? a urine sample? – which stood on the sideboard.

'No thanks awfully, I'm fine,' said Hunter. And everyone else seemed to think the same.

We mingled and chatted. It was only as we boys were leaving in a gaggle that Hunter called out to me, 'See you in Norfolk, perhaps!'

'Right ho, sir!'

The exchange made us all laugh. We had no sooner come out on to the foggy pavement than we all began our Treadmill imitations. As it happened, Hunter and I were to overlap that summer, but not in quite the way I imagined and not until I myself had undergone a series of emotional experiences which did something to heal the pains still suffered whenever I thought of Miss Beach.

*   *

In the days when it still seemed certain, in my private hopes, that I would be a writer (by which I meant a novelist) I used to assume that I would make good use of Barbara, or rather of the Barbara experience. As life wore on and it began to be clear that, whatever else the Fates had in store, it was not to fashion me into a weaver of yarns; the difficulties of describing sexual intimacy became clearer to me. By the time I had abandoned any hope of depicting Barbara in a novel, I had seen through all the technical problems. It is only failed writers, I have come to think, who are even aware of such difficulties. Real writers somehow confront their material as only they can – head on. They aren't perfectionists. There are consequently moments of ludicrous failure. Their greatness carries it off. That is what I have come to feel about D. H. Lawrence, for example, whose titanic stature as a writer is not really diminished by the fact that some of the steamier scenes in *Lady Chatterley's Lover* come close to unintentional farce.

This was the least of my difficulties when coming to write that unfinished, unpublishable fragment of a novel about Barbara. While I struggled with it on iron bedsteads or in transit camps during my wasted two years of National Service, I was sex-starved, disgruntled, bored. Contemplating those carefree weeks in Brittany from the barracks in Northampton, or in the awful tedium of Cyprus, I was in no position to do Barbara justice. I quite ignored the fact that writing down the experience was in itself an act of betrayal, undressing Barbara in public and revealing (were Madame de Normandin ever to read the book) what had been a secret. But even apart from this, I was still years away from recognising that any description of oneself indulging in sexual acts is almost bound to seem ridiculous to a third party.

Then again, even if I were to overcome the technical difficulty of recounting those scenes with Barbara, the actual description of what went on which, when I was writing about it, seemed all important, I would still have come up against another difficulty, namely the sheer improbability of it all. The fact that it actually took place – that Barbara and I made love on a number of occasions – was enough to justify writing it up as a piece of narrative. All that seemed necessary was to change some details. Barbara's name, for instance, which *sounded* so French when called through the food hatch by her mother or by Madame de Normandin, did not look French on the page.

The last time I looked at the manuscript, before consigning the exercise books to the flames, I noticed that she had several names – Marie-Celeste, Brigitte, Françoise – I am surprised that I did not call her Albertine and have done with it. I also found, on my final, embarrassed perusal of the thing, that I had changed the *venues* of our strange and fateful interviews. The beach hut has been transposed to somewhere more flattering to my sense of adventure. Bedrooms, bathrooms and even the dining table at Les Mouettes were scribbled in a list of possible settings.

I was under the ancient delusion that the mere fact of something having happened was enough to authenticate any narrative about it. I thought that truth was bound to shine through. God knows what I thought fiction was. But I was sublimely unaware that all plausible narratives, whether historical or fictitious, require art to make them plausible. The Barbara episodes in the beach hut had in reality happened quite arbitrarily, with almost no reference to anything which was going on in the household around us. I *think* that we liked one another, but we really had very little conversation. My contacts with her may have done wonders for my sentimental education, but they did nothing for my French.

'*Que penses-tu, si tranquille?*' she once whispered in my ear. And, on another occasion, '*Une parole, seulement une parole, je t'implore!*'

How could one possibly convey all this with anything approaching verisimilitude, while giving a true picture of the imaginative effect of that month in Brittany – the whole household at Les Mouettes, the other people, the landscape, the weather? My life with Barbara happened offstage to all this, like something in the life of dreams.

Then again, would I ever be honest enough to reconstruct my inconceivably clodhopping and ill-informed attitude to sex itself? It may have been the case that our hut sessions gave some sort of pleasure to Barbara, but it was not a matter to which I devoted any thought at the time. I supposed myself in love with her, though I suffered for her absolutely none of the pangs which had wrung my heart at the very thought of Miss Beach. Certainly, I should never have predicted that, as the experience receded, Barbara would have left very little impression on my memory, certainly far less than Madame de Normandin herself. As a very young man it just would not have occurred to me that I would retain a clearer recollection of quite commonplace conversations with an old lady than of my first essays in sexual gymnastics. Madame de Normandin remained a far more vivid figure even as a physical entity. Her neat, white hair in its delicate net and her intelligent, hedgehoggy face (an upper-class Mrs Tiggywinkle) remained in my mind perpetually, long after Barbara's features had become a forgotten blur. The fact that partners in bed, or in beach huts, can vanish completely from one's consciousness, so that one forgets not merely salacious details but even ordinary ones like names and faces, is one of the stranger tricks played by time. Barbara's chief importance in my emotional history was, in any case, a negative one. Until that French holiday I had been intensely involved in the world of school. Life as a boarder at a public school is lived at a level of emotional engagement seldom experienced afterwards. You are cooped up with sixty other boys for two-thirds of the year, sharing dormitories, bathrooms, studies and meals. It is, in any case, a period of life when feelings run high. Anger, resentment, admiration, jealousy, infatuation, disgust all coursed through one's system as a matter of daily experience. No wonder the Renaissance drama was something which made such an appeal. After Barbara, the whole flavour of it was muted. I recognised school for what it was, just another transit camp in the English Gulag, and I could not wait to leave.

FOUR

Aunt Deirdre was always the one who made any practical arrangements. It was she who discovered Madame de Normandin's advertisement in *The Lady*. I forget the details, but young, paying guests were offered board, lodging and French conversation in a large family house on the northern coast of Brittany. Shortly before the end of term, one of Aunt Deirdre's letters informed me that I was signed up for half the summer holiday *chez* Normandin.

By then, I had become insufferable. It was small wonder that my uncle and aunt wanted me out of the way. Fair enough, they both got on my nerves. But, rather than avoid them or lie low, I was occasionally drawn, quite irresistibly, to take the war into the enemy camp and to offer unprovoked attacks which were specifically designed to be hurtful. At this period, my uncle avoided me whenever possible. Sometimes, however, he took a meal with us, rather than with Sargie up at the Place. Or I might catch him creeping out of the lavatory, or sidling from the front door to his study. Then I could take the opportunity to give him my opinions about the Christian religion in general and his own apparent interpretations of it in particular. It did not really matter what I said on these occasions so long as I inflicted pain; and, on my uncle's soft, pampered features, pain always registered fast and easily.

It is only on those whom I have loved that I have ever

knowingly inflicted pain. The guilt of it remains for ever, my words selected with such malice and the startled expression on the victim's face as the effect went home. These are the faces which return during nights of insomnia, forever hurt in my memories, and inconsolably so. It is said that time is a healer, but it is not necessarily so. Memory has the power to encapsulate moments of pain, to freeze them, so that though the person who suffered has drifted on into other worlds and other states of feeling or non-feeling, the remembered moments of pain can stay. Sometimes in spells of profound depression, it is these moments alone which surface in the memory. Everything else is a bland, misty background against which these figures stand out sharp and clear – women in tears, or my uncle, drawing back the corner of his lips and sticking a pipe in his mouth, trying to conceal the extent to which I was hurting him.

Sometimes, I would start from the position that only a dunderhead could believe in the miracles of the New Testament; and, another thing, couldn't Uncle Roy *see* that a loving God and an omnipotent God (that is, a God capable of stopping pain by magic as Jesus was supposed to have done) was a contradiction in terms? If he could heal one blind man, why not all blind men? Then, having knocked down my uncle as an intellectual inadequate for believing in this stuff, I saw nothing inconsequential or unfair in attacking him for hypocrisy. Anyone, I would tell him, could see that he did not believe a thing; he only wanted to be a priest for reasons of snobbery, or because he liked wearing funny clothes or because he wanted to live in a grand old Georgian rectory. If they were really Christians, they would live in rags and wander round begging like Jains or St Francis of Assisi.

The restraint of my uncle and aunt during these taunts was remarkable. They never once reminded me that it really had been Granny's responsibility to look after me after my parents died. (Of course that possibility was unthinkable, with her feet, her 'heads', her general need to protect herself from any demands from any quarter.) But my uncle and aunt did not *have* to have me. They were not my legal guardians. By now I had simply grown into a disgruntled, loudmouthed lodger in their house, who paid no rent. It never even occurred to me at that period that the trust fund, set up from insurance payments after my parents were killed, nowhere near covered my living expenses. My pocket money, school fees, clothes and food were all provided out of their own resources. In grown-up years, the question of how life is to be paid for has been dominant. Not in my teens. Perhaps they should have made me more aware of this side of things. As it was, I saw my uncle and aunt (more especially my uncle) simply as irritants who set out to annoy me. I quickly nosed out the surely understandable fact that they had only devised the French sojourn because they wanted me out of the house. At one point in that dreadful row, the night before I left, I actually threatened not to go. The panic on their faces was terrible.

'Your aunt's paid now,' said Uncle Roy in exasperation. 'You've *got* to go now.'

'I expect it'll be quite jolly, old thing,' said my aunt. Her line, when I was being obstreperous, was to continue for as long as possible the pretence that the conversation was not departing from her own standards of cold-fish amiability. Then one would go too far and she (the equivalent of yanking the dog on its leash) would suddenly snap, 'Oh *do* shut up,' or some such call to heel.

'You just want to get rid of me!' I stormed.

'I wish I was going to France,' said my uncle.

'Oh yes? If you wanted to go to France, you'd have gone. You haven't been to France since the war. You never go anywhere. You just sit here in your stupid clothes, playing at your stupid, made-up religion and we're all stuck with it, just because you want to mince up and down between here and the Place licking Sargie's . . .'

'Oh, *do* shut up, old thing,' said my aunt.

My speech shocked them both. It shocked me. It seemed to be releasing spurts of hatred I did not really feel. The wounded look came into Uncle Roy's face and I wondered whether he would burst into tears, or whether the worm was about to turn, and he would strike me.

'I think the sooner you go away the better,' he said quietly and got up to tiptoe out of the kitchen.

'Just what I said. You're all trying to get rid of me!' I yelled.

Uncle Roy had reached the kitchen door, but before he could grasp the handle it turned and the door opened. Felicity was standing there. I don't know if she had been listening at the door or whether her quiet reading in another room had been disturbed by my shouts, or whether she had been coming into the kitchen anyway. Tea was on the table.

But she was there and she had become rather terrible.

'Get rid of you? I wouldn't blame them if they did, you selfish little creep!'

'Now, dear,' said Aunt Deirdre.

But Felicity's wrath was up. I had insulted her father just once too often and she was about to give me the rejoinder which *he* should have dished out months earlier. Her freckled face was drained of all colour and one vein stood out, very blue, on her left temple. A big girl, she was really frightening in her anger. I thought she was going to biff me.

'Ma and Pa have had just about enough of you! You moon about in this house – you never offer to help – you never even make your own bloody bed.'

'That's enough,' said my aunt.

Uncle Roy looked as though it was not half enough for him. His eyes gleamed.

'I don't know what you are meant to learn at that school where Ma educates you at great expense but it certainly has not been manners. And don't think it's charm, either, ducky! You've turned into the most charmless little prat . . .'

There was quite a lot in this vein. You get the general idea. It was conveyed to me that I was an ill-mannered oaf who was not worthy of the kindness which her parents had lavished upon me over the years. If I wanted to earn the right – Christ help us – to complain about being given a month's free holiday in France, a privilege for which most boys would have given their eyeteeth, then I should have to do something more constructive than loll about the house moodily, occasionally squeezing my blackheads in the hall mirror.

Every word bit home. Before the end of her speech I had got up to go, shoving past her and slamming the kitchen door. While I belted upstairs, she had opened the door and was yelling something about the truth being too hard for me to take and her parents being saints who had been given more than anyone could be expected to stand.

I went to my room in a burning rage. I would have liked to

kill someone – preferably Felicity and then myself. I think I wept a lot. I saw that everything she said was true, but I couldn't do anything about it. I hated myself much more than she could ever hate me and yet I hated her too for seeing so clearly and for being so just in her rebukes. I felt no penitence, only self-horror.

I must have lain on my bed for hours. At one point, my aunt called up in her 'joke posh' voice, sometimes used for smoothing troubles, 'Sup-per'. The imminence of this repast had been heralded by unappetising smells wafting up the back kitchen for about an hour previous. Rather later, her voice at my bedroom door said, 'I've made a cottage pie, old thing.'

Pride would not allow me to answer. I was too overwrought to eat. My mouth filled with brine, my stomach churned, my eyes scalded but, although I yearned to apologise to her, I couldn't.

About an hour later, she opened my bedroom door without knocking and breezed in, as though none of the previous scenes had taken place.

'Have you packed, old thing?'

'More or less.'

'Got enough socks? Got your bathing togs?'

'Did they say they'd provide towels?'

My voice shook as I asked. It was like going through the clothes list for Seaforth Grange, only now, instead of Vanessa and the Binker and Darnley, it was a lot of foreigners that I was about to meet. I had never been abroad.

'It said "big family" in the advert,' said my aunt. 'I should think they can run to a towel. What is the French for towel? Something funny, isn't it, something you wouldn't expect?'

I tried to say *serviette* but, greatly to both our embarrassment, I found myself choking on the words. My aunt was sitting beside me with an arm loosely on my shoulder – for her a supremely demonstrative gesture.

'Come on, old thing.'

Emotions weren't really Aunt Deirdre's thing. She was better when I'd blown my nose and she was breezily making the cocoa in the kitchen. It was surprisingly late. Uncle Roy had gone to bed. Felicity I did not see until I got back from France.

Such is the distorting power of narrative that the reader might well have derived the impression that Felicity had remained totally silent all her life, only to give voice to a vitriolic denunciation of her cousin in the paragraphs which I have just written. This would be to give a quite false impression. At Cambridge, Felicity had blossomed in just the way her parents might have wished. She had made a handful of 'nice' friends, played hockey in the Girton Second XI and got a very creditable degree. She had even been taken to a May ball by a man called Graham, reputed to be writing a thesis on Schopenhauer. Now, she too was writing a thesis, the working title of which was 'Some Epistemological Problems Since Moore'.

When she heard the title, my aunt said, 'Oh, thank goodness I'm not clever like the rest of you!'

Having no particular plans for the long vacation, Felicity had come home. She was going to earn a bit of extra cash by helping Sargie sort what he called, with ironic portent, 'The Lampitt Papers': that is, the boxes of Jimbo's old junk which had been languishing at Timplingham Place ever since the writer's flat in London had been cleared.

Felicity was Sargie's goddaughter. She felt protective towards him, rather as she did towards her own father.

'We don't want people snooping through all the stuff until we've made sure there's nothing there,' she had said firmly, happily falling in with the suggestion that she should help Sargie with the task. Hunter's proposal to bring out an edition of Petworth Lampitt's letters had been received guardedly by Sargie. He was glad to think of someone keeping Jimbo's memory green, but he was wary of 'publishing scoundrels'. Hunter's arrival for a preliminary snoop, due to occur some time when I was abroad, was something for which the greatest possible caution was needed.

'There aren't going to be any of Jimbo's letters *here*,' Sargie had said. 'I mean, a chap doesn't keep his *own* letters.'

'No, but Mr Hunter will be able to find out who were Jimbo's main correspondents. Then he can bother *their* families.'

A particular look of self-satisfaction had come into Felicity's face when she said these words. She thought she was being so clever.

The words which had passed between me and my cousin were too harsh for us to face each other over breakfast on the morning of my departure. She stayed in bed until I was out of the house. My uncle, back from early church, was wary over his porridge. Well he might have been. Although I had resolved, after my aunt's good-night kiss, to be 'good' for my last few hours in England, I found the sight of Uncle Roy prissily blowing into his silver porringer irresistibly provoking.

My aunt was journeying with me from Norwich to London, seeing me on to the boat train at Victoria and then lunching with her friend Bunty. There was even talk of her buying a new mac at the Army and Navy.

All these plans went smoothly and, although the quarrel of the previous evening made me uncomfortable, it also made me realise the wisdom of the French arrangement. Uncle Roy and I were for the time being immiscibles. This was a fact which simply had to be accepted. My relief in parting from him had been an almost physical thing. There is a strange illusion which I can remember Darnley practising on me at Seaforth Grange. Somebody presses very hard on your head with the flat of their palm for two or three minutes. When the pressure is released, you have the curious sensation that you are floating upwards, levitating like a Hindu mystic. This was what it felt like saying goodbye to Uncle Roy. To a lesser degree it was what it felt like when I kissed Aunt Deirdre at Victoria Station, though in this case, it was not so much that she irritated me, more that, in parting from her, I experienced a delicious sense of complete freedom. I was going to France on my own! It wasn't a school term. I did not have to do what anyone else told me to do. Within the fairly generous limits set by the law, I could do anything. As I looked out of the train window and saw the platform at Victoria recede, watched London turn to suburb and suburb to Kent I had my first realisation that the previous sixteen years had been lived in a sort of cage. There were people out here who were at large, free, unanswerable to anyone. There was life beyond the cage door. So far, everything which I had ever done had been governed and modified by the arbitrary rules of a game made up by other people. At Seaforth Grange, it was the Binker's game, in which almost everything you could think of doing was illegal – putting your hands in your pockets, reading, talking, going for a walk on your own, omitting to defecate after breakfast, going into a shop. My present school was more free and easy but even so the atmosphere was restrictive. Ordinary freedoms enjoyed by most boys of my age – being able to smoke a cigarette or take a girl to the cinema – were regarded there as highly flagitious.

At school, there were actually rule books. Absurd as they were, you at least knew roughly where you stood with them. At home, there was no book – merely a vast, unwritten, suffocating code, in its way quite as restrictive as the Binker's. Here the punishments were subtler. There were no canings, no gatings, no lines to copy. But there were hurt looks and feelings of intense embarrassment if you so much as spoke of stepping out of line.

I was hemmed in by a further invisible fence – my own shyness and awkwardness. I was still paralysed with fear of the village people at Timplingham. I could not have brought myself to hang round the village pub or talk to the two or three females in the village who were under the age of forty. But, even if I had wanted to, I should have been made aware that while not actually forbidden, this sort of behaviour would have been impossible in the eyes of my uncle and aunt.

And now I was moving into a world where – as I then fondly supposed – 'anything goes'. My head was filled with Rousseauesque misconceptions about freedom as the natural human condition. England scudded past the window. The train was full of holidaymakers with suitcases and merry faces. Very gingerly, and with the sense that I was doing something pretty wicked, I loosened and then removed my tie.

'Put a tie on, I should,' my uncle would say, on the hottest of days, if there was any question of my accompanying him on a visit to the Place. We would get there and find Sargie in a string vest and shorts.

There was no absolute rule in the world that you have to wear a tie. No one in that train was going to come up and say, 'Put a tie on, I should.' No one would have turned a hair if I had lit up a cigarette.

For the first time in my life I was a free agent. A sense of my freedom stole over me – not *like* a sexual experience, it *was* one. I was at large in the universe, a young bull. I stretched up to put my holdall on the rack above my head. Then, since there was room in the carriage and I did not much like my neighbour,

I wandered up and down the train. It was about five minutes later that I asked, 'Is this seat taken?' and returned the smile of a blousey, brown-skinned girl from Brussels.

*   *

How much, in advertisements, depends upon punctuation. My aunt had been under the impression that she was dispatching me to spend my summer holidays with a large family, house on the coast of Brittany. Before my arrival, I had managed to reconstruct all the de Normandins in my mind. *Monsieur*, rather like Monsieur Dubois in our French primer at Seaforth Grange, would be a precise figure, suited, moustached and with an amazing interest in pens, ink, desks and exercise books; talking about them all the time. *Madame*, who also liked to say things like 'The exercise book is on the desk', had a tiny waist, which showed no sign of having given birth to the young de Normandins, in whose possession these items of stationery and classroom equipment were to be found. Jean, he who wrote in the exercise book with the pencil, would be my age now, a surly brute in all likelihood, perhaps with a taste for the sort of novels still admired by Felicity – Camus, Sartre – and sexually precocious too. His younger sister, Mathilde, would by now, I hoped, have become a nubile creature who had lost her obsessive desire to accompany her mother to the grocer to buy coffee, tea, butter and other comestibles.

'What else did she buy at the grocer, Darnley?'

'*De l'encre, monsieur.*'

'Don't be ridiculous. You don't buy ink at a grocer's.'

Hands going up all over the class, with evidence of grocer's shops known to supply ink when required.

'What is it now, Darnley?' Lollipop Lew asks bewilderedly.

'Well, sir, supposing there was ink and you wrote a letter, not in English, but in the language we're doing . . .'

'You mean a French letter, Darnley.'

In the riot which followed, things got thrown. A window was broken, I seem to remember.

No wonder my French was appalling. Though I had advanced from the primer and the prosaic activities of the Dubois family, I was still nervous at the prospect of conversing with all the de Normandins.

It was a surprise, when I had settled into Les Mouettes, to discover that there were no de Normandins at all. Madame de Normandin's daughter, who turned out rather grandly to be called the Marquise d'Alifort, arrived when I had been there about ten days. She made periodic sorties to her mother's house, staying for about three days at a time before returning to her house in the South. She was all that was left of Madame's family. Three brothers of the Marquise had been killed in the First World War. Madame de Normandin and her daughter both lost their husbands in the Second.

Les Mouettes had been a family home. A turreted, granite affair, it would have been hard to classify architecturally. Is there such a thing as Seaside Gothic Celtic Twilight Revival? By Sargie Lampitt's snobbish standards, it would have passed muster: it wasn't a bought house. Madame de Normandin's grandmother had built it in the 1880s. It was large enough to house twenty people with ease. Before the war it had been the de Normandins' summer home. Monsieur de Normandin had been a diplomat – the house was scattered with mementoes of his various postings. The tiny circular drawing room with its signed photographs (George V and Queen Mary; the Princess Bibesco; Daisy Fellowes) was crammed with *vietnaméserie* picked up in Saigon. The library upstairs had a lot of Turkish junk, some of it, I now suspect, rather good.

I have never been easily able to ask people direct questions about themselves. If someone tells me their story I am (almost always) interested to hear. Likewise, if, before being introduced to someone for the first time, a third party gives me what diplomatic or military types would call a briefing, I listen with fascinated interest. But I am bad at admitting to their face that I do not know the details of someone's biography, even in circumstances where no disgrace attaches to ignorance and it would be extremely surprising if I *were* to know. I can't bring myself to say, 'I do not know anything about your past life. You mention a husband – to whom were you married? Is he dead? Did you have children?' or 'You mention Cairo – what were you doing there?' Rather, when a total stranger says to me, 'When Johnnie and I were in Cairo,' I tend to nod knowingly, as though it would be bad manners not to have known who Johnnie was and why he went to Egypt.

If all this is true of me now, it was yet truer when I was sixteen. I never once asked about Monsieur de Normandin during my entire month at Les Mouettes, even though I did a lot of sage nodding whenever Madame de Normandin referred to her husband. Years later, when staying with some friends, I happened to find a new biography of de Gaulle left for my bedside reading. It was much more readable than such books usually are and my interest was sufficiently held for me to read, having opened the thing at random, until the Fall of France. It was only in this way that I learnt how the Baron de Normandin, at needless personal risk (his diplomatic status could have allowed him to slip out of the country via Vichy and spend the war in the United States or London), had attempted a last-minute resistance to the establishment of Pétain's quisling government. He had remained in Paris after the Occupation and openly challenged the legality of the Vichy regime. Within a week, he had been shot by the Gestapo. Les Mouettes itself, where Madame de Normandin had lived continuously since the Liberation, had been occupied by the Germans: one reason, as she explained, for the bizarre variety of furnishings. The Turkish tables, Chinese screens and garish rugs had for the most part been stowed in cellars or lumber-rooms before the invasion. Much of the nicer furniture had been damaged by the troops billeted there.

I never heard Madame de Normandin, or anyone else at Les Mouettes, refer to the Germans as the 'boches'. The brutes who had moved into her house in the summer of 1940 and, when they discovered that it belonged to the Baron de Normandin, had thrown some of the nicer furniture over the cliffs, were always referred to as 'our visitors in 'forty'. Indeed, the outrage was described with such gentle irony that I at first missed the point altogether and supposed that some *Lady* readers had answered Madame's advertisement, come to Les Mouettes and, in a fit of high spirits, decided to destroy the furniture.

'The period of Louis Quinze was not, we suspect, altogether to our visitors' taste. They threw my husband's *secrétaire* over the cliffs, and his bed and a writing table. All the same period – made by Riesener. There is one, you know, in your Wallace Collection in London. It was similar.'

I just nodded, as if what she was saying was general

knowledge. I regret this now. It would have been better manners to express curiosity about an extraordinary story and to ask for more details. Perhaps I had been partly inhibited by Aunt Deirdre who had told me not to mention the war to any of the de Normandins.

'They'll all have things they would rather forget. It's only because they are ashamed of what happened after Dunkirk.'

The tone had implied that the French nation as a whole had been guilty of some absurd solecism – speaking 'ee bah gum', for example, or calling my aunt by her Christian name – and that she would rather that the family adopted her policy of 'taking no notice'.

In fact, I think that Madame de Normandin enjoyed recalling the war. Memories were a source of pride to her, rather than the reverse.

Madame de Normandin was very myopic and, rather than attempting to get anything into focus, she usually gazed upwards as she spoke, always rapidly and usually bilingually. These mealtime colloquies were designed, as she frequently reminded us, to teach us the art of conversation. Doubtless, this would have been a useful skill to acquire, but during my first week at Les Mouettes I was inhibited, partly by an intense shyness of saying anything at all and partly because I found my fellow guests uncongenial. There was absolutely nothing wrong with them. I was simply frightened of them, being used either to coevals of my own sex at school or to the quiet Rectory routines at Timplingham. Entirely unabashed either by my silences or by the somewhat different gaucheries of the other young people, Madame de Normandin made conversation relentlessly. She spoke, as it were, in subtitles, putting all the difficult words, and many of the easy ones, into our own language.

'*Alors*, now then! *Tout le monde a passé un bon matin à Perros-Guirec. Qu'est-ce qui se passe au club? Le tournoi, n'est-ce pas?* The tournament? The tennis tournament?'

'We just knocked a ball about, *madame*.'

'*Français, s'il vous plaît, Atlas.*'

'*Alors, nous avons . . .*'

These syllables were enough to reduce At Birk's two sisters to derision. Madame smiled patiently (one felt that it was an expression which had graced many an embassy dinner) and tried to help At on his way.

'*Je vous en prie, Wilmington! Atlas, continuez!* Go on! *Vous avez dit* . . .'

'*Oui, oui, madame* – Wilmie, quit foolin', can't you? – *nous avons* – what's "net"?'

'*Filet.*'

'Anyway, *nous avons joué au tennis.*'

'*Tennis,*' she repeated, correcting At's pronunciation. '*C'est ça.*'

By then the last little mountain of artichoke leaves had assembled before each plate and it was time for Madame to ring the bell.

Barbara came in to clear away the plates. She was about my age and she wore her dark hair in a pigtail. She was not strikingly pretty. More than any obvious perfection of feature, it was her smile which captivated me; and the fact that she did not smile at everyone. Her face was particularly impassive when she took At's plate.

'*Voilà, chérie, seulement pour toi,*' he said with a lewd laugh. My own accent was not up to much but I was already starting to hear the language in my head. At, who could be quite fluent when he chose, seemed not to have noticed the sound of French at all and spoke it with the same nasal drawl with which he spoke his own language.

While Barbara was in the room, Madame de Normandin spoke English. It was a convention dating back to her husband's lifetime that servants did not understand anything but French.

'And this afternoon, you are all to take Julian down to the sailing school at Perros-Guirec. That's right, isn't it?'

'Would you like to do that?' This kind inquiry came from Coral Birk, the eldest of the party.

'Sure he would,' said At.

I nodded, and tried to smile.

'D'you go sailing in England?'

'I haven't done.'

'But you'd like to learn, huh?'

'Oh, yes,' I lied. 'I mean, ah, *oui.*'

It was not at all how I had envisaged the French holiday. It had never occurred to me that there would be other English-speaking guests. I felt that Madame de Normandin had tricked us. For the next few days I was packed off to Perros-Guirec with the Birks and told to enjoy myself. My tennis was hopelessly less good than At's – not a fact in which I take any pride. My sailing skills turned out to be even worse. I acquiesced in the idea of signing up for lessons without beginning to imagine what they would be like. In an open boat with seven other people I would surely not be called upon to *do* anything? While the sails flapped above my head I could sit back and feel the salt on my skin and the sun on my hair; I could stare back across the bright, blue ocean to the strange, pink, porous rocks and cliffs of the coast-line, and the little seaside resort with its coloured umbrellas and cafés. The sailing school took the more rigorous view that having paid for instruction I should be instructed. Our instructor was a bossy little woman with short hair, the Gauloise forever dangling on her lips as she yelled at me furiously. I had no idea what she was saying. (Madame de Normandin with subtitles was still barely comprehensible; this sporty loudmouth did not even realise that my French was too poor to understand her elaborate directions.) I only knew that I was doing almost everything wrong. For instance, there is a large wooden pole at the bottom of the sail which swings to and fro across the entire surface of the boat. If you swing this without warning people, they get hit on the head. Whenever it was my turn to hold the pole, I either forgot to shout or, more shaming, felt too shy. What were the right words? It was only good luck which prevented me concussing the rest of the crew whenever I took the boom.

'He's just so stupid,' I overheard At saying one afternoon, as he rubbed the bumps which I had given him on the back of the head.

'And so, like high and mighty, like, you know, he doesn't want even to talk to us,' said Wilmie.

But Coral, who was the eldest and kinder, said, 'I guess it's all a little strange to him and he's a little girl-shy.'

'Like me,' said At.

'Like hell,' said Wilmie.

'Do you think Barbara loves me? You know the way she looks at me when she clears those plates away.'

'At Birk, Barbara thinks you are a shit. Can't you see that?'

I could certainly see it at that moment, as I came round the corner of the clubhouse to where they were eating their ice-cream cones. He was big, he was blond; the fact that he was covered in spots did not detract from his swaggering handsomeness. I hated his ability to be *open* – to make jokes about his own emotional state. I hated his loud voice and his decent, honest smile.

'Hi, Julian, have an ice cream.'

'No, thanks.'

'Hey, come on! Let me buy you an ice cream!'

'No.'

'Leave him alone, At.'

Increasingly – who shall blame them? – they did. I just couldn't enter into their *bonhomie*. I felt paralysed by it. And Coral was dead right to say that I was 'a little girl-shy'. I was disconcerted by her own shorts and teeshirt revealing so much flesh. I did not desire her – not when I was with her, anyway. I was overcome with awkwardness to have to spend time with someone who was so unselfconscious. She took my arm one day when we were walking down the road together. It was a purely sisterly affectionate gesture (her other arm was linked in Wilmie's) but I froze as she did it, instantaneously hating her action and my own involuntary cold-fishery. Besides, I had by then begun my own obsessive preoccupation with Barbara, with the thickness of her brown hair, falling down her back, and with that back itself, as I imagined it beneath the bow of her white apron. I thought too of her legs, of her large, pale hands as they took away my plate at table, of her strangely deep voice. Through all the tedium of sailing and tennis, and through all the badinage of Coral, At and Wilmie, and through all Madame de Normandin's stately meals and through all the long nights, in my remote turret bedroom with its view of the garden, the beech trees, the pines, the cliffs and the sea, I thought of Barbara. That unwavering concentration upon another person whom we hardly know, which we call falling in love, is unlike any other human relationship. It is different in kind from the way we think about those actually known to us – our family and friends – and has more in common with the incantations of witches or the intercession of those who pray than it has with any ordinary rational or sympathetic process. Long before I had touched Barbara, I knew exactly what the small of her back would feel like when pressed by my fingers and what it would be like when my chest was pressed against hers. As soon as a glance told me, quite unambiguously, that she would allow me to kiss her, everything changed. I took the risk that someone would spot us. She was on a landing, taking some sheets and towels out of an ottoman and looked up when I passed. Without saying anything, I put my arms round her waist. There was no resistance. All that remained, after our lips had parted, was to speak to one another, to make an assignation.

'Carbon?' I said, puzzled by her attempt to explain in my own language where we might meet again.

'On the side of the sea.'

'Oh, the cabin. The bathing hut.'

'Yes, the urt.'

After luncheon the next day was the soonest we could get away. As At remarked at the time, it was some meal. It was the last meal which the Birks ate in that house. The train would soon be taking them to Paris and then on to Geneva where their father worked for the United Nations. No one bore the Birks the smallest ill will, least of all Barbara's mother who had been tipped handsomely by Atlas and, in consequence, pulled out all the stops for the last meal she cooked them.

I had never come across proper cooking before I went to Les Mouettes. I did not even know that it existed. The grand meals which Darnley's mother paid for at hotels in Malvern were really only a step up from Aunt Deirdre's cuisine, with plenty of over-boiled vegetables and roast potatoes made out of leather. School food was universally horrible. The only improvement which I noticed after going to public school was that one was allowed to supplement high tea with eggs or tins of one's own. I wonder what Barbara's mother would have made of the food which Mrs Binker, or even Aunt Deirdre, so regularly set before their charges.

That last meal she cooked for the Birks was a triumph. Even by her own impeccable standards this was a series of dishes done to such perfection that one was half aware, even while eating it, that the memory of the meal would remain for ever. Almost all experience is instantaneously forgettable. Most of what we do remember is only fixed in our minds by chance. For another person to place something in our consciousness deliberately, so that we never forget it, that is art. Treadmill as a teacher had it, Thérèse as a cook. The meal began with a spinach *soufflé* which was like a thing of nature, a puffy light green crust sprouting from its bowl like a bush coming to leaf. And then there was *raie au beurre noire*, the freshest strands of succulent skate as white as snow amid the black butter and the little, dark green capers: once again, one felt that the food was for the first time in its natural habitat: a naked mermaid was suggested, sitting in seaweed. And then there were pieces of roast beef, pink and tender, served with *pommes dauphinoise*. And then there were *haricots verts* from the garden, served separately when we had all finished our meat. And then there was a fresh, very oily, green salad with which to eat the Camembert. And then, to crown it all, *omelettes soufflées aux liqueurs*, frothing, bubbling in their great buttery pans as Thérèse and Barbara ran in, squealing with the excitement of this success, for sweet omelettes never looked lighter or smelt more spirituous than these. Every time the mother and the daughter appeared throughout the meal, there were exclamations of delight at their genius, and no one seemed to notice the smiles and nods which I exchanged with Barbara, since everyone was smiling and nodding too, in happiness at the meal, and perhaps because everyone was fully able to tolerate the departure of the Birks. At, Coral and Wilmie themselves were eager to be back with their parents. Madame, when they had gone, commended their exuberance but deplored their lack of manners. So, the parting was a merry one.

Though, or perhaps because, it was her last meal with the Birks, Madame did her best to keep up a level of what she considered good conversation. It was not a level to which the rest of us aspired.

'Will you be going to Perros all on your own when we're gone?' At asked me. Now that we were about to part, I liked him and I think he rather liked me.

'*Parlez français*, stupid,' said Wilmie.

'So, who's stupid? *Est-ce que vous allez* . . . er . . . *au* . . . er . . . *club de tennis quand* . . .?'

It had never occurred to me that I would play any tennis once

At was on his way back to Geneva. Horror must have registered in my face because Madame de Normandin came at once to my rescue.

'*Julian est beaucoup plus intellectuel que sportif,*' she said decisively.

I do not think this has ever been true – the intellectual bit anyway – but it was a relief to discover that I would no longer have to pretend to be *sportif*. Madame said there were plenty of things to do, down on the little beach, at the bottom of the cliffs below her garden. I said that I had thought of spending the afternoon there.

'So, you see, Atlas, Julian will be able to occupy himself,' she said kindly, while Barbara brought in the beans.

'I know who I'm gonna miss,' said At, putting his arm round Barbara's waist. It was hard to know whether Madame, with her faded eyes fixed on the ceiling, noticed this little moment of endearment.

'So Julian'll be all alone,' said Coral.

'*Jusqu' à l'arrivée des Mount-Smith,*' said Madame. 'Until the Mount-Smiths arrive. They are my very good friends. The grandfather of these boys was a close friend of my husband.'

I had not dared to hope that I would have the place completely to myself when the Birks had gone. But the idea of the Mount-Smiths was, to me, lowering. I felt instantaneously jealous of them for knowing Madame de Normandin so well.

We had finished our beans and their consumption seemed to have cast Madame into a contemplative mood. She clasped her hands together and closed her eyes. She was going to make one last attempt to draw some coherent sentences from her young female guests and on a subject of what might be supposed to be of general interest.

'*Alors, Wilmington, dites-moi, s'il vous plaît, qui est votre auteur préféré?* You see, we are having some intellectual conversation for Julian.'

'Excuse me?'

'Your favourite author, dum-dum,' (this prompting from Wilmie's brother).

Atlas Birk's sister flicked him with the last of her green beans. One got the feeling, from the giggles which followed, that Wilmie was under the impression that reading, books, literature, were invariably obscene, or at least vaguely improper.

'*Et vous, Atlas,*' persisted Madame de Normandin. 'Who is your favourite? Mark Twain, or perhaps someone more modern? Jack London, perhaps.'

'I read a little Hemingway.'

Coral confessed to a fondness for Margaret Mitchell. The conversation was getting nowhere.

Madame de Normandin announced that she chiefly liked to read authors for their excellent style. I have never met anyone else with this rigorous ability to distinguish between style and content. Nevertheless, I did not believe that Madame was being pretentious. Coral asked Madame who were the greatest stylists.

'In French – *Pascal et Voltaire.* In English – I believe Agatha Christie and Winston Churchill.'

This led easily into an anecdote which Madame de Normandin recited regularly every few days about coming out into the Champs-Elysées just before the Liberation and seeing a solitary Union Jack. What could it signify, this flag? Was the King coming to Paris (he whose signed photograph she kept with the others in her drawing room)? No, no! It was not the King. It was Churchill.

The climax of the story, as she rehearsed the familiar scene of de Gaulle and Churchill walking together down the Champs-Elysées to the tumultuous acclaim of the crowds, was that the great prose stylist's lapels were wet with tears.

This recitation took us as far as the cheese.

'*Mais, nous n'avons pas demandé qui est l'écrivain préféré de Julian?*'

The Birks assumed a worried air, as if the whole of their remaining time at Les Mouettes might be devoted to a discussion of my literary preferences. I muttered my reply and, rather to my surprise, Madame de Normandin had heard of him.

'*Mais oui, Promenades à Venise* – what is this in English? *C'est un livre qui m'intéresse beaucoup.*'

'*Lagoon Loungings.*'

This was the one I had not read. Madame spoke of Venice, one of her passions. Petworth Lampitt, whose private correspondence was at that minute being revealed to the gaze of Hunter, passed swiftly out of the conversation. The name meant nothing to the Birks and, in spite of her polite interest, next to nothing to Madame. The excitement of the sweet omelette was enough to bring all talk of the Lampitts to an end.

Not long after that, I suppose I must have said goodbye to the Birks. Coral and Wilmie both said it had been good to know me. It was kind of them to say so, because I do not think they knew me at my best. At, with a big amiable smile and a clasp of my shoulder, expressed the hope that we would meet again. There was even talk of my looking them up in Geneva. But I have no real memory of their departing. The rest of the afternoon was spent on the beach. When I emerged from the little wooden cabin there, I had had an experience more memorable even than Thérèse's cooking; an experience after which the whole of life was different.

*   *

Some days later, I left Barbara on the beach and returned to the house towards half-past five in the afternoon.

From the first days at Les Mouettes, it had been a pleasant walk – a steep, sandy path with high banks and hedges on either side thick with the flowers of summer. It was almost like a subterranean tunnel, particularly when one passed the spot about halfway along which was overhung with wind-blown pines. By now the path between the house and the beach was associated with a pleasure more intense than anything in previous experience. When I trod the path, even if it was only for a bathe and there was no assignation arranged, I involuntarily felt stimulated. My climbs back up the hill, such as the one that afternoon, were suffused with deep happiness, only marred on that occasion by the knowledge that the Mount-Smiths would be arriving, a pair of brothers at present being educated at Downside.

Madame de Normandin had repeated several times since the Birks left that it would be nicer if there were some other guests of my own age and sex. The truth is that with very few delightful exceptions I have never got on especially well with persons who fell into this category and the other indications given off by the word 'Downside' were far from reassuring. Downside was a Roman Catholic monastery. Now, I knew that Madame de Normandin kept a missal wrapped in a black lace mantilla in the glove compartment of her Deux Chevaux and attended Mass several times a week; but I did not think of her as R.C. I was used to grown-ups spending a lot of time in church. Though I thought of my own life as largely shaped as a reaction against Uncle Roy, I had in fact imbibed many of his prejudices and I had a gloomy sense that Romans, as he called them, were not really the thing. Never knowingly having met an English Roman Catholic, I had no idea what, particularly, was wrong with them. But I knew that Downside boys would be awful.

Emerging from the cliff path, one crossed a patch of rough ground, entered a small gate into a shrubbery and then emerged into the garden of Les Mouettes. Passionate anglophile that she was, Madame believed that she had created, with her few flowerbeds and abundant bushes of hydrangeas, a veritable English garden. But there were no borders, no roses. There was none of the abundance of the Rectory garden at Timplingham. It would have astonished Madame de Normandin to know that a woman like my aunt spent hours of every day digging and weeding, and dead-heading and transplanting, and trundling wheelbarrows down muddy paths. She frequently spoke of the wonders of British gardens and obviously thought that her own was comparable with them. But *why* English gardens were so green and colourful and abundant was probably a mystery. If she had known how much time the English spend on their gardens, I am fairly sure that she would have thought it was an absurd waste of time, just as my aunt, who prided herself on what she called 'good, plain cooking' would have been scandalised by the artistry, the day-long kitchen toil, of Thérèse.

When one had crossed the garden, it was either possible to turn the corner by the large hydrangea bush and enter the house by the front door, or to weave one's way behind a hedge into a yard and enter through the back kitchens. This was what I did, so that I could hang the key of the beach hut on its hook by the dresser. My heart was full of the questions which Barbara had whispered in my ear. Did I love her? Really? Yes, yes, I had insisted. 'But if you love me, why do you not talk? Why is it – just *this*?' It *was* just 'this'. I had an almost painful awareness of the fact that, though fascinated and delighted by her, I was not after all in love. And this had been clear to me from my first emergence from the hut.

When I came into the back kitchen, I encountered a woman smartly dressed in black, whose neat hair was a shade too blonde to be credible. She both was and wasn't looking at me intently, for one of her eyes met mine and the other, over which there appeared to be no control, stared in all directions. The disconcerting thing about the eyes was that I did not know from second to second which one was wandering and which was staying still. If I withdrew my attention for an instant, the stable eye had started to wander, and I would find that the glide had now come to rest its observant and ironical gaze on me.

Having been in France a little while, I was beginning to feel like a native. It was slightly humiliating to be addressed in English before I had even opened my mouth.

'Good afternoon. My mother is still having a little rest. Let me introduce myself. I am Madame d'Alifort. You must be Julian Ramsay, yes?'

'Yes.'

When we had exchanged civilities, she said, 'I had no sooner arrived this afternoon than we had the most terrible news, my mother and I.'

'Oh, dear.'

'Oh, yes. The boys, the young men, who were to have been your companions for the rest of this fortnight, Dominic and Gerard Mount-Smith, have sent a telegram to say that they have had a death in the family.'

'How awful.'

'It really is. Their mother apparently has died, most unexpectedly, in hospital.'

From the way she squinted I could guess that Madame d'Alifort was puzzled by the grin which I was unable to prevent stealing over my face.

'It is very, very sad, isn't it?'

'Oh, terribly.'

Almost no event is objectively sad. Only sympathy can make it so. A minute's reflection on what the Mount-Smiths would actually be suffering sobered me up and stopped me smiling. But it could not make me *feel* sad. I had so little wanted the Mount-Smiths to be there, so convinced myself that they would be ghastly, that all I was capable of feeling was relief at their non-appearance.

Madame de Normandin and Madame d'Alifort might have had their own reasons for private distress at Mrs Mount-Smith's death. They were family friends of a sort. They were also going to lose a fortnight's money for the two Mount-Smith boys. I had the impression that the quite modest sums charged for board and lodging made an appreciable difference to Madame de Normandin, quite possibly that she needed the money. But there was another problem, perhaps more glaring, and it was me. Madame de Normandin, who was nearing seventy years of age, had her own distinctive manner of dealing with young houseguests. The only times when she felt personally responsible for them was during meals and for about an hour after dinner, when her conversations would continue over coffee in the library.

'*Dites-nous, Wilmington ma chérie, quel est votre paysage* – landscape or scenery, is it not – *votre paysage préféré?* What is your favourite scenery?'

'Excuse me?'

'Just say Swiss, Wilmie.'

More often than not, in the previous week, there had been sudden but semi-plausible announcements, before the end of dinner, that Wilmie, Coral and At were going to the cinema, a fly-blown little establishment which they had discovered in Perros-Guirec. I saw *Stage Coach* there, with subtitles, but full concentration on the film was impossible, what with Coral's knees pressed against my trouser legs and the generally overpowering smell of the lavatories, which seemed to dominate, however much the audience tried to drown it with Gauloises.

Into the gap left by the Birks the Mount-Smiths had been destined to step. It never occurred to me for a single moment during my time at Les Mouettes that my own presence there constituted a potential nightmare. How many grown-ups of their age (I suppose Madame d'Alifort was about forty-five) would relish the prospect of three weeks spent in the company of a moody, foreign adolescent who could not properly speak their language? The fact that I so visibly brightened at the prospect of having Les Mouettes to myself must have made it all the harder to tolerate. Had I not been there, Madame de Normandin could perhaps have gone away herself, gone back to stay with her daughter in the South, where there was more company and comfort. Yet never, by the flickering of an eyelash, did Madame de Normandin betray any such feelings to me. Perhaps she realised that things could have been worse. She could have been walled up for a month with At. (But perhaps she would have preferred that.) The only thing to be said in my favour was that years of living with Uncle Roy and Aunt Deirdre had given me plenty of practice at adapting myself to the routines of a quiet, elderly household.

Les Mouettes had all the advantages of the Rectory at Timplingham, with none of its drawbacks. It had beauty and seclusion but I had no sense here, as in Norfolk, of being trapped miles from anywhere in a household of persons intensely uncongenial to myself. For Aunt Deirdre's cottage pies, I had all the abundance of Thérèse's ingenuity and invention. Instead of Mrs Batterbee, waddling about the Rectory with a carpet sweeper and dispensing an odour of self-righteousness and armpits, there was Barbara.

Our clandestine meetings in the beach hut played such a large part of my own picture of how the days were to be spent that it was almost surprising to find Madame de Normandin anxious that, without some plan, I should be unable to occupy myself. Neither she nor her daughter could have had any conception of how thoroughly practised I was at solitude. Indeed, it may be said that I learnt it too well at Timplingham and have never entirely shaken off the sense that time spent in anyone else's company, however pleasant, is a departure from the norm, to which one only returns when alone.

Clearly, the hour or two between the arrival of the Mount-Smith's telegram and the serving of dinner was devoted by Madame de Normandin and the Marquise d'Alifort to a discussion of policy. They did not know anything about me. Supposing, for all his good nature, they *had* been stranded for a month with Atlas Birk? Over the soup, the Marquise, squinting this way and that, explained to me that, since I was now their solitary guest, some routine, some timetable, some *horaire* – she was so desperate that the synonyms poured from her – must be maintained. She wanted to protect her mother, I see that now. Madame de Normandin interrupted with many a delicate apology, as though my solitude, the death of Mrs Mount-Smith, the absence of the young scholars of Downside

School, were all calamities so insupportable that it would require in me the patience of a saint to endure them.

'My mother's eyesight is failing,' said Madame d'Alifort insistently, in English.

'Such a nuisance for everyone,' said her mother.

'She must not be strained. But perhaps you could, for example, read her the newspaper after breakfast. This would be useful for your own study of the French language and be of great help to her.'

I readily agreed.

'But she cannot supervise your activities later each day.'

'I wouldn't expect . . .'

'He would find it too boring!' exclaimed the mother.

'You can of course always take the *autobus* into Ploumanach or Perros. Then again, there is the little beach.'

'Our poor little beach!' exclaimed Madame de Normandin. 'Julian is loyal to it, I think. He seems just as happy there as at the, how would one say, *pleasure* beaches. He takes a book. Absolutely *anything* satisfies him!'

Barbara's English was not good enough to appreciate any comedy in all this as she brought in the next course.

'You are always most welcome to luncheon here with my mother,' continued the Marquise.

'And in the afternoons,' said her mother, 'when you are not sitting with a book on our poor little *plage*, I shall drive you for expeditions.'

'My mother is not meant to drive,' said the Marquise.

'I can show you Brittany,' said Madame de Normandin.

I think that the next three and a half weeks were the happiest of my life, a selfish confession since, in spite of my moments on the poor little *plage*, it was a month of delicious uninvolvement. I never came to know Madame de Normandin or the Marquise d'Alifort any better in the space of those three weeks. The same polite level of conversation was maintained. The same amiability was displayed and, I believe, felt. Madame's impeccable manners towards myself actually made me into easier company. She civilised me, just a little. There must have been moments, during that time, of awkwardness, or loneliness, or at least of minor depression or sorrow. No other period of life has been without them, so they must have been there at Les

Mouettes, those spells, lasting anything from a few hours to
several days, in which life seemed miserable, boring, oppress-
ive. But I have no recollection of any such time at Les Mouettes.
Memory paints a purely sunny canvas. I remember waking,
morning after morning (in memory it all seems much longer
than a month – it is a whole phase of life which has left a
stronger imprint on my imagination than many longer spells
such as my two years in the army) and feeling happy to be
alive. That joyous sense of total independence which I had felt
in the boat train at Victoria never left me, all the time I was
away.

And then again the place itself, Les Mouettes, had such
magic. One was always woken by the cawing of rooks in the
beech trees which grew close to the house. Rising, I would
open the little window of my tower bedroom, and look across
the slope of the garden and down to the flat-topped pines
which blackened the view of the sea. Everything at that hour
was usually grey with the pallor of a sea mist – *la brume*.
Sometimes it would lift and a day of bright sunshine would
follow. Equally beautiful to me were the days when the mist
never lifted, and when the air was damp and salty all day. It
was particularly good to bathe in this weather. Sometimes the
beach was so white with fog that Barbara and I could emerge
from our hut as naked as Adam and Eve to bathe in the sea,
with no chance of being seen from a distance of five yards away.
Or again, on misty afternoons, my wrists might be busy with the
hand-operated windscreen wipers as Madame de Normandin
rattled her Citroën down the high-hedged lanes at a daring
twenty miles per hour. Her daughter's claim that Madame
de Normandin's eyesight was failing was no exaggeration. I
sometimes wondered whether it was worth wiping the haze of
the dew from the windscreen. She saw everything, I imagine,
through a perpetual *brume*. She sat behind the wheel, as she
did at the dinner table, with her head held back. She did not
appear to be looking at anything in particular. She knew the
roads so well that she appeared to be driving by instinct.

In her company, I came to love the world of the Celtic. Every
few miles, we scrunched to a halt beside some primitive granite
church. She always remembered exactly what there was to see
in each place – here a standing stone or an old cross, fantastically

carved with serpents or Scriptural scenes; there a particular piece of old glass or an unusual font. It was all much more primitive than anything I was used to from the splendid Norfolk churches in the environs of Timplingham (and which, when seen with Uncle Roy, were nothing but a bore). The squat Breton saints who looked down from their niches seemed like children's dolls. Moreover, they were saints peculiar to the Celts – St Chattan, St Enedoque, St Ystyple, St Poran, St Brian, St Tugdual. The female figure with a child might be the Blessed Virgin, but she could equally easily turn out to be St Eboubibane. The lawgiver in these parts was neither St Paul nor Moses, but St Yvo.

Madame de Normandin apparently held this Celtic pantheon in the same affectionate regard as she did her neighbours.

'Cher petit saint!' she would exclaim as she surveyed one of these wobbly old wooden dolls in its place of honour. The tone of voice was identical if, on driving through some nearby village, she might say, 'Why – there's Madame de Lanfrancourt.' Then the Citroën might judder to a halt, and Madame would climb out to exchange civilities with some old lady walking out of a drive or hobbling into a grocer's shop.

Comparing her behaviour and that of her neighbours with the way we behaved at home, I concluded that Bretons had better manners than Norfolk types. There was no hint of condescension when Madame called the postman or the gardener 'monsieur', nor of servility in their address to her. Between Aunt Deirdre and the villagers in Timplingham there was a carefully graded hierarchy of attitudes and relations, with nothing so liberating as the convention of 'm'sieur' and 'madame' as a mode of addressing just about everyone. If Aunt Deirdre had addressed the postman as 'sir', he would rightly have concluded that something was amiss.

There were perfect manners, too, in the fact that, although we visited lots of churches together and although Madame told me many of the legendary stories about the Celtic saints and shrines, there was absolutely no awkwardness from a religious point of view: certainly no sense that I should accompany her on her frequent visits to Mass. She cannot have been a bigot, for one of our happiest outings together was to Tréguier, where I was enchanted by the crooked little cathedral, the steep, winding, cobbled streets leading down to the water's edge and the estuary.

We went to Renan's house, open to the public as a museum. Ernest Renan had left the Roman Church in the same year, 1845, that John Henry Newman had joined it. English readers of his *Vie de Jésus* have mostly regarded it as a romantic, even a sympathetic portrait of its subject. Renan's inability to believe in the miraculous elements in the Gospel could scarcely shock a nation many of whose clergy were honest doubters. In France, in the nineteenth century, things were very different. The divisions between those who believed and those who did not were more sharply accentuated, both religiously and politically. Madame de Normandin, who had been in her teens when Captain Dreyfus was sent to Devil's Island, was in many ways a highly nineteenth-century figure, patriotic, Catholic and Gaullist, with distinct monarchist sympathies. One might have expected her to sympathise with those nineteenth-century clerics who, scandalised when the people of Tréguier erected a statue of their most famous literary son, retaliated by shoving up an enormous (and hideous) Calvary by the railway station, in reparation for Renan's supposed blasphemies. The occasion had been attended by Madame de Normandin's mother, who remembered the huge crowds and some mitred bishop blessing this gruesome memorial to *odium theologicum*.

Madame de Normandin herself, however, like many pious people, regarded the clergy of her Church with a distant sort of derision. As far as she was concerned, they were functionaries whose task was to dispense the sacraments; there was no more need to interest herself in their opinions than in those of others on whom she relied for some particular professional expertise – her dentist, for example, or her plumber.

So – without guilt or apology – we went to Renan's house and inspected the relics which such places always contain – his old coat, stray bits of manuscript, photographs. Renan was a passionate Hellenist. Sepia photographs of Athens adorned the walls. We were shown his famous invocation to the goddess Athena. It was impossible, Madame de Normandin said, not to feel affection for Renan's intellectual honesty and for his love of beauty. He had come from a poor family. His career in the Church had 'made' him. When he had confided his religious

doubts to an academic superior, he had received a cynical smile
which had shown that, whatever he believed in the secrets of
his heart, he could easily have carried on functioning as a
professor of theology.

This was the level of Renan's inner heroism. What accounted
for his local popularity, however, was that he remained so
thoroughly a Breton. Indeed, when one looked at the photographs of his tubby little figure or surveyed the controversial
statue which stood between his house and the cathedral, Renan
looked simply like the last in a line of fat little Celtic saints,
another Tugdual or Samson whose dumpy body had been
framed by nature in the manner of the primitive Breton sculptors.

Even had Madame de Normandin and her daughter never
cropped up again in my life, I would still think it was worth
recording our visit to Renan's house. For, said she, Renan
had never really written better than when recalling his own
childhood and youth. It was a common enough thing, in all
generations since Rousseau, to try to recall the most significant
scenes of our early life. But, said she, Renan's *Souvenirs d'Enfance
et de la Jeunesse* was an admirable example of the genre. As we
were leaving the house, she bought me a copy. That evening
after dinner in the library, she handed me a paper-knife to cut
its porous, smudgy pages and asked me to read it aloud to her,
an exercise altogether more restful than her carefully constructed conversations and one which was in itself delightful.
I saw at once why she admired the book and considered it
worthy of comparison with Churchill's *My Early Life*.

For myself, the book articulated what it was I had fallen in
love with when I became captivated by the land of the Celtic.
Renan's love of early Breton lore and history were all of a piece
with what I myself was nebulously in love with – the standing
stones and menhirs in rough grassland and heather, the pink,
rocky coastline, the windswept hedges, the primitive churches,
the faces of the villagers round and brown as leather beneath
peaked caps or white lace coifs. The world evoked by Renan
was one which, with the necessary nostalgia of the memoirist,
he believed to have vanished for ever; and much, by the time I
came to know Brittany, had changed. The idiots from the
asylum, for instance, no longer wandered the streets of

Treguier. But in many ways the Brittany of Renan survived until the decade after the Second World War. The extraordinary, elaborate costumes, for example, worn by the old women, high lace constructions quite as ingenious as the Gothic spires at Treguier or Quimper, were not affected for the benefit of trippers. They were a genuine survival.

So was their piety, apparent at a village *pardon* on August 15, when Madame de Normandin and her household all followed the *curé* and his acolytes as they carried the statue of Mary out of the village church and down to a ruin of a small chapel on the clifftops, singing hymns which mingled a sentimental devotion to the Mother of God with a shrewd hope that the sea harvest for the coming year would be abundant. There were no hymnbooks, as in a Protestant service, and the accents of the worshippers were thick – that is, when they sang in French at all, some of the ditties being in Breton. But the general impression conveyed was a profound veneration for virginal purity and a very strong desire for lobsters. Even with my cynical Rectory upbringing (and I took part in the procession partly with the gleeful certainty – I wonder if I was right – that Uncle Roy would consider it silly) I approached it with a residual Manichean respectfulness which was quite inapposite. I thought, because it was 'religious', that it ought to be solemn. When I made out some of the words, I was all prepared to be scandalised by the jarring blend of excruciating superstition and commercial self-interest. And sometimes the jabbering crones were telling their beads and sometimes they were gossiping among themselves, which initially struck me as wrong – surely if they were 'really religious' they would have been unable to gossip at such a solemn moment? I do not know where these ideas came from. Perhaps they weren't ideas, so much as attitudes acquired by Sunday after Sunday of having to put on a smart suit to go to church, day after day at school of being told that one did not talk in chapel. Religion, which I did not even begin to understand, was something connected in my mind with being on someone else's idea of good behaviour. And there I was, walking along, side by side with Barbara! It was with myself that I felt most priggishly uneasy.

But, as the procession continued, these feelings of awkwardness wore off. Barbara and her mother sang the hymns quite unselfconsciously. I have no idea what their religious beliefs were, where they stood on the probability of the Virgin Birth or the moral allowability of sex before marriage. Nothing, I gradually came to feel, could be less relevant to what we were doing as we followed the *curé* and the lace-draped doll, carried on two poles and a sort of stretcher by an old man with earrings and a miscellaneous gaggle of altar boys.

The whole point of what I felt on that occasion is that I cannot put it into words. There was this strange collection of people, among whom I walked as a total stranger. What they were doing was inexplicable, alien. Yet, for about five minutes of the procession, it stopped being alien. The doll went on ahead. Behind followed the old women in their coifs and then the rest, taking up the rear – a crowd of a few hundred. Our voices were out of harmony, out of tune, out of time. We left behind us the tarmacadamed road and followed a rutty track down the lane which led to the cliffs. Beyond the Madonna, which swayed from side to side on the shoulders of the boys, was a clear blue sky and the sea. For a very short space of time – I have called it five minutes, but it may have been less – I was caught up in it all. At first, to my great embarrassment, I thought it was all going to make me cry; not merely water at the eyes, but really blub as I used to do when I was a little boy. There was a feeling of tears about it.

Since that day, I have tried on a number of occasions to articulate what it was that the procession began in me. It certainly did begin something which has continued to this day. And sometimes I have wanted to explain this as some sort of spiritual quest. And sometimes I have told myself that the procession was an example of natural religion – it worked, because the people took it all for granted. Religion, I have tried to say, is only possible in a world where most people take it for granted. Once you start analysing it and saying how much of it you believe, then it gets lost. But that isn't really quite what I felt or began to feel at the actual time of the procession. It was all much more nebulous than that. The *sort* of feeling it was followed the lines of 'At last I can see what religion *is*.'

This thought subsequently got rationalised into negatives. 'It isn't a matter of theology; it isn't a matter of the Sarum Rite; it isn't even a matter of good behaviour.' I got even hazier when

I dropped the negatives and started trying to say what it was. Hazier still trying to remember it and disentangle this from subsequent 'spiritual experiences'. Perhaps it would have been better not to mention it. But it wouldn't be truthful to censor it. I remember it as just about the last thing I did on my holiday at Les Mouettes. Probably that is a false memory. I do know that, after the procession, there were no more secret meetings with Barbara. She said goodbye to me, perfectly demurely, in front of her mother and of Madame de Normandin in the dining room at Les Mouettes. We did not kiss or anything. Nor did Madame de Normandin kiss me when she left me at the railway station.

'*Au revoir*, Julian,' she said.

But a quarter of a century was to pass before this wish was fulfilled.

FIVE

The sense of our own identity is fluid and tolerant, whereas our sense of the identity of others is always more fixed and quite often edges towards caricature. We know within ourselves that we can be twenty different persons in a single day and that the attempt to explain our personality is doomed to become a falsehood after only a few words. To every remark made about our own personal characteristics we would want, in the interest of truth, quite disregarding vanity, to say, 'Yes, but . . .' Or, 'That may have been true once but it is true no longer.' And yet, although we know this to be the case about ourselves, we can go on devouring works of literature, novels and biographies, which depend for their aesthetic success precisely on this insensitive ability to simplify, to describe, to draw lines around another person and say, 'This is she' or 'This is he.'

Petworth Lampitt achieved his effects as a literary caricaturist by sketching in the boldest of outlines. His Prince Albert is a figure whom we could recognise at a hundred yards, a two-dimensional creation made up of a handful of supposedly Germanic traits – efficiency, courage, soulful musicality, etc: an Enlightenment polymath born out of time and trapped in the purely decorative world of tartan linoleum and antlers made into loving-seats which all Lampitt's admirers took to be the authentic Balmoral or Osborne. His Albert was a man who could have been Frederick the Great but who was trapped like a German doll in a musical box compelled to do the bidding of his diminutive female owner, the victim of a domestic tyranny which hovered, like so many other domestic dramas, in the borderlands between tragedy and farce.

Taught by Hunter's *Life* we have probably all by now supplied reasons for Petworth Lampitt's particular obsession with the Prince Consort and his ability to have drawn a portrait at once so convincing and so misleading. Lampitt's misogyny and his well-manicured political radicalism supposedly go back to his experiences in Timplingham Place with his parents. Hunter's way of doing a biography is as different as possible from that of his most successful subject. Whereas Lampitt's portraits were self-confessedly imaginative (he was, indeed, halfway to the novelist's belief that we reach the truth about people only by inventing them) Hunter provided his readers with a superabundance of detail and what he himself like to call 'material'. Every notebook or postcard which Lampitt wrote has been gone through, its significance sifted. We feel that Hunter is being as fair as an experienced advocate who will if necessary (or even if unnecessary) take days to lay his evidence before the court, rather than influence the jury by distortion or paraphrase. And yet how often a defendant on trial, listening to just such a catalogue of his alleged deeds or misdeeds, must have thought that the mere length and detail of the evidence did nothing to diminish the unreality of the proceedings. If anything, the reverse. 'Yes, it is true,' he will think, 'that I did thus and thus, but no account of the matter can ever convey to a jury what it was like to do it: the thoughts passing through my head, the moods then possessing me. When I committed these crimes I was for all serious purposes a different person. Quite a different person from the man you see standing before you. The recitation of dates and facts by the barrister, as if he were the recording angel, is not real as I now am real.'

Hunter's *Life of Lampitt* was praised on all sides when first published for its accuracy and its subtlety. It was only those who had *known* Jimbo Lampitt who thought that this enormous, patiently assembled portrait, constructed from all the 'material' on which Hunter could lay his hands, bore no relation whatsoever to the man they had actually known and was actually less truthful than one of Lampitt's own historical caricatures.

It is only in relations of the deepest intimacy that we can allow to another person the same complexity of nature which we know to be our own. That is, with such individuals, we can stop making presuppositions and merely accept, as we do with our own selves, that there is no need to define them, no need to seek for patterns or shapes, no need to say that she or he is such and such a type.

Even more rigid than biographers in their desire to classify and depict, families impose on their own members the characters which they expect of them. The simplest way to respond to tyranny is to submit. Women whose sons and husbands have decided that they are shrews need never, at home, be anything else. The friends she meets when she is out of the house perhaps find all manner of qualities in a woman which her family have never seen and would not really want to see. If her churlish son or husband were to see her laughing with a friend, good-humouredly and without (as is her domestic wont) flying off the handle, they would murmur suspiciously that this was 'not what she was really like'. The pleasant, likable, varied character enjoyed by her friends would be, by this judgement, merely a front, put up to conceal the 'real' self, a figure who is either crying over the washing-up or shouting at Dad.

So it is that teenage sons whose fathers know them as mind-less rudesbies are found in other contexts to be ingenious workers, clubbable companions, affectionate lovers. By con-trast, men suited by temperament to the few, simple modes which make 'perfect husbands' can present very different figures to the world, figures who are little short of odious. The man who is happy to sit on a sofa at nine o'clock in the evening, holding the same hand on to which he placed a ring quarter of a century before and watching the televison set, can be transformed by nine in the morning into an office bully, free with his amorous attentions to stenographers and his withering unkindness to subordinates.

When we say 'It isn't like him,' we betray not so much our imperception about an individual (as though we might have spotted that the domestic mouse could also be a sergeant-major in a typing pool) as our general incomprehension of human personality. Pronouns are themselves just shorthand, since when we say 'I' or 'you' we really mean only that part of ourselves revealed for the time being to the other and seen through the other's eyes. We speak of the mad as people who aren't all there. But none of us are all there all of the time, that is, there is present in none of us at each moment of the day all the different modes of personality which might occasionally overtake us or be, for the time being, the most convenient mode of expressing ourselves. If we are not all there to ourselves, still less are we all there to others, presenting to the other every disparate particle of our consciousness, as it were, as fixed and artificially moulded as a 'character' in fiction or biography.

This series of rough and ready perceptions about human character, however, cannot quench our natural interest in the lives of those around us. For investigative purposes, we do carry around a rudimentary idea of what certain people are like. This is not because we think that Dickens in his crudest caricatures was nearer to the truth about human nature than masters of the ambiguous like Proust and Henry James. Rather, it is because, if human intercourse is to continue at all, we have to start somewhere and these ideas of other people which we carry about in our heads have some of the serviceability of maps. We know that the red line isn't a road, that the splodge of brown isn't a range of hills. We know the limits of the map's usability but we would rather have it in our pockets when out walking than leave it at home.

My ideas about Felicity, partly because I had lived with her at such close quarters for so long, were of this simple, maplike kind. I do not think they were all wrong, any more than her unsympathetic vision of myself, however little it took account of my inner life, could be dismissed as bearing no relation to the figure I cut in the day-to-day life of the Rectory.

Making my way back to England after a month at Les Mouettes, I knew that I was a quite different person. It vexed me that I should soon be treated as the self I had outgrown and discarded. I also feared that this vexation itself would turn me back into the figure that Uncle Roy and Felicity had (as it seemed at the time) somehow forced me into being.

I attributed my changed personality not to the obviously civilising influence of Madame de Normandin, but to my visits to the beach hut with Barbara. It was therefore quite out of the question that I could *announce* that I was a different person, even if it were possible without awkwardness to say anything so weird.

In fact, though I lecherously savoured my experiences on the little *plage* as I remembered them in the train, their memory was already dim by the time I pulled out of Liverpool Street. As far as memory goes, sex is not different from anything else. A few episodes, not necessarily those which appeared remarkable at the time, form arbitrary tableaux in the mind. For the rest, one is aware that such and such a thing took place, but it is only as it were as a third person narrative in one's brain that one believes in it. The reality of the thing itself fades into insignificance. This is as true of Eros as it is of meals, conversations, places and nearly all the people we ever meet. That, incidentally, is another reason for viewing with enormous distrust the archaeological endeavours of men like Hunter. In actual lives – lives, that is to say, which are lived rather than constructed by biographers – the past recedes and becomes a barely noticeable haze in the background. Things which seemed important in one particular week are shown, by the mere fact of their being forgotten, to be ultimately insignificant. Faces drift in and out of focus. The effect of a biography such as Hunter's *magnum opus* is to paint all these scenes and figures in the same tones. The mountains twenty miles away are as strongly coloured as the sitter's gown in the foreground. Everything, by virtue of being printed on the page in the same typeface, is given the same weight – friendships of enduring importance, encounters which strictly speaking made no imaginative impact at all, social chitchat scribbled on a postcard, hasty judgements of another person scribbled in a secret diary. In Hunter's defence it has to be said that this method of composition, denying what the painters call aerial perspective and hurling all the material at the reader with no sense of its unimportance, may in its own clumsy fashion be less distorting than some right-minded attempt to view a human life 'seriously'; for then the criterion of selection sets the focus and the picture becomes like one of those strange productions of artistic photographers where everything in the foreground is out of focus and all attention is fixed on some small detail in the middle distance. In the case of a poet's life, for example, the earnest chronicler might wish to single out from the correspondence or journals of the subject only those details which were of a piece with his perhaps modest verse productions; whereas a truer picture might have been that the poetry only ever came from a small part of the individual concerned and that for most of the time, most of the personality was dominated by domestic trivia or alcohol.

But while, as I have said, such adjustments and allowances are made on our own behalf without thinking, it is an almost impossible leap of the imagination to make them for other people. In the train back to Norwich, I glowed with the knowledge of how different I had become in France. Why, the very words in my head were different: I was even dreaming in the strange, bilingual language which I had adopted from my kind old hostess. But although I had witnessed this change in myself, I had not realised that change is a condition of human life which applies to other people as well. I assumed that when I got back to the Rectory it would be a different me meeting the same old them, as though Uncle Roy, Aunt Deirdre and Felicity were as unchanging as the surpliced wooden figures carved on the beam ends of the parish church. How untrue this was, I had all the evidence of my senses to tell me. Felicity, in particular, had been many different persons in the time that I had been living with her. The wholly silent, probably disapproving adolescent turned into the homesick undergraduate in her first year at Girton.

'She's spoken more on the telephone this week than in the whole of her last year at home,' Aunt Deirdre remarked at the time.

And then Felicity had settled down at Cambridge. The fact that she had made several friends suggested a diversity of sympathy not always apparent, nor looked for, in the circle of the family. Nevertheless, the word 'Felicity' still conjured up for me something lumpish and static, and I was in the habit, hard to shake, of only selecting such details about her life as corresponded with the pre-existent caricature of her formed in my brain.

Thus, although there was nothing particularly funny about Felicity's friends, to my mind they were all exquisitely ridiculous, the mere fact of their having chosen to spend time in Felicity's company being enough to suggest that they were at best undiscriminating, at worst desperate for society, even a little crazy. Other girls went to dances and nobody laughed. The fact that Graham had taken Felicity to a May ball wrote him down (as far as I was concerned) as a figure of pure comedy. Photographs of the occasion proved that Felicity looked rather sweet, with a tightly waisted evening dress worn off the shoulders. Felicity was neither plain, nor a frump, even though I chose to believe that she was both. The photographic evidence that she had shapely arms, shoulders and breasts made no impression on me at all. When I looked at the picture of her in her ball gown, I just imagined her delicately mottled skin turning to gooseflesh in the wet evening air. I seem to remember wondering, too, whether she had been able to abandon the sandals and ankle socks which at that date were her daily wear and which, for some reason, I found particularly annoying.

This belief, that Felicity was a frump, a joke, an irritant, had allowed me to reach the age of sixteen without ever considering that Felicity had emotions comparable with my own, emotions which had to be taken seriously. Therefore when Aunt Deirdre, having met me at the station at Norwich, broke the news about Felicity, I burst out laughing. It was the inevitable, the only, reaction.

My aunt was at the wheel of the Trojan as we chuntered out of town on the Newmarket Road. During my absence, she had rather severely cropped her hair so that in her simple open-necked white blouse she more than ever resembled a slightly overweight Boy Scout. For the ten minutes or so that it had taken her to negotiate her way out of the station car park and queue at the traffic lights, she had been giving me a rundown of things which had happened in my absence. A Mr Hunter had been up at the Place going through boxes of Jimbo's letters and papers – or as many as Sargie had let him see. Mr Hunter said that there was so much interesting material that they really ought to have a full-scale biography of Jimbo, but Sargie was not sure. He had asked Uncle Roy's advice, who thought there should be a book not just about Jimbo but about all the Lampitts – a history of the family. Sargie had tried this one on Mr Hunter and it had not gone down so well. Oh, and the carpet sweeper at the Rectory finally gave out, but mercifully Mrs Wimbush was going to let Aunt Deirdre have hers second-hand because Dr Wimbush was buying her a new vacuum cleaner, lucky thing. Uncle Roy – a great event – had got his smart, new summer suit from the tailor. Oh, and that wretched woman *said* she had written a novel, but people did not know whether to believe her and no publisher in their right mind would buy it.

'She was bragging about it in the post office yesterday when poor old Mr Jameson – you know, from the cottages – was standing there waiting for his pension.'

'Do you think we'll all be in the novel?' I asked.

'Shouldn't be surprised. Bet I'm the murderer!'

My aunt always spoke as if every novel contained a murder, which was true in the case of the ones she read.

For the moment I was more interested in the work that was going on at the Place: the sorting of Jimbo Lampitt's papers. Even more, I wanted to know what Hunter was really like. I still minded terribly about Miss Beach. I think in a way I still do. But I can't pretend that I am still in love with her, whereas, a mere four years after I had seen Hunter's silky hands caressing her back, I think I was still then in love with Miss Beach, a fact which Barbara and France had really done nothing to dispel.

'You know, Granny and I once saw Mr Hunter in Worcester,' I said. 'Having lunch in Bobby's with one of the school matrons.'

'The Mr Hunter who's working on the papers?'

'Yes.'

'How did you know it was him?'

'I didn't. But when he came to give a talk to the Lampitt Society last term I recognised him.'

This version of events was one which I found it easier to give than the truth. Miss Beach was not a subject to bring up with my aunt.

'Extraordinary things you do remember. Actually,' she added, going very red and putting on a poor show of non-chalance, 'something rather exciting has happened with your Mr Hunter.'

'Oh?'

'Don't say I mentioned it – in fact, don't talk about it at all, certainly not to Felicity.'

'Don't mention *what* to Felicity?'

'You see, we think she's developed a bit of a pash on Mr Hunter.'

And it was at this point that I ungallantly roared with laughter.

'You're *not* to tease her about it, Julian, you really mustn't. It's . . .'

But my aunt changed gear and stared ahead at the great Norfolk sky, unable to say, quite, what 'it' was. Had she ever felt 'it' herself, this most extraordinary feeling? During my teens it was unimaginable to me that Aunt Deirdre and Uncle Roy had ever been in love. The very language they used about it – they talked of people being keen on one another, or having pashes – seemed to rule out the possibility of their having any experience of the phenomenon themselves. I did not realise that brisk talk could very readily betoken not ignorance but a whole range of sadder, subtler things: the disappointment of passion fading into the fuddy-duddy boringness and mutual dislike of a middle-aged marriage or, quite simply, the embarrassment which sensible people quite often feel when they look back on themselves in love.

When we got back to the Rectory it was time for luncheon. Spam, beetroot and cold potatoes were in readiness. We ate them, just the three of us, Uncle Roy, Aunt Deirdre and I. Felicity was out.

'You've told him . . .' my uncle ventured.

'Something may come of it, who knows, but we aren't saying a *thing*,' was Aunt Deirdre's reply.

Since, in general, their policy was to treat everything as classified information, I was not surprised that the Felicity-Hunter thing was being kept so firmly under wraps. I wondered how successful they were being in keeping the liaison from the village.

'You're wrong to think I'd joke about it,' I said, by way of an announcement that, since going to France, I had changed.

Getting the message, Uncle Roy merely raised sceptical eyebrows.

'London must have been packed.'

'It was rather.'

'All those *people*! And going to the Festival thingummy!' He raised both hands with a gesture identical to the one he used for praying at the eucharistic altar. 'They must be *barmy*!'

'Quite mad,' said my aunt, firmly dissecting a baby beetroot and putting half in her mouth. She munched crossly, with sharp little movements of the jaw which looked as though they were designed to teach the beetroot some sort of lesson.

The possibility of seeing the Festival of Britain Exhibition at Battersea had crossed my mind some time before the boat train pulled into Victoria. Most of the tourists with whom I was travelling were talking of it. I still wanted to see it. My uncle and aunt's shared conviction that anyone who wanted to see it (or indeed go anywhere, do anything) must be insane only quickened my wish. But I was 'good' and suppressed any word of dissent from the Rectory line. Of course anyone who wanted to see the most exciting exhibition held in London for a hundred years was off their heads.

'Needless to say,' said my aunt, who had taken a sip of water to swill the chastened beetroot on its passage, 'that wretched Maddock woman took her children. She will call them kids.'

'Well,' said Uncle Roy with a smile. And then, before allowing the witticism to fall from his delicate lips, he dabbed them gently with his napkin. 'We all know that kids are the offspring of nanny-goats.'

It was not the first time he had given utterance to this particular drollerie, but it made my aunt whoop with almost savage amusement.

'We were all delayed for a good ten minutes in the shop the other week when she gave Mrs Beynon – you know, Jill – a blow by blow account of how they got to Liverpool Street and how they got to Battersea. And she will call Mrs Beynon Jill.'

My aunt called Mrs Beynon Jill but this was different.

'You could see,' she continued, 'that everyone thought her a complete fool for taking the twins at their age.'

'I should think it would make very little impression,' said Uncle Roy. 'Babies remember nothing. I was two or three before I started to have memories.'

'The twins are five,' said my aunt.

'Even so,' said Uncle Roy.

'Oh, quite' – for this was a moment of Rectory solidarity against the Wretched Woman, rather than an occasion for marital point-scoring – 'and think of the crowds. Think of two five-year-olds getting lost! And of course there are always funny people about in a crowded place, not to mention all the bugs you are bound to pick up.'

'To my recollection those children have never been baptised,' said my uncle, who seemed quite unconcerned to have got their ages wrong. Six months, five years, what was the difference in a mere non-Lampitt?

'And then she said in that "ee bah gum" voice of hers,' and here my aunt adopted her prissy 'imitations' voice which was not in the least 'ee bah gum', ' "Oh, Jill, there's a village post office and stores in my novel but you mustn't think it's *all* based on yours." As if,' continued my aunt in her normal voice, 'anyone would want to read it.'

'Oh, I want to read it,' I confessed. 'What's the title?'

'They do say that it is all about people in the village,' said my uncle. 'But I expect it's mainly about . . .' The hands went up again in a gesture of prayer. The sentence was obviously unfinishable by lips which could not mention sex or any other kind of marital intrigue.

'There've been tremendous dramas on that front while you've been away,' said my aunt; and I wondered whether she would have gone so far before my holiday. Perhaps she sensed that going to France had been emotionally educative.

'The husband always seemed very pleasant whenever I met him,' said Uncle Roy.

'You speak of him in the past tense,' I remarked.

'He was the one who gave you all those books for the fête the year before last,' said Aunt Deirdre, playing for time.

'Not all of them suitable,' added Uncle Roy.

'He may come back anyway,' said my aunt. 'People in the village are saying they don't blame him, but of course we can't take that line so we just say nothing.'

'What's Mr Maddock supposed to have done?' I asked.

It was foolish of me to think they'd say. They all found out about three years later anyhow when her first novel, *The Melon Garden*, reached the mobile library van.

'Catching up on all the gossip since you went away?' said Felicity's voice behind my head.

I turned, and there she was. I hardly recognised her. She looked – beautiful! Really! She had lost some weight, but it wasn't just that. Her face glowed with an almost ethereal joy.

'You've done something to your hair,' I said.

'Isn't it good?' said Aunt Deirdre. 'Now, darling, lunch is here if you want it – we started without you because we thought you might not be home.'

'Oh, I'm exhausted!' she exclaimed. 'Raphael and I have been through fifteen trunksful of stuff this morning. Imagine! No, I shan't eat here, thanks, Ma. I've left him down at the White Hart and said I'll go back and join him there. I just nipped home to say he'd love to come to tea this afternoon.'

'Oh, *terrific!*' said her mother.

'So,' said Felicity turning to me, 'what was France like?'

I made some reply or other but she wasn't interested. She was in a daze of happiness, almost mad with it. I don't think I had ever seen her happy before. Not *really* happy. There were moments like when she got her first and she said she was 'chuffed'. Chuffedness and happiness were visibly different. It was almost frightening.

'Raphael says not to make anything special for tea because he's got to have dinner with Sargie,' said Felicity.

'Yes, but he's got to eat.'

'I've hardly seen Sargie since Mr Hunter arrived,' said my uncle in a funny sort of tone.

'Yes,' said my aunt with assumed gaiety, 'we see your uncle much more often now Mr Hunter's around.'

When Felicity had trotted out again like an excited child to meet its first playmate, there was an embarrassed sort of pause. It was broken by Uncle Roy.

'Sargie says he can't find out anything about Mr Hunter's people.'

'Did you know he was with Jimbo on the day he died?' I asked.

'Mr Hunter?'

'He gave this talk to us at school.'

'It doesn't sound quite suitable,' said Aunt Deirdre.

'It baffles Sargie. Apparently Jimbo never mentioned this young man to anyone and yet Mr Hunter speaks as if he and Petworth, as he will keep on calling him, were the best of friends. And yes he was with Jimbo when he died.'

'You never said that before!' Aunt Deirdre shot him an accusing glance.

'You didn't ask.' The putdown was smiling, smug. 'No, Mr Hunter was a witness at the inquest. There is no secret about *that*. The funny thing is that *no one* seems to have heard of him before. Sibs had never heard of him and she saw Jimbo most *days* by the end.'

'You see why we aren't entirely happy?' my aunt said to me.

I felt as you did at school when the teacher finished explaining something and you realised that you hadn't been paying attention for the crucial part of the lesson. Only, on this occasion, I had been paying close attention to what they had been saying about Hunter and still their message, if there was one, had eluded me. They were obviously worried in a general way that Felicity had fallen in with – not to say fallen in love with – a mystery man whom no one knew anything about. But I felt vaguely at the time and much more sharply now that they had a specific worry: one which in Rectory terms was entirely unmentionable. If it was the worry I now think it was, I now rather admire their prescience. It never crossed my mind at the time.

Not long after four o'clock, Hunter and Felicity appeared, openly holding hands as they walked up the drive in the sunshine. Felicity was staring at Hunter with an expression which made me see why schoolboys and others said love was 'soppy'. At the same time there was something moving about the pair of them, even though I now believe that, had I known more, I should have seen something spurious in Hunter's smile. With my uncle and aunt, he was all charm. I think the secret of this, which did not occur to me at the time because it was too staringly obvious, was that he genuinely found them charming themselves. It had never occurred to me that anyone, still less anyone from the outside world, would actually *like* my uncle and aunt. But then I had very little experience of seeing them together with strangers.

Neither of them was in the least used to entertaining. 'Village people' came to a garden party once a year. Sargie very occasionally staggered in and out of the house but he seldom ate with us. For the rest, the only regular visitors to the Rectory were old schoolfriends of my aunt's, such as Bunty, and their visits were few and far between.

Even without the drama of Felicity's pash, therefore, Hunter's

visit would have been something of an event. My uncle had
been upstairs to change several times before the young man's
arrival, wondering what gear would be suitable for tea with a
possible son-in-law. A whole range of clobber had been got out
of the wardrobe, ranging from his cassock, which my aunt very
properly shouted at him to remove, to the bright green Harris
tweed golfing trousers. A compromise was reached when he
finally settled for the jacket which went with these controversial
items of clothing and a pair of grey flannel trousers.

It was evident, when we were all in our places, with plates on
our knees in the drawing room, that Uncle Roy did not trust
his wife to keep us properly nourished.

'See if Mr Hunter would like more tea,' he said sharply at
several moments.

In spite of Mr Hunter's 'I'm quite all right really,' Uncle Roy
kept jumping up to peer at the contents of his guest's cup with
a curiosity which would have been excessive if water lilies had
begun to sprout on its surface. Similarly, Hunter had no sooner
put the last of a biscuit or a sandwich or a piece of cake in his
mouth than my uncle and aunt would leap up and vie with
each other to make him eat more. Radishes, spring onions, a
freshly baked Victoria sponge were all on offer and there was
the implication that offence would be taken if he did not sample
some of everything.

'Please, Ma, I *told* you Raphael's having dinner tonight,' said
Felicity.

Hunter thrived on all the attention and ate obediently. Even
more than this – for anyone, after all, can eat a cress sandwich
– he displayed a masterly ability to parry any inquiry concerning
his background, family, avocation or present mode of employ-
ment. I suppose that my uncle and aunt chiefly wanted to find
out whether Hunter was rich, and whether there was madness
in his family, but they skirted round both subjects with what
must have seemed to them like subtlety.

'I suppose this interest of yours in Mr Lampitt's documents
is all part of your work,' said Aunt Deirdre.

'I'm hoping to make it so,' said Hunter.

'Is it what they call research? I'm hazy about these things.'

'That's more science,' said my uncle hastily trying to cover
up what he took to be a gaffe by his wife.

Hunter, however, conceded that research was one word for it.

'I think we've all tended to get Petworth Lampitt quite wrong,' he drawled. I knew the line. But my uncle, who had not had the benefit of having heard Hunter's talk to the Lampitt Society, picked up the wrong end of the stick with alacrity.

'I agree with you there!' He filled his pipe and fiddled with matches. He looked at last as if he would stop offering Hunter things to eat and settle down to some really good talk. 'What fools they'll all look, the moderns, in a few years' time.'

Hunter's face did not betray any pleasure at the moderns, whoever they were, being made to look fools. He moved his head from side to side like a stage Frenchman.

'Sargie always maintains that Jimbo is one of our great *stylists*,' said Uncle Roy. 'Mind you, Sargie himself is a very good writer. Did you ever read his book about the House of Lords?'

Hunter smiled, 'I'm afraid . . .'

'Lady Starling – his sister.' There was a faintly interrogatory tone when my uncle supplied this gloss; it really was scarcely conceivable that anyone should not know who Lady Starling was, but he wanted to be sure.

'Rather a severe lady?' asked Hunter.

'Severe! Sibs?' Uncle Roy laughed indulgently. 'She is famous in the family for being a complete doormat.'

'I only met her briefly at Petworth's funeral.'

'Anyway, Lady Starling says that Mr Sargent – Sargie, that is – is almost a revolutionary. A good example of her famous overstatements. Really, I could write a book about the Lampitts. Wonderful lot. Sibs is married, as you know, to Sir Rupert Starling. Working in the Treasury as he does, he is bound to take an equivocal line about some of Sargie's theories. I'm not really sure what line Sargie *does* take these days about reforming the Upper House.'

'I'm sure Mr Hunter thinks the moderns . . .' My aunt was trying to clear up what she saw was a failure of understanding on both sides, but my uncle shut her up, rather crossly.

'He was just hearing about Sibs. As I say, Lady Starling lets people walk all over her. An extraordinarily sweet person. She lives,' he added with the unspoken implication that this made her even sweeter, 'in Cadogan Square.'

My aunt, determined not to be frustrated in her pursuit of the particular, changed tack and decided that she might at least get some clue as to Hunter's address.

'Do you live near Cadogan Square, Mr Hunter?'

'Not really. But with undergrounds, buses and things – one gets about.'

'Of course. I just wondered with your work – I mean, whether you had to live . . .'

It was five o'clock and still my aunt had been unable to persuade Hunter to admit that he lived anywhere or did anything.

'It's such a frightful bore getting about in London, don't you find?' she said in despair. 'And with this Festival!'

I guessed that Hunter admired the Festival and all it stood for, but he was hedging his bets. He began a sentence and left it tactfully in the air, to be finished by anyone who chose.

'Isn't it . . .?'

'I want to go,' said Felicity earnestly.

'Darling, think of the crowds!' said her mother.

'Would you have missed the Great Exhibition of 1851, Pa?'

It was a good question. Uncle Roy's pipe was now alight and he allowed himself the luxury of a quotation.

'"From Timbuctoo and Tooting Bec they came, from the Lancashire mills and the villas of Lahore . . ."'

Hunter looked quite blank.

'Surely you remember that bit?' asked my uncle.

I did. It was one of the best set-pieces in *Prince Albert*. It was said that Yeats had considered including it in the *Oxford Book of Modern Verse*, as he had done Pater's passage of purple prose about the Mona Lisa.

'Marvellous stuff,' said my uncle.

'And yet,' said Hunter, 'I think we shall find that Petworth's importance lay less in the books than in the *man*. In fact, I think we shall find that Petworth's true significance only emerges when we have been through all that mountain of stuff at Timplingham Place.'

Like Mrs Maddock, Hunter pronounced the name as it was spelt, rather than 'Timming'em'. He took Felicity's hand and stared into her eyes as he spoke. His desire to get his hands on the papers sounded like a lovesong to her, which perhaps in its way it was. Without her help he would not be able to see any of it. Sargie had made that clear from the outset.

'It isn't always wise to rake over the past like that,' said Aunt Deirdre. 'I mean, in your case, you'll behave responsibly. But one does sometimes feel, "Let Sleeping Dogs Lie".'

'Oh quite,' said Hunter, with a very mysterious smile indeed.

As he sat there, young, handsome, refusing a piece of cake, he might, for all they knew about him, have been an angel whom they were entertaining unawares.

The silence which ensued allowed Aunt Deirdre to put a direct question.

'Were you at Cambridge too, Mr Hunter?'

'Cambridge as well as . . .?' He leaned forward, seeming anxious to get the meaning of my aunt's inquiry absolutely straight.

'As well as Felicity. I thought perhaps . . . I mean, it would be nice.'

Everyone blushed at this for some reason.

Felicity, through her teeth, said, '*Ma!*'

'No,' said Hunter, 'I wasn't at Cambridge.'

'I'm an Oxford man, too,' said my uncle, warming to his young friend. 'Exeter was my college. Which was yours?'

'Sorry,' said Hunter, 'I misunderstood. I didn't in fact go to a university.'

'Oh!' My uncle looked astonished. He could not have looked more surprised if Hunter had confessed to never cleaning his teeth.

'It must have been difficult to get . . . well, to become a . . .' My aunt stared at Hunter. Become a what? Surely he would help her out now? What was he, or what did he hope to become?

I was still innocent enough to suppose that everyone eventually became something. I did not realise that most lives flit by before the person, strictly speaking, has become anything. But, even at this unformed level of understanding, I think I was beginning to guess that Hunter intended to become something and that he had seen in the unlikely quarry of the Lampitt Papers the means towards his mysterious end. Given the extra- ordinary unpromising nature of his material – an outmoded author whom he did not even admire, a bundle of 'stuff' which was almost surely rubbish, Sargie and his 'impossible' temperament – there was a touch of genius in all this.

Seeing that the others were getting nowhere in their attempts to pluck out Hunter's mystery, I decided to play a certain card.

'You and I were both at Seaforth Grange. Do you remember, we talked about it when you came down to address the Lampitt Club.'

'That's right,' he said with a smile. I could write a whole book on the way that Hunter has smiled at me. His smiles were different with different people. When directed at me, there was always the implication that I was taking the mickey out of him, but that he was indulgent enough to put up with the tease.

'Have you seen Robbie lately?' he asked. 'I'm sorry to say that Margot has not been at all well – phlebitis in her left leg.'

'How awful,' said my aunt. 'Who are we talking about?'

'The Larmers,' said Hunter softly. 'You know, from Seaforth Grange.'

I could not believe my ears. That a human being, someone who could smile and eat cake and hold hands with girls, was prepared to be on terms with the Binker and his wife was astonishing enough. Yet weirder was referring to the Binker as Robbie, as though he actually liked the man. But to be sorry when Mrs Binker was in pain; this was going too far.

'I try to see them whenever I go back to visit my parents in Malvern,' said Hunter. 'A wonderful pair. Such a shame in a way that they did not have children; and yet, as Margot is always saying, the school is their family. We're all their children in a way, aren't we, Julian?'

The truth was that any child born to the Binkers would, in a decent society, have been taken away immediately and put into the hands of the State. The thought that, by their system of tyranny, persecution and sexual perversion, the Binkers were models of how good parents should behave beggared belief. It silenced me.

'I don't think Julian got on awfully well with Mr Larmer, did you, old thing?' asked my aunt.

'Ah,' said Hunter. Once more, the indulgent smile to conciliate a difficult customer. 'A pity. Most Old Seaforthers retain quite an affection for Robbie. He was a great friend of both my parents before I ever went to the school.'

'What does your father *do* in Malvern?' A match point, to judge from her expression of triumph. But Hunter lobbed it back across the net with nonchalance.

'My father's retired. He has been for a very long time.'

But it wasn't singles. It was mixed doubles.

'What *did* he do?' asked my uncle. That surely won them the match?

Not so. Felicity, waiting by the net, slammed her father's ball back into the other court.

'What on earth does it matter what people's fathers do?' she asked crossly. 'Anyway, we're off now. We thought we'd have another hour with the boxes before Raphael changes for dinner.'

The mystery of what Hunter *père* did for a living was never revealed. Years afterwards, someone told me that he had been something big in chocolate. I don't know if that was true.

For the next couple of weeks, Felicity and Hunter continued to work together on the Lampitt Papers. I did not see much more of them together but, from her absences, it was safe to infer that Felicity was getting deeper and deeper *in* to whatever it was she and Hunter were in together. Her parents began to speak openly about the possibility that she and Hunter might get married. Then, from something Sargie had said to Uncle Roy, the imminent announcement of their engagement seemed certain. I don't know exactly what he'd said to Uncle Roy, but it was a prediction to the effect that we should be hearing wedding bells before long; and, since the prediction fell from the lips of a Lampitt, we all took it as infallible. I even began to wonder what it would be like when Hunter was – as I thought of it – a member of the family.

But this was not to be.

One morning, Sargie appeared at the Rectory. On his sporadic visits to my uncle's house, he never bothered to ring the doorbell. He always walked into the front hall and yelled 'Roy!' in the tone other people would reserve for addressing dogs.

'That's Sargie,' said Uncle Roy, putting down his porringer.

It being the hour of breakfast, he was still wearing his cassock and bands, having come over to the house directly from church. He hurtled to his Master's call and the rest of us – Felicity, Aunt Deirdre, me – sat in the kitchen and heard the two men talking.

'I've told you. Just buggered off.'

'But he'll be back.'

'Didn't say so.'

'He can't just have *gone*,' said Uncle Roy.

'It doesn't worry me. I'm in two minds about his nosing through all Jimbo's things and I think the idea of writing a biography of Jimbo is simply crackers. Told him so. No, the worst of it all is, he'd promised to drive me into Norwich this morning, and now he isn't here . . .'

'I can always drive you.'

'Could you, my dear? It would help.'

Realising from this exchange that Hunter was being discussed, Felicity jumped to her feet. Now it was just Aunt Deirdre and I, sitting alone in the kitchen and listening to the three voices echoing tragically round the hall.

'Raphael's not gone away today, surely?' Felicity's voice.

'That's why I came round, darling girl.'

'But he'll be back? When did he say he'd be back?' Felicity sounded not so much angry or incredulous as frightened.

An expression of tenderness came into Sargie's voice as he said, 'He did ask me to come and tell you that he was going.'

'But we haven't nearly finished the work on the papers and he never said anything to me. He wouldn't just go off and *leave* like that.'

By now Aunt Deirdre and I had come out to join the party, and we all stood round Felicity in a circle.

'Oh, there's no need for you all to *stare!*' she exclaimed. Making a poor concealment of her distress, she hurried upstairs.

'Oh dear,' said Aunt Deirdre.

'He'll be back, you see,' said Uncle Roy. 'They probably had a very slight tiff.'

'That's what I came to say, my dear.' There was a look of real sorrow in Sargie's long, lugubrious face. 'He may come back, but something tells me it won't be soon.'

Aunt Deirdre and Uncle Roy both spoke at once. He said, 'But Felicity and he were more or less . . .' And she said, 'Oh, this is the *limit!*'

Sargie shrugged. How much he had been taken into Hunter's confidence, it was impossible to say. How much, indeed, was there to confide?

'It puts *me* in the most frightful spot.'

'*You*, Sargie? Oh, *really* – what about poor Felicity?'

'You see, he's made me promise not to give the poor girl his address for the next six months. And I am her godfather.'

Hunter's departure had an appalling effect on Felicity. The simple way of describing it would be to say that she went back to the beginning and became as morose and taciturn as she had been at the age of fourteen. But whereas her former silences were just grumpy and annoying, there was now something definitely tragic about her. She was hugging to herself an awful, private grief.

'He'll be back – I'm sure he'll be back,' said her father.

'Oh, you just don't *understand*.'

She did not eat. She had endless baths. By the look of her, she did not seem to be sleeping.

'Are you quite sure you're okay, old thing?' asked her mother on Felicity's last morning at home. 'I'm sure you shouldn't be going back to Cambridge on your own.'

It was obvious that Felicity was the reverse of okay, but her unhappiness was so terrible, so heartbreaking to witness, that I guessed that her parents almost welcomed her departure. Some days later, I myself went back to boarding school.

*   *

Aunt Deirdre said, 'We should never have let her go.'

This remark was made some months later, towards the end of October. When she said it, Uncle Roy looked more pained and sheepish than I have ever seen a man look. I was home for half term, when we had a week off school. By then, the Felicity drama, which had begun for me as a farce when I had roared with laughter at the very idea of her being in love, had plunged into tragedy and sordidity.

Felicity was home again but staying in bed all the time. I had absolutely no idea what was wrong with her. Given her parents' habitual policy of treating everything as a secret, their silence in the matter did not strike me as particularly suspicious. They would have been just as 'hush-hush' about a minor gastric upset or a bout of 'flu and enjoined me not to mention it in the village.

Even so, on this occasion, they were pretty pressing about the need for discretion.

'You're not to mention Felicity is in the house. Not to anyone in the village,' said my aunt.

'We're not even telling your Uncle Sargie. It would only upset him,' said Uncle Roy.

'It's rather upset *us*,' snapped my aunt. She clearly thought this was no moment to be considering Sargie's feelings. 'It's upset poor old Fliss.'

This childhood abbreviation of Felicity's name was hardly ever used now. It betokened a feeling of great tenderness in my aunt. But still I did not twig what was going on.

'It's not catching, is it, what Felicity's got?'

'Well . . .' My uncle seemed doubtful.

'Only I've got the lead role in the school play this term and I don't want to . . .'

'Of course you can go in and see her,' said Aunt Deirdre. 'But be gentle. She's not up to much.'

Just before I put my head round her bedroom door, it occurred to me that something really awful might have happened to her – like having burns all over her face. That was just the sort of thing her parents would not be able to bring themselves to mention.

But she looked reasonably normal. The flushed ethereal beauty which had momentarily possessed her when she believed herself to be loved by Hunter had vanished. She had gone back to being slightly plain and now, for the first time, she was inclining to be scrawny. All the pudge which she used to share with her mother had gone. Her skin was waxy and shone in the gloom of her bedroom. The dark rings under her eyes looked like becoming a permanent feature. She was flopped against the pillows. In one hand there was a *Daily Telegraph* but she was not reading it.

'I wondered if there was anything you needed?' I began gingerly.

Felicity's face made it obvious, even to a sixteen-year-old cousin, that there were many things she needed – things like love, different parents, a happy temperament: all things I was helpless to supply.

'Hallo,' she said, slightly as if there was a shared joke between us. 'What's happening outside?'

'Nothing much.'

There was an achingly long pause.

'I've hurt them so much, Ma and Pa. I mean, apart from all the pain it's caused me, I don't think they'll ever recover.' She spoke slowly, bleakly.

'They're just worried – hoping you'll soon be better.'

She opened her eyes very wide at the idiocy, the sheer ignorance, displayed by this remark.

'I'll never really get over this.'

'Nonsense. You will.'

'I just feel . . .' She looked away.

'What?'

'Oh, it doesn't matter any more what I feel.'

Years later, Felicity herself told me that she had been found by a fellow graduate student in her lodgings in Cambridge. She had been bleeding badly and was rushed at once to Addenbrookes Hospital. A week or so later, she was rescued by her parents. She had tried to keep it all from them, but the college had found out. They had behaved humanely. At that period, they could so easily have dismissed her from the college and brought her academic career to an end.

'The Principal's been very good. They're letting me stay – Ma told you that?'

Since at that time I was unable to guess why my cousin had been taken ill, I was equally unable to guess why the college authorities should have been anything but 'good'. I did not realise that Felicity had broken the law of the land.

When one takes into account how inward and shy Felicity was, how she needed to summon up reserves of bravery to ask for a cup of tea in a café or a ticket from a railway booking clerk, it is almost unimaginable how she was brave enough to procure this treatment for herself. Just saying the words would have been an achievement of extraordinary courage. Having sold her few War Loan bonds and cleared out her account at the post office, she had obviously been able, just, to get the services of some low-level incompetent. She never revealed to me how this person, who lived in London, had been introduced to her.

At sixteen, I hardly knew what an abortion was. Knitting needles and back kitchens were something boys did not talk about at a boarding school. For almost all of us, sex was a thing of pure fantasy. Its realities and consequences never had to be dwelt upon. I am fairly sure that, after my summer with Barbara, I was the only boy in my house who had even the most rudimentary experience with a girl.

I think that, at some stage of our awkward little conversation, Felicity realised that I was completely ignorant of her reasons for being in bed.

'What about you, anyway?' she said.

'School's awful except for the drama.'

'What's that Mr Treadmill putting on this time?'

'It's a play by John Ford.'

'Oh yes?'

All at once, it was I who became shy.

'Hope you've got a good part,' she said.

'The lead.'

I laughed nervously. I hoped she was not going to press me to say the title of the play. She lay there looking so terrible; it was as if the Hunter experience had tortured her physically, as well as in spirit.

'You do the obscurest plays,' she said. 'What was it last time? *Ralph Roister* something?'

'Treadmill says this one's tremendously hackneyed but it's a wonderful play with great poetry,' I said.

'Oh, *Hamlet*?' There was almost sprightliness in her voice as she made the suggestion.

'No,' I said, '*The Broken Heart*.'

SIX

It seems as if it is going on for ever, childhood. Then, like a bad dream, it is over. With the arrival of morning, you lie there. All the monstrousness which has possessed your mind during the hours of darkness is stilled and tamed. Whatever horrors the coming day will bring, there will be nothing so garish, nothing so raw. This is not because life's external events get better as the years pass; nor, conversely, because the outward events of childhood are necessarily miserable. It is because the dreamlike self-concern and self-absorption of childhood can never be recaptured during adulthood except in cases of extreme mental disturbance. Henceforward, other people and events not directly relevant to oneself take on sharper outlines.

Belonging to my own particular generation, I had a last staging post to serve in the English Gulag: two years of National Service. No one ever supposed it pleasant. But it was far worse for the boys who had enjoyed 'normal' childhoods, with parents, homes and all. Most of the men I met during my basic training had never slept a night away from their mother's house. For me, the discomfort of army life, the rudeness of the N.C.O.s, the pointless discipline, the blancoing of things which did not need to be white, the hurrying to do in five minutes things which could easily have taken an hour (if they were worth doing at all), were all just an extension of the insane patterns of life which had begun when I first met the Binker.

At school, it was hard not to fall for the con trick that it actually mattered whether you did 'well' or 'badly'. By the system of marks, exams, reports and so forth, it was instilled into us that if we did not do 'well' at school we would not do 'well' when we left. The army, transparently, was not like that. I had no wish to become a professional soldier. I decided just to get by. The system was designed to break young men, but I had been broken years before beyond hope of repair. I joined the Norfolk Regiment and did my basic training somewhere near Northampton. The huge sprawling camp was a sort of hell: hundreds of Nissen huts stretched line upon line in a bleak bit of hunting country, where it never stopped drizzling for six weeks and where the sergeant-majors never stopped shouting their idiot instructions. At the earliest possible opportunity I renounced my status as a potential officer and took the slithery course of not-really-trying. This was a mistake since, in the army (perhaps in other areas, too?), not-really-trying is just as much effort as trying-really-hard. The only difference between the two modes of activity is that not-really-trying receives no reward. After a while, it gets depressing, too – but then so does just about everything. Shoddy equipment. Lazy drill. It was not long before the R.S.M. announced in front of all the others that I was a 'nasty-low-down-piece-of-shit-what-did-I-say-that-you-are?'

One of my greatest good fortunes in life, never having made up my mind what sort of person I am, is that I am usually ready to go along with other people's opinions of me. Not because I think they are necessarily right, but because in any area so nebulous as psychological portraiture one person's guess is likely to be as good as another's; or, if not, anyway of interest. The willingness with which I accepted the sergeant-major's assessment of my personal character was written down as insubordination. You couldn't win.

But there was far more leave from the army than you got from school. We had every weekend off during the six weeks of basic training. I returned regularly and thankfully to the Rectory at Timplingham, refreshed above everything else (though it sounds a ridiculously priggish thing to say) by the fact that my uncle and aunt were not in the habit of swearing. The unimaginative use of bad language in every sentence by just about everyone I met in the army had a tremendously lowering effect on the spirits.

'Martin – my cousin who fought at Ypres – said the worst thing about the trenches was the way the men peed in their boots,' said Sargie, fairly far gone on dry martinis. Uncle Roy and I were lunching at the Place and Sargie's sister was there, Sibs Starling.

She was a surprisingly tall woman. I do not know how the legend began that she was a 'complete doormat'. It is not a phrase which would seem immediately appropriate to anyone who had actually met Lady Starling. My uncle, however, had thus described her so frequently that I was unable to disentangle her from the phrase. It clung to her like an Homeric epithet and had made me envisage her as tiny, cowering.

I should think she was five-foot-nine. Once, she must have been dazzlingly beautiful. She had a much rounder face than Sargie's, with deep-set eyes and a cupid's bow of a mouth. Like her brother, she smoked her cigarettes through a holder. Though she was, perhaps, nearing sixty, she retained the mannerisms of a much younger woman, even of a teenage girl.

'Sargie, don't talk about pee just before we eat.'

'Night after night they did it, apparently.'

'We've heard it fifty times before.'

'But in their boots. Can you imagine? That's the dear old human race for you. They deserve Vernon and his Labour Party.'

'Sargie, you are awful.'

She evidently enjoyed the awfulness, but whether for its own sake, or because it threw into relief her own cool good manners, who could say?

Much later on, when we had gone into the meal and were eating chops and mashed potatoes, Sargie still reverted to the subject of urination in boots.

'I mean, just imagine, putting your shoes on in the morning. It's the great difference between the working classes and everyone else. They won't see ahead. That's why kindly people like Vernon – and myself in the old days – felt we had to do all their planning for them.'

The lunch was memorable to me not just because it was the first time I'd met the doormat, but because it represented a sort of watershed in Sargie's relationship with Uncle Roy. In a way, it was the beginning of the end. Given Sargie's deviousness, my uncle's secretiveness, the wonder is that I followed anything of what was going on.

What had happened was this. Some time after running away from Felicity, Hunter had resumed contact with Sargie and, little by little, wormed his way into the older man's confidence. None of us knew anything about it at the time, but Hunter had started to persuade Sargie that it was not really safe to keep Jimbo's trunks and boxes lying around in Timplingham. The damp was beginning to get at them. It was agreed that Hunter should take the more 'significant' of the boxes into safe-keeping.

By the time I had begun my National Service, I suppose Hunter had probably purloined about three-quarters of the Lampitt papers. None of us knew about it, because Sargie had chosen to keep his friendship with Hunter a secret. With the whole sad episode of Felicity in the background, he could not very well have talked about it to Uncle Roy. Merely to have *seen* Hunter after that would have been, and perhaps was, a species of betrayal.

I was away from home so much that all subsequent developments – of how, in effect, Sargie let Hunter take him over – were unknown to me. I never did discover how much Uncle Roy knew. Very little, I suspect. Even if he had known that Sargie had admitted Hunter into his confidence, my uncle would never have spoken about it. The whole thing was too wounding on too many levels.

Sargie started to say that he found the countryside unutterably depressing, always had, that he wanted a little place in London, couldn't afford one. There was no one of any interest in Timplingham and he had spent his entire life there doing nothing except watch rain drip down windowpanes.

It was against this background, some of which was known and most of which was unknown, that the luncheon happened. Talk was undirected. Sargie, becoming increasingly inaudible, commiserated with me for being in khaki. His sister and Uncle Roy talked about Lampitts. Sibs had three children. The two Starling boys were by now in their early thirties. One of them had done frightfully well in the war and another – or perhaps the same one – had done equally well in the City. There was a much younger sister – Anne – who was a student. Presumably she was doing well too – that seemed to be the way with the Starlings.

Like Sargie, Sibs mumbled. The quiet voice was partly, perhaps, responsible for the doormat idea. There was nothing submissive in her general demeanour. Quite suddenly, when most of the meal was over, she turned to me and said, with a smile, 'Do tell Sargie he's being a complete idiot.'

'Oh, shut up, Sibs.'

'No, tell him,' said Lady Starling.

I looked at her glass. Then at her face. We had been drinking water. Before the meal she had had, at most, two glasses of sherry.

'Why?' I ventured.

'This mad idea of getting rid of this place.'

'What!' Uncle Roy almost shouted. 'What's this? Getting rid of the Place? Sargie! Honest*lee*! This can't be true!'

'Suppose you have to know. Tell them, Sibs. Too bloody sad. I can't talk about it.'

'No,' said Sargie's sister, firmly refusing to let him off the hook. 'You have got to tell them. They will tell you what a crazy, wicked idea it is. Just think of what Mother would say.'

At the mention of their mother, Sargie winced.

'Always said . . . only a bought house.'

I had the idea that Sargie might be pretending to be more plastered than he actually was, to let him off having to share with us his plans for Timplingham Place. After all, it was his house, to do with as he chose. But the idea of Timplingham without Lampitts was, from Uncle Roy's point of view, unthinkable. Although it had always been obvious and I had laughed about it, it only then became abundantly clear to me that the Lampitts, and Sargie in particular, represented the emotional centre of my uncle's life. If someone had threatened to shoot his wife and daughter – I am not saying that he would have reacted to the news with indifference, but the effect could not have been more cruel than the possibility of the Lampitts clearing out.

'Thing is, place very expensive.' It was only just possible to hear Sargie's tiny little voice. 'Builder's been. Dry rot. Floors, the lot.'

'You're making no kind of sense,' said Sibs sharply. 'All this started just because a ceiling fell down – when was it?'

'Six weeks ago,' said Uncle Roy. 'And then there were those burst pipes last winter, weren't there, Sargie? But look, you always get things going wrong with old houses. Half our ceilings are on the point of collapse at the Rectory.'

'Exactly!' said Sibs. 'You see, Sargie, you can patch up here and there.'

'You don't have to pay for it, live here, feeling bloody miserable all the time, whole place falling into ruins.'

The semi-coherence and near inaudibility of Sargie's remarks were the more disconcerting because he did not look drunk. Sitting at the head of the table in that nice old dining room, he looked positively distinguished. He might have been a judge presiding over a rather grand private meal at a club, or the Master of a Cambridge college conducting a meeting of his governing body. He never went red or dribbled at the lips. Alcohol made his voice quieter and gradually obliterated his sense of humour. It also tended to have a poor effect on his legs but at present he was not trying anything so ambitious as standing. I realised, looking at his tumbler, that he had been filling up with Gordon's while the rest of us drank water.

The dining room at the Place was panelled and more beautifully proportioned than any room I can remember. It had been rather spoilt, forty years earlier, by old Mrs Lampitt who had painted it a powdery shade of flat, pale blue. The paint had been slapped on thick on all available surfaces. Now, just as thick, it was coming off. Flakes the size of cabbage leaves curled in the middle of panels to reveal scrubs of whiteish wood or, further up, blackened expanses of mushroomy wall. The pictures, mainly of Mrs Lampitt's side of the family (they had been Bainbridges), were blackened and matted with years of exposure to damp and cigar smoke.

'All right for you, Sibs. Lovely house in Chelsea. You don't have to live here all the year round.'

'Nor do you.'

'Do.'

'You don't.'

A nursery squabble.

His sister continued, 'You could come up to London if you

wanted. Jimbo always wondered why you came up so seldom. And that's the *other* silly thing.'

Once more, Lady Starling had turned in my direction and appeared to be appealing for my help against Sargie. This was just a conversational mannerism. She would have enlisted the alliance of the sideboard if she had been alone with her brother. She raised her eyebrows at his folly.

'What's that?' I asked.

It made Sargie sober up fast.

'We're not going into all *that* now, Sibs, so just shut up for once, can't you?'

Sibs cast a glance at Uncle Roy and appeared to get the message. It was lost on me at the time. Sargie meant that she was not to talk about Jimbo and therefore the Lampitt Papers, and therefore Hunter, in front of Uncle Roy.

But I did get a *frisson* of unpleasantness, the first sign that everything between the two friends was about to change. That wonderful double act – Sargie and Roy – which had been playing in the background of my life for as long as I could remember, was about to be wound up. Timplingham Place was threatened. Things fell apart; the centre could not hold.

A little more light was shed on the matter in the car going to Norwich. Since she was driving away in any case, Lady Starling offered me a lift to the station and I cut short my weekend leave in order to go with her.

'My brother is a very selfish man,' she said to me, drawing in her cheeks as she spoke. Against the engine noise of the Princess I was not sure that I was catching every word. Her beautiful lips hovered around the words, sucked them like boiled sweets.

'Everything in our family has always had to revolve round him. Always. He was Mother's favourite, of course. You know that. Spoilt him, absolutely. I think it is because there was such a gap between him and Vivian. Sargie and I were the babies. And now he's doing this to Mother – to us.'

It seemed coarse to remind Lady Starling that their mother was dead and beyond minding what happened to Timplingham.

'What's Sargie up to exactly?'

'Selling the Place, I suppose. There's nothing we can do to

stop him unfortunately. I wish Roy would stop him. He used to have such an influence. We even thought Sargie might have become – you know, religious. Are you religious, Mr Ramsay?'

'No.'

I had never been called 'Mister' before by anyone. Instead of taking it as a compliment, I took it as a rebuke for referring to her brother just as 'Sargie'. But I could hardly say 'Uncle Sargie' to her – when he wasn't my uncle; and having known him for so long as 'Uncle Sargie' I could hardly have called him 'Mister Lampitt'.

'No, Roy's lost his influence over my brother, I am afraid. Sargie was so . . . well, you know, after Felicity. I don't myself believe that that was my brother's fault.'

'I'm sure not.'

I was amazed that anyone could have suggested such a thing, but also appalled that Felicity's troubles, which I had considered so secret, should be a matter of general knowledge and discussion.

'He might' – she really sucked at the next few words – 'have kept more of an eye on them. A man and a girl in a library.'

With the last syllables of 'library', her voice sank to silence and her lips became so pursed as to disappear momentarily altogether, before opening out again into their wide selves. I thought there was something predatory about her face: a hawk, not a starling. I stored the joke up, instinct telling me that the truth it contained would be useful to me in the future.

'I don't like the sound of Mr Hunter one bit,' she said, shoving the Princess into second in order to overtake a tractor. When we were past it and on a straight bit of road again, she said, 'You know all about my brother Jimbo, I suppose?'

'I have read his books. I knew that Raphael Hunter wanted to write about him.'

'I mean about Jimbo himself. His weakness.'

'No, no. I never met . . .' After the 'Sargie' solecism, I could hardly say 'Jimbo'. But it would seem equally absurd to say, to his own sister, 'I never met Petworth Lampitt.'

She obviously thought better of any more talk on the subject of Jimbo's weakness, whatever it was. At first I guessed it was drink. Then she said, 'You can never trust them. Horrid little men.'

'Who?'

'People like Mr Hunter. Ugh!'

She shrugged and shivered theatrically, a schoolgirl down whose gymslip someone had just put a slug.

'Really, Lady Starling, there's no need to drive me all the way into the station.'

'I had no intention of doing so.'

'I can walk from here.'

'I know.'

She spoke as if we were coevals and that she could afford to be rude to me. Older people, I've found, are usually polite to the young. Sibs spoke as if she *was* young.

She switched off the engine for a minute.

'It's nice we've met,' she said. 'I need allies. Perhaps you'll be an ally in the future. Being the youngest member of the Lampitt family isn't easy.'

She gave me a weak smile. There was something very like sexual attraction between us which, in spite of her words, bred instant distrust. I realised that she did not like me and that I found her terrifying. It seemed nothing to do with the present, but rather to be bred in us by instinct as the preparation for some future stage of the journey.

On my way back to Brentwood in the train, I reflected that there were probably at least forty first cousins who could be described, more or less accurately, as members of the Lampitt tribe and who were a good deal younger than Sibs Starling. But she regarded herself as the youngest of the Lampitts.

I thought it was crude of her to hint that Hunter and Jimbo had had some sort of queer relationship – if that was what she *was* implying. I was curiously innocent about such matters. English boarding schools are supposed to be hotbeds of all that kind of thing, but it was not until I joined the army that I came across the phenomenon in any very vigorous form. Bloom was the first thoroughgoing homosexual I ever got to know; and at that stage I had no means of knowing whether or not he, or anyone else I had ever met, was 'typical'. Certainly, his exploits made anything I had ever heard about at school seem pretty tame. I am not just talking about achievements in the flesh. It was amazing to me, for example, that someone of only my age could be so culturally well-informed. He knew all about opera, which was something of which I was totally ignorant. I had simply had no opportunity to find out about it. I had never seen an opera. My uncle did not possess a gramophone.

I came across Bloom after my basic training was over and I had been transferred to a camp at Brentwood to await my next posting. He and I were in rather similar positions, being men of allegedly officer material who had elected to stay in the ranks.

Most of my memories of Brentwood are of peeling potatoes and listening to Bloom's extraordinary reflections on the universe, interlaced with accounts of his erotic adventures. Clearly, he was preparing to become a flamboyant undergraduate. Educated at one of the big old London dayschools (Haberdashers, I think), Bloom had got a scholarship to the university which was waiting for him when his two years in khaki were up. I envied him this pretty acutely, having nothing arranged for myself. His company certainly made a change from the amiable, but on the whole somewhat neanderthal members of my own platoon. By way of small talk, many of my fellow soldiers were capable only of grunts, usually mouthing a very few synonyms for sexual intercourse. Basic training with them had been what is called an 'experience', but I did not feel that I was making friends for life. Then, spud-bashing in Brentwood, I found myself sitting next to the dark, sharp-featured and slight figure of William Bloom. After two months in which conversation had been, to put it mildly, limited, it was a startling change to hear someone say in the tones of a flutey dowager, 'This kitchen is positively Stygian!'

All my reactions to Bloom in the first instance were hostile: what he would have called predictably provincial. I was embarrassed by his willingness to show off in front of the men, by his refusal to adapt himself to his surroundings. Most of them would have had no trouble with the word 'kitchen', so long as no one asked them to write it down. But to use a word like 'Stygian' in their presence was to emphasise the gulfs which lay between us.

I had found it was perfectly possible to get on with the other men in the ranks. At various points I even tried to persuade myself that, despite differences of speech and background, we were all the same really. We all wanted to get through army life unscathed. We were all frightened by the experience, all mildly resentful of it. Nearly all of us responded in the classic fashion of youth by false irony and humour. That was what my first few months in the army were like. Some of them mocked the posh way I talked, but there was no nastiness.

Bloom was something different. A number of them hated him from the start, under the impression, which I think was totally misplaced, that he was trying all the time to make them feel small.

I first became aware of him during some absurd piece of drill.

'Squ——aaaad! Move to the left in twos!'

The corporal gave this order in the rhythmical, exaggerated tone which N.C.O.s all adopted when giving commands. Bloom, a strikingly handsome, small, dark man, looked much older than the rest of us, though he was only my age. He was standing beside an amiable farmhand from the depths of Suffolk, ruddy-faced, muscular and stupid as hell. It was interesting to study this boy's face as Bloom said, perfectly audibly to everyone, 'Here we go, dear, with our *pas de deux*.' On another occasion, to a similarly uncomprehending listener, he said as we moved into quick march, 'Isn't this sheer *Aïda*?'

These outbursts cost him rebuke, sometimes even punishments, from the N.C.O.s. From his fellow soldiers such observations earned him ostracism and sometimes actual physical violence. He was not trying to be 'grand' and, in fact, as I learnt when I got to know him, Bloom was largely without social snobbery, if by that is meant a reverence for rank and title. The truth was that Bloom could not stop himself talking to his fellow soldiers in this way. He genuinely made no distinction between persons, which is why almost everyone found his company disconcerting.

At first, I thought it was not just silly, but offensive. When I later met up with him in the kitchens and began those conversations over the spud-bashing, I added to my distaste for his silliness a profound, physical revulsion from the seamier details of his erotic conquests. Like all great imaginations, Bloom's was one which found riches where the rest of us would have seen nothing at all. Many of his lovers, seen purely on the level of imaginative *trouvailles*, had a sort of brilliance. But I was so unused to the tastes he displayed that I was merely revolted and found myself hating Bloom as much as the other men did.

Then I told myself not to be such a stupid little prig and I began to concede, inwardly to myself, that Bloom was the first, the only, interesting thing to happen to me since I joined the army. The sexual talk was actually fascinating. When someone of roughly your own sexual persuasion is confiding in you, there is strictly speaking no interest in the talk at all. There may be collusion, but no *interest*. You understand what they are talking about before they say anything. As far as it extends their sympathy, the talk between two likeminded people on these levels is about as interesting as the song which some of the men at Brentwood liked to sing in the showers:

> I like eggs and bacon
> I like eggs and bacon.
> But if you think I'll tell you why
> You're fucking well mistaken.

What Bloom liked was altogether more imaginative and surprising.

'That little corporal from E Barracks squealed like a weasel when I got inside him last night. I said to him, "When on earth did you last go to the toilet?"'

'What did he say?' I chucked a finished spud into the huge vat of salted water which divided us.

'Talk about cleansing the Augean stables or dear David Herbert Lawrence' (he pronounced the name for some reason as if it were German, with an accent on the last syllable) 'purging the whatever it was.'

'He is like a weasel, Harker, now you mention it.'

'Never again, anyway.'

'I just can't understand what you see in them all. To me he is just a boring little man in spectacles. You presumably . . . I don't know . . .'

'Hear Mahler's Eighth Symphony in my head whenever I see him approach? No. I like to taste what talent there is going, that's all. You should try it – broaden your horizons.'

'There were one or two one-night stands in Northampton – before we came here,' I said.

'But they were girls, I expect.'

'Yes.'

'You're like the most boring type of provincial Englishman who'd rather starve when he goes abroad than eat any of the local dishes. Meat and two veg or nothing.'

I admitted that I was a person of very marked emotional limitations.

It wasn't all smut or opera, Bloom's talk. He had an admirable capacity for gossip. He seemed to know everything which was going on in the camp and, because he found it interesting, he was able to make it interesting: which N.C.O.s had got women into trouble, what was for lunch the next day, where we were likely to be sent on our foreign posting (Cyprus and Germany were the likeliest possibilities), everything. He also maintained an astounding capacity to keep in touch with what was going on in the outside world. He read theatre criticism and book reviews. He was the first person I ever met, incidentally, who had read Debbie Maddock's novel. First he talked about the reviews. 'A new star in the firmament apparently. One Deborah Arnott. I must read her when I next return to civilisation.'

After he had returned from his next weekend leave, he had indeed read *The Melon Garden*. It was only when I heard the title that I realised that Deborah Arnott was the same as our Debbie, the Wretched Woman of village-shop fame. From Bloom's description, I gathered that *The Melon Garden* was the story of a sexually attractive and highly imaginative young woman immured in a Norfolk village with a tediously mousey little schoolmaster husband.

'One identified with the more sub-Lawrence moments,' said Bloom. 'There is a memorable scene in a barn with a dairyman; but on the whole the quality of the prose was too painful.'

I had thought it would be a tremendous feather in my cap to claim acquaintance with the author, but Bloom seemed disappointingly unimpressed by my knowing her. He sniffed and said something quite noncommittal, as though we all knew novelists.

It was not Deborah Arnott, however, but Proust, in the Scott-Moncrieff translation, that Bloom was reading when I returned to the camp that afternoon, having parted with Lady Starling some hours before. In my recollection, soldiers spend most of their time, when they aren't doing soldierly things like drill, just lying on their beds. I suppose in the army you are tired most of the time – and, for those of us who weren't officers, there were no armchairs or comfortable mess where we could loll and smoke.

Bloom was arranged on his bed wearing a short-sleeved vest and some blue, checked overall-trousers, a memento of an afternoon in the stores with a member of the catering corps. He had stockinged feet. His serpentine posture was reminiscent of the Rokeby Venus. He threw down the little blue volume – *The Cities of the Plain* – and said,

'Oh, it's all too hideously true!'

'Proust? I've never managed to get started with him somehow. Sargie Lampitt reads him, I think.'

I had told Bloom all about the set-up at home. By now we were quite good friends. Funnily enough, he knew some distant Lampitt cousin. I began to tell him about meeting Sibs Starling. It was hardly headline news. I did not blame him for the look of abstraction which passed over his face. He responded to none of my Lampitt-prattle. Straightening out from the Rokeby posture and lying flat on the bed, he said between puffs of his cigarette, 'I'm in love.'

'Another weasel?'

'No, no.' He was perfectly serious. I almost wondered if he wasn't close to tears. 'I said in love. With weasels it's just like eating. One just fucks anything which happens to be there. I'm talking about love. The real thing. Shakespeare's *Sonnets, Tristan und Isolde, La Prisonnière*, the whole horror story. Has it ever happened to you?'

'I think it did when I was very young.'

I began to talk about Miss Beach. What I had felt for her, and in a way still felt, was on a much more exalted scale than anything I had felt for Barbara, or for the one-night stands in Northampton. I thought that I understood the distinction he was drawing between the 'real thing' and the merely available. He wasn't listening to anything I said. He interrupted my discourse with a loud moan.

'Oh, my *God!*'

For the first time in our conversations, he was totally serious. For a moment of sheer egotistical horror, I thought that he was going to say that he was in love with me. We were alone in the dormitory. It was hours before most of the men would be back from their weekends. But the next few sentences dispelled any such anxieties.

'You know the way love makes you frightened? I'm terrified of him. Terrified I'll say or do something which will put him *off* me.'

'You still haven't said who he is.'

'I spotted him the first day I arrived here. Our eyes met. Has that ever happened to you? I *knew*. And yet I didn't know. That's the awful thing about being queer. You can never be sure. He's only spoken to me once.'

'He's a soldier, yes?'

'I thought and thought of ways we might meet. I've written him letters, but of course posted none. Then we just happened to bump into each other in a pub down the road.'

'Oh yeah?'

'It wasn't *like* that, fuck you. He asked me what regiment I was in and we started to say what hell army life is. He's applied to do this Russian course. It's a cinch. They send you off and teach you Russian – it's really almost like being at university, he said, only without the awful people.'

'Has he been to university?'

'No. He's like me. He's got a place when he's finished with all this nonsense.'

'So you have a rosy future together?'

'Don't even say it, not as a joke! Julian, he's just so *beautiful*.'

I wondered, rather crudely, how far intimacy with this Adonis had progressed, but it did not seem an appropriate line of inquiry. There was a quality of reverence and sadness about the way Bloom described his new friend which made it obvious that things were still at a romantically nebulous stage.

'The thing is, I'm frightened that, if I show him how much I mind, it will scare him off.'

'He doesn't feel the same about you?'

'I don't know. I mean, he wouldn't have started to talk to me in the bar if he hadn't – well, *liked* me. On the other hand . . . Normally I hate intensity. God, I'd run a mile if I thought some silly little queen had got serious about *me*.'

'You would?'

'Of course. *Hate* it. The trouble is, I can't tell if he's bent. I can't even tell if he realises that is what I'm trying to tell. Do you see what I mean?'

'It sounds complicated. You hope he is – bent?'

'Well, everyone is really,' he said.

'I don't agree.'

'It's just that some men, most perhaps, have been conned by their mothers into thinking that they actually *need* women. Half the babies' – he made a gesture towards the row of empty beds in the dormitory – 'think they can't open a tin of peas or iron a shirt, so they fuck a woman and she in return acts as their servant.'

'If you think that, you're barmy. People really do fall in love with girls, *fancy* them, William. Most people aged twenty aren't thinking about ironing.'

'You only look on the surface of things.'

'That's where most of life happens.'

'You're so wrong,' he said, dangling one stockinged foot over his raised knee. Then he said, 'I'd do *his* ironing for the rest of his life.'

'When are you seeing him again?' I asked.

'That's just it. He said he might be around in the same bar at about seven o'clock this evening. The thing is, Julian, it wasn't really an arrangement. He just said it casually. I can't tell whether he really wants to see me again, or whether he was just being polite.'

'Would you like me to come along with you?' I asked. 'If he stands you up, we can just get drunk together. If he does turn up, I can make a tactful exit.'

Bloom looked slavishly grateful for this offer which was made, I regret to say, less in a spirit of altruism than one of pure curiosity. I was fascinated to see the beauty which had been able to transform my loftily cynical, world-weary friend into a spoony teenager.

At about six we were dressed and ready. A few minutes later we walked out of the camp and down the bleak, arterial road which led into Brentwood. The pub where the assignation had been made turned out to be one of those featureless buildings, vaguely neo-Georgian in inspiration, which were put up during the 1930s all over greater London. The lounge bar was carpeted and panelled. The windows were too high for looking out of.

It was hard to see why anyone chose to go there, but there were some customers. At one table, two men and two women, all aged about fifty, drank shorts and took it in turns to tell smutty jokes. The women appeared to be married to the men, which made their presence in that place all the more mysterious. After all, they had homes to go to. There were a couple of loners at the bar – a man in a mackintosh drinking his way slowly through a pint of bitter and a seedier figure, more bottle-nosed, who was getting through a lot of whisky.

Since I now believed that Bloom's preferences could extend in just about any direction, I looked at each of these figures interrogatively, wondering which of them had inspired this besotted devotion of his.

'Oh, no,' he said, reading my looks, 'none of these.'

'How did you come to find this place?'

'It's so near the camp. I just dropped in here one evening. Most of the men avoid it for some reason.'

'For quite a lot of reasons that I could think of. What'll you have?'

'Half, please.'

'Bitter?'

'Yah. I want to stay sober in case . . . Christ this is him.'

The door of the lounge opened and a tall, languorous figure wearing the uniform of a lieutenant in the Middlesex Regiment entered. His face was conspicuous for its overhanging eyelids, great ovals over each eye, and for his huge mouth. As he approached, I looked at him purely from the point of view of curiosity, to see what constituted (in Bloom's eyes) the ideal of beauty. But, by the time he had reached us and said, 'Ramsay, what on earth are you doing here?', I had recognised him as Darnley.

He had grown about eight inches since we last met and he no longer wore specs. I knew that time had made analogously dramatic adaptations to my own appearance.

'Clever of you to recognise me.'

'You've met *before*?' Bloom asked.

He glared at me with angry suspicion. It was several weeks before I could get him to believe that Darnley and I had not somehow set the whole thing up as some kind of prank. Also, never having himself attended an English boarding school,

Bloom assumed that promiscuity in these places was so universal that Darnley and I must be ex-lovers. He was unshakable
on the question. Not that it mattered. The whole moment in
the pub was jarring and unfortunate, calling in all three of us
for instant readjustments of what we had previously thought
about one another. It certainly changed my picture of Darnley
to think that he might hang about in bars in order to meet 'a
man like Bloom'. He for his part, as he confided in me years
later, assumed that I had been brought along as Bloom's 'fancy-
boy'.

'Bloom's having half of bitter, I'm having a pint. What'll it be
for you?' I asked.

'Mackeson's if I may.'

He smiled nervously and we all found ourselves a table in
the corner. When I came back with the drinks, Bloom was
grinning.

'Heard the news?' he said. 'Miles has just told me.'

'What?'

'Stalin's dead, horrible old shit.'

I had never heard anyone rejoice in another person's death
before and I was shocked by it.

'It just came on the news before I came out,' said Darnley.
'You surely aren't upset by it?'

'Well,' I laughed nervously and raised a glass, 'here's to Uncle
Joe.'

I knew absolutely nothing about Stalin. Being with the other
two, who were both somehow more sophisticated than I was,
I wondered whether I knew anything about anything. Perhaps
I should just clear off back to the camp and leave them to spend
the evening together as they chose. But, out of politeness, I
asked Darnley for his news. Since Seaforth Grange, he had
been to Westminster, won a scholarship to Oxford and somehow ended up with a commission. He was now on the point
of doing this Russian course, a mild bout of pneumonia having
prevented him from starting sooner. For all I knew, he still had
a sense of humour, but the anarchic little figure whom I had
liked so much at Seaforth Grange had sobered up a bit.

'How about you?'

I found that my biography could be contained in about three
sentences.

'Wants to go on the stage!' trumpeted Bloom.

I remembered Mrs Webb and Granny saying that this would be Darnley's destiny.

'Oh, yes?' he asked. It somehow seemed to fit in with my being with Bloom and, as he drained his glass slowly, I felt he was reassessing me, reconsidering all our years together.

'It's only one idea,' I said. 'I did quite a bit of acting at school. I know I'm good at it.'

'Curious thing,' said Bloom, 'is that he has hardly ever been to the theatre. Knows nothing about it. Now, dears – drinks!'

When Bloom went to the bar to buy his round, there was a gleam of the old Darnley. As soon as Bloom's back was turned, Darnley, without standing up, put one hand on his waist and managed, simply by squirming from side to side in his seat, to convey the mincing manner with which our friend walked. As a final flourish he lifted a limp hand and waved it about like a handkerchief.

I roared with laughter. There was some reassuring complicity in this. By the time Bloom brought the drinks back we were feeling more friendly towards each other, but sadly there seemed nothing to talk about. It was inevitable that we should fall back on memories of Seaforth Grange.

Our memories were slightly different. We both remembered the big things, like Darnley ordering a cart-load of manure to be dumped outside the chapel on Speech Day. But he had forgotten some of his more engaging little jokes.

'Do you remember "Fielding's quite a different boy"?'

'I remember Fielding,' he said.

Oddly enough, I didn't. I just remembered the joke. The boy Fielding was of no interest to me.

'His sister's a friend of one of my sisters.'

'I forgot you had sisters.'

'Two – and a step-sister.'

There was no point in explaining to him his own joke about Fielding. What made the memory sweet was the thought of Darnley and me as twelve-year-olds, sitting far out near the boundary of the cricket pitch while the umpire shouted at us.

'Do you remember that pathetic man Lollipop Lew?' I asked.

'The one who married the art mistress,' said Darnley.

'I don't know about that.'

'You know,' said Darnley. 'The one you were dotty about, or pretended to be.'

'I was.' I almost added, 'I am,' because the idea of Miss Beach marrying Lollipop Lew was surprisingly painful.

'Not Miss Beach?' I said. 'He didn't marry Miss Beach?'

'Is that what she was called? We called her Beryl, don't you remember? The plain one with glasses. I never knew whether you actually liked her or whether it was one of your teases.'

He smiled at Bloom conspiratorially, as though he too must have noticed my habit of saying things which I didn't mean.

'How do you know she married the French master?'

'Do you remember those awful lessons?' He laughed and put on his Lollipop Lew voice. '"Gee swiss, tew ayse . . ."' I remember them together. We all collected money for the wedding present. Surely you were there? No, of course, you left a term earlier than I did for some reason, didn't you?'

'I think I did.'

'She ran off before the end of the summer term, but by the next term she was back with Lollipop Lew. Probably there are lots of little Lollipops scampering all over the Malvern Hills by now. It was what? Five years ago? Six?'

That was a long time in our timescale.

'She was going to marry a man called Hunter,' I said. 'Then he went off with Vanessa, the matron.'

'My dears,' said Bloom, 'your school sounds so infinitely more exciting than mine.'

'I vaguely remember the Vanessa business.' He turned to Bloom by way of explanation. 'We had this rather marvellous matron who came and gave us good-night kisses in the dormitory. Really cuddled us. I suppose she was a bit of a nympho.'

'Like one,' said Bloom.

'Do you remember, we saw her with Mr Hunter when we went out to lunch together in Worcester? There was a tremendous fuss.'

'Oh, was there?'

He laughed and, seeing our glasses empty, went to buy his round at the bar. Obviously some memory of that day in Worcester had remained with him, because when he came back with our beer, he said, 'I hope your grandmother's all right?'

'She's fine. I saw her the other week.'

'Ramsay's got this marvellous granny,' said Darnley.

Now that I was almost grown up I was embarrassed by the hint of condescension here. I even nervously interpreted 'marvellous' to mean that Darnley recalled my grandmother's slightly accented London voice. Was he even confusing her with her much more Cockneyfied friend, Mrs Webb? Still, it was nice of him to ask.

'She liked you a lot,' I said.

'We had fish and chips together. You probably won't remember.'

'Of course I do,' I said. 'You know, Hunter – the man we saw with Vanessa – has cropped up since.'

'Who's Hunter?' said Darnley. I could tell he didn't give a damn. 'Oh yes, the chap who married the matron. No, I never really followed that. But the art mistress and Lollipop Lew. Look, let's stop calling each other by such damn silly names. I'm Miles, you're Julian.'

'And I'm William,' said Bloom.

'Yes,' said Darnley, 'of course you are.'

Since we were by now quits and had each bought a round, I rose tactfully after my third pint and said that I would leave them to it, get back to the camp. They wouldn't hear of it. However Bloom and Darnley had intended to pass the evening, my presence changed it. That was the first evening I got really drunk. One of them generously substituted whisky for beer when it was their turn to buy the drinks and after that the dingy little lounge bar began to sway like a stormy ocean. I can remember the swaying movements of the bar changing to swift revolutions, so that the coarse quartet at the next table began to spin round and round my head like whirling dervishes. And I can remember getting out to a grass verge more or less in time and being sick, partly on the grass, partly on my boots. I don't know exactly how I got to bed.

About a week later, Darnley left that camp and started his Russian course, and we did not meet up again until we were both in civvy street.

All love dies, except perhaps the love which parents feel for their children. When it is gone, a bit of oneself is left behind, irrecoverably lost. We *know* that we loved such and such a person; but the sensation itself and the being who actually did the loving, these cannot be brought back. Often, it is imaginatively impossible even to remember what it was that we loved about a particular person. In affairs of the heart, where Eros plays an obvious role, the switches can be violent, terrible, destructive. With friendship it is otherwise. Though some friendships last, sort of, for life, most don't and what the friends once had in common diminishes to something which exists only in memory or which atrophies into habit.

Poets like to tell us that love is everlasting and that 'what will survive of us is love'. But, even in the span of our earthly lives, we discover that love is the least permanent of things, the most subject to change and death. As I sobered up in the showers next morning, with a churning head and traces of vomit still discernible in my nostrils, the shocks of the previous night came back. First, meeting Darnley at all and wondering if he was queer. But worse than this was the thought of Miss Beach married and my feelings for Miles himself cooled. It was as sure a whiff of mortality as a death in the flesh.

It was a time of disruption and severance. In Timplingham, too, between Sargie and my uncle, the estrangement was becoming more pronounced. It had begun with the painfully delicate matter of Felicity and Hunter, but perhaps it was on the cards anyway that Sargie would eventually tire of Uncle Roy, or that my uncle would decide that his friend had for once gone too far.

I was stuck in the camp at Brentwood for longer than scheduled. There was some sort of hitch. We were all meant to have been flown out to Germany. We had our last weekend of leave and bid a fond farewell to our families. Then there followed three anti-climactic months in which we did nothing. Rumours started to fly about that we weren't going to Germany after all. Aden was mentioned. Cyprus. Africa. I hated the idea of any of these places. Some of the other boys were excited at the prospect of travel. I am often beguiled by the promise of future happiness, but on this occasion I wasn't. It was obvious to me that, wherever we went with the army, it would be identical to Brentwood. Only, abroad, it would be Brentwood with sunstroke, diarrhoea and the likelihood of getting shot added as tempting extras on the menu.

Throughout this more than usually dull period of waiting

about, my aunt wrote me her weekly letter, as she had done throughout my days at school. They looked the same, the Brentwood letters – the same, small Basildon Bond paper and envelopes bought at the village shop. But by her standards these letters became painfully frank. The cause of all the anguish was what was happening up at the Place.

Sargie had decided to buy a small flat in London. Sibs had found him one off Kensington High Street. He was not thinking of leaving the village altogether, but henceforward he would only be there occasionally. There was talk of putting Timplingham Place up for sale. Then it seemed that, in its present condition, the house would attract no buyers. My Uncle Roy and Sibs got together, and made Sargie promise never to sell the Place.

A little routine began to establish itself. Sargie, carrying Joynson-Hicks in a basket, set off for London each Monday or Tuesday and returned to Timplingham at weekends. Before long, predictably, he was saying that he missed the dear old village, hated the constrictions of the little flat, didn't know anyone in London any more.

It all began to look rather hopeful. My Uncle Roy even went to spend the odd night in Kensington to keep Sargie company and it seemed as if their friendship was on the mend. Then Joynson-Hicks took it into his head to wander off. Unfortunately, it was while Uncle Roy was in the flat and he was blamed. The whole neighbourhood was scoured, the Metropolitan Police informed. But Joynson-Hicks was lost in London and he never came back.

The incident precipitated an intense depression in Sargie. He returned to Timplingham with his grief and, just at the blackest period of this emotional decline, another ceiling collapsed at the Place. The builder was called and he proposed the final solution. Why not level Timplingham Place to the ground and replace it with a lovely new bungalow? Sargie could have central heating, toilets which flushed easily, all the trimmings.

My aunt told me of this proposal with many underlinings and exclamation marks. I assumed that no one in their right mind would demolish a beautiful, eighteenth-century mansion in order to construct a hideous bungalow: a fair assumption to make. I forgot that Sargie was not in his right mind – that he had never been in a worse mental condition since the original breakdown thirty or more years before.

Because of the delay over my next posting, I was allowed one last weekend leave. I returned to Norfolk at the height of summer, when the village was always at its most beautiful. The elms near the church were in full leaf, and all the parkland round the Place was lush and abundant – a canvas by Constable.

I could not have returned at a more dramatic moment. Even as my aunt and I came in at the Rectory front door, we found Sargie and my uncle in the middle of an acrimonious conversation. My first thought was one of pleasure that the worm had turned, because my uncle was showing real anger with Sargie. In my simple-minded way I had always seen the friendship as a matter of Sargie exploiting Uncle Roy. But Sargie needed Roy just as much as he was himself needed by my uncle. The dispute which I now witnessed was rather terrible. Both men were in pain and too much hung upon the outcome of their quarrel.

'I've said you were right all along, Roy.' Sargie was crestfallen, apologetic.

'I don't need telling. Anyone could see that it was a crazy idea, pulling down the Place. Sibs told you so. I told you. We all told you.'

'Please, Roy. Just this once.'

'Why *should* I be the one who makes all the decisions for you? I rang up Jackson last week and told him *not* to demolish the Place. That was because you asked me.'

'I wanted you to, Roy. You're better at telephoning than I am.'

Sargie still looked a highly distinguished, if rather grotesque old gentleman in a double-breasted suit of expensive cut and a large, silk bow-tie concluding his long, lugubrious face. His tone of pleading, however, was that of a child.

'You rang the builder,' said Uncle Roy, 'and flatly contradicted my message. You said you wanted the house pulled down after all.'

'I've told you, Roy. He rang me. He talked me into it. He even implied that I would be breaking a contract if I didn't have this ruddy bungalow built.'

'For God's *sake*, Sargie!' My uncle bellowed this. 'It's your house, not Mr Jackson's. Let him sue you. Just let him try!'

'Trouble is, I *do* want the bungalow. In a way. Don't think my health would stand another winter in that place.'

'Now you're just being silly.'

'Please, Roy. Ring Jackson, Roy. Please.'

'And then you'll ring him back and cancel all my instructions.'

'I'll kill myself if you don't ring Jackson.'

'Oh, you're *ridiculous!*'

'I see.' Sargie was by now hamming it up. 'Your oldest friend kills himself and it's just ridiculous. Something to laugh about. Ha, ha. You're all right, of course. You've got your family, you've got Deirdre.' He turned and looked at us. I don't know how long he had been aware of our presence. 'You've got your beastly religion to keep you going. I don't have anything, Roy. Nothing. And you won't even lift the telephone, not once, to save my Mummy's house.'

His lower lip was trembling.

'But why on earth can't *you* ring the builders?' asked my uncle. 'You can use my telephone, if you'd like.'

'But I only spoke to them an hour ago and confirmed that the demolition work will start tomorrow. I can't ring them back and cancel it all again. They'll think I'm barmy.'

'Suppose I did ring them,' said Uncle Roy. 'Then you would change your mind again in five minutes and want the opposite.'

'You could ring and say you were the Rector.'

'I am the Rector.'

'But you could sort of say – oh, that the demolition was forbidden. Say it was an historic building.'

'It is an historic building.'

'Oh, please, Roy. Please ring the builders.'

'I'm sorry, Sargie. I'm fed up with it all. I've had enough.'

There was a silence.

Then Sargie said, 'I see.'

It was one of the most painful exchanges I had ever witnessed. Sargie turned round, walked past my aunt and out into the Rectory drive. When he passed me, I saw that his eyes were full of tears. He shambled down the drive. I don't think he walked so unsteadily because he was tight. He was reeling from a blow. My uncle too looked as though he had been hit. Without either of them wanting it, they had just talked out of existence the two things they cared most about – Timplingham Place and their own friendship.

I saw my uncle's point of view. He had, apparently, already rung Mr Jackson four times, with four contradictory sets of instructions from Sargie. He was unable to make a fifth call. Now, unless Sargie made the call himself, The Place would be demolished. The furniture had been moved out. Most of it was in store, but the larger pieces had been given to Vernon Lampitt, who had succeeded to his father's title and now lived twenty miles away at Mallington Hall.

When Sargie had disappeared down the drive, my uncle shut himself up in his study and smoked a great deal until evensong.

At supper, he said, 'I just hope he'll have been shaken into making a decision for himself.'

'A decision! Sargie!' My aunt's derision was understandable.

'I think we'll find he'll have rung up the builder.'

'You mean, they won't be pulling down the Place after all?' I asked.

'Good old Sargie,' said Uncle Roy.

The next morning, the suspense of the situation woke me early. I was alone in the Rectory with my uncle and aunt, Felicity (by now a university teacher) being away doing her job.

When I came downstairs fully dressed at half-past seven, I found Aunt Deirdre sitting at the kitchen table anxiously drinking a cup of very strong tea.

'There's plenty in the pot if you want some.'

'No thanks.'

'You're not going over to the church are you?'

'No.'

'Your uncle has already gone.'

She herself, I noted, had more or less stopped going, except on Sundays. I wondered if Uncle Roy was alone over there, reciting the Ten Commandments to an empty building.

'Sargie won't let them pull down the house, will he?' I asked. I was very nearly nineteen. Still, this was one of those situations where one instinctively looked towards a grown-up for reassurance.

Aunt Deirdre just shrugged and pulled a face. I had always been aware that she did not really like Sargie. That morning, I got the distasteful impression that she almost hoped the Place would be destroyed, just so that everyone would blame its unfortunate owner for ever and ever.

'I always remember old Mrs Lampitt saying, "Sargie's a babe." He lets other people make all the difficult decisions for him. He's battened on to your uncle for twenty-five years. Now we are going to see what it's like when Sargie makes up his *own* mind for a change.'

'Isn't that a bit hard? Sargie's a sick man.'

'Who have you been talking to?'

'No one. It's just obvious that he is – well, weak.'

'All that psychology is a load of twaddle. Weak and sick are two very different things. No, I can remember his mother saying, "I'm afraid we've let Sargie have things too easy." How right she was – but whose fault was that?' Aunt Deirdre sipped from her breakfast cup furiously. 'And he was such a clever person, too,' she said. 'He could have been brilliant but it was all wasted.'

'I thought he was brilliant.'

'Was or is?'

'Perhaps I will have some tea after all.'

While I poured tea into a cup, Aunt Deirdre continued.

'He's just let life go by. He's wasted it! And that's the worst of sins. And he's dragged your uncle into all his time-wasting too.' She gave an enormous sigh. 'Oh, do you think we should still be *here* if . . . if . . . ?'

When she said 'He's just let life go buy,' there was the strong implication that, faced with time's tendency to pass, there was something else one could do with it, if one only had the guts or the enterprise. I was silenced by this. Would life, anyway, have been different in another place? What was she thinking? That my uncle might have become a bishop? Surely not. Or that they might have been happy? Ah, that was a difficult one to answer.

Uncle Roy himself appeared not long after our silence began. He was wearing the cassock and cloak which he wore on early morning trips to the church.

'It's started,' he said quietly.

'You don't mean it's going ahead?'

He went out again immediately. Neither my aunt nor I needed verbal prompting to follow him. We walked down the lane opposite the church until we reached the point where the Place came into view – the house framed by the beech avenue which led up to it and the clumps of elm behind. A light mist hung over the scene. No one could doubt that there was some machinery being driven about up at the house. Sargie, as we learnt afterwards, had got himself taken up to London by car immediately after the quarrel of the night before.

After a short silence, there was a bang and then a second, much deeper booming noise. The house was lost in smoke which mingled in the morning mists. When these smokes dispersed, we could still see the old Place. We stood, the three of us, and saw the roof and the walls of the house shake as if they were made of cloth. Then another explosion and more smoke, dust, rubble. Then a silence. Above our heads, birds flapped their wings and there was a great cawing of rooks. A few days later I was sent abroad and I did not return to the village for fifteen months.

SEVEN

'You got a nice tan on you, where you been then?'
'Cyprus.'
'In the army?'
'Not any more, thank God.'
'That's my soldierboy.'
In any professional life there can reach the point where the practitioner, however expert in a chosen field, starts to lose interest. The surgeon's hand has not lost its cunning, but he is bored and the success rate of his operations begins to decline. The tireless criminal advocate begins to lose cases not because he is no longer clever, but because he no longer cares whether or not his clients are acquitted. The imparting of knowledge which, to the young teacher, had been a matter of consuming zeal, has turned into a mere routine. His lessons, once legendary for their intellectual fireworks, now send the children to sleep. To give her the benefit of the doubt, something of the kind might very well have happened to Cindy (or whatever her real name was) who concluded our business together in a manner so perfunctory that, had it not been in England, one would have thought it deliberately insulting.

She got off the bed immediately and for a moment I admired her plump silhouette against the dingy Nottingham lace curtains. She had a top flat in Craven Street off the Strand. It is a part of town of which I am very fond. That day, the proximity of the river seemed to give a particular quality to the light in the drizzly sky.

I had not planned to spend my first hour in London in this fashion. Having left luggage at Charing Cross, I had merely intended to wander about the streets and taste freedom, knowing with a sense of incredulous happiness that the independent existence was about to begin. Cindy had engaged me in conversation almost as soon as I set foot outside the station and the next half-hour was the result of impulse. It was not that I grudged her the thirty shillings. I just felt vaguely cheapened by the experience itself. I had never paid for it before. To have done so was a blow to vanity.

'Well then, darling,' she said, 'see you again.'

'Hope so,' I said.

I was back in the country where nobody means anything they say to one another. Had I met her an hour later, Cindy would probably not have had the slightest recollection of having met me before. The drizzle had turned to quite heavy rain by the time I was outside in the street again. Nevertheless, a walk seemed the obvious way of clearing the head. I crossed the Strand, and wove my way in the direction of Leicester Square and Piccadilly. Sometimes I stopped and looked about me with disbelief. It really was true. I was out of the army. I wasn't at school. I was very nearly twenty-one years old. I was free! Free! As I passed the theatre at the bottom of Charing Cross Road I stood and looked at the photographs of the actors displayed outside. It seemed only a matter of time before my own face would be looking down with theirs. The legend would be posted up outside: 'ANOTHER BRILLIANT PERFORMANCE BY JULIAN RAMSAY.' Or 'I LAUGHED TILL I CRIED.' Where to start? That was the only question.

I crossed Leicester Square and walked down Piccadilly, half wondering, in a grand manner, whether to buy my aunt a little present of something at Fortnum and Mason. Before I reached that emporium, however, I paused by the window of Hatchards bookshop. The whole of one window was filled by a pyramid of stout duodecimo volumes, each bearing the title, in yellow capitals against a green background: *Petworth Lampitt: the Hidden Years, 1881–1910, by Raphael Hunter.*

Since Felicity's misfortune, now nearly five years in the past,

Hunter had been an unmentionable word at the Rectory. I had therefore no means of knowing what progress, if any, had been made with the sorting of Jimbo's stuff. Sargie, since the demolition of the Place, spent more and more time in London. My aunt's letters hardly made mention of him and my uncle never wrote to me. The whole Lampitt family and its concerns had been pushed out of my mind by the experiences of the previous twelve or fifteen months. I had hardly given any thought at all, since joining the army, to the question of whether Hunter would one day persuade Sargie to let him edit some of Jimbo's letters. The idea of a huge biography of the man was not something which I remembered being on the cards, though doubtless it had always been Hunter's ambition. I recalled the funny look which had come over Miss Beach's face at the name of Lampitt. Had Hunter even then disclosed to her his ambition to become 'the greatest English biographer since Boswell' (the words were not mine but those of a reviewer in the *Sunday Times*)? Did Hunter, after those years earlier, sense the extraordinary *potential* of the man Petworth Lampitt? Potential, that is to say, in the nebulous area of what makes a successful book?

'Petworth Lampitt was the archetypal Edwardian man of letters, but, as this fascinating new study shows, he was something much more . . .'

The blurb of the new jacket which I soon found myself reading inside the shop went on to hint that Lampitt was chiefly of interest because of his enormous range of acquaintances. 'Here was a man who grew to manhood in the aftermath of the Wilde trial and who knew a complete cross-section of English society . . . We meet here many famous names in surprising settings . . . The first volume of Mr Hunter's enthralling study is a reassessment not only of a much-neglected writer but also of English society itself . . .'

These were big claims. Perhaps the publishers were bound to make them, since they were charging a guinea for the book. I had been out of the country too long. I did not know that this biography of the first thirty-five years of Petworth Lampitt's life was already a best-seller. Its huge popularity was partly owing to the fact that there had been talk, which the judicious publishers had done nothing to quell, of a prosecution for obscenity. Had the relevant passages of Lampitt's *later* diary been published in that year, it is conceivable that they might have been liable to prosecution. As it was, Hunter's second volume appeared after the triumph of *Lady Chatterley*, so that he was free to write more or less what he chose. The activities themselves, in this volume, were never described in Lampitt's diary entries, but rather in Hunter's own cotton-wool prose. Opening the book at random, my eye fell on the sentence 'Petworth had found in Dr Hastings [evidently some schoolmaster] the father-figure he lacked in his own ineffectual parent . . .' Hunter's subject was 'Petworth' throughout, never 'Lampitt'. It gave a peculiar quality of coy intimacy to the book which was somehow unthinkable with the majority of male subjects (other than monarchs or popes) of whom biographies had ever been written. Could one read a life of Johnson which referred habitually to 'Samuel'? A life of Osip rather than one of Stalin?

I flicked to another page. 'No one can ever say with any certainty whether, after the incident in the punt, Petworth and Oscar Browning were ever lovers in the accepted sense. But a deep bond had been formed . . .' Another flicking revealed, 'It was probably Hugh Walpole who introduced Petworth to Turkish baths as a way of life . . .' And then another page, quite near the end: 'Petworth's tragedy, like that of many of his kind, was that he was doomed to form attachments with men who were wholly heterosexual in temperament. It was a tribute to his charm that he succeeded with so many and on so many occasions. The incident with Lloyd George was typical: the herald of hundreds of such episodes in the years which lay ahead . . .'

Lloyd George? I looked up the name in the index and found the appropriate page. Petworth Lampitt, when in his late twenties, was taken by an uncle to luncheon in the House of Commons. They shared a table with David Lloyd George, then Chancellor of the Exchequer. The 'incident' – perhaps the lawyers insisted on vagueness, or perhaps Hunter preferred it that way – appeared to have been a case of fellatio, or at least some intimate embrace, in the corner of the library. Nor were they alone in the room. Sir Henry Campbell-Bannerman was sitting by the fire (admittedly fast asleep) while, in another alcove, Hilaire Belloc and George Wyndham were shouting out lines of French poetry. This carefully contrived tale was given reference notes

(P.L.P. 2487: this stood for Petworth Lampitt Papers; the obscure style of numbering was devised by Hunter himself). As I turned the pages I discovered the pattern of the tale very clearly and saw at once why the book had been given a prominent place in the shop window. It is not quite true to say that Lampitt, in Hunter's account, had it off with every man you ever heard of. But the catalogue was decidedly impressive. Cardinal Manning – a guest of Petworth's grandmother in Rutland Gate – had allowed his archiepiscopal hand to stray over the child Petworth's sailor-suited person. I thought of William Bloom. Here was his vision of the world: or, come to that, Proust's. It was a world teeming with inverts, most of whom were cleverly posing as 'straights' or celibates. The psychological (not to mention circumstantial) improbability of the narrative did not stop it being compulsive reading. Was Petworth Lampitt a supreme fantasist whose surviving journals and memoirs had hoodwinked Hunter? Or was it actually possible that a young man of supreme personal attractions might succeed in captivating a person who, in any other circumstances, would have no interest whatsoever in their own sex or indeed in anyone else's? Women, it would appear, fell for Petworth Lampitt quite as readily as men, but he was incapable of giving them what they so indecorously implored.

'I am not ambivalent myself, but the cause of that ambivalence is in others,' as Lampitt once quipped to George Bernard Shaw, just about the only man in Hunter's book who did not at some stage or another take off his trousers for 'Petworth''s amusement.

I had paid my guinea and caught my train, and settled in a compartment with Hunter's book before I began to see how much he was the master of innuendo and suggestion. The first time you glanced at the teaparty with Manning, it seemed as though Hunter was sparing the reader's blushes and forbearing to state an obscenity. The next time you read it through, it was obvious that no evidence whatsoever existed to convict the Cardinal of child-molesting. All that existed was a number – P.L.P. 913 – which might have referred to some inaccurate memory of Petworth Lampitt himself or which equally might not. When closely perused, all we saw was the fact that Manning once had tea with old Lady Lampitt and that Petworth, aged

seven, was allegedly present. It is Hunter who says, with a
clever use of negatives, that 'it is not for us to say whether this
incident was what inspired Petworth's Firbankian short story
Watered Silk . . .' which was evidently some unpublished and
vaguely improper *jeu d'esprit* about a bishop misbehaving himself.

The day when I read Hunter's book through, beginning at
the beginning, lay in the future. My train-perusal was a matter
of turning here and there, collecting impressions.

For me, the biography was doubly absorbing. On the one
hand it was the story of a writer whom I admired and whose
inner life appeared to have been, to say the least, highly
coloured. On the other, it seemed like the confirmation in print
of an extraordinary, private fantasy – not mine, not Hunter's,
but Uncle Roy's. For the eroticism of the story only took up a
tiny proportion of the pages. Here was an index bulging with
Lampitts, the whole tribe of them. And yet it all had a curious
unreality for me, precisely because I had been taught to lisp
their names since early childhood. Needless to say, the Lampitts
in Hunter's pages were shadowy figures when compared with
the characters who peopled my uncle's narratives. Where other
children were told fairy stories or folk tales, I had been reared
on Lampitt legends. My dragons and demons were all cousins
or uncles or aunts of Sargie's. It was inevitable that Hunter's
approach should have been duller than that of Uncle Roy.
Whatever his motive for writing this enormous book, Hunter
had none of the obsessive love which had dominated my uncle's
grown-up life. And then again, my uncle's method of retelling
the old tales was vividly oral whereas Hunter existed behind a
cloak of the flattest prose imaginable. If my uncle was Homer
then Hunter was a classical dictionary. It seemed strange to
read of all these characters stripped naked of epithet or anecdote. Sibs Lampitt merely appeared as 'Petworth's youngest
sister Sibyl, who married Rupert Starling, a Permanent Secretary at the Treasury'. There was nothing about Lady Starling's
famed resemblance to a certain item of floor-covering. Bobby,
who went out to be a farmer in Rhodesia, was alluded to, but
without any of the stories inseparable from his name. For a
moment in the train, I put down Hunter's book and thought of
Uncle Roy, convulsed with mirth, as he tried to repeat what

Bobby had said to that waiter in Brighton. It was the day he proposed to Slish, of course. It would not have been funny if written down. It needed Uncle Roy going pink at the gills and shaking as if he would suffer from apoplexy.

'In my book, a duckling is a young duck and not an old horse.'

This was the celebrated put-down with which their food had been sent back to the kitchen. The proposal of marriage was slipped in while the waiter was remonstrating with the cook. But none of it was funny or interesting unless it was told in my uncle's voice, enlivened by my uncle's love. As he dabbed the corners of his eyes with a silk handkerchief, he would say, 'Extraordinarily witty man, old Bobby.' And then, growing quiet, he would murmur, 'Typical Lampitt story, that. An old horse.'

In half an hour, I would be met by my uncle at Norwich Station – our first meeting for well over a year. As I prepared for the encounter, the full force of his personality came before me. For years, my complex feelings about Uncle Roy had forced me into making simple judgements of him, nearly all hostile. During my year away, I had not really missed him; but I had been homesick and I had missed the whole Rectory set-up. And now, just before we met again, I enjoyed a sort of revelation about him. I do not know whether it was an accurate vision, but I suspect that I never came nearer to the truth about him. For years, the chief thing which embarrassed me about Uncle Roy was his relationship with the Lampitts and with Sargie in particular. It all seemed humiliatingly toadyish. In this view, Uncle Roy appeared as a pure snob, making obeisance to a lot of people who 'in fact' (whatever that was supposed to mean) 'were no better than we were'.

But, with Hunter's book in my hand, I realised that the Lampitts with whose exploits I had been brought up were all creatures of Uncle Roy's fertile imagination. He was an artist, a novelist *manqué*, a natural one who did not realise his vocation or his gift. He possessed the one thing needful. Doubtless the figures with whose stories he regaled me, or anyone else who would listen, were in some sense real people, whose births and deaths had been recorded by a registrar. But it was my uncle's vision which breathed life into them and – as I had discovered for myself when I met Lady Starling – these 'real' people often bore no relation to the characters teeming in my uncle's brain.

Of Uncle Roy, needless to say, Hunter had written not a word. There was, however, a certain amount about Sargie who, although twelve years Jimbo's junior, had shared the same house, the same nurse and the same extraordinary parents. Much of the 'material' unearthed by Hunter was certainly new to me. My aunt had admitted that Mrs Lampitt was 'a strange old girl', but she had never explained how. Some of her eccentricities (for example, her insistence for the first six years of his life that Petworth was a girl called Petronella) doubtless helped to explain the sad story which Hunter felt constrained to tell. I don't know what it explained about Sargie, but it made one rather less surprised that he had turned out so rum.

Rather unimaginatively, I assumed that the publication of a book entirely devoted to the Lampitts would naturally be the first subject which my uncle would wish to discuss. I was beginning to look forward to my aunt's euphemisms for Petworth's amorous adventures. At the same time, I quite genuinely rejoiced in Hunter's book, because I thought that, for the first time in my life, I would be able to discuss something with my uncle as a fellow adult, without adolescent sensations of annoyance. What better than a book about his favourite subject? Hunter's flat prose would surely unleash a whole torrent of stories and corrections – memories of old Mrs Lampitt and of Timplingham Place in the old days.

By the time the train arrived, I was really looking forward to the reunion with Uncle Roy. It was a tremendous shock, therefore, as the train pulled in at the station and I glimpsed him on the platform, to find within me all the old childhood irritation and embarrassment welling up, as if I were a thirteen year old. I tried, in the few seconds which remained before greeting him, to take a grip on myself and to tell myself that he was a perfectly amiable man, who had only my best interests at heart and who had absolutely no desire to provoke in me either embarrassment or rage. But both were there, bubbling away inside me, as I stepped down on to the platform.

Uncle Roy was wearing his bright green Norfolk jacket and matching tweed knickerbockers. A pipe was between his teeth and, as often on stations, he was so deep in conversation with a porter that at first he did not notice my approach. When he did see me, he hurried up and took my hand. It was not the gesture of an uncle greeting a relation whom he had not seen for a long time; much more that of the host at a party who has found just the right person to lead up to a favoured guest.

'This man's father was a gardener at Mallington Hall,' were Uncle Roy's words of greetings.

'That's right, sir,' grinned the porter.

'Now,' said Uncle Roy, looking around, 'you have some luggage.' I allowed the porter to carry what there was – a large suitcase and a holdall.

'No,' said Uncle Roy, though I hadn't as yet opened my mouth, 'we were just saying before you arrived that we were *afraid* that *old* Lord Lampitt – that's the present Lord Lampitt's father – was a tiny little bit of a humbug.'

My uncle's shoulders were shaking. I could see an anecdote coming on. It was the one about old Lord Lampitt (Dickie) making a speech in 1914 against food hoarding, while in fact he had a sack of flour and another of sugar in the boot of his Rolls. His heir (who, as the Honourable Vernon Lampitt, had sat in Attlee's Cabinet) was, in Uncle Roy's judgement 'an immensely able economist'. I found myself asking silently and furiously what Uncle Roy ever knew about economics.

'Oh, Mr Vernon's clever – His Lordship I should say now,' said the porter.

'There was always the hope, you know, that he would succeed Sir Stafford Cripps as Chancellor of the Exchequer. Instead it went to Gaitskell. But he is an immensely able economist.'

'Maybe,' said the porter, who wisely took nothing on trust, least of all when it was spoken by Uncle Roy.

He followed us to the car park and looked askance at the coin which Uncle Roy had placed in his hand as a reward for struggling with my bags. I thought there might be a danger of his cursing us, or even of offering a show of physical violence.

'It's been very enjoyable talking to you,' said Uncle Roy with a lordly smile. When the man was gone, my uncle added, 'What an extraordinarily nice man. And how nice to see you. I'm afraid to say that the Trojan finally conked.'

He opened the door of a dilapidated Rover, which it was unkind of someone to have sold him.

'Your aunt prefers this car,' he added as we jerked forward,
'but I miss the old one.'

It was just my luck to have come across a porter with Lampitt
connections.

'I was telling that man about Bobby going out to Rhodesia.
He didn't really know much about *our* branch of the Lampitt
family.'

'I've just bought Mr Hunter's book,' I said. 'But perhaps
you've already got it.'

My uncle concentrated purposefully on the road.

'Your Granny's looking forward to seeing you,' he said. 'I
warn you, she's grown a bit older in the last year. Nothing to
worry about, but she's deafer.'

'Aunt Deirdre wrote that Granny's come to live with us.'

'Did she say that her great friend had died?'

'No! Not Mrs Webb?'

'Extraordinary memory you have. We thought it was better
not to write it. You never know with a letter. It might fall into
the wrong hands. No, poor Mrs Webb had a stroke at Easter.
She didn't recover. Your grandmother has been staying at the
Rectory ever since. We never meant to have her, but – she can't
really manage on her own, you see.'

'Without Mrs Webb, she'll be lost,' I said.

And this death, this passing, made me forget the essentially
frivolous subject of Petworth Lampitt's love-life. We were more
or less silent for the remaining few miles of the journey.

One notices the smallest changes in the scenes of childhood
memory. Timplingham without the Place was bad enough. But
now there was a horrible petrol station on the edge of the village
and more bungalows where green fields had been. The post
office had been painted a different colour. Jill, who no longer
ran it, but lived in one of the new bungalows, thought yellow
was a 'ridiculous colour in a village', a judgement entirely
endorsed by my aunt. In the next couple of weeks, Aunt Deirdre
was to fill me in on most of the village news, including the fact
that the Wretched Woman had another novel on the stocks,
but had gone to live in Hampstead with her 'kids'. For the
moment, though, Aunt Deirdre's concerns were more immediate. The Mulberrys were blaring as we entered the house –
perhaps a symptom of Granny's increased deafness. Tinker was

yapping in the kitchen. Aunt Deirdre came forward to kiss me.

'Brown as a berry!' she exclaimed. Then, in quite a serious voice, 'I made a cottage pie because I didn't know when you'd be getting in.'

I didn't have words for the death of Mrs Webb, so I just hugged Granny and kissed her powdery old cheeks. And Felicity was there too. I think the peck we gave one another that early summer evening was our first kiss.

'She's frightfully grand!' said Aunt Deirdre as I kissed her daughter. 'Junior Dean, no less.'

'It doesn't mean anything,' said the philosopher, adding, 'How are you, anyway?'

'I'm okay.'

Felicity followed me upstairs. Her parents stood in the hall and shouted after us.

'Your room's had a face-lift,' yelled Aunt Deirdre.

'Yes,' said Uncle Roy. 'The diocese has at last offered to give the place a lick of paint.'

Felicity helped me with my holdall. Instinctively, when we were alone in my bedroom, I opened it and took out Hunter's book.

'We'll need to have a talk about that,' she said, putting her hand on the book. 'But there's no need to have it now.'

'Uncle Roy didn't want to talk about it in the car.' While I spoke, I was taking in the effect of the 'face-lift'. An alarmingly jaunty, floral wallpaper danced its way all over the room, waging war not only on the books and the furniture, but also on the view from the window, the subdued colours of a Norfolk evening, the village rooftops, the octagonal, flint tower of the church, the narrow river Timp running muddily through the paddock beyond our vegetable garden.

'It doesn't exist, of course,' she said.

'I'm sorry?'

'As far as Ma and Pa are concerned, that book does not exist. They won't talk about it.'

'Isn't that a bit silly?'

'It's hurt everyone very, very much,' she said, quietly.

This, the most obvious thing about Hunter's book, that it was bound to be hurtful to all who knew and loved the Lampitts, was something which had just not occurred to me.

'Sargie's in pretty poor odour with the rest of the family, needless to say, for letting that man anywhere near the stuff.'

'Raphael Hunter, you mean.'

'God, I hate him,' said Felicity.

This exchange made me burn for more news about the whole story of Hunter and the Lampitts, but there was a cottage pie to be eaten and news to be exchanged. I had thought that they would want to know all about my year in Cyprus, but all we heard about that was Granny's observation that she didn't like Archbishop Makarios and that Mrs Webb had never been able to abide a man with a beard.

What they all wanted to know were my plans for the future. I was astonished by the speed with which they got on to the subject. I murmured something about acting. I had hoped that this ambition would be something which was obvious to them, but that they would be patient while I thought of ways in which I might start on the career of my choice.

'I wondered whether you would think of following your father,' said Granny. 'I know it's thirteen years since he passed away, but there will be those at Tempest and Holmes who remember him. In fact, I know there are, since I still get a card at Christmas from Mr Pilbright who was in accounts with your father.'

I looked at Granny's face to see if she was being serious, as of course she was. It was a horrible moment.

What was wrong with thinking that I should live as my parents had lived? My father had been an assistant manager in a shirt factory. Had he lived, he might have ended up as a director; anyway, a full manager. He would have exchanged his semi-detached house in Richmond for something a little bit further out of London, perhaps in Ewell. But, for me, this way of life was not something which I had even contemplated. There was no *reason* why I should not become one of those thousands of people who had a job which bored them, and a mortgage and a suit to wear to the office.

'You'll have to settle for something,' said my aunt firmly.

'Mr Pilbright was ever so kind after David's funeral,' said Granny. 'Do you remember him, dear?'

'Vaguely,' said Uncle Roy.

The subject of my father's death was excruciating to him. It was hardly ever mentioned.

'He said, "If there's *anything* I can do to help." And he really meant it,' said Granny. 'As I say, he still sends a card at Christmastime.'

'I'm not sure that I'm cut out for that sort of work,' I said.

'There's no money for a university,' snapped my aunt. 'I mean, even if you *had* passed those exams.'

'I wasn't thinking of a university,' I said.

'What were your ideas?'

The women were persistent.

'It takes a bit of time,' said Uncle Roy gently. 'I expect you've had several thoughts.'

Seeing him at the end of the table, dreamily smoking his pipe, I realised that my uncle had hardly done anything for the previous quarter of a century. Oh, he had driven Sargie to Cromer and he had read the Prayer Book services and he had worn clothes. But he had never been obliged to go to an office or tolerate the condescension of Mr Pilbright in accounts.

I genuinely don't know and it would be impertinent to speculate whether Uncle Roy felt a true sense of religious vocation. But during that conversation I had a very clear vision of how *silly* I had been, during all those terrible quarrels of my teenage years, when I had tried to catch my uncle out in some theological argument or accused him openly of hypocrisy. Certainly the clerical life was not for me. But it had rescued Uncle Roy from suits off the peg, and semi-detached houses in Ewell and Mr Pilbright of accounts. I had other dreams. I wanted to write a great book; act a great Hamlet; have a great and complicated love affair. None of these things could be accomplished unless I could persuade my family that I did not need to take a job. And how could someone who was penniless do that?

These were now huge, urgent considerations. I had to find a plausible alternative to my grandmother's suggestion. Otherwise the shirt factory beckoned. My only objections to it were snobbish or aesthetic. They weren't *rational*. The sensations of freedom which I had tasted in London that morning and which had helped to drive me so impulsively into the arms of Cindy were quickly evaporating. None of the ideas about the future which existed in my mind could be voiced without embarrassment. I could not, in that company and at that moment, say, 'I'm hoping to write a book,' or 'I rather want to go on the stage.'

Instead, I said, 'I thought of living in London for a bit.'

'What on?' asked my aunt mercilessly. 'You have no money.'

'We could probably find you accommodation,' said Uncle Roy. 'Sibs would help, I'm sure.'

'That would be very kind.'

'Just to start with.'

'We had a charming letter from Sibs the other day. It looked at one point as if Gavin was going to follow in Father's footsteps and become a civil servant. But instead he has gone into banking, like Francis. Anne is studying art – the history thereof.'

'Who's this?' asked Granny.

'Lady Starling, mother,' her son shouted. 'No,' he added in a quieter voice, 'Sibs has been absolutely wonderful lately about keeping in touch, with Sargie being so barmy.'

'Barmy?'

But no explanation was offered. For the moment the subject of my career was dropped. The twin beacons of Lady Starling's boys had been held up to light my way. Even Lampitts had jobs. It was a woeful thought. The question of whether Sargie had in fact lost his wits or whether the phrase merely suggested that he was still being tiresome would have to wait until I was alone with Felicity.

It was still light after supper, so Felicity and I took a walk together in the midgy evening air. Barminess, Sargie's or anyone else's, was a good enough subject for laughter. I chuckled as I asked about it.

Taking the road out of Timplingham, the very slight incline actually increases one's sense of the infinite sky which stretched above us. The drizzle had cleared. Wind blew. That familiar soughing for which I had so often and so painfully been homesick in the Meditteranean moved the trees.

A few years of giving tutorials (at Oxford now) had made Felicity much more coherent. Perhaps unhappiness, perhaps the austerity of the meals in a women's college, explained the fact that she had lost so much weight. She was much more handsome: tall, lean, intensely serious, a being quite other from the adolescent, silent girl whom I had frightened with a toad.

'Pa's been through hell,' she said.

'With Sargie? Has he actually been certified?'

'You've been away so much, it's hard to know where to begin,' she said, stopping to light a cigarette. She was now smoking a lot. 'That man Hunter has a lot to answer for.'

'From you, certainly.'

'I don't care about him any more personally. It's as though none of that happened between him and me. Honestly. It's not a question of "hell hath no fury". Though I do see now the way he treated me was all of a piece with his totally ruthless desire to exploit everyone who crosses his path. Look at what happened. First, years ago, he latched on to Jimbo Lampitt. I don't know whether that was a simple case of what it looked like. Perhaps we shall have to wait for Hunter vol. II or even Hunter vol. III to find the answer to that one.'

'You're surely not suggesting that Hunter and Petworth Lampitt . . .'

She offered me a cigarette and I took one.

'I don't understand Raphael,' she said, 'and I don't really want to understand him. God knows why he wanted to write this foul book in the first place. It isn't as if poor old Jimbo was even a very good writer.'

'Oh, I disagree with you there.'

'Well, he wasn't Gibbon.'

'Isn't it legitimate to write the life of a writer even if he wasn't Gibbon?'

'Not if it hurts people,' she said.

'Who's it hurt?'

'Oh, just about everyone, that's all. Everyone who matters. Sargie is absolutely devastated. It's his own fault in a way, but not in another. Raphael simply took him over. I know how that can happen. It was starting that summer when he first came to the Place and I was working with him. But after Sargie moved to London, the takeover was complete. Now, of course, Sibs and the rest are saying that Raphael should never have been given the Lampitt Papers. But he just *took* them. What could old Sargie do?'

'Did you know all this racey stuff about Jimbo? Is that what you and Hunter were reading that summer five years ago?'

'You know, the funny thing is, I went through an awful lot

of the old boy's papers that summer, even before Raphael descended on the Place, and I never found anything remotely interesting in them. Oh, there were some letters from famous people . . .'

'Which famous people?'

'Oh, I don't know. Hugh Walpole. Lascelles Abercrombie. There were one or two from Henry James. But nothing to suggest that he was leading this rampaging, alleycat sort of life.'

'You have to admit it was clever of Hunter to find out about it.'

'Clever?' She stopped to light up again. 'That's one word for it. I did not go through everything, of course. Jimbo left so much. I don't think the Lampitts realise how much there was. It's all very well for Sibs to say that Sargie should have read the papers before he gave them to Raphael. But I'd like to see *her* go through it all. There were at least fifteen large trunks all bursting with papers.'

'And Hunter just appropriated them?'

'They really were getting mouldy at the Place, I believe. Just look at it now!'

We leaned on a wall and looked across the fields. In the old days, this would have provided a view of the splendid old stables behind the Place. Now there was nothing except Sargie's bungalow, where a light was burning. The fading sky did very little to disguise its uncompromising brashness; as if the new bricks were not bad enough, Sargie had yielded to the builder's suggestion of a royal blue front door, frosted glass and a carriage lamp.

'Raphael just took Sargie over,' she said. 'Poor Pa was edged out. They would never have quarrelled if it had not been for Raphael. I am convinced of that.'

'There have been phases before when they were off one another,' I said. 'I think they'll come round to one another again.'

'The old things were tiffs. This was a real rift. And it was deliberately created. I feel certain of that. I am sure that Raphael wanted to stop Sargie seeing the people who loved him. He wanted me out of the way and he dispatched me in the most efficient possible manner.'

'Isn't that going a bit far?' I asked.

'He did not want me to know the contents of those papers. I'm sure of that. And I'm absolutely sure that his desire to keep me out was stronger than . . . his desire for me.'

'But this is to make him into some kind of . . . *devil!*'

'Julian. Either he *knew* that those trunks contained the most awful secrets of Jimbo's sex life; or – which is what I suspect – he knew they didn't. Either way, he did not want a witness spoiling his story. He knew that an innocent galumphing girl would just never go away from her godfather's house, unless she *had* to go away in disgrace.'

'You're not serious?'

'It's all right. I haven't gone round the bend, though sometimes I've thought that I would, just thinking about it all . . . The point is, we'll never know. We'll never get our hands on the Lampitt Papers. Raphael will make sure of that. In my opinion, the biography is equally disgraceful whether it is a pack of lies or a deliberate, if truthful, betrayal of trust. It has to be one or the other.'

'But why – what are the motives?'

'You know, in the last few years, it has become clear that it wasn't just that Raphael wanted the papers for his wretched book. He had a compelling need to make Sargie betray those who loved him best. Sibs was a victim, you know. She thought she was in control, but she just let Raphael walk all over her.'

'A complete doormat, in fact.'

'Why do you say that?'

'Nothing.'

'She even rang Pa to ask if Sargie was still *alive*. She'd written to him three times, asking him to meals and things, and he simply wouldn't reply. She tried ringing his flat, and whenever she did so Raphael answered and said that Sargie wasn't available. Hunter moved into the flat. He's living there now, I believe – which is why Sargie is sitting over there in the bungalow drinking himself silly, poor old boy.'

'Couldn't you all have done something to rescue him? Get a doctor or something?'

'Well, there you are,' said Felicity. 'Paranoia creates what it fears. For years Sargie has been imagining that all the Lampitts had been holding councils of war and talking about him behind his back. Now they really did.'

'Lady Starling summoned a council of war?'

'Sibs had the whole gang of them round to Cadogan Square to decide what to do. Vernon wanted them to get a power of attorney over Sargie – have him certified – anything to get the papers out of his hands.'

'So they had begun to suspect what sort of beans Hunter's biography was going to spill?'

'There'd been rumours. In a highly calculated way, the little slug had gone round London feeding people with titbits. The news certainly reached Oxford. I was dining in New College one day – Sargie's old college – and my host, not knowing that I knew anything about the Lampitts, raised Jimbo's name. The usual thing. "Does anyone nowadays read James Petworth Lampitt? My bookseller advised – buy in while he's still at the bottom of the market. First editions of *Prince Albert* are still purchasable for a few shillings. When the world gets to know of his liaisons with all and sundry, my business sense tells me that he will *appreciate*. Nothing like a little sex for improving an author's standing with the book-buying public." I naively said that I thought Jimbo had been a bit of an old woman, but hardly a Lothario. Upon which, my genial philosopher said, "I'll spare your blushes, Felicity, but how many old women of your acquaintance give blowjobs to the Prime Minister of the day? This throws an altogether new light on the women's colleges."'

'Quite good.'

'As may be. But, you see, if my philosopher friend's appetite had been whetted, that meant that a key five hundred people knew about Raphael's so-called research. And they were the five hundred people who determine, in the end, whether a book will be successful or not.'

'The public determines that – the public alone.'

She merely laughed at my simplicity. I took another of her cigarettes.

She said, 'Apart from anything else, it threw the most appalling light on Raphael's own relationship with Sargie. It has tarred Sargie with Jimbo's brush, this making out that Jimbo was a sort of Oscar Wilde.'

'Good Lord. You don't mean that anyone thinks that Sargie and Uncle Roy . . .'

'It has tainted *everything*.'

From the grass where we walked – not ten feet ahead – a pair of larks rose almost vertically into the air. Our eyes followed them until the brightness of the yellow sky made it impossible to stare further. There was no visible sun, but the clouds were full of light.

Obviously – if anything was now obvious – the very thought of Uncle Roy having some sort of inverted association with Sargie was totally preposterous. It would have been impossible to find a friendship which on its own terms was more innocent. Yet the meaning of Felicity's words was perfectly clear. Hunter's biography was bound to sully the atmosphere. Perhaps – this was what she seemed to be saying – that was why he wrote it.

'He's like some horrible parasite crawling its way into the system,' she said. 'He could beguile anyone.'

I could not answer this without raking up her own affair with Hunter. I need not have been so delicate.

'He got me,' she said. 'I was *so* in love with that man, Julian.'

'I know.'

I wondered if there had been other men since. Felicity and I were not used to sharing confidences. She knew nothing of my inner history. I would have known nothing of hers, had she not been made ill by it.

'I still don't really understand why it was so important to batten on to Jimbo,' she said. 'Why write a biography of him, of all people?'

'Oh, that I think I do understand,' I said. Although it was an evening for confidences, I still felt too shy to admit that I understood what it was to have a literary ambition. 'I daresay he wanted to get started, in a literary way. To write a book about anything. Jimbo was to hand.'

'Was he?'

'Oh, it looks to us like some inexplicable conspiracy. First, Hunter intrudes himself into Jimbo's life, then he steals the papers. But don't you think that from his point of view, it might all look different?'

'How do you mean?'

'Suppose he was in love with the idea of himself as a writer.

It would mean that anyone who fitted in with this idea of his would become an object of fascination to him. So he was in love with Jimbo's memory. In love with the girl who helped him sort the papers.'

'That's your explanation for what happened between me and Raphael?'

'It might explain why he became infatuated with Sargie.'

'I never thought of Sargie as a queer,' she said.

'I don't suppose he is. There are ways and ways of taking people over. Hunter's way of taking *you* over would be different from his taking over Sargie.'

We walked along the path at the side of the field and back again into the road. The walk was more than halfway over and now we were turned for home. The evening light was fading and the rooks were noisy in the sky.

'It's broken Pa's heart, all this,' she said.

'I don't quite see why, or how.'

'You know how paranoid Sargie is.'

'Yes.'

'Well, when Sibs and the others became really frightened about Raphael they came to Pa and begged him to do something. So he went down to London and took Sargie out to lunch. There was the most frightful row. Sargie said that Pa had been paid, all these years, to spy on him for the other Lampitts. They really are estranged now. I don't mean they will never meet or never speak again. But Pa never goes near that bungalow and Sargie never comes down to us. In terms of Pa's life, it's sadder than anything. Much sadder than the ending of a love affair.'

'He's got your mother,' I said, realising, as I said it, that this cut both ways.

We walked back to the house in silence. Something rather deep had happened during our walk and it would take time to absorb. Among other things, for the first time in my life, I had been compelled to take Uncle Roy seriously. I had been able to perceive him as a sentient being like myself, capable of hopes which could be dashed and feelings which could be hurt. I had no idea how much consolation could be derived from his religion. But, as I lay in my bath after the walk, it was of those early morning rituals in church which I began to think: my scuttling across to serve his altar on winter mornings before the light appeared. I thought of the very morning when Jimbo Lampitt had died and of my uncle in his funereal Mass vestments: a vaguely frightening figure at that moment, indulging in something which was on the edge of being magic.

Descending in my dressing gown, I found Uncle Roy in the hall, staring through the glazed front door at the night sky. He was swaddled in his own mannerisms to such a degree that I felt unable to penetrate to him and offer the sympathy which I now so acutely felt. I noticed that, since I went to Cyprus, he like Felicity had lost quite a bit of weight. The white collar and the bow tie hung loosely from a neck which had become scrawny and birdlike. The Oxford bags into which he had changed were not merely voluminous. They now seemed tragicomic, like trousers in a farce or a mental ward, waiting at any moment to fall to his ankles. He was only in his mid-fifties, but he had started to look old.

'I think it's going to be a nice day tomorrow,' he said.

'The weather forecast has just said the opposite.'

I hated myself for saying this, but my instinct to point out that almost everything he said was wrong was unstoppable.

'We'll see.' He smiled, unperturbed by anything so modern as a report emanating from the wireless. 'I think you'll find it's fine in the morning.'

'Do you still have an early service on Thursdays?'

I asked the question hesitantly. He was no fool. He must have known that I had not undergone a religious conversion in the previous year. My desire to present myself at the altar was potentially embarrassing to us both. At that moment, however, I could think of no other way of showing my uncle that, in spite of all our difficulties together, I actually loved him. If I'd been a girl, I could just have gone up and given him a big kiss.

'Yes – yes – we still have the 7.30 on Thursdays. But really, there's no need . . .'

'I was wondering if you'd like a server?'

I suppose by pious standards I was suggesting a blasphemy. I wasn't a believer. I was in a state of mortal sin. But I did not think much of a God who would damn me for what I was proposing and I prayed inwardly to this God who did not exist to make Uncle Roy accept my offer.

He repeated his unfinished sentence about there being no

need. But he was touched and he read the signals right. He said he would be most grateful if I could serve his altar in the morning.

I set my alarm clock for 6.45 and woke earlier, my mind churning not so much with thoughts as with a whole jumble of images past and present – girls I'd been in love with, chaps I'd known, things which had happened in the army, things from much further back. School. Mummy. The train pulling out of the station and Mummy standing there, surrounded by men in uniform, and waving goodbye for ever.

Woven into all this undirected collection of feelings, there was my memory of the previous evening's conversation with Felicity. As I dressed, I opened Hunter's Life of Lampitt and looked at the photographs – Petworth with Lytton Strachey and Duncan Grant at Charleston. Petworth with Cynthia Asquith. Petworth, Arthur Machen and Yeats. These disparate moments of *their* lives had all been gathered together, artificially made into an historical whole, which they had never been at the time, by the painstaking but surely uninspired pen of Raphael Hunter. I could not believe in Felicity's theory that he had invented Jimbo's emotional life, because I could not believe that anyone capable of writing such flat prose could be so imaginative.

As I tied my tie and put on my shoes, I thought of Hunter. What motivated him? In Felicity's vision, he was a purely manipulative figure who had intruded himself into the life of the Lampitt family – and thus into our life – for the purposes of some obscure form of self-advancement. To me, as I looked back over the years, Hunter began to seem different.

There he had been at the beginning, embracing Miss Beach. And would his curiously youthful, fascinatingly dull smile be there to greet me when I tottered towards the end? I half-wondered whether he was not some sort of magician, capable not only of the spuriously fictitious art of biography, forcing outlines which had not been there on the haphazard existence of old Jimbo, but also an occult master capable of controlling and shaping the lives of the living, perhaps even pulling the strings of my own existence. Such a fantasy would seem, in the light of future developments, to have been not wholly wide of the mark. At the very least, if not a controller, Raphael was some kind of recording angel, a figure who arbitrarily connected with some of the most intimate moments of my emotional history far too frequently for it simply to be a coincidence. Hunter's destiny and mine appeared to be mysteriously linked. At times, as with the experience of watching him embrace Miss Beach, I was compelled to have my experience filtered through Hunter. At other times, as with our very different perceptions of the Binker, or our quite different relationships with Felicity, we were destined, like figures in Oriental religion, to represent two sides of the same phenomenon, the dark and the light, the positive and the negative. My heart was already preparing itself unconsciously for the idea that Hunter was not just a figure who would keep cropping up but, much more strangely, that he was a figure without whom my own life was not quite imaginable.

Perhaps the whole concept of imagining one's own existence, seeing it as a finished entity, is a misguided one. Whether or not this is the case, I had the sense of Hunter's presence that morning, either as a fellow actor or as a master of ceremonies, but always a figure on the stage with me, or waiting in the wings, one whose exact role in the drama had yet to be disclosed.

My dressing was complete. The whole palaver of getting up for the early service – tiptoeing on landings so as not to wake the rest of the household – inevitably made me a twelve-year-old once more. I even experienced a particular kind of early-morning collywobbles in my stomach which I had forgotten existed.

Outside, it was pelting with rain. Monsoon conditions. As I squelched my way through the churchyard, I could see a light on in the vestry. My uncle was there. He had already lit the candles on the altar, and placed the bread and wine on the credence table. The church felt extremely damp and cold. It was as empty as ever.

I walked up the aisle, staring into the shadowy roof at the rows of carved, surpliced figures on the beam ends. And there she was, looking down over the pulpit, baring the incomparable Timplingham Titties as she had done for the previous five hundred years. Perhaps, rather than being the aberration of some lecherous carver, this curious piece of sculpture hid some profounder theological purpose. As the prospect of serving the altar drew nearer, I thought sheepishly (with embarrassment more than with guilt) of Cindy and of some of the other erotic moments in life. Quite involuntarily, I remembered the extraordinary excitement (with the one-night stand in Northampton) of discovering that they too could *come*. It was a revelation which filled me with guilt in relation to Barbara. Her *'lentement, chéri'* and her *'ici, ici'* now had meaning for me. These images flashed through the mind when I should have been praying. And then I thought of another moment with Barbara, walking along with her in that religious procession and thinking I might blub. It wasn't guilt, it wasn't morbid eroticism which prompted those tears. It was something much odder, something which I had not got round to thinking about and which probably should never be approached by the medium of *thought*.

Waiting in church for the service to start, though, I did have a thought. If there was a God of love, I thought, then presumably an indulgent and even an amused eye was turned to the bizarre ways in which we tried to make ourselves happy. The naked wooden breasts exposed so flagrantly over the pulpit were perhaps not so out of place. Instinct told me that Aunt Deirdre was wrong to think them 'a pity'.

I bowed to the altar, not because I believed that there was any magic there, but not just to please Uncle Roy, either. I don't know why I bowed. Uncle Roy was kneeling at the back of the Lady Chapel with his face in his hands.

I went into the vestry where his green chasuble was spread out on the vestment chest. At 7.25, he came backstage and threw this item of attire over his head. At 7.27 he put the maniple over his left wrist, and I led him out of the vestry and up the north aisle to his altar. Rather surprisingly, there were about five village people kneeling there for Mass. My aunt wasn't among them.

The Prayer Book service was the same as ever I remembered it. The Lord's Prayer in my uncle's monotone began at the very moment that the little clock over the north door struck the half hour. After the Collect for Purity, the Ten Commandments.

'Thou shalt not commit adultery,' said Uncle Roy.

In response, I said the words which were printed in the book, but with absolutely no confidence that my heart, in the years to come, would be inclined to keep this law.